Also by William E. Kennedy

Tramp: A T.K. & Associates Detective Story
(Middle Grade Novel)

The Singing Bone

William E. Kennedy

Kennedy Literary

Jamestown, ND

For information on author appearances or book club information,

E-mail: billkennedy0@gmail.com

ISBN-13: 978-0-615-89031-9

The Singing Bone

First Edition

10 9 8 7 6 5 4 3 2 1

Dedication

This book is dedicated to my father, William J. Kennedy, who never spoke about his great-grandfather, his grandfather, or his father. But the memories of William J. and the men that made him the man that he became are as strong as my love for all of them.
Their blood flows through my veins every day.

Letter Ten to Franz Xaver Kappus
Rainer Maria Rilke

And then when one realizes that the presence of the distant sea and its melody is added to all this, perhaps as the innermost tone in this prehistoric harmony, then I can only wish that you trustingly and patiently allow that grand solitude to work in you. It is no longer possible to be erased from your life. It shall be immanent in all that you experience and all that you do. It will act as an anonymous influence, akin to how ancestral blood constantly moves and merges with our own and links with that of the individual, never to be unlinked. It is gently decisive at each crossroad of our life.

An Irish Tale
Anonymous

The Singing Bone hums when a blood memory rises up from the past. There has been no narrative, no discussion of the event that is recalled. It is as simple as a chin passed through the generations, but more revealing and dangerous to the descendent. The singing bone lies amongst the tiny bones of the middle ear. It is a very rare and special event when it is touched.

STONE FAMILY TREE

Michael Stone 1831-1895 - Nora Adams Stone 1836-1895

One son

William Stone 1870-1927 - Julia Geare Stone 1870-1934

One son

Thomas Stone 1905-1973 - Margaret Nelson Stone 1913 – 1980

One son

Liam Stone 1943 - Kathryn Smith Stone 1943

One son

Colin Stone 1970

Contents

THE SINGING BONE
PART ONE 1980

1. Closet 8
2. Superior Lodge 27
3. Ledgers 43
4. Delay 50
5. Therapist 55
6. Kathryn Stone 59
7. The Novel 61

STONE AND SON
PART ONE 1849 – 1890

1. Michael and Nora Stone 63
2. New Orleans 76
3. Peoria 78
4. Green Grocer 84
5. Ledgers 89

THE SINGING BONE
PART TWO 1980

8. Kathryn Stone 92

STONE AND SON
PART TWO 1890 – 1935

6. William and Julia Stone 93
7. The Bridges 97

8. William and Julia Stone *100*
9. Son Is Born *102*
10. Growing Up Thomas *105*
11. Coogan's Lot *113*
12. Attack *116*
13. The Other Story *121*
14. Another Attack *125*
15. Prohibition *127*
16. Bag Man *130*
17. War Story *138*
18. Solution *143*
19. Move *147*
20. Sisters *148*
21. Basketball *151*
22. Train *157*
23. Colliers Magazine *161*
24. Al Capone *163*
25. Ralph Capone *166*
26. Ralph Meets Thomas *172*
27. Job Offer *176*
28. The Job *179*
29. Death *185*
30. Julia Stone *188*
31. Ann Geare *189*
32. Thomas Stone *192*
33. Safety *196*
34. Sunrise *203*
35. Irene Lucas *204*
36. James Conlin *207*
37. Ledger Entry *210*
38. Al Capone *212*
39. Nathan Lucas *213*
40. Irene Stone *215*
41. Crash *219*
42. Gone *224*
43. Thomas Stone *227*
44. Divorce *229*
45. Saturday Night *234*

THE SINGING BONE
PART THREE 1981

9. Liam Stone 242

STONE AND SON
PART THREE 1935

46. The Swimmer 246

THE SINGING BONE
PART FOUR 1981

10. Kathryn Stone 253

STONE AND SON
PART FOUR 1935

47. Thomas Stone 255
48. Backyard Party 258
49. The Future 263

THE SINGING BONE
PART FIVE 1982

11. Finish 266
12. Reading 269

THE SINGING BONE
PART ONE

CHAPTER ONE
CLOSET
MARCH 1980

Liam Stone stood at the closet door in his Mother's bedroom. He reached out to touch the brass doorknob, but hesitated, something he had never done as a child. Unwrapped Christmas presents, candy given up for Lent, shoeboxes of black and white photographs had drawn him into the room on clandestine searches. Today, his hand trembled as he pushed the door open. He could feel her scented arms wrap around him, but she wasn't there. Margaret Stone lay on the embalming table at Boland's mortuary, her neck broken in a single car rollover on a dry, sunny, Highway Eighty.

Dust particles, cut by rays of sunlight through a single window, suffused the closet with sudden life as he stepped over the threshold into the fragrant four-walled womb. He reached over to the window, loosened a tattered sheer, grasped the curved handles at the base of the window and forced it open. A cool wind blew shells of battered houseflies into the shallow grave of his deceased father's black wing tips.

He pushed his toe against the worn heel of the cracked shoes. Margaret had not moved them in the seven years since her husband's death at the age of sixty eight. Thomas Stone's business suits were in the rear of the closet, each hanger two inches apart, an order she had left untouched. Her dresses were within grabbing distance of the door.

Liam stepped past the dresses and suits, touched each sleeve before he reached the felt hats that lined the back wall, rubbed a finger along a cracked leather sweatband, absorbed the pungent mix of sweat and hair oil. He snapped the brim of the gray fedora, replicating what he had seen his father do thousands of times. Each hat had been blocked when it was retired and placed on the shelf facing the changing sky outside the window. Liam thought of his father. What made him laugh? What made him cry? What made him angry? Did he control the outbursts? Did he close the door knowing someone needed a hug? Did he leave home in the morning knowing he left a hole in the day?

He turned and held his father's hat in front of the suits, a row of elegant, orderly men, marching to work, shoulders square, left arms in position to carry a leather briefcase. He lifted the black tunnel of a pinstripe sleeve, held it to his nose. The faint scent of a sweet after-shave buckled his knees. He sank to the closet floor, pulled the jacket to his chest.

Why did you leave me?

He remembered the one A.M phone call seven years before; words from a scratched 78 record turning at 33 1/3 revolutions, the receiver feeling like silken ash as he listened to his mother's quivering voice.

"I'm sitting across from your father. I've been here for an hour. He's dead in his chair. I know he's dead. I can't move."

Liam took a deep breath, thought of hanging up, forced back a smile. The angina had finally stopped his father's heart. He could see the bottle of nitroglycerine tablets left untouched on the coffee table.

"Mom, I'll get there first thing in the morning." The line fell silent, something that always made him uneasy. He struggled to fill the void and was surprised when his own voice sounded firm.

"You have to call Doc Ryan now. He'll come over and take care of Dad. Then call Fr. Conlin."

"Just get here."

St. Bernard's rectory had two parlors. One large comfortable room on the left of the entry hall was known as the "Leave Your Wallet at Home Room." Committee's for Bingo Saturday's, Mother – Daughter breakfasts, Father – Son Breakfasts, sat around an oblong oak table with ornate legs and discussed budgets and personnel. Beer, soft drinks, nuts and sandwiches were served. The Irish pub atmosphere was complete with the soft sound of John McCormick's voice in the background. Some skillful parishioners got away with only their hours committed.

Across the hall the smaller and colder of the two rooms was used for personal meetings between parish priests and parishioners. It was known as the "Why Me?" room. Marital discord, child rearing, angry neighbors were discussed privately with the priest giving advice that somehow always sounded like a penance.

"Tell her you still love her, and say five Hail Mary's. Let me know how it works out at your next confession."

A stone fireplace anchored the east wall with a wooden crucifix centered above the mantle. The largest and most comfortable of three chairs in the room belonged to the pastor, Fr. James Conlin. It was an overstuffed deep brown leather chair that the parishioners had given him when the bishop announced his appointment. The other two chairs were straight back rough wooden peasant chairs with plank seats.

Liam and his Mother sat in the two peasant chairs as Fr. Conlin pushed embers around in the grate bringing up a brief blue flame.

"What about the burial?" asked Liam.

"He'll be buried in the family plot at St. Mary's next to his parents." The priest knocked the ash from his cigarette into a brass ashtray.

"What about a Mass?"

Fr. Conlin crushed the cigarette by swirling it in the ashtray until the red glow was extinguished.

"No Mass," the priest answered.

Margaret put a twisted hankie into her purse, snapped it shut and walked to the front porch. The screen door slammed loudly as the spring pulled it back against the door jamb.

"Doesn't look like now is the right time to talk to your Mom about becoming Catholic, does it?" The priest said.

Liam stood and walked out to the rectory porch where his mother was pulling a bit of tobacco off the tip of her tongue, a lit Camel in her hand. Liam knew that she wanted to stop, but wouldn't. Quitting had not helped Thomas. He had quit the lifelong habit just three months before his heart stopped.

"Mom, come on back in. We're almost done."

"Don't mind me, I just want to stew," she replied.

Margaret's permed white hair didn't move as a cold March wind came up the stairs. Liam put his arm around his Mother and recited,

March winds bring kites a flying,
April showers bring May flowers.

"Remember that Mom? Sitting on the front porch, watching

the clouds go by like racing ships, hoping for early rain and flowers."

Margaret's eyes scrunched as she smoothed her straight tweed skirt, twisted away.

"Liam, I can't go back in there. I won't listen to him anymore."

"You mean Fr. Conlin? All he wants is for you to start instructions. You can be a Catholic now."

"Instructions? Instructions? I know as much as he does. No mass! It's like Thomas served a prison sentence with no chance of parole. Now it's over. I'm done."

Liam tried to take her hand to coax her back into the rectory, but stopped when her face hardened.

"Leave me alone."

Liam took a deep breath, brushed a shock of black hair off his forehead,

"You stay here, I'll be out in a minute." He returned and sat across from Fr. Conlin. The priest looked over Liam's shoulder towards the porch.

"She won't be coming back, will she? " He asked Liam.

"No, she won't," Liam rubbed his palms together, sat straight in the chair. This was not as hard as he thought it would be.

"She'll be OK Father, she needed some air. How are we going to do this, without a Mass?"

"I'll say the usual prayers, a few words about your Dad, then you can read your eulogy. You'll write one of course. We'll keep it simple, go to the cemetery and then back to the house."

Liam slumped against the rigid chair back, realized that he hated the priest's habit of giving directions, never asking the question,

"What do you think?"

The priest's words resurrected the same sense of retreat that he had felt when discussing career plans with his father.

"Mechanic, you want to be an airplane mechanic? What a waste. Do something with that head of yours. Make me proud."

"That's it then. See you tomorrow Father."

Liam rose, wiped his hand against his trousers, shook the priest's hand with his strongest grip.

Flat gray clouds touched the crown of the church, ready to release the last half frozen drops of winter moisture onto the brown stubble and black streets in front of the red brick church.

Liam collapsed the umbrella he had been holding over his Mother.

"It's time Mom, we have to go in."

"It looks like the whole city is here. I didn't know he had so many friends," Margaret said.

"They're your friends too, lets go before Fr. Conlin comes out to get us," Liam said. As they approached the eight foot Cedar doors, the clouds opened, releasing a hard edged sleet that rang on the metal roof drowning out the Gregorian organ notes that filled the church.

Fr. Conlin stood in the entrance to the church, shadowed by the heavy wooden doors, his arms crossed in front of his waist, hands inside the loose sleeves of a long white alb. Margaret nodded imperceptibly as she and Liam went by. The priest said nothing as he closed the doors.

Margaret slid into the first pew. Liam followed and sat on the aisle. He reached over and ran his left hand lightly over the mahogany surface, wondered if his father felt it. He put his right arm around his mother's shoulder. Her eyes twitched, a sign that tears would come very quickly.

"I finished the eulogy last night," he said, "Short, to the point."

Margaret leaned into his shoulder,

"You know that all he ever wanted from you Liam was your love." She hesitated,

then said firmly, "I just want to put this behind me, get out the door."

Liam sorted his Mother's sentence in the back of his consciousness, next to,

"It's not that simple," then pulled her closer.

Father Conlin took his place at the head of the casket, two steps down from the altar that appeared to be on a separate unlit stage. The only light came from candles around the casket and narrow gray beams squeezing in through the tops of the stained glass windows.

"Thank you all for coming," Fr. Conlin spoke slowly as he looked directly at Liam and his mother, then scanned the crowd and adjusted the purple vestments he had selected for the ceremony.

As Fr. Conlin spoke, Liam looked at a small faded photo that he carried of the 1924 championship basketball team; stern, clear eyes, slicked back hair parted in the middle, neatly knotted narrow ties, straight backs. His father sat in the middle of this long table surrounded by Conlin, Coughlin, McLaughlin, O'Brien, Larson, Moriarity, Schmidt. The winning eight.

He turned to see who sat in the pews, saw bifocals, balding heads, liver spots, parchment skin thin enough to see through, stooped shoulders, paunches, gnarled hands, canes sticking up over the curved wooden backs separating the rows.

"Thomas was with us for 68 years. Some of you knew him your whole life, as I did." Fr. Conlin's voice echoed out into the vault of the main church.

"We grew up together, we played together, we fought, we criticized, and we tried to help each other. We relied on each other for direction, but in the end, we made our own decisions. Thomas helped many of you over the years. He had an amazing capacity to go out of his way to help his friends and even people he didn't know. His house was always open to you, to me, to the many priests and nuns that have been part of this parish over the years. His wife and children will miss him. I will miss him. But he has found his rest in God's almighty arms. A more deserving man could not go to St. Peter today. I can see him, hear him, as if we were talking basketball strategy. 'How can we beat those taller teams?' His answer was, 'Use your instinct, move, pass. Let Tony shoot. Stop them with constant pressure. Don't let them shoot.' To many of us, he was a second coach, even after he got into the insurance business. He faced great obstacles over the years. He overcame them with the same energy that he brought to Spalding's championship team of 1924. But as he grew older, he added one new element to this energy. Love. I've never known a man whose courage was exhibited so clearly through love. His love for his family, for his friends, his church gave him a compassion and resolve that we all benefited from. We will continue to benefit from our friendship with Tom as long as he is in our memories. I am proud to have had Thomas Stone as my friend. He will be buried in St. Mary's cemetery next to his parents, Julia and William. After that, you are all invited to the Stone's house for some of your own food."

The reference to the food brought smiles and nods from the women of the parish that had dutifully delivered their casseroles, Jell-O dishes, hams, roasts, pies, cookies, cakes and beer to the Stone house that morning.

Father Conlin's words rolled past Liam, to be absorbed by the eager ears behind him. The priest's sermons always found their mark. He could move the congregation to joy with his Christmas sermon and take them straight to hell during Lent. They waited anxiously, hoped for some insight into their own suffering. They worried about their lives, not Tom's. His journey was over. Theirs would go on and on.

"Now, his son Liam, will say a few words. A few words, right, Liam?"

Margaret sat motionless, staring at the casket. Father Conlin glanced towards Liam with mock sternness. Liam responded with the same sternness,

"Of course, anything you say Father. I'll follow *your* example."

Sighs of relief were heard as the congregation realized that the two men were sparring good-naturedly. Liam stood, took a step towards the casket. Margaret took his hand, held it to her cheek.

He wasn't sure how he would get through the eulogy. Would his Mother see his lack of emotion, would the priest see through his lies? His father was gone, but he had left a long time ago. No matter how often he came back to the house on Illinois Avenue, each mile that he drove in Central Illinois took him further from his son. He barely existed while he was alive, what was different now? The only image that Liam had to hold on to was the woman sitting alone in the front pew. She needed him now more than ever.

He looked to the right and saw the life size crucifix hanging between the thirteenth and fourteenth stations of the cross. Thirty feet down the aisle was the confessional that had greeted Liam every Saturday from his seventh birthday till he left for college. As far as Liam knew, his mother and father had never entered that heated box. He touched the marble altar rail just behind him, the same altar rail that he had received communion at since he was seven. He had never seen his father or mother at that rail.

"Thank you, Father, for being Dad's friend all these years. And thank you all for coming to say goodbye to my father, Thomas Joseph Stone. Some of you knew him much longer than I did. Some of you know more about him than I do. My memories are framed by his love. Not love alone, but love that stands next to anger and tempers it. Love that stands next to disappointment and gives hope. Love that stands next to pain and soothes it. I don't understand much of the pain that I know he felt. He would kneel next to his bed every night and pray. I thought this was normal until I got into my dorm in college. Not many of those beds had kneelers hooked to the frame."

"His prayers were private. He never prayed out loud, even in church. Was he praying to be released from suffering or was he praying for a way to give more love? His actions say that love won. He had a strategy, much like Father Conlin described for the basketball team." Liam turned to the priest who had returned to sit in the pastor's chair next to the altar, "Thanks for the intro to the team, Father, a great lead in."

"But his human strategy won hearts, not money, not games. He will be with us as long as we remember him as a man that overcame by giving."

Liam watched his Mother smiling. He wondered if she saw Tom's face from 1936, the year of their marriage? Liam was the same age as his father was that year, thirty one. She had often remarked how they had the same bold smile, the same full lips, the same straight nose, the same lift in their step.

But I'm not like him. I wouldn't leave her.

Her head fell to her chest and the tears Liam had seen just behind her eyes rolled down her cheeks. As he finished, she wiped her eyes and for the first time since Liam had come home, he saw her straighten her back..

Father Conlin moved quickly to the church entrance as Liam finished. He looked to see that the doors had been properly opened. Two altar boys followed the priest with candles in tall ornate holders, leading the rest of the congregation. Margaret walked slowly down the aisle towards the door. The priest shook hands, touched heads, smiled, as he did after every mass and funeral. He hesitated as Margaret passed, his eyebrows up as if he was going to say something. Margaret passed and he nodded.

At St. Mary's cemetery, Liam threw the last handful of darkened sod onto the casket, stepped back and swatted at the gnats hovering around his head. He reached down, scratched at his ankle bones, noticed blood on his fingers. He heard the squeak of the gears that lowered the casket into the grave. Margaret leaned heavily onto his shoulder.

"It's over," she said.

"Yeah, Mom, it's over."

Margaret stayed in the house on Illinois Ave. Liam pleaded with her to sell it, move into a different neighborhood.

"No, I've lived in this house for 36 years, I'll die in this house."

"If that's what you want, it's good enough for me," Liam said, not knowing that she would decide where and when to die, and it wouldn't be in that house.

Liam stood, hung the pinstripe jacket back in its position at the head of the marching line, pulled a large cardboard box out from under his mother's dresses. Lifetimes were jammed into that box, births, picnics, weddings, graduations, his wife Kathryn's first visit to meet his parents, images of smiling faces, toasts, arms locked together.

He laid the photos side by side on the floor, thought of each as a possible chapter in a novel. The older photos with no names on the backs, the sepia toned ones posed in blank studios with nothing to reference, were of little interest. When he had first discovered them at around six, he demanded to know who they were. But his father had told him that "they were dead, it didn't matter."

Now he felt an odd attraction to them but the pictures he cared about most were the ones his Mother was in. Here she was standing next to the closet door with a padlock in one hand, the other pointing at the door. A big smile on her face as if to say,

"Two doors open when Liam walks in, the front door and our closet door. The closet is now officially closed to him."

The last photo on the floor was mounted on a loose sheet of black paper. A cracked black and white image of the whole family standing in front of the house in winter coats, hands holding onto hats, ready for church. Four black photo corners held the image in the middle of the page. Below the photo, his mother had written in white ink,

"The whole gang ready to go." It was dated Christmas, 1953.

Liam remembered how just before that Christmas, at the age of ten, he had crawled under the long wool coats hanging in the back of the closet and discovered a box wrapped in plain brown paper. Very carefully he peeled the tape back, pulled the top section of the box back, and saw the unmistakable orange and black Lionel train boxes, remembered he had seen the same cars at Block & Kuhl's Department Store.

His father had mumbled something like, "Santa's coming soon."

He closed the box, pushed the tape back onto the paper as firmly as he dared, and crawled out of the closet, resolved to act surprised. He certainly didn't want his parents to know that he finally had figured out that they were the real Santa's.

On Christmas Eve, he sat in the back seat of the car as they returned from St. Bernard's church from the final Advent service. His Mother and his Aunt Ann, had stayed home. Liam was nervous, afraid to say anything.

"What's wrong with you, Liam? Cat got your tongue tonight?" asked his father, as he turned to his impatient passenger. "Hurry, Dad, I know he's been there with something great. And why did *two* people have to stay home tonight? It only takes one to put out milk and cookies."

So far, nobody knew that he knew. Under the tree were the smoking steam engine and six cars, riding unsteadily along the track laid around the pine Christmas tree. "How did Santa Claus know I wanted a train? Did he get it at Block & Kuhl's?" he said to nobody in particular. "Can I get a set of switches? Where do I get those smoke pellets if I run out?" Somehow he had pulled it off. They hadn't suspected a thing. His curiosity and confidence were matched perfectly.

Liam thought of his family's ordered life that started with Sunday mass. They were always on time and stayed until the priest was off the altar. Their regular pew at 9:00 A. M. Mass on Sunday was third from the front, on the middle aisle.

He never asked his father why he didn't go to communion. He never asked his mother why she didn't kneel during the Sunday mass. Nobody seemed to care. He and Aunt Ann filed up to the altar rail every Sunday, took the consecrated host into their mouths, firm in their faith that it was the body and blood of Christ. Sunday had a pattern as predictable as the penance given in confession. Get up, bathe, no breakfast, have to fast before communion, get in the car, drive three blocks to church. Come home, eat breakfast, wait for the visitors. Every Sunday, one of his father's friends, a priest or a few nuns, would visit the Stone house. There were no games of catch on Sunday.

Liam's favorite visitor was Ralph Whelan, an ex FBI agent. He was just under six feet and three hundred pounds. Ralph had wanted a son, but the fates brought him five daughters, each more beautiful then the one before. After each birth, he gained twenty-five pounds. When the fifth gorgeous little girl arrived, Ralph gave up trying, or rather, his wife, Beatrice, stopped letting Ralph try.

It would take Ralph five minutes to get from the car into the front room. By the time he got to the couch beneath the bay window sweat ran down the sides of his round cheeks that he'd mop with an already wet handkerchief. Then Liam's running began.

"Liam, get Ralph a beer."

"Liam, get Ralph another beer."

"Liam, get Ralph a towel."

Ralph brought stories of insurance fraud, bank fraud, and all other kinds of fraud that the FBI assigned for his investigation. Liam heard parts of stories, never the beginning, middle and end. When he asked his dad if he knew any of the crooks, the answer was, "Maybe, maybe not. Get Ralph an ash tray, will you Liam?"

Was his family different? All you had to do was look around at mass and see parents not going to the altar rail. But not every Sunday. Liam's parents were the only ones never to go.

The week bought a separate routine. On Monday, Thomas Stone stayed in Peoria. He went to work in the morning and came home at night, like every other father Liam knew. On Tuesday, Thomas separated himself from the other fathers. He got in his car and drove to the small towns that comprised his territory as a special agent for the Illinois National Insurance Company. He returned on Friday night.

Every Tuesday Liam asked "Where to today Dad?" as he watched his father shave and smoke his first cigarette in the bathroom next to Liam's room. One hand scraped off whiskers and the other moved a Lucky Strike between his mouth and the glass ash tray on the sink.

"We'll look at the schedule after breakfast."

By the time Liam got downstairs for breakfast, Thomas had eaten his All-Bran and smoked his second cigarette.

"Come on up after you finish your breakfast. We'll check out the travel for the week," Thomas would say as he patted Liam on the head.

Liam swallowed as fast as he could, raced upstairs to the front bedroom. He looked over Thomas's shoulder for a final look at the weekly agenda, handwritten in duplicate with carbon paper; shiny paper that left blue smudges on Liam's hands after he folded it into three exact sections, put it in an envelope addressed to company headquarters in Springfield, and handed it back to his father. A third Lucky lay in the grooves to burn itself out in the glass ashtray that Thomas had carried from the bathroom.

"Looks like Streator today, tomorrow Galesburg, Thursday, Peru. Home Friday, maybe we'll play catch."

"O.K. Dad. I'll have the gloves ready."

Liam watched him put on his suit coat, pick up his leather brief case, walk down the stairs, kiss Margaret, say good bye, and go out the back door to the car. By the middle of June, his left forearm and hand were deeply tanned, except for the white rectangular shape of a Hamilton watch on his wrist. He drove with the window down as he traveled throughout central Illinois: 9 o'clock position, right hand at the top of the steering wheel, left arm resting on the open window frame with left hand resting lightly on the wheel. His technique was perfect. No accidents in over 25 years.

On Friday nights, Liam played in the front yard, pushed a toy 52 Plymouth across the sidewalk, toward the worn pocket of his baseball glove that lay just in front of the concrete steps.

"He's almost off the highway, turning onto Knoxville," he said out loud as he maneuvered around rocks and clumps of dirt. "He knows the street, here he comes down the hill, almost home." He would look up, convinced he would see the car pull up in front of the house. He kept track in a spiral notebook of the times he looked out at just the right moment to see the Plymouth pull up to the curb.

July 10, 1954

I pushed the car home on time today, I am my father's navigator,

sailing into unknown harbors. My captain is always with me.

He didn't know what to call these moments. It was as if he was in a free zone, void of sound, except for a slight ringing in his ears that accompanied every entry. He never intended to show them to anyone. He hid them in a box in his own closet, and took them out only when some strange new association crept into his consciousness.

Liam thought of the mix of childhood freedom and pain as he put the pictures back in the box. How could he have spent so much time with Thomas Stone and feel as if he were skipping rocks across the depth of his life, waiting for the ripples to return and give him answers? How had he lost the ability to look out and see the world unfold as if he were driving down an Illinois highway with his father?

At one time he could absorb his surroundings and sense what was going to happen next. This was confidence, built on a lack of fear, but it had gradually been replaced by mistrust. 'What if?' became the opening question of the day, not, 'where to?' He retreated into his own conspiracy of silence, the urge to see the unknown replaced by comfortable habits acquired one by one. A shell masoned by fear had gradually covered his arms and hands, stopping them from reaching for the tracks in the dirt and writing in his notebook.

He walked out of the closet and carefully pushed the door shut, walked to his father's Steelcase file, pulled open the bottom drawer to look for a tattered brown folder marked "Divorce." It was always in the back of the drawer, conspicuous, but out of a small child's reach. The other folders were pure ivory. He tried to imagine the woman his father had married in 1927, she was the reason for the church's sanctions, no sacraments for his father, his mother not becoming Catholic. But the cabinet was surrounded by silence, the file was there, but empty. He wished he knew more about this mysterious woman. He sensed that his Mother had destroyed the contents of the dirty brown file after his father's death, trying to free herself from the memory of Thomas's first wife

Liam returned to the chest next to the closet door, opened the top left drawer and reached under the folded white handkerchiefs. The watch was still there. He tried to remember the last time he had felt no fear, knew what would happen next. Maybe the watch would bring back his sense of clarity.

He sank onto the chenille bedspread, engulfed in the late afternoon shadows of trees that rose above the shingled roofs. He turned the silver pocket watch over and over. His fingers traced the circumference from the winding knob and pendant loop down to the broken hinge. Black gothic arrows pointed to XII at the top of the marbled white face. The engraving was still clear on the back: "National High School Basketball Champions, 1924." He loved this watch.

Liam had found the watch in the same drawer in late 1954. He wanted to see how it worked and show it to his friends. While his mother was in the basement ironing, he went to the kitchen and pulled an old bent silver kitchen knife out of the utensil drawer, returned to the bedroom and started to pry at the side. Eventually he won the battle by twisting the back off. Two ruby eyes stared back at him, almost winking as they seemed to guide the interlocking wheels to a regular beat that brought a smile to his lips until he tried to close the back. The hinge was attached but he had bent it. The back swung up to close at the knob, but off to the side enough to prevent the solid snap that Liam had expected. He tried to bend the hinge, but sensed that any more pressure would separate it completely from both the frame and the back of the watch. The airy sense of discovery and accomplishment dissolved. Sweat erupted on his upper lip and temples. His hands appeared to be paws as he opened the dresser drawer and shoved the broken watch under as many handkerchiefs as he could pile on and still close the drawer. He retreated out of the bedroom, down the backstairs through the kitchen.

"Hey, Liam, where are you headed?" His Mom asked over her shoulder. She had finished the ironing and was peeling potatoes in the kitchen sink.

"Out back, Mom, I'm going to get that casting lure out of the apple tree. I'll use this old kitchen knife."

"O.K. but be careful. Don't use that wooden ladder from the garage, and don't drop the knife on the ground."

"I won't."

Sweat ran into his pants and down the back of his legs as he fumbled with the screen door. He got to the young crabapple tree and slid to the ground against its narrow trunk, facing the afternoon sun as it shown down the common driveway between the Stone's and Walker's houses. He wanted the light to scour the sin off his soul.

"I can't tell Dad, I can't tell Mom, I sure as hell can't tell Father Conlin."

This was Wednesday. Thursday passed, Friday came and his father was home from LaSalle. Liam waited, expecting to see him in shirtsleeves, belt in his hand. Saturday passed. Sunday morning, standing at the side entrance to St. Bernard's, his father smiled at him.

This is it, thought Liam. He was scared to death that during mass, Father Conlin would put the watch on the altar for the whole church to see. He'd have to kneel on the marble altar rail with his hands clasped, head bowed in prayer, asking forgiveness from the priests, the nuns, his friends, their parents, and Mom and Dad.

A normal mass. The Stone's went home.

Maybe he hasn't found it.

Liam decided to tell his father. Better to tell the truth, admit the mistake, take the punishment.

"Dad, can I talk to you?"

The nausea came back, exposing the black stain he imagined was still on his soul.

"In the living room?"

Liam closed the pocket doors to the dining room and the front hall way. He stood facing his father with his head turned slightly to the right in case his father's right hand swung. Maybe the blow would glance off.

"Dad, I broke your Championship watch, just the hinge. It still runs. Maybe we can get it fixed. I'll pay for it out of my lawn cutting money."

Thomas put his hand into his waistcoat and pulled out the broken watch, turned it over and over in his right hand. His face had darkened to a shade of purple red that Liam had never seen. His teeth were clenched and Liam thought he heard a grinding like gears in an old car. Thomas put the watch back into his pocket and walked out of the living room up the steps to his bedroom. The silence was as sharp and painful to Liam as a belt across his backside.

The topic of the watch never came up again between Liam and Thomas. But something had gone away with the admission of guilt. Liam didn't trust the reckless instinct for discovery any more.

He would wake every morning and repeat a variation on the nun's instructions to forge good habits, that they would replace the bad ones.

Stand still, don't move, it will go away. Good habits take the place of bad habits. Repeat the good thing over and over. The bad will go away.

Liam stood in the faint yellow light that shone in from the street lights, put the watch in his pocket. He remembered a clear view into the houses across the brick street, but now his vision was blocked by canopies of pin oaks and dutch elms. From the main floor he could hear his ten year old son Colin opening doors, closing them a second or two later. A slight smile creased his mouth as he thought,

We'll stay here tonight, he'll love staying in my old room. Maybe I'll tell him about the watch.

Liam felt as if he were rolling down a steep hill without brakes or steering. He reached out and pushed his hands against the sides of the window frame.

Why didn't I insist that he talk to me about the watch, the game, the divorce, how he met Mom. Now they're both dead.

Four nights before, he had thought it was his mother calling. He knew when she needed to talk. He could feel the loneliness with the vacant rings, but when he picked up the phone he heard the pharmacist from the hospital, where she worked in the personnel department, speaking with his southern Illinois drawl, simple, straight forward, just the right amount of grief and concern.

"Liam, it's Scott Simpson, I have some bad news."

Simpson paused, breathed a sigh, continued,

"Your mother's been killed in an automobile accident."

Another pause.

"Can you come?"

Liam's heart seemed to slow, the ringing in his ears that came at odd times with no warning, pushed the physical world outside his awareness, no emotion.

Act. Don't think. Get the garment bag. Get the plane.

"She's at the mortuary. There is a lot of work they have to do."

"There's a flight first thing in the morning. Where should I go first?"

"Come to the hospital, pick up her things, then probably to the house."

"Did you call Father Conlin?"

"Do you want me to call him?"

"Of course."

"There will be a service at the church and then to St. Mary's cemetery, right?" Liam said evenly.

"If that's what you want. Is it?" Scott replied.

"Yes."

Margaret had been returning from visiting her sister in Chicago. A trucker traveling north on highway eighty on a clear afternoon, reported that a car heading south, swerved to the right, off the highway, appeared to recover and return to the road, then flipped two or three times before landing on its roof. She was killed instantly when her neck snapped. Liam envisioned his mother suddenly releasing the wheel as she fought for control. He could see Thomas standing on the highway, at the top of a hill, with outstretched arms, beckoning to Margaret,

Now you've taken her away.

Since his father's funeral, the dialogue between Liam and his Mother had recovered much of the trust they had shared when he was in grade school. He would call from his office, and she would say before he said hello,

"Hello Liam, I know it's you." She didn't pause, continued talking.

"I was just thinking of the library. Remember how proud you Were when you could read books from the 5th grade shelf?"

"Yeah, Mom, I was in 3rd grade. But there were just better books on that shelf. I don't know if they were any harder. I was just having fun. My favorite was about 'Chief Black Hawk.' You said 'Red Badge of Courage' was for older kids, but you let me read about Henry Fleming and how he overcame his fears. It's still one of my favorites."

He called and listened for her to say that she missed Thomas, that it was harder than she ever expected. But she would never open her wounds for others to see. He could tell by her voice, no matter what the words were, that she missed Thomas deeply. Liam sent his poetry to her:

You are too sensitive
I saw that long ago
left alone will tell
your grief.
Is it enough to go on?
I see your face move.
Feel your shudders
As a fragrant
earth tremor

She called him and said in a controlled voice,

"You really know what I am thinking."

"Yeah, Mom, I do."

Colin yelled from downstairs.

"Dad, where are you?" At the same instant, the phone rang. It was his Aunt Grace calling from Chicago.

"Liam, you're there?"

"Yes, I came as soon as I could. I expected you would be here. Colin came with me. When can you get here? I thought I would start with the mortuary, but if you prefer, we can do it together."

"Did Kathryn come?" Grace said.

"She couldn't get a sub."

"I'll be there tomorrow. Will you be OK? Where are you staying?"

He ignored the OK? question.

"Colin and I will stay in my old room, still two beds there. I'll get some food. We'll be fine, plenty of room for both of us now."

Colin ran up the stairs, ringing the bells attached to an old leather harness.

"Dad, who was that?" He said as he jumped into Liam's lap

and rubbed his hands on his Dad's day old stubble. Liam struggled to focus on his son's question.

"Your great aunt. Won't it be fun seeing her again?"

. "What's her name again? I don't remember her very well. Where will we sleep then? Is Granma going to sleep next to Granpa? I think she would like that. Let's do that. Then you and Mom will have a place too, right?"

Liam's eyes stung as he listened to the rapid barrage of questions.

Colin started in again,

"Dad, what was Granpa like? I don't remember him. Did he live here with you? When did he die? Will they be together now? Let's eat, o.k? I'm really hungry."

"How about McDonald's? Colin. You can have the double burger, and I can have your fries."

"You can have half my fries if you order two bags. Then tell me about Granpa."

Liam looked at his son and wondered where the unlimited curiosity came from. His questions could only be answered when he paused to think of a new one.

Was I ever like that? Maybe I've lost something that he is trying to give back to me.

"OK, dinner and then I will tell you everything I know about Granpa. And I may tell you a few things about your old man. How's that?"

"Weeellll, OK." Colin dragged out the answer,

"I'm just kidding, you can tell me about you too," his smile almost hiding the freckles that blended across his face.

Margaret's funeral was a simple burial ceremony at St. Bernard's. Her casket rested in the same space below the altar rail that his father's had seven years before. There was no mass. She had not become a Catholic after Thomas's death. She had not set foot in a Catholic church. Fr. Conlin made a few comments about Mary's support of the parish and her family. It was a short speech without his customary flair.

Liam and Colin sat in the front row, the same pew he had shared with Margaret seven years before. In one hand he held a black and white glossy photo from 1936. Thomas and Margaret had just moved into Thomas' parents' house. They stood in the back yard framed by the latticed porch. He had on a white pin stripe double breasted suit, straw boater, saddle shoes. She had on a bold hat, short shirtwaist dress and elegant pumps. They were smiling directly at him, he imagined her saying,

We did our best, Liam, it's up to you now.

His other hand squeezed a piece of spiral note paper that held the words he had written that morning after waking from a recurrent dream. He was still agonizing over the poem when Fr. Conlin called his name. He had a few stanzas he was satisfied with, but was still changing words as he walked to the head of the casket. Finally, aware of the slight murmuring, he raised his head.

"Please excuse the delay," he held up the single white sheet of paper for them to see the crossed out words, hoping they would be sympathetic with his agony.

"I wanted to read a poem that I wrote for Mom while she was still alive. It came from a dream that I started having after he died. But I'm not sure if I should read it. I was once asked by a priest to write a poem for Easter Sunday. When he read it, he said 'Good Friday, Liam, read this on Good Friday. There's more death here than resurrection.'" Liam looked up with a small smile, saw a few nodding heads, heard repressed laughter. "It is difficult to say that you're glad that someone is dead, especially if you love that person as much," Liam stopped, wiped his hand across his forehead, "as much as I loved Mom. But I know she's not been happy for the last seven years. She wanted to be with him. She told me that some things were hidden from small sailors, that eventually they had to find their own safe harbors. She said she prepared me to find my own way. Now she is gone, I know she's happy, now we are faced with a new river that flows on." Liam stopped, looked down at the poem that he would not read, "She is happy in the arms of the man that she loved."

CHAPTER TWO
SUPERIOR LODGE

Umbrellas of color hung along bare ski runs that sloped toward the main lodge. The mix of yellow hickory and walnut with red oak and scarlet poplar was framed by black-green stands of pine that offered a sense of permanence on the long descent to the basalt shore of Lake Superior. The lodge was built to witness the consistent flow of seasons from the hills; lush green summers through the colors of fall to the frozen white of winter; and separate them from the equally predictable beauty and sometime violence, of the largest fresh water lake in the world.

Father James Conlin sat in front of large casement windows between two hand carved pillars. The chairs and tables were smooth blonde pine decorated only by rounded legs that tapered slightly to the wide plank floor. Each table was covered with two cloths, the lower visible from the sides. His table had the best view of the lake, ready for contemplation or conversation. He looked around and smiled, pleased with his choice.

Rough hewn high beamed ceilings held the sounds of dishes, utensils and voices without returning them at vicious angles to private ears. Waitresses moved quickly through the North Woods dining hall in the same style uniform that they had worn since the 20's, black short sleeve shifts, starched white aprons, black oxford shoes; a sharp contrast to the majority of diners in their plaid flannel shirts and faded denim jeans, ready for trekking or just happy to look like natives of the Minnesota boundary waters.

Fr. Conlin had walked into the lodge with a slight lean. He seemed to control the warm interior and cold blustery sky at the same time. His steel gray eyes surveyed the rows of diners like a benevolent hawk scanning his territory; a finely tailored black jacket and Roman collar said priest, but his manner said executive.

"Are you sure I have a clear view of the lake and a good waitress?" Father Conlin asked the hostess.

"Yes Father, the best table, and the best waitress, each day, just for you."

The young hostess, working her first fall color change at Lake Superior Lodge, guessed his age at 75, until she stood closer and spoke to him. A long blade-like nose, soft almost smooth skin, neatly combed back gray hair and his habit of speaking into a person's eyes with no hand movement, changed her guess to 65.

Jim spoke in a hushed tone,

"I'm diabetic, you know, I have to keep close watch on when I eat, when I take my insulin shot, and I have a friend meeting me here at 11:30."

His waitress, who had been moved from another station under the guidance of the hostess, brought a glass of cranberry juice to his table at 11:10, came back at 11:20 with a worried look on her face,

"Can I get you another cranberry juice Father? Your friend isn't here yet,"

"He will be here. It's only 11:20. I told him 11:30. He does whatever he's told ever since I baptized him."

"Let me know if you need anything, I will be going back and forth from the kitchen," she said as she turned to the four men sitting at the adjoining table, "You guys want anything?"

A black leather satchel sat at Jim's feet. He would need to take it to the men's room soon. But he worried about not seeing Liam when he entered the dining room. Perhaps he should wait a few minutes past 11:30 to insure a first look at Liam, standing, looking for him; a worth while risk that would give him a slight edge in the conversations to come. He wondered if Liam at 38 would look more like his father than he did at Margaret's funeral a few months ago. It would be easier if he looked like his father; a conversation with a boyhood friend, his best friend. But he couldn't wait too long and run the risk of even the slightest insulin reaction. He wanted this meeting to work for both of them, but he needed to be in control.

Jim swirled the ice cubes against the glass, looked out through the curtain of glass to fir trees hanging on to a granite escarpment. Their roots reached back thirty feet, absorbing whatever moisture was left by the upright pines. Tomorrow the firs could be washed out to the horizon. How many years had they hung on? Perhaps as many as he had.

The lodge faced southeast, catching the morning sun as if it came on a straight line from Miami through Chicago. The Lake always surprised him. He still expected to see Michigan or Wisconsin on the horizon. He remembered his uncle, his mother's brother, telling him that he couldn't see across the big lakes to the other shore. He didn't believe that story any more than he believed in Limbo or Purgatory at age 10. He was 13 when he stood on the shore of Lake Michigan and told his uncle what a genius he was.

The noon sun broke through the scrambled clouds shining directly on meringued white caps. Scattered points of light seemed to form a crystal lattice that moved slowly towards him. In each point he saw an event in his life. Plucking one would collapse the fragile structure. He could only massage the edges, hoping for some insight into its relation to the others. He thought of the ships that lay at the bottom of the lake, entombed in catacombs, each assigned a row and number. Perhaps he could be next. He pushed the watery apparition aside, saw himself in a small plane, flying out over the lake, running out of gas. Nobody would see it for what it was. It would be a tragedy caused by the collision of high and low pressure systems. Bishop O'Reilly would write in the Diocesan newsletter,

Driven to see if his old flying skill remained, 76 year old Fr. James Conlin took a Beechcraft Debonair out for a brief flight. Against the wishes of the planes owner and Jim's instructor, Tim McLaughlin, he took off just before the storm hit. His plane crashed 2 miles off Stony Point Bay. Local rescue efforts by the National Guard Air Wing proved fruitless and were called off as the storm intensified. We will all miss Jim.

The idea of a last flight and its explanation scared and exhilarated him.

An original thought. How many do I have in a day? Not many. How many have I had in my life? I chose the church, I chose the teachings, I believe in them, but how have I used my own intellect, my own passion?

Other less creative ways of exiting had occurred to him since he was diagnosed with diabetes, just one year after a quadruple bypass surgery had saved his life. Pills, guns, ropes. But somehow he woke every morning and found a purpose. He lay motionless for the first few minutes reciting Hail Mary's and Our Father's. Abstract, unemotional, rote recitations of ageless prayers; the first piece of a frame that surrounded each day.

Finally, rising, showering, shaving, going to the priests dining room, the depression would slowly dissolve. The next action was a life saving affirmation. In previous years, the daily consecration of the host gave each day its purpose. Now at exactly 7:45 A.M., just before the eggs, bacon, toast, and coffee were put on the table, he went to the rest room and pushed the insulin syringe against his stomach, felt the fluid enter his body. The day began, the routines took over.

Is this how Tom Stone lived his life? Repeat the same routine day after day? Liam deserves to know. He will expect the truth. No more pious avoiding, protecting. Isn't that what Tom did? Protect Liam? Close the door whenever a tough subject came up. No wonder little Liam had a smile on his face all the time. Didn't know the world had more pain than presents.

Fr. Conlin thought of the call he had made a few days before.

"Hello."

"Liam?"

"Yes."

"Jim Conlin."

"Father, how are you."

"I want to see you. Can you join me at Lake Superior Lodge Monday at 11:30? I

have made two reservations for Monday and Tuesday night. " He expected Liam to say, "What is this about? I haven't heard from you since Mom died. You haven't answered any of my calls."

Instead, he heard a note of relief,

"Of course Father. I've got a meeting with my publisher, but I can postpone it. All she's going to do is complain about my lack of material anyway." Liam then asked, "How are you getting to Superior? I heard you wouldn't drive on a highway because of the diabetes."

"Timmy McLaughlin is flying me. He's got a small flying school

Close to the resort and he promised me good weather."

"You mean Tony McLaughlin's son? We went to high school together."

"That's the one."

"Well, that's it then," Liam said, "I'll see you Monday."

He saw Liam standing at the check in counter, garment bag over his arm. He wore all black; turtleneck sweater, wool slacks and a leather blazer. It was 11:29 A.M.

I knew it.

Liam gave the bag to a porter and turned to walk into the dining room, past the fire place big enough to stand in, and the stuffed six foot snarling polar bear. Their eyes caught and they both smiled.

Liam strode quickly to the table, reached out for Jim's hand and grasped his right shoulder with his left hand.

They're both touchers. Like father, like son. Fr. Conlin felt that the way a man presented himself at first was sometimes an indication of what he was not. A cover from somebody else's book. Not in Liam or Tom Stone's case. You got what you saw, to a fault. He remembered that people often mistook the two for brother's, especially after Tom had cut his slicked back hair into a crew cut in 1959. Broken wire rim glasses had led to a shocking change. Short hair, Buddy Holly glasses. A huge change that followed twenty years of no change.

"Father Conlin, how are you?"

"Just fine Liam, thanks for coming on such short notice."

The young waitress walked over as she saw Liam sit down.

"Father, would you like another juice? And what can I get for you, sir?"

"We'd better order, do you mind, Liam? I'm diabetic, you know, and I have to take my insulin shot pretty quickly."

"No, that's fine, I know you're diabetic, I'm starved," Liam looked at the waitress with a smile confined to his left cheek.

"What do you recommend?"

"The roast beef is very good, or the pot roast, but we are best known for our walleye served on wild rice."

"Pot roast with fries for me, and an iced tea this time," responded Fr. Conlin.

"Do you have a chicken breast sandwich and a mixed green salad with vinaigrette dressing?" Asked Liam.

"Sure, with the skin or without?"

"Without, and mustard, please. And I'll have a diet coke with lemon."

Liam opened his napkin, arranged the fork on the left and the knife and spoon on the right, spread the linen on his lap, picked at the lint on his black wool trousers, looked directly into Jim Conlin's eyes and said,

"Why am I here?"

"Excuse me, Liam, I have to go to the rest room and take my shot. I won't be able to answer any questions without it. But that's why we're here, to answer questions. By the way, where did you get that jacket?"

He didn't wait for an answer, stood, and walked to the rest room. Within minutes, the food arrived. Fr. Conlin returned as the last bit of warm steam rose to the wooden rafters.

Liam asked,

"In time?"

"Won't know for a minute, but I've gotten pretty good at this," Jim replied and continued,

"Food looks good, has it been here long?"

"Just got here."

"How have you been, Liam?" asked Father Conlin, as if they were old friends that had seen each other once a month for lunch.

"Fine, just fine."

"Tell me about what you've been doing for the past few years. I haven't kept up with you kids like I used to."

"I understand, I know you didn't see Mom much after Dad died. Guess there just wasn't much for the two of you to discuss. Her staying away from the church and all."

"Right, I went to see her a few times, but we seemed to be in different worlds. I just wish I could have helped her a little," the priest said.

"I never brought it up, becoming Catholic, I figured she knew what she wanted. She didn't even talk much about Dad, we talked about grand kids and books and how my writing was going. She was really excited when I sent her my first book of poems. But I could tell she was very lonely, she would call sometimes and say,"

'Just thinking about you, were you thinking about me?'

"Funny thing was, most of the time, I *was* thinking about her. I visited her a few times in Peoria, and she came to Minneapolis once or twice, but mostly, we talked on the phone."

"I know she was proud of you, your writing is what she talked about the few times we did see each other. I kept hoping I would turn around one Sunday and see her, but it didn't happen," the priest said.

They finished their meals and had coffee as the last of the sportsmen filed out. The sun had moved to the northwest wall of the lodge and the water seemed to be darker, rolling in smooth arches against two large rocks twenty yards from the pebbled beach. The dining room was quiet except for their spoons hitting the coffee cups, dishes being removed, sugar containers being filled, napkins, silver, and glasses recovering the square mahogany tables.

"When did you know you were a writer?" Father Conlin asked.

Liam leaned back, hesitated as if he didn't want to answer the question, as if he knew this was a delaying tactic, but answered.

"I had six jobs in twelve years; Dad had two, as far as I know, during his whole career."

"I've only had one," Fr. Conlin replied.

Liam smiled, said, "Lucky you," then continued.

"Each job looked great at the start, but the end was always the same, 'You've got a lot to offer, Stone, but not in this situation. Better for both of us, if we end it here,' or I would see something that looked better, more money. I was a great interview. Usually got the job, for awhile. Finally, we were having Thanksgiving dinner a few years back, Colin was asking me why I changed jobs so much. He said, 'Dad, you should send your poems in. *Those* guys will like you better than the ones you work for now. Mom could go back to teaching.'

"I guess I had been avoiding the commitment that it takes to write. It seemed easier in a way to have a place to go to every morning and people to meet and papers to sign. Kathryn said she would go back to work teaching, give me time to get a publisher and start making some money. She believed, still does, that I can make a living as a writer. She says writer, not poet. Once I made the commitment to writing, the stuff just seemed to flood out from somewhere. I was afraid of the chasm that I had to get over, but I just started building these little cantilevered pieces and finally got to the other side. Each poem is like that. The difference now is that I have the confidence to stare across the pit," Liam's words came faster, tumbling over each other in their haste to get out.

"I went to readings, read some of my stuff when there was open reading. People seemed to like it. Especially older women, I mean sixty and up, and over worked mothers. Guess I understand them. Anyway, I sent some poems to a poet on the English staff at the U and he suggested I send a them to the local presses. I got lucky. I got an advance from "White Cloud," a small publishing house in St. Paul. They got me on local talk shows as a late blooming writer. Sold enough for White Cloud to want another book. I'm working on that now. But I couldn't do it without Kathryn working full time."

"She's been great, she loves teaching. I feel guilty sometimes that she does everything for other people. Not enough for herself. But someday, someday. I have an idea for a novel, but every time I try, the dreams that work as poems, get in the way of writing a good story. I can't get past these images of fast rivers, dirty sand, broken shells, bright lights. And always some Irish connection. Dad never talked about his father, his grandfather, where our people came from. It wasn't like he was ashamed, more like he didn't have time."

Jim listened patiently. He was tempted to turn to the side, as he did in the confessional, put his hand to the side of his head and nod in understanding as Liam blurted out his life story. *Not much to forgive here, I wonder when he'll start asking questions?*

"I'd like to get to the reason I asked you here," Fr. Conlin said.

"Sorry, sometimes I just get going. I haven't seen or spoken to You in so long, I guess I felt I needed to bring you up to date. Then maybe I'm just nervous, why *are* we here?"

"Do you still have the house?" Fr. Conlin asked.

"It's on the market, but the agent tells us that the right buyer hasn't come along. Why? What does that have to do with you and I sitting here eating lunch?"

"Did you know that your father had been married before he met Margaret?"

"Yes, I knew. But I never spoke to him or Mom about it. There was a folder in his file cabinet marked 'Divorce,' now it's gone. I think Mom destroyed whatever was in it. I started to look at it a few times, but I knew that if he wanted to talk about it, he would. I asked him once what it was like growing up in Peoria. He asked me what I meant. 'You know, how did you feel about your school, your friends, your parents.' He told me that he would never talk about his feelings. 'Why, that just wouldn't be right,' he said. So, I figured it was better left untouched. It's only recently that I really want to understand what he went through. That's why I came up here. I figure you're the last one left that really knew them. He was gone so much, we were always busy with sports or school or jobs, it didn't matter much to me that he had been married and divorced. It didn't bother Mom."

They did a great job of protecting him, maybe too good of a job.

"You mean, *you* were so busy. Nobody could ever sing 'Good Night Irene,' your Dad wouldn't allow it. It was not something any of us ever joked about," Father Conlin said, and was suddenly aware of the quiet in the room.

"There was that time when I was a freshman at Spalding…Father Brown, the principal, wanted to see me," Liam said.

"Yes, I know that story, you came to me, asked me not to tell your parents."

Liam turned his chair to the right and faced the lake, then looked back over the dining room. He and Jim Conlin were the lone diners. The edge that had disappeared with the after lunch coffee, returned to their voices.

"You came to see me for advice, but what you really needed was someone to talk to. You told me a story," the priest said.

"You tell *me* this time Father, I can't seem to remember the punch line."

Father Conlin leaned a little forward, lowered his voice and began.

"This is what I remember, jump in any time. The principal told you that you could be a better Catholic, that someday, you would thank him. He told you that you were illegitimate, that your Dad was married and divorced before he married your Mother. The church didn't recognize a marriage performed by a justice of the peace in Indiana. That's why he and your mom never went to communion."

The room was free of noise, the tables had been reset, all the sugar containers were full, the only sound came from the lakes submerged waves erupting on the shore and pulling back into their own blackened throat. Father Conlin watched Liam's jaw tighten, his hands grip the edge of the table as he came to the end of the story.

"The principal told you that Tom could get back in the church And your Mom could become a Catholic. All they had to do was sign a document that said that they would live as sister and brother for the rest of their lives. He wanted you to tell them about this great opportunity. In so many words, you told Fr. Brown that there was a better way, he just hadn't figured it out. Is that about right?"

Liam was slumped into his chair, his chin in his left hand., his elbow held up by his crossed right arm.

"Why bring this up now? Why not when he died? Why not right after mom died?"

Father Conlin, pushed his coffee cup away and said,

"We all tried to protect you Liam. I fell into the same trap. You remember what I told you. I told you to go home and forget it. Your Mom & Dad had their own lives and didn't need your principal interfering. You seemed satisfied then. In fact, you started telling me about how you had memorized your first poem as a punishment for acting up in English class. You were different from the rest, a little smarter, a little quicker; we all wanted that promise to come alive. But protecting never works. You start relying on other people too much. I've wanted to talk to you, but I didn't know what difference it would make. I thought you could get by without knowing more about your Dad and what drove your Mom. They're all dead now, I don't have a lot of time left. If I don't talk to you now, it would be like I was lying to you, and that is worse than protecting you. "

"Who else is dead? I know about Mom and Dad."

"Tony McLaughlin, remember, the county sheriff, he was the center on the team. He died last month."

"I know as much about that team as I do about the divorce. Dad didn't tell me about it. Mr. McLaughlin was not one of the regulars at the house. You know that. What's the rest?"

The sun brushed through the panes of glass leaving spots of pale yellow light on the table between the two men. Father Conlin absently traced a line with his finger through an oddly shaped circle that moved slowly towards Liam.

"Some of the details are gone, but the important part is to tell you as much as I know about your father. How well do you think you knew him?"

Liam appeared agitated, "Get to the poin…" hesitated, and said,

"I remember little things that he did. Not much of what he said. I remember his cough in the morning as he shaved, a cigarette burning on the edge of the sink. I remember playing catch, going to get a haircut on Saturday mornings. I remember some angry reactions; swearing when the window fan wouldn't fit in the hall window. I *don't* remember sitting down to talk about his job, if he liked it, we never talked about sex. In fact, I don't remember ever using the word when he was around. He was gone a lot…."

The last sentence faded slowly as each word was spoken. He looked down into his hands resting on the table next to the small spot of light that had traveled across the table.

"He was gone, he was gone," Liam whispered.

"Liam, what is it? What are you thinking about?" Jim said softly. He had heard and felt these reactions many times in the confessional. His urge was always to say 'aha, now you see it,' like a refrain from an old song. Instead, he leaned forward and repeated,

"What is it?"

Liam put his hands over his ears, shook his head side to side.

"He was gone, I never felt anything when he was gone. I didn't *miss* him. I didn't want to see the anger. I just wanted to play catch with him. I played all the sports: football, basketball, baseball. They were a kind of shield, a protection from talking. I don't know, I didn't know where it came from."

"What came from?"

"Having to play sports. They took up all the days. I have a beat up picture of him as a high school senior staring at the camera.

Maybe a team or a class picture. But they're not in rows. They're sitting around a table, a long rectangular table. They're all staring at the camera. But he *is* looking directly at me. Every hair is in place; his face is long and thin, chiseled. His lips aren't full, but have finely defined edges. He is trying to tell me something, but I can't hear the words, they're too far away."

Liam leaned back, dropped his hands from his ears.

"I'm sorry Father, to put you through this. I never grieved for him. My ears would hurt, a loud ringing, every time I got close to grief, or maybe it was anger, I stopped, forced myself to buck up."

Jim sighed, sat back and listened, as Liam started in again.

"I have very specific memories of you, Father. How in some ways, you acted as a surrogate. Interesting image, don't you think, physical father, spiritual father. I was always a little afraid of you. Did you know that you had as much to do with shaping me as he did. Did you know that you had that power? Is it something you do consciously?"

Liam's voice started to rise, but he seemed to catch the change, leaned over the table as his voice lowered,

"Is that what this is about? You seeing if I ended up your son or his? Or maybe you want to tell me about yourself, before it's too late. Somebody here needs to know you. You're human like the rest of us, and want to leave knowing some of it matters. The hardest part for Dad, myself, maybe you, is living up to other's expectations. The church's, your friends. I don't have any expectations. I accept you for who you are. Is that it? You hope that I will listen and not judge. That I'm like him?"

Liam stopped, "Sorry, Father. I guess this is not going the way you expected."

How do I answer that? He wants to be like his father. I'm the only one that can tell him if he is, Father Conlin motioned to the waitress, looking for a diversion, not for himself, but for Liam.

"Is it OK if we stay here?"

"Do you see anybody that would object?" She circled the room with her finger.

"We must look a little out of place, all in black. Maybe we should wear jeans tonight?" Fr. Conlin said.

"You know, stay in black, it adds a little diversity to the crowd," she smiled at both of them.

"When I think about your father, I think of extreme courage, love, loyalty, and stupidity. They all go hand in hand. Stupidity usually leads to the others. I'll tell you what I know. The rest is up to your own imagination, or research. In the end, no matter what you hear," he paused, "or read, you have to decide for yourself. Nobody can fill in all the details, especially what he was thinking. I think that being an only child brought out the best and the worst in him."

Liam rubbed his hand through his thick black hair, pushed the chair back from the table and crossed his legs.

"What do you mean, 'read?' I don't know of any official History of the Stone family. Anytime I asked questions about people in the pictures, he and Mom would say, 'You wouldn't know them, they're dead.' And if I asked a question about their childhood, especially Dad, he would say,

'Why do I want to talk about that?' and then change the subject. He sure wouldn't have written anything down. Or would he?"

"Just listen for a minute. Your Dad and I grew up on the south Side of Peoria. For a while it was pretty bland. Then the War, "

Liam smiled and said,

"You mean the "Great War?""

"Of course, I mean the 'Great War.' Anyway, after the War, Congress passed the Volstead Act and liquor was illegal. By the time we started high school, there were speakeasy's on every corner. Our favorite was Rocky Sullivan's on Aiken. We'd walk up, knock on the door, and say,

'Pete, or Harry, or anybody for that matter, sent me.' It was owned by the father of a friend of ours. He thought it was better if his son's friends drank within walking distance of home under his supervision. Remember, not everybody had electricity, radio's or cars in those days. Entertainment for teenage boys revolved around sports, girls and booze."

Liam interrupted Fr. Conlin,

"So what else is new?"

"What else is new is that prostitutes and racketeering came along with the illegal booze. Your father was always writing, I don't know when he started, he may have been *printing* stories in first grade. Once in a while he told me what he was writing about, but most of the time, he said it was none of my business. I didn't like going into his house, his mother wanted to read to us all the time. 'Listen to this,' she would say, 'you'll learn something.' She must have started him on the writing. Her heroes were authors, Stephen Crane, Melville, Dreiser,

Mark Twain. She saw him as her little writer-hero. We had to sit straight, talk when spoken to, and when Tom started to write down what he saw on the street, what went on in his father's grocery store, she loved it. His father hated it, figured it would eventually lead to problems. You don't know any of this, do you?"

"No."

"William, your grandfather, and namesake, didn't understand Why he was writing about the neighborhood. He'd grab Tom by the shirt sleeve and pull him real close, 'Why are you writing about those goons? And who said you could use one of my ledger books?' Your grandfather was a very funny man, until he got angry. I saw him angry once, had to do with the two kids that ran the booze and protection scams."

"What do you mean, 'kids?"

"They were 3 or 4 years older than us, 17-18 when prohibition started. They were already part of the mob. Tom had some notion that by writing a story about them, he would save their souls. Walk em into St. Patrick's, into the confessional. I told him to just stay away from the bums, and the girls on the street. Ironic that in the beginning, he wanted to convert all the sinners. I just wanted to play basketball."

"Who are you talking about? Not my father. He was ready to help people, but write it down? He wrote schedules, described buildings that needed fire insurance, detailed automobile accidents. And he didn't read anything but the Journal Star," Liam countered.

"They hid things from you, tried to protect you. Maybe, just maybe, you didn't want to know. You were in your own world, so busy with your games. Remember, I asked you about the house. Have you gone through it?"

"Yes, I remember, and no, I haven't gone through it. We just put it on the market a few months ago. I haven't been back since Mom died. The pharmacist from the hospital is taking care of it."

"Start there. Before it's sold. I've thought about this a lot and it's the best way. You need to hear it from him."

"C'mon Father, how can I hear from him? I don't trust mediums or Ouija boards."

James Conlin heard the sound of Lake Superior splattering against the window. He looked out and was sure he could see Thomas Stone standing on the watery horizon, glaring at the lodge. He was holding tightly to something. It looked like a black book with red edges. He wondered if Liam saw the same misty apparition.

"I told you he wrote in these ledgers. The last time I heard about them was right after he married your mother in 1936. He said he was through writing. They're in the house somewhere. He hid them. You have to go back and find them." The words came out of his mouth as if they were wrapped in cotton.

"Look, Liam, I don't feel so hot. Best if I go up and rest a bit. How about if I meet you back here for dinner. You make sure we get the same table."

At 6:15 P.M., they sat at the same table. All they saw in the window was their own reflection and the reflection of the same plaid shirts that had been there during lunch. Jim ordered lake trout and Liam ordered walleye. Both specialties of the lodge. As at lunch, Father Conlin got up and went to the men's room to inject his insulin just as the food arrived. He seemed to return quicker this time, a familiar route in place. The knife bounced off the fish as Jim tried to cut it. The fish appeared to have a protective coating. Liam smiled and said,

"That fish does not want to be eaten."

Jim tried to cut it once more and put the utensils down on the table.

"Wouldn't you know, probably came from Lake Michigan," he said with a touch of irritation, "I need something pretty quick."

Liam cut a piece of his walleye and put it on Jim's plate as he motioned for the waitress.

"What have you got quick? The trout has a shield around it," Liam said as he punched into the side of the suspect fish.

"I'm really sorry, I've never seen that before. Usually the Lake Trout from Chicago are pretty good. How about an egg salad sandwich?"

"Five minutes," Jim said, "And hurry."

Jim ate the piece of Walleye, looked up at Liam,

"Your dad and I had run-ins with those two guys I mentioned at lunch. They called themselves Cobb and Dempsey. I think he started writing about them to get rid of them. Or at least to handle how he felt. They wanted Tom to be their bag man."

Liam dropped his fork. As it clanged against the plank floor, the young waitress walked by.

"Where's the sandwich?" Jim asked with a mix of anger and disappointment.

"Coming right up Father."

Liam leaned forward and whispered.

"What do you mean, bag man?"

"Just like it sounds. They wanted your Dad to pick up protection
money from neighborhood merchants. Put the money in a bag and deliver it to them."

"You guys were what, 12-13 years old?"

"We were old enough to go into Rocky Sullivan's and have a beer, we were old enough to be considered for a mob job. At least your dad was."

"Tom told his Dad, your grandfather. He stopped them."

"How?"

Jim Conlin's face gave the first sign of the insulin reaction. Sweat ran down his temples and there was a twitch in his left cheek and eye.

"Father, are you all right?"

"No, I need cranberry juice *now*."

The waitress was coming through the swinging door to the kitchen with the sandwich when she heard the priest's plea. She quickly grabbed another large glass of cranberry juice and served it with the sandwich. Jim swallowed the juice in one gulp.

"This is why I don't drive on the highway. There are two of you over there, right?"

Liam reached over and wiped Jim's forehead with his napkin.

"What can I do Father?"

"Nothing. I'll be fine. But I better go back tomorrow morning. Call Tony's son, tell him it's important that I get back before noon. I don't want to take any chances. He'll do whatever he needs to get me home. But you need to promise me one thing."

"Of course."

"Find the journals your Dad kept. We want you to read them," Fr. Conlin's voice sounded like a file being pulled over a ragged piece of iron.

"Who's "*we*"?

"Your dad and I."

Jim Conlin felt a tightening in his throat, a hand seemed to be closing on his windpipe,

"Go away, Tommy, I know you said not to tell anyone about the ledgers, and I haven't for all these years, but he is in front of me, not you."

Liam grabbed the priest's hand, "Father, who are you talking to? Where should I look for the ledgers?"

"Nobody," he said firmly. "I don't know exactly where they are. They're sure not in that closet of theirs. You would have read them long ago if they were. Look in the basement, maybe the garage. There's quite a few, so look for a taped up box of some kind."

The owner of the lodge was now standing next to the priest,

"Father, we have a doctor staying with us tonight, would you Like to see him?"

"No, I know more than a doctor. Just let us out of tomorrow night's reservation. We'll both be leaving first thing in the morning."

"Fine, we can make that happen."

The room was quiet, every eye was turned to the two men in black, dressed as if they were on their way to a funeral in Grand Marais.

Father James Conlin died a week later of coronary complications due to diabetes. He was 76. Bishop O'Reilly presided over a formal funeral mass that included six remembrances from bishops, monsignors, priests and lay people. Liam Stone was a pall bearer. James Conlin was buried next to his own mother, twenty five yards from Thomas and Margaret Stone.

CHAPTER THREE
LEDGERS

The house on Illinois Avenue stood in the middle of a flat block facing north, four houses from the intersection of two worn red brick hills; the best sledding hills in town if you had the courage to go through two intersections with no stop signs. The metal runners of a Flexible Flyer would stop at 606 when the snow was packed just right, before the plows uncovered the bricks. But this was spring. It had rained hard the night before, washing the dark red brick streets clean of dirt and small packs of half frozen leaves left over from the spring thaw. Liam drove down New York after Fr. Conlin's funeral, unnerved with his own ambivalent anger at the priest's formal internment. It bothered him that his father did not receive the same ceremony. But it was this anger mixed with Fr. Conlin's last words, "Want you to know," that brought him back to the house for a final search.

He turned left onto Illinois and cringed as he stopped in front of the two-story clapboard house. The lawn had been cut but the sidewalks were overgrown and the realtor's sign had chickweed grown up around it. The "For Sale" sign really said, "Vacant House."

No wonder it hasn't sold, the real estate agent says it's a changing neighborhood, the right family hasn't come along. Looks to me like it's lack of care.

Liam had called the real estate agent the day before and asked her about getting into the house.

"Just open the lock box, 12-4-12. Excuse the dust, not many lookers. But we're marketing the heck out of that house. "

"Yes, I'm sure you are. I'm going over tomorrow. I want to make one last list of the furniture that we'll be taking out."

"Oh, I wouldn't do that, it doesn't show well without furniture."

"From what I hear, it doesn't show at all," Liam retorted.

He stopped, glad he had said it.

"I'm sorry, I don't mean that you're not doing a good job." He couldn't stand the idea of finding another agent.

"We know it's a tough market. I won't take all the stuff. I'll leave enough so that you can show it at it's best. I probably won't be back after this. Mr. Simpson will handle yo..., the house from now on."

"I am sure it will sell very soon," she said with an uplifting lilt that caused him to think, *Why do they all sound like that?*

He stood on the sidewalk in front of the house, looked up at his parent's bedroom. The middle shade had been pulled to the side, an unknown person wanting to see the view. He hated the idea of anyone touching the inside of the body,

No it's a house. I lived in a house, not a body. Where do I look first? Jim said the basement or the garage. If I was Tom Stone, where would I put a box of books I didn't want anybody reading, and why wouldn't I want my own son reading them anyway? Why didn't he destroy them? What weight did they offer to hold his pattern in flight? One more box, I just need to open one more box.

He walked up the cement steps onto the wooden porch. The gray paint was worn through where he and his mother would sit and watch the clouds move across the afternoon sky. They would talk about books, writers, going to a Wisconsin lake for a week later in the summer. Maybe he could drive part way. No emotion, just a breeze tracing an idea between a mother and son. He stopped. His heart pumped quickly, as he turned the dial, 12-4-12. Just as the real estate agent had said, out popped the key. He opened the door and felt the stale dry air rush towards the street.

He walked past the front stairs leading to the second floor, past the living room, through the dining room, into the kitchen, pushing through fragrant scrims of memory; his mother's Estee Lauder fragrance lingered in the entry hall, as they left for a party,

"We'll be back by 10:30, you be in bed, mind your Aunt Ann."

"OK, Mom, I'll be fine."

Her sweating as she carried the laundry up from the basement into the kitchen,

"Fold these towels, will you Liam?"

"Sure, Mom."

His father's Yardley after shave at the back door drifting to the garage, leaving for Galesburg,

"Have the gloves ready Liam, we'll play catch on Friday."

"Right, Dad, see you Friday."

He returned to the kitchen table, sat and looked at the rooster with the word "Velkomen" painted below it on the wall.

Where? Where would he put them?

His ears whistled, a sound he had learned to ignore years ago, jerked his head around to face the kitchen sink. He was sure his father was leaning over the white porcelain in a white v-neck t shirt, white oxford shirt tied around his waist as a towel. His oval horn rimmed glasses sat on the counter as he scrubbed his head with a plastic brush, ridding himself of the loose gray hair left after the barber gave him his weekly crew cut.

"This was the biggest change in my life after 1936. Got new glasses, got a crew-cut. A new man. Have you changed? What the hell are you doing, going from job to job. And those poems you write, get a job you're good at. Routines, yeah, I have routines."

He shook the towel and hung it over the bar on the wall.

"Look around Liam, not much here. It's old history, why do you want to know? Go home."

His voice drifted out to the driveway, gone again, maybe back on Friday.

I'm not like him, he got his hair cut every week, I get mine cut once a month.

He got up, swung his hand over the stove burners to see how close he could come to the heat. An old game. Don't get caught, his mother's words came back,

"You'll burn yourself. Stop that."

"Right, mom, I was just checking."

He pulled the back door open, unlocked the screen door, crossed the porch and went down the wooden stairs into the yard. Yellow dandelions and pale green crab grass crowded the broken cement sidewalk. The limbs of the flowering crab tree his father had planted in 1950 hung untended almost touching the first spurt of a spring lawn bound to go to seed. Reddish white tubers of rhubarb pushed their way through the unraked leaves that had blown up against the neighboring apartment building's four stall garage.

The back half of the yard had kept chickens for the Stones. Liam had often watched their heads come off in the thick stubby hands of Ed Sigley, a neighbor from Centralia, Illinois, dressed in faded denim overalls with one shoulder strap hanging, bare skin showing at the side just below his stained t shirt. Ed killed and cleaned the chickens for the Stones. Then kept two as his payment.

A barrier of Scotch thistles left their prickly residue on Liam's pant legs as he pushed the bi-fold doors of his parents garage to the side. They opened with a sucking sound, loosing whirlpools of dust. Dried elm leaves, veined dead hands, tried to push him back onto the driveway. It was cold outside, ice was still on the lagoons, but inside the empty garage, life erupted in symphony with the grass and weeds in the yard. Spiders raced to cocoon their harvest of flies. All found birth, life, and death, in the heat behind the closed doors. Liam stood motionless, waited for the air to clear. His eyes stung. He pulled his left eyelid down over the pupil, trying to dislodge a cinder, moved slowly to the left, around the oil splotches that still had sawdust at their edges. Steel rakes hung on the wall with the sharp prongs facing out. He could hear his father,

"Jesus, Liam, hang that rake with the prongs against the wood. Somebody will sure as hell impale themselves. Especially the way you park the car."

His ears rang. The audiologist had suggested a hearing aid to improve his hearing and reduce the annoying noises that seemed to come from nowhere. But he wouldn't put a device in his ear that said age, he would just nod and smile as if he heard every word.

But now it was bells clanging, the masts of sailing ships chiming in a cold wind. All signs of stress, fatigue, lack of exercise, too much caffeine, or just plain fear.

He pushed the sound away as the dust settled revealing a rectangular shape cowering in the back corner, under a pile of magazines.

That's it, Aunt Ann's beer. She drank one every night before she went to bed.

Liam would watch Ann sit at the kitchen table pouring the beer into a glass and sipping it just before she went to bed. She would then give him a kiss good night and go up to the back bedroom, the room they shared from the day he was born till she died in 1952 at the age of seventy eight.

"What's that smell, Auntie?"

"That's my Irish toast. The doctor says it helps me sleep."

"Do you have trouble sleeping?"

"Not with you here, Liam. You come up soon, don't forget to brush you teeth."

His Dad bought the beer by the case and kept the empties in the corner of the garage. There were always two cases. Nobody noticed that the bottom cardboard box with the red Gipps insignia emblazoned on the side never left the garage. After Ann's death, his father had said,

"Leave the cases there, I'll return them to the liquor store later."

He never did.

They remained with the other detritus, rakes, wheelbarrows, oil cans, wooden baskets, oil soaked gloves, Colliers magazines tied with a brown string, all stacked in corners and hanging from the walls of the empty one car garage. The bottom beer case was the perfect hiding place. Ten, twelve, ledgers would fit easily. His father could have replaced the top case every month, leave the bottom case with the words.

He pushed the stack of Collier's off the top of the cartons. Opened the case exposing 24 empty brown bottles all inhabited by moving creatures, some of which he could not, or didn't care to, identify. He moved it carefully to the floor, trying not to disturb whatever was going on inside the bottles. He put his hands into the openings on either end of the bottom box and lifted. It was much heavier than the first case. His hands slipped from the holes and he fell backwards to the concrete floor. The case hadn't moved.

"Fr. Conlin was right, they're in here."

He lifted the case, realized it wasn't as heavy as he had expected. As he turned to go to the garage door, he heard a sloshing sound. Ann had never gotten to the case on the bottom. He put the case of full bottles back in the corner, put the empties on top and wondered if he could get a refund. A sudden breeze rattled the iron rakes against the wall. Liam looked up to where he sensed the breeze originated. The sun was now shining through the half-closed doors, briefly dissolving the shadows in the back corner. He could see a battered screen door laying across two rafters that ran parallel to the sides of the garage, but it was at an odd angle and looked as if it could fall at any time. With the shadows gone he could see that it was butted up against a wooden box resting on a shelf between the screen door and the back garage wall. He picked up a wooden ladder and placed it against the rafter where it joined the wall. Exposed nails and ragged tar paper scratched his left hand as he climbed the round rungs,

No wonder I didn't come up here. Too many sharp edges. A part of the garage, bits of my father, hidden from me.

The ladder rose just above the edge of the shelf. He almost stepped onto the top rung as he started to bring his leg over the edge of the wooden platform, but heard his father admonishing him,

"Don't step on the devil rung, Liam."

"What's the devil rung, Dad?" he had asked the first time his Dad had talked to him about the dangers of ladders.

"The one on top. He's waiting there to push you off."

He decided to stay on the ladder, keep one hand on the rafter. A piece of pine had been cut in a rectangle and placed on the rafters. Liam would never have seen the shelf or the wooden box, if he had not looked at just the right moment when the sun was passing the front of the garage. The short side of the box was flush to the back wall of the garage. Liam pulled the container towards the edge of the shelf, he swiped at spider webs around his head and he wondered if the devil was anywhere near. A vacant sparrow's nest rested securely on the top of the box, he lifted it and moved it to the side, careful not to disturb the possibility of its future use. He pushed at the box. It was heavier than the full case of beer.

Liam put his fingers under the warped pine cover and carefully pried it open. The four nails securing the cover had formed valleys in the top of the box from constant opening and closing. Sweat ran down his cheeks, the back of his shirt stuck to his shoulders and rib cage. He wrapped his fingers around a pebbled black ledger with red edges. He pulled it gently from its resting place, held it with both hands, and felt a dizziness that rocked the soles of his shoes against the round wooden rung.

The devil is here, he thought, as he grasped the edge of the shelf. He took eleven ledgers down the ladder, one at a time, laid them in order on a piece of brown wrapping paper that had been stuck on a nail, and then took the box down the ladder. He put the books back in the box in the exact order in which he had found them. He finished in darkness. The sun was gone and the doors to the garage had slowly moved back to the center, not accustomed to the open position that he had imposed on them. He moved quickly to the space left between the doors and slid through with the box held at his waist. He sat on the back porch steps and cleaned each book with a soft rag. There were letters that appeared to be carved neatly into the center of each black pebbled surface. He rubbed the dirt out of the indentations exposing angled numbers and letters.

1885 TRANSACTIONS

These aren't just Dad's books, Christ, these must be his dad's.

Inside were pages of names, dates, types of meat, prices paid, all broken into weeks, written in a sharp cursive style that looked vaguely familiar.

Could be Dad's writing. Just like his weekly agenda. But this has to be his father's hand writing. I know less about him than Dad. Nobody talked about him, just that he was a butcher with a temper. Not even a picture in the old albums. Just a name, William J. Stone, with two dates, 1870-1924. Now I have this. Thank you Jim Conlin. You probably didn't know what you were giving me.

The next nine books were all transactions from the grocery store. Liam was getting discouraged.

So, he kept good records, big deal. Nice books, but so what.

Then the eleventh book, There were no markings on the outside.

This had to be it. Liam wanted to absorb the words as oxygen, let them flow to every part of his body. He was facing his own history through the words that his father wanted to keep away from him, but as his fingers wrapped around the edge of the ledger's cover, his ears rang again, whistled, chimed, a vise pinched tight, crippling his hands.

I can wait another day. I'll read them at home.

On the last flight to Minneapolis that night, he held the ledger box firmly in his lap until the stewardess insisted that he put it in the overhead or under the seat in front of him.

"Fine, fine, I'll put it on the floor. " He said with more than a little irritation, "I'll need this again, right after take off. It's very important."

A heavy set business man in the middle seat next to him said,

"What's in the box? Are you a lawyer?"

"No, no, just some old family records."

"Must be pretty important. I'm going to visit my grand daughter in Minneapolis. Maybe you know her parents, the Andersons?"

"Sorry, I don't know any Andersons in Minneapolis."
He turned to the window and acted as if he were sleeping.

CHAPTER FOUR
DELAY

"Where are you going to put them?" Kathryn asked as she stood over the box with her arms folded.

"They can't stay any longer, I'm tripping over them every time I come in here."

Ten days before, Liam had placed the ledgers on the corner of the oriental rug in his study, just to the side of the brown love seat sleeper couch. He thought the black and red books contrasted nicely with the petrol blue and burgundy fibers of the rug. Colors were essential to his associations as a poet. Stone was a mid tone gray name, Liam was a deep silver, Kathryn was an ocean shade of blue.

Her eyes had drawn him to her fifteen years before. He bought jewelry, agonizing over which shade of blue matched her eyes the best. All her presents ended up sapphire or lapis in color, no matter what the material. He knew that the most important thing to her was not the gift, but the fact that he tried to make the day special.

"If you don't make these days special, no one else will. Every day will be just the same. The children need to see us making a difference not just for them, but in the way we treat each other," she told him the first and last time he forgot her birthday.

"I'll make room in the "S's," Liam said.

"There's no room in the "S's. You'll have to get another bookcase started. Maybe we can move some of my teaching books."

"You don't have to do that, I'll take some of the duplicates to the Booknest. Tom's always looking for first editions in decent condition."

"My real question is, 'when are you going to read them?'" Kathryn looked up into Liam's eyes, took his elbow in her hand.

"I know you're in your 'diversion' stage. How long is it going to last?"

Liam looked down at Kathryn, sighed, and said,

"I've already looked through ten of them, just a sort of accounting. OK, OK, you're right as usual. Tonight, I'll start tonight after Colin's guitar lesson. I'll be through by tomorrow afternoon."

A week later he was still touching the edges of the pebbled boards. He would pull one out and rub the cover, loosening a little of the embedded dust, enjoying the aged texture. They were a sharp contrast to the mylar covers on the dust jackets of the rest of his collection of contemporary first editions. He had made room in the S's, considered that a pretty good first step towards opening the eleventh ledger and reading it. But every time he pulled number eleven out, the ubiquitous ringing in his ears jumped a decibel. He had always attributed the noises to childhood mastoiditis.

In the 40's it was not uncommon for a surgeon to treat middle ear infections by opening the skin just behind the ear, exposing the infected bone and scraping the infection away. After Liam cried for two weeks while holding his ears, Doctor Ryan recommended a double mastoid operation. The recuperation for Liam meant keeping his hands off the stitches. His head was wrapped tightly with gauze and his Mother watched him every minute. At night he slept under a sheet pulled tight against the crib mattress. Margaret kept the crib next to her bed and slept with one hand on the crib rail. Only his head was left uncovered. He hated that crib.

Now the sounds were different. Not the sharp pain of infection, but a low rumble that changed timbre as he moved.

Couldn't be dad, I don't believe in ghosts. But what's the connection? Some allergy to an eighty year old spore hidden away in the garage? Or am I just afraid of what's in the last of these books? Dreams, confessions, actual events I'm afraid to know about?

The daring pleasure of the first contact with the ledgers had been replaced by a woolen rug of anxiety. Something about blood and memory hung in the back of his consciousness. Red, burgundy, ruby, the color of Tibetan monk's robes. Reaching to touch the ledgers was beginning to be painful. Both ears and eyes burned, then cooled as the red released into the palms of his hands as perspiration. He sat back into the brown velvet chair across from R's, S's, and T's.

He looked up and saw his father standing next to the S's, somehow younger than the last time in the kitchen in the old house. His hair was black and slicked back, rimless glasses with thin metal bows, a white shirt without a collar, buttoned at the neck, his arms folded across his chest.

Now what's wrong? You wished for this. You wanted to know everything. Jimmy told me how important this was to you. OK. Now do something about it. Stop procrastinating. Pick your spot and go after it. Didn't I teach you anything? Honor, perseverance in the face of difficulty, family? Listen for the bone. That's the best place to start. And don't count on me to pull you along. For Chrissake, do it on your own. You really have a problem with that, don't you. Waiting for the 'Deus ex Machina.'"

Liam sat back into the brown velvet love seat across from his IBM Selectric. *Must be my imagination. But it's so clear, I can hear him speaking. What bone, what are these damned riddles about?*

He went to the first book, determined to go through each one page by page. Maybe there was more in the first ten than just records of buying and selling meat or which farmer owed money to the Stones. He opened number one, carefully flipped the pages, went through the next nine, turned them left and right, up and down, just as if he was gauging the condition of a first edition that he had been searching for. He picked up number eleven and felt a bulge in the back end paper. The bulge shouldn't be there. He went to the bathroom and got Kathryn's hair dryer. He plugged it in under his desk and blew warm air onto the ledger's sealed edges. He then put a bone folder at the edge of the paper in the upper right corner and slowly forced it between the paper and the board. He peeled the end paper away, exposing an envelope that fell onto the floor.

The upper left corner had a printed return address, Stone's Garden Store, 228 Second Ave. S., Peoria, Illinois. An angled date with sharp corners, October 5, 1880, was hand written in the middle of the thin rectangle. He leaned over to pick the envelope up, touched the date, felt liquid dripping from his right ear lobe. He reached to wipe it off but a single drop fell to the browned paper leaving a crimson spot.

"Kathryn," Liam called out as he slumped to the floor dropping the ledger.

She came into Liam's study and saw him curled on the floor covering both ears with his hands. The ledger lay on the floor with the unopened envelope next to it.

"You know Liam, I could just go to the lake, sit on a pier, read a book. That could be next, but I never get to next. Instead I see you laying on the floor holding your ears. You really need to see a doctor. I'm calling urgent care right now."

"I just can't get past this noise in my head. It's like an underground engine rumbling up a sort of path. It's getting louder and now I'm bleeding."

Kathryn slowly picked up the ledger and the envelope, put them back on the shelf with the other ledgers, then turned to Liam,

"Come on," he could hear the exasperation in her voice. "You're getting in bed while I call."

Kathryn put a towel under Liam's head, no more blood was escaping, checked to make sure that Colin was in his room and called the medical center.

She stood at the phone and spoke loud enough for Liam to hear her.

"The pain seems to have subsided, we'll come tomorrow morning.
You're sure a specialist will be available?"

She paused.

"Yes, yes, Dr. Onitsuka will be fine. We'll be there."

Liam woke Kathryn at three A.M. as his leg swung back and forth to some unheard beat. His pulse was racing, his back soaked with sweat. She watched his strange dance for a minute and finally shook his arm.

"Liam, wake up, you're having a bad dream."

"The baby was floating in the water, she was dead."

"Have you been eating yogurt and walnuts?" Kathryn paused.

" How do you know it was a girl?"

"I was on a ship, I saw my great grandfather, I know it was him, drop a baby into the ocean. He was crying, the baby was his, his wife was pulling on his arm, yelling at him not to let go. He had to bury the baby to keep the other people safe. God, there's no room, it's so crowded and it smells so bad." He looked around the room before his eyes rested on Kathryn, sat up and wiped his forehead with his arm,

"The noise in my ears is different, it doesn't hurt like before. There's more of a pattern now. I can't seem to stop it. It just keeps coming."

He looked at Kathryn, afraid that she wouldn't believe him, that he was making the whole thing up, looking for sympathy. He realized that his own honesty was limited only by memory. Soon he would see his own memories as labyrinths, hidden from each other. They would slowly fade, making way for new memories that filled his bodies lacunae, each delivering a fully formed world that could be observed one piece at a time. He would write about these new worlds with no idea what would come next, whether or not the images were linked. He would think of a metal board with magnetic balls that found a collective home, different each time the board moved. It would be a waste to attempt prediction. He would learn to listen and observe the balls arranging themselves. He would be in a free zone, immune to the barbed hooks of emotion.

But this night, Kathryn said to him with great conviction, "Forget the ear guy, you're going to see Shirley Bernstein."

CHAPTER FIVE
THERAPIST

Liam had not read ledger number eleven or the content of the hidden envelope as he entered the office of Dr. Shirley Bernstein. Ms. Holden, the receptionist, sat behind a small desk, scratching on a piece of white paper with an old fountain pen. Liam recognized it as an Esterbrook, the same brand that his father always had available on his desk. Her white hair was permed tightly around a round smooth face, small lines seemed to connect the edges of her lips and eyes. She greeted him when he arrived, with a quick nod and smile as she pointed to the single chair in the room other than the one that she sat in.

"Ah, Mr. Stone, the doctor will be with you shortly, please sit down," she said as if she had known him for years. She didn't look up again. He sat in a straight backed chair, his palms smoothing the textured wool of his trousers. He glanced at a three month old issue of *Time* magazine, but his attention was on the closed door immediately next to Ms. Holden.

Will I see the other person come out? What if I know them? What if they know me?

A faint buzz came from the receptionist's desk.

"You can go in now."

"Thank you, great reading material."

She finally looked up,

"No sense in distracting you with new news."

Shirley Bernstein sat behind her desk smoking a Lucky Strike. She was a small woman in her late fifties, black hair flecked with grey pulled back off her face into a bun. She and the room were soft and shapeless, surrounded by diffused light and lingering cigarette smoke. Their corners came visible when she spoke in her quiet, defined, voice. Only then did he notice the rimless glasses sat on a linear nose above thin waxy lips. A door was just behind her to the right. Liam soon learned that it was the patient exit door.

"No rules, just tell me what you want to. I'll ask a few questions, make a few comments, but it's really up to you, say the first thing that comes to your mind," was her opening statement as Liam sat down in an overstuffed leather chair. Her speech pattern reminded him of Aunt Ann, but with a slight New England accent. She moved to a wooden high back chair directly facing him across a dark oriental area rug. He waited for her to speak again. And waited.

Ten minutes went by, Liam crossing and uncrossing his legs, hands held in his lap, Shirley puffing on one cigarette after another.

"I'm having trouble with my ears."

"Isn't that another doctor's domain?"

"*That* doctor told me last year that there was nothing wrong with my

ears, other than a loss of hearing on some high pitched levels and I should learn to ignore the ringing when it came. I'm pretty good at ignoring. But it's different now."

"So, you think there's some other cause for these problems with your ears?" she said as she coughed into a tissue.

"What?" he said as he tried to focus on her last question, bothered by the cough.

"So, you think there is some other cause for these problems."

"Yes."

"And what would that be?"

"Can't you tell me?" He felt a sudden apprehension about the doctor. Maybe he should have gone to the ear doctor. He didn't have to talk or listen to the ear guy.

Shirley moved her hands between a pad and paper, cigarette and ashtray, kleenex and wastebasket.

"You have to tell me a little more before I can help." Her voice had a calm edge that reminded him of backyard conversations between his mother or aunt whenever he needed some reassurance that it was OK to speak of what many of his friends called "weird associations."

His mom would say, "Your dad will play catch with you, I'll talk to you." Aunt Ann would tell him, "Just say what's in your heart, it's all that counts."

"I have dreams that aren't dreams and I'm afraid to read a ledger

that my father wrote in a long time ago, before he married my mother. He's trying to stop me from reading it."

"How does he try to stop you?"

Uh oh, now I'm really going to look stupid.

"Um, he lets me see him frowning or sneering, or he says Something kind of mean."

Boy, that does sound stupid.

"Where is your father now?"

"He died in 1973."

"I see." She paused, made a note on her pad.

"Have you thought about what brings him to you?"

"It has something to do with these ledgers that I found. A priest

Told me to look for them in our old house, then he died."

"Ah, a priest. And he's dead too."

"What do you mean, 'ah, a priest?' And yes, he's dead too."

"Let's stay with your father." Shirley made another note on her paper.

"Did you find the ledgers?"

"Yes, in the back of our old garage. I found them a few weeks ago, after the priest's funeral. I can read the first ten with no problem, they're *his* dad's records of his grocery business. Then I found an envelope hidden behind the end paper of the one I can't read. The envelope, I think, was my great grandfather's, but every time I pick up number eleven or that envelope, I hear noises I've never heard before. There is some pattern that I can't figure out. Then the other night a drop of blood came out of my right ear and I sort of collapsed. I woke up from what I first thought was a dream, but it wasn't. It was more of, of, a memory."

Liam jerked forward, put his arms around his knees, started to rock back and forth. His face was contorted with quick breathing. He looked up at Shirley and said, "What was that?" and continued to rock.

"It's called a start. Why does the word 'memory' bother you?"

"Because when he was little, he could remember things that happened before, then he stopped remembering. He didn't like it. "

Shirley stopped making notes, leaned forward with her hands clasped, said very softly,

"That little boy is you, don't call him 'he.' You have to integrate him."

"I called him 'he?' And it's me that I'm talking about?"

"Yes, you are talking about yourself."

"Then I'm the one that wants the memories to return, not some other person?"

"Yes, you are the one. Now, why do you want the memories to

come back?"

"I want to know more about my father, and this seems to be the only way."

He leaned back into the chair, feeling exhausted, but somehow relaxed, minutes as quiet and soft as his mother's arms ticked by. A lightning bolt had hit a rod somewhere in his body and exited without harming him. He touched his ring and watch to see if there was any carbon residue, felt none and smiled, eager to continue, but his fifty minutes had expired.

"Can I come back?"

"If you want, I can put you in on Thursdays at eleven."

"What should I do in the meantime," he replied as he put his sport coat on, pulled his shirt cuffs out so they were exposed one half inch past the coat sleeve.

"Read the ledger, if you can't read it, stay close to it. Let yourself remember. Try to get rid of the editor inside your head, some people call it their monkey mind, I call it fear. The noises won't go away, but they will change timbre, change their arrangement, as if they were part of a large orchestra."

"How do you know this?"

"The same way you do. Now the session is over, other patients are waiting. Please leave by this door, see you next week"

"Wait, how will I know when we've, I mean, I've, finished?"

"You'll stop coming," Shirley said from behind the intermingling smoke of the cigarette she held in her hand and the one between her lips.

CHAPTER SIX
KATHRYN STONE

"How was the session?" Kathryn asked Liam as she watched him hang his jacket in the closet and carefully smooth the sleeves and space the hangers evenly. He walked to his desk, pulled out the wooden chair and sat down. She hated the chair, it squeaked every time he shifted his legs or the chairs legs. He said he would fix it, but she knew it was number twenty six on a list of fifty two things around the house he would never fix.

"Good, good. She smokes a lot, but seems to understand. A little superior too, kind of priestly. I can't seem to get away from it. She said I can come on Thursday's, that I'll know when it's over," the words tumbled over each other as if they were bouncing over hidden rocks just below the surface of the river that now seemed to carry him forward.

"But did she say anything else, why all this stuff is happening to you? I worry," but she stopped, seeing that Liam was already reaching for the ledger, he had flipped the "on" switch of the selectric, the low hum permeated the room. She made one more attempt.

"So, an hour a week, one more distraction; but if it makes you feel better and you can finish your poetry manuscript, it will be worth it. You get a call every week now from White Cloud asking about your progress."

"That will have to wait, I'm going to write a novel, at least that's my idea. It will be about fathers and sons, what they do to and for each other. I've got these ideas that won't go away. Shirley says I just have to remember. What do you think?" The last four words were almost indecipherable.

"At first you thought you were Walt Whitman, than Ezra Pound crossed with that idiot Velikovsky. Last week Robert Lowell was all you could talk about. Why can't you just be Liam?"

Kathryn lowered her voice. Her eyes moistened with the realization that she could not help, that he would go through this alone. Her world was now even smaller than when he rotated between writing and being a husband and a father. She saw a man obsessed with a search, a boy looking for his father. She understood his need, but started to measure the qualities she admired in Liam, his intelligence, his empathy for others, his ability to listen, with the selfish child she saw in front of her.

CHAPTER SEVEN
THE NOVEL

Fragile sheets of onion skin lay in front of Liam next to the envelope dated October 5, 1880. Next to them, propped up on a wire easel, was a small sepia toned tintype of a man and woman standing together, their hands joined between them, his hands bare, hers in delicate knit gloves. Their eyes stared directly into the camera as if looking through a window hoping for some answer to why they were still alone, the only Irish couple in their new home without five children and one on the way. Liam stared at the photo and then at the onion skin. The edges were brown and ragged as if a flame had eaten at them each time they had been touched.

So this is what they give me if I listen. I already know this story. He folded the sheets carefully, placed them back in their envelope without reading them, and put them back in their hiding place, placed the ledger back in the "S's." Lines of dust from the sun reflecting off the particles that always rose as he moved around the room danced from the window to the bookcases.

The rhythmic pattern of an old car engine slowly disappeared from his submerged internal sounds, replaced by a dull *thump, thump* that coursed up through his throat, mixing at a small bone next to his middle ear. He picked up his pen and started to write. He heard his son calling,

"Dad, Dad, come on down, we need to play catch,"

but listened to the singing in his ears. He stood up, crossed the room through the rays of sun that struck the floor just at the threshold, and closed the door.

STONE & SON

A NOVEL

BY

LIAM STONE

STONE AND SON

PART ONE

CHAPTER ONE
MICHAEL AND NORA STONE
1849

Michael Stone's eyes opened just before he heard the clacking wheels and in that hazy state of self-doubt felt an arrow enter his chest. He knew it would exit to the right of his spine, through the hard mattress, then stand at a slight angle in the wide plank floor. Each morning he was tempted to look under the bed, but stopped, not wanting to know if the nightmare was real.

He checked to see if Nora was asleep, pulled the comforter over her shoulder, brushed her red curls with his fingertips, turned to the right and swung his legs off the bed. As he pushed his heels down on the bare floor a chill rose up under the coarse fabric of his sleep shirt. He shuffled towards the shutters, rubbed his hand along the edge of the washstand that held a blue porcelain pitcher and bowl and dipped his finger into the pitcher's clear water, regretting that he hadn't emptied the bowl of its inky residue the night before. Then stopped at a small pine desk.

Both pieces had been cut by his friend, Emmett Ryan, in payment for Michael improving Emmett's neglected reading and writing skills. A marbled green pen lay next to a bottle of black printer's ink. Michael rolled the pen back and forth, left it next to a scarred brown leather folder where he kept the loose pieces of onion skin used for his journal. At first it was the feel of the paper that he loved, a fragile texture that absorbed his undefended, unexplained words. But he soon cherished his own sentences as a balance to the suffering depicted by his employer, the printer Mr. O'Malley, in his broadsides against the British and the obituaries requested daily by those that could not read nor write.

He ran his hand quickly along the rough plaster wall leaving a faint trail of ink that he could not remove from his hands. This habit of touch surprised and calmed him each time it was repeated. He knew that Nora would wipe the wall clean daily, never trying to change his sense of order.

The clack-clack grew louder as he reached the shutters, a rhythm he associated with death. The louder the sound, the longer the space between the metallic noise, the more bodies he knew would be on the wagon. He pulled the shutters open, vaguely aware of Nora's request to oil them and that he had promised; he closed, then opened them, hoping the sound would go away with use. He bent his spare six-foot frame to look out and see if it was the sound of the funeral wagon that had pulled him out of his nervous sleep. The street was wide enough for two wagons if no arms or legs hung over the side, if the children's bodies did not slide off the top of the older gnarled corpses. A block past the shop, the rain soaked cobblestone street turned left out of Skibbereen on the way to a mass grave.

Michael held his sleep shirt close to his chest, pushed a shock of unruly black hair away from bloodshot eyes and rubbed his hand back and forth over sunken cheeks feeling the two-day growth of bristle. He had not slept well since receiving the letter. This morning it was not the letter that woke him, it was the hard-edged clack-clack. He looked down through the perpetual Irish mist, anxious to see if he would recognize the passengers, and saw his best friend. Peter Laxton stood beside his own jaunty cart drawn by a bony sway backed mare. He had one hand on a woman's shoulder, holding her body in place. His other arm squeezed a small blanket wrapped around what could have been the spoils of a night raid on an unguarded larder.

Michael raised his hand and started to speak when he realized that the dead woman was Peter's wife, the bundle their dead baby. Peter glanced up and nodded. Michael knew that the anger thrown from Peter's swollen eyes and reddened face was not aimed at him. It was as if Peter Laxton was defying Victoria, and perhaps God, by keeping his head high as he led the makeshift funeral wagon to the communal grave. There he would say goodbye to his only family.

Michael woke each morning without looking ahead into the day. Better to move quickly, not think about the Riley's, the O'Malley's, and Nora's parents, the Adams. The risk of death was spread evenly through the town. Three year olds and their grand parents were equally subject to the quick death; not a slow, steady starvation but sudden heat, chills, dry staccato coughs, delirium, and collapse into a deep endless sleep. Many woke to a warm body next to them that had stopped coughing. The drill was emotionless; wrap them up, put them in the patrolling wagon, off to the recently opened ground, gone in an instant, as if they had never been there. What was left was a hole, black and liquid, that went away for minutes, but always came back.

They had talked about the black fever, how it hit those close to starvation; maybe a blessing, quick and sure. But even with enough food, the risk of contracting the fever was greater now than at any time since the first putrid potatoes had been pulled from the ground four years before.

Nora Adams Stone struggled out of bed, pulled her nightdress down over her newly swollen belly. She was five months into a pregnancy that her father, Timothy Adams, had predicted would never happen.

"Those Stone men living by all that salt water seem to forget why they got married, hardly a child among them. Should be called the barren boys."

The pregnancy brought one final comment from the father of eight,

"Odds were in his favor."

She placed her left hand on the small of her back, the other hand over the spot where she could feel a movement as if her first child struggled to touch her hands. She moved slowly to the window, an early morning smile on her face, her right hand traced the wall along the path Michael had carefully established.

"You try to be so quiet, but I hear you every time; get out of bed, touch the floor, your desk, then the wall, then the window."

She moved around him and started to lean over the open frame; Michael quickly put his arm around her waist, certain that a hand moved under her skin, reaching out to him.

"Is that Peter? What is he doing out so early? Oh, no, is that Madeline?" She turned, grabbed Michael's sleeve, and twisted it at the same time she felt the movement of her child. She wasn't sure if her tears came from the joy of the sudden touch or the sight of another of her friends about to be thrown into a grave in order to save the living.

"Move away Nora. Nothing we can do. Madeline had the symptoms first, but the only food for the baby was her milk. We can't help them. Nobody can, not even the priest." Michael closed the shutters, pulled the hesitant Nora towards his desk and said,

"I won't have this happen to us."

At age twenty-three, Michael was the youngest printer in the county. This gave him a sense of superiority that he often used as his only sin at weekly confession; not quite arrogance, more a confidence that he would make the best decision.

Michael's father had set the seeds of hubris. Robert Stone was an Anglo married to an Irish, Cliona O'Driscoll. They lived in Baltimore, fifty miles west of Skibbereen, the last town at the southwest corner of the Irish mainland. A sail maker by trade, Robert was proud of his skills and told his son that it would be *his* own skills and ability to make the right decisions that would bring him happiness and a place in heaven. This sounded more efficient to Michael than the prayers and good deeds offered by the priest.

But Michael's interest in books and printing exceeded his father's desire to teach him sail making. When the opportunity came to go to Skibbereen and work as an apprentice with O'Malley, a master printer in the Cork Union, Michael told his parents that this was his chance to pursue a trade that would allow him to prosper. He left Baltimore, sure that there would be enough food for two, only with him gone.

After four years as an apprentice, he was accepted into the union as a journeyman printer. On that same day, red haired, dark skinned, Nora Adams entered the shop and any doubt about his decision to leave Baltimore disappeared

She had walked into the print shop with a rolled piece of paper in her hands. She stood in front of the stacking and sorting counter and pulled long red tendrils back from her forehead, exposed deep set agate blue eyes framed by a narrow face the color of autumn dusk.

"Would you print this? It could help all of us if the landlords start managing their land properly?" She said.

"Of course I'll print it. You just have to pay the three shillings. But, I don't want to get your hopes up too high. They will need more than a sheet of printed paper to change their ways. And I surely don't want you to be disappointed."

"And what makes you an expert on landlords?

"Talking to you makes me feel like I'm an expert on a lot of things,"

Jesus, Mary and Joseph, did I really say that!

"Well now, you just do what we pay you to do. Then we'll see what kind of an expert you are."

He soon learned that Nora's confrontive personality and dark skin came from a survivor of the Spanish Armada that had crashed off Cape Clear in 1588. Nora's mother had instilled a sense of pride in her daughter that she was descended from an enemy of the British. Nora pushed her chin out and smiled whenever she was called Black Irish and said,

"Proud I am to be descended from a race that wouldn't put up with the likes of Victoria."

If Michael waited any longer, *he* would be the next to escort a wife and child to the rotted gravesite. He took the letter with the American post-mark out of the bed-stand.

"I want to read you the letter from Emmett."

"Michael, what could Emmett possibly say that .."

"It's a blessing Nora, God has seen fit to give us a way to escape this famine."

"It is not famine, it is starvation. I'm not sure God appreciates the difference." Nora said firmly as she took the letter into her hands.

"This letter is a blessing, but it's wasted if we stay here and watch the English take our food as fast as we can get it out of the ground. I see them pack the ships for Liverpool every day. Emmett has an answer. We will raise our child to have a life that has been taken from us," Michael said.

Nora sat on the edge of the bed with the letter on her lap.

"Do you remember the last time you saw him? You thought that all he wanted was money. He wasn't your friend that day."

Emmett had arrived in mid-July, smelling of travel, a dirty canvas pack on his shoulder.

"Come to the pub, Michael, I need to talk to you." Emmett did things on the spur of the moment, never had a plan. He was afraid of losing arguments, money, tests, games, and avoided all of them, leaving the impression that he had no worries. Today there was a sadness in Emmett that Michael had never seen before.

Michael thought at first that Emmet's father had sent him to look for work in the print shop, something that Michael was steeled to refuse. Emmett had improved his reading and writing skills, thanks to Michael, but he was unkempt, seldom shaved, wore his clothes till they stood up in the corner; an opposite to Michael's orderly habits. He got his carpenter's pay from the owner of Rocky Sullivan's, the pub on the corner across the street from the print shop. The owner got cash from the local union, took what Emmett owed for liquor and gave him the balance. A good system if Emmett kept track of his consumption.

Their friendship was based on Michael's sense that he could help Emmett some way; give him direction or advice that would improve Emmett's lot in life. But Michael did not give handouts, people needed to earn his respect and his help.

They pushed aside the heavy drape that acted as a door in the winter and the summer, letting in a sudden light that brought hands up and complaints from the bar about germs that should stay outside. A man in a dark wool jacket and paneled cap leaned heavily against the bar, head resting in the crook of his right arm. Next to him was a five-year-old boy perched precariously on a stool, dipping his finger into a jar of Guinness.

"Hey Martin, how's your Da?" Emmett nodded towards the slumped over figure, smiled at the boy, picked him up and sat him solidly on the stool.

"He's just sleeping. I think he has an ache," the boy said.

"That man's not fit to be a father, Rocky should boot him out of here." Michael said.

"It's Rocky's son in law. His daughter died. It's easier keeping track of the boy where he can see him." Emmett pulled Michael's sleeve and said,

"Let's sit in the corner where we can talk."

They sat at a square wooden table covered by circular stains from pints of Guinness, and the smaller impressions from brandy glasses that often accompanied the pints when a few extra shillings were available.

"I don't have a lot of time Emmett." Michael said.

"It won't take long. I have to be in New Ross in two days. I'm going to America. I just wanted somebody to know what happened before I left. You know that I've been working in the mine shoring the walls. Most of the time replacing what's already there that's deemed dangerous by the owners. It's a step up from the digging."

Emmett waved at the young bar tender that had opened the bar just an hour before. He was sweeping up last night's debris into a container in the middle of the floor.

"Two more pints Harry."

"One, Harry. Do you know everybody here?" Michael asked.

"One of the benefits of being a regular." Emmett replied with a laugh.

Michael's eyes dropped to the table as he shook his head

"We were in number ten. The foreman said it was enough, no need to spend more money. Sent us on our way."

"That was two weeks ago. They called the crews back. My father was the first back in. Two days ago, the shoring gave way." Emmett twirled his pint between his blackened fingers, rubbed the rim with cracked fingernails.

"He was crushed with five others."

"You can't blame yourself, it's not your fault." Michael said as he reached over and grasped Emmett's shoulder. Emmett pulled away with a force that sent his pint to the floor.

"I know Michael, it's not my fault; but that's not the point. The foreman want's me to go in now and replace Da. I can't do that. I won't end up like him. Ma has my sister Carrie to look after her. I'm taking the next boat. I needed to tell somebody instead of just disappearing. You've been stand up with me. I didn't want you to think I just ran away."

Michael paced back and forth between the bed and the window, pushed his toes along the rays of sunlight that softened the hardwood floor.

"I think Emmett just wanted to know that he still had a friend here. He came with more of a confession than a call for help. Maybe that's what confessions are. Please read the letter, Nora. Tell me that you see an answer for us."

Nora opened the envelope.

"I can tell when you have made your mind up; here, you read the letter to me." Nora leaned back against the wall, a look of bemused resignation on her face.

My Friend Michael,

This is the first time that you get to see the fruits of your teaching. I am sorry for not writing earlier, but everything takes longer than you plan. It took longer to cross the Atlantic than I thought it would. Longer to get up the Mississippi, then even longer up the Illinois River. I followed a priest named Halloran who told us that he knew of a town with jobs and tolerance for the Irish. He had arranged passage for many on the boat with that same promise. I wish I had met him earlier. Could have saved a few crowns.

That's how I got to Peoria. Father Halloran introduced me to the Keystone family that runs the coal mining and soon I was pulling the bits of black brick out of the hills. Mind you, not from the shafts the likes of which killed my father, but out in the sun and the rain. We dig down a few feet and there it lies. Some say when we are done, the hole will fill up and be used for swimming. Imagine Michael, if you knew how, you could go swimming. Maybe by now, you and Nora have babies and they could learn before you do.

Come as soon as you can, Michael, I promise a job and a much better life. I know you are proud of your skill as a printer, but that is not as sure as what I offer. If you get here by next spring, there will be plenty of jobs with the coal.

Your Friend

Emmett Ryan

Michael slowly folded the letter, put it in the envelope and laid it on the nightstand. Nora sat up, folded her arms across her stomach.

"This is Emmett Ryan; not a priest, not my father, not Mr. O'Malley. Do you really think that he's doing this with no other motivation than being a friend? I wonder what he's up to," Nora stood and walked to the window. "Or maybe, he really is your friend and for the first time in his life, he wants to do something for somebody else. I can tell you've already made up your mind. I suppose you know when a ship is available and how long the voyage is."

Michael's hands unclenched, his eyebrows rose, and he said with palpable relief,

"I do. It takes forty two days. A new ship, the *Blanche,* is available on January 2, but we would have to reserve the space quickly. Following Emmett is not important, staying alive is. I want us to have a life that the British are bent on destroying. The transport agent assured me that there is time to cross the ocean and be in New Orleans well before the baby is due." Michael had fallen to one knee and taken Nora's hands.

"God has given me you and this child that I carry," Nora said, "He will see us across the ocean. Is this the first boat we can get on?" Nora put her arms around Michael's neck, kissed him and laid her head on his shoulder. He did not see the tears streaming down her cheeks.

On January 2, 1850, Nora, Michael and 468 other Irish emigrants were on board the Blanche.

The passage started with music and dancing on the deck as they left New Ross. Two days later, as they headed west past Baltimore and then Cape Clear on the southwestern tip of Ireland, some thought they had reached Newfoundland. This early optimism soon turned to despair.

Unknown to any of them, the ship had been built to carry 380. The owners had installed extra bunks in steerage to increase their profit margin. Each passenger had a six-foot by twenty four-inch bunk. Wall and floor planks were laid to expand and contract as the ship rolled with the seas, sometimes opening and closing so quickly that small hands and feet were crushed in their grasp. The complex odor of heat, cold, mold, and human waste, mixed to prevent any relaxed moment. Time was spent in fitful sleep and waiting for a turn on deck for fresh air and a chance to cook over the only open fire on the ship designated for steerage passengers.

Part of Michael's waiting consisted of daily writings; spare phrases that kept him connected to the moments of misery, death, and hope on the ship, and reminded him of his goal; a life for Nora and their child. Four weeks into the voyage as he wondered if the soft dust that floated constantly in the air could be bad for the lungs, he wrote:

> *"I am among the fortunate. A member of the crew asked if I could help with a task that his other mates would not do. I would receive an extra ration and fruit if I searched the hold for the dead. I agreed, knowing the need to keep Nora as well nourished as possible. Finding the dead is made easy by the sound of weeping or the smell. I am careful not to touch the enflamed skin as I wrap the body in a sheet provided by the crewman, carry the body to the aft deck and drop it overboard as the ship leans into the water. It is not a physical challenge. I am still strong and free of the fever. It is, however, the hardest thing I have ever attempted under God's eyes. The adult bodies are mostly low in weight and there is only a prayer that accompanies them as I carry them out of the hold. It is the children that cause one most pain, but the saddest of all sights is the live mother. Sometimes they won't give the child up and I have to wait till she falls asleep before I can pry her fingers away from the small body. I can only do this knowing that I will keep my Nora and our unborn alive."*

On the fifty-ninth day, the captain told the packed steerage that they would be stopping in New York for provisions. He said it would only take two days to get the needed supplies. But the South Street Seaport harbor master feared that the Blanche carried the black fever. He told his dockworkers that no member of the anchored crew was to reach dry land and no worker of his was to go within fifty yards of that "black" ship. One small dinghy would be towed out, anchored, and left for the Blanche crew to pick up the supplies. It took five days of shuffling between the dinghy and the ship to bring the required water, biscuits, flour, molasses, sugar, oatmeal, rice and tea, for the remaining two thousand mile trip to New Orleans. The ship left New York on February 25th, fifty-four days into the voyage. The captain said,

"Two weeks sail, then we're there. God willing."

The sea warmed as the ship traced a route along the eastern coast of the United States, always in sight of land, but never touching it. Nora's spirits rose and fell, as she would ask Michael,

"How much further Michael? Do you think we will make it before…?"

"It won't be long now my love, the crew says a few more days and we will turn west through some small islands. They say you can smell the fruits and flowers from the islands as you pass through. Then we turn north and head straight for New Orleans. We will make it, the Blessed Mother won't leave us now," he said, but his own thoughts were back in New Ross. That night he wrote two lines,

We should have stayed in Skibbereen till the baby was born. I should have been patient. Emmett be damned.

In the early light of March 30, 1850, the Atlantic was behind. The islands had shared their fragrance. Michael stood on the aft deck, a hairy piece of twine in his hands. He crossed himself and said in a whisper,

"Please Jesus, let that be the last." He watched the crew pulling the sheets up and down trying to catch any wind that would move the ship and bring a little coolness to their salt encrusted faces. He saw no wake behind the Blanche, only a flat gray color that reminded him of the coast just south of Skibbereen before a storm. It was this glassy sea that he dreaded the most, a sea that could break and force its ragged shards into his skin.

It was then that he felt Nora's first screams. He raced down the ladder to the steerage and saw her staring at a deep burgundy mass in her hands.

"It's a blood clot, just that, but we need to get her to the cabin," Grace and Harriet Callahan said in unison. Michael's anxiety abated briefly as he looked at the two spinster midwives from Cork. Nora had told him that it was the Blessed Mother looking after them when she met the sisters on the first day of the voyage.

"Michael, you get the first mate, tell him we need blankets and water, three to four days ration. Tell him we'll use mine and Harriet's," Grace said.

When it had become clear that the baby had a good chance of being born at sea, Michael had asked the first mate for a space for Nora to give birth. A small cabin was designated for Nora to deliver and nurse her child for as long as she needed. It had a table, a bunk and a small writing desk with a chair. Most importantly, it had a door that could be closed. The first mate would bunk with another crewmember while Nora used his cabin.

Michael knelt on the bare plank floor behind Nora, holding the blanket folded as a pillow under her head. He placed his hand on her cheek each time she screamed,

"Oh God, it hurts, why does it hurt so? What did I do wrong? Michael, where are you? Don't leave me. Did I do something wrong? Grace, where are you? Thank God, you and Harriet are here, I need a woman's help. Michael, I need to see you, hold my hand." Between contractions he thought he heard a choking sound, but Nora's lips were closed as she relaxed after each jerk of her head against his chest.

"It's all going to be fine," he said to her over and over as he exchanged glances with Harriet and Grace who were trying to hide their concern with rigid smiles and periodic, "ahs."

Suddenly their forced smiles disappeared, the "ahs," replaced by simultaneous gasps from the two sisters.

"What? What?" Michael's voice cracked as he strained to read the expressions on the midwife's faces.

The baby girl had burst into their hands with the umbilical cord wrapped tightly around her neck; the final oxygen had been delivered minutes before the red curls appeared. Harriet slowly unwrapped the deadly tether from around the small neck, cut it with a scissors, quickly tied the cord and handed her to Grace while she attended to the afterbirth. Grace wiped the still infant as clean as she could before handing her to Nora.

"She is with God, Nora, we did our best, please forgive us. Hold her now, as long as you want. Michael, you must baptize this child, before the devil gets her soul. Here is the water; you know the words, don't you? 'I baptize you in the name…"

"I know the words." Michael said through clenched teeth.

Nora held the warm body next to her chest as Michael poured water over the child's forehead, forcing the words,

"I baptize you in the name of the Father, the Son, and the Holy Ghost."

As he spoke, Nora wiped bits of blood from the child's face, her pale lips pressed against the reddened forehead of her daughter for the first and last time.

"I love you Mary, I love you Mary, remember me, I will see you in heaven."

Michael suppressed a scream, felt the guilt that had been borne in him since deciding to leave Ireland with Nora full of their child explode in his stomach as a vile black liquid.

The Latin words from the Confiteor that he had memorized in order to become an altar boy at the age of seven, pounded just behind his eyes,

Mea Culpa, Mea Culpa, Mea Maxima Culpa. My fault, My fault, My most grievous fault. If I had just waited, if I had thought more of them than I did myself, Mary would be alive. I am a murderer.

But there was no forgiveness, no relief from the pain he would carry with him for the rest of his life.

Nora looked up at him, as if she could read his mind.

"No," she took his hand,

"It is not your fault, the Blessed Mother is with me, she said that we will have more chances. It's not your fault. We made the decision to leave Ireland together, as husband and wife, as mother and father. It's nobody's fault. Oh God."

"Nora, you know what I have to do."

"Not yet, let me hold her awhile, I want to say goodbye. Oh God."

As Nora said this she closed her eyes and rolled to the right, one arm wrapped around the infant, the other under her still distended belly, the cabin wall within inches of her face. Michael sat on the floor, listened as Nora's gasps finally smoothed into the rhythm of the ship crossing the swells of the Gulf. He reached inside his jacket and pulled out a piece of the onionskin and a stub of a pencil. He wrote slowly and deliberately,

It is over, our baby Mary will soon be in the water, released as the others. Nora is breathing, alive to my ear, but will she be alive when she wakes? She is the only light left in the world, blocking out the priests, the landlords, the owners of this death ship, all who only think of themselves. My salvation lies in a resolve to see her smile again.

Michael folded the sheet and put it in his pocket. He reached over Nora's shoulder and pushed her fingers away from the inert form lying between her body and the cabin wall. He pulled Mary carefully into his arms, wrapped her in a small blanket.

"Can I help?" Grace asked.

"No, you stay with Nora, I have to do this alone." He replied.

He made his way through the cramped steerage, almost falling over sleeping forms, excusing himself as he bumped into men and women that hardly noticed his passing. He felt as if he was working his way out of a snake's stomach, squeezing out of a death smell, covered by rancorous itches that he could not scratch, finally emerging into the night, free of the gurgles, moans, screams, that meant "help me."

One last body, just one. But he hesitated at the rail. The smell of warm salt rose from the Gulf, waves slapped the wooden hull, the black abyss beckoned two, not one. He would hold her tightly as they hit the water; air bubbles would rise around them as they sank into the out stretched arms of a figure in a green robe.

The ship dove down the side of a swell, wind sudden in his face, his black hair straight out behind his head, his eyes shut against the sting of the salt water and he heard Nora scream. He carefully took out a knife and cut a small lock of Mary's red curls, put them next to the onionskin in his pocket. He dropped the water soaked blanket in a bundle at his feet and pressed his lips against the wrinkled blue skin of his dead daughter.

He thought that he would pick up the blanket, wrap her tightly, hide her under his bunk, touch her every minute, but the black water came back with the sound of an Irish gale at midnight and sucked the flaccid form out of his hands. He leaned over the rail, opened his mouth to yell at the sea, but was mute, as he watched her bob momentarily, and then disappear with the retreating wave.

Michael and Nora Stone arrived in the port of New Orleans on April 2, 1850, 90 days after leaving New Ross.

CHAPTER TWO
NEW ORLEANS

Nora Stone, her arms folded as if she held a child, sat motionless against a bale of cotton, staring past the ships in the harbor. The port of New Orleans was filled with single mast sloops from Spain, square-rigged barques from France and Italy. But most of all, it was Irish that streamed out of the sailing coffins onto the docks looking for further transportation north or west.

Michael stood first in line in front of a low wooden table, Emmet's letter in his hand. The white steam driven paddle wheeler, Columbia, rested behind the representative of the Keystone Mines. Golden sunlight shone past Michael's shoulder into the pale, smooth face of a man in a tall beaver hat. The brim was pulled down protecting his eyes from what Michael knew to be an unwelcome glare. He stepped to the left and put the man into the shade offered by his shoulders.

"Thank you sir, I don't often sit outside and it is honestly a bit uncomfortable." Sweat ran down his cheeks as he continued,

"You come highly recommended by Mr. Emmett Ryan. A good friend indeed. Sign here, Mr. Stone, the trip to Peoria is paid for by the President of Keystone. He's chartered a portion of the Columbia. There will be housing for you and your wife, and a fifty-dollar bonus after you finish six months in the mine. Lucky for you, your friend had the foresight to write to you. There aren't many spots left in the shafts."

"What do you mean, the shafts? I was told this was a strip mine, work on the hills, not inside them," Michael said.

"We have a need in the shafts, after you work there, the other mines become available. Sort of a reward," the man said, his left cheek rising to show a black space where incisors had once been.

Words that Michael had heard before,

"Not to worry, everything will be taken care of for you."

Words that took his control away,

I won't be part of another's idea of safety, I will think first of Nora.

"And when does the steamer leave?" He asked as he stepped out of the line of the sun's rays, bringing the mine representatives hand up to just below the brim of his hat.

"Tomorrow, but if you wait, the position I am offering may not be available. And the cost of the trip will be from your pocket if you decide to take the Columbia north."

Michael turned and walked directly to Nora.

"Emmett was wrong, there are no strip mines, only the holes. We will take the Columbia to Peoria, and I will look for other work. I will not go into the shafts and take the chance of making you a widow."

Since little Mary's burial in the Gulf, Nora's strength had seeped out between the wooden planks of the Blanche as if she were using all her energy reaching out to pull the small body back into her womb. Michael watched Nora retreating into a haven where their child could be seen and heard. Then she spoke,

"But, won't Emmett be upset? After all, he is the reason we're here. You wouldn't have known of the mines if it weren't for him." Her face was turned toward the Gulf as she spoke, each word soaking up the oxygen around her. Then her eyes sought Michael, her voice rose, her cheeks, that had paled during the crossing, now darkened with a sudden rush of blood,

"I know why he didn't mention the shafts. He needed you to walk into that mine so that he could walk out alive."

CHAPTER THREE
PEORIA

Michael and Nora spent the next two weeks in the unaccustomed comfort of a steam driven paddle boat. Two tall smoke stacks reached into the musty air, belching smoke that could be seen for miles on either side of the Mississippi River. The huge single paddle wheel behind the boat churned the river into a brown soup of silt and mud being washed to the New Orleans delta from the river's origin in Minnesota.

Meals were served on tables with white cloths and real silver ware. They had a private cabin, a door that actually locked, separating them from other people and almost blocking the many languages that floated through the wooden slats. In some ways, it was the honeymoon that had never been within their grasp.

Nora's strength returned in bits as she walked the circumference of the boat twice every day. Her anger with Emmett Ryan rising as the child seemed to struggle from the cloudy water and reenter her womb. She felt a phantom push from inside as she nodded to the other women and their children taking the river sun full into their faces. Then she was empty again, anger replaced by despair, as the steam boat's whistle announced another emerging city had slipped by. On the third day she found herself mouthing a long ago memorized prayer,

"*Hail Mary, full of grace,*" then new words surprised her, made her reach for the railing, gasp for breath,

"*You had your time with your child, let me have mine.*" She was surprised not so much by the anger, but by the positive energy that surged through her body. It gave her hope, hope that she needed to get through each day, hope that set her plans for another child.

Michael's poisonous guilt woke him every morning, fluttered near the surface of his consciousness, then retreated just enough for him to face the day in his own way. He wanted to launch the blame in an arc that would land on another human. But it could not land on Emmett Ryan. No matter how much he believed that his friend had deceived him, it was still his decision to cross the ocean. He was alone with the guilt that he felt was his deserved punishment and there was no priest, no God, that could absolve him of the blackest mark a man could have on his soul, the death of his child. The God that he had often seen pointing out a single road, had not raised a hand.

They stood on the deck of the freshly painted steamer, felt the crowning scent of white blossoms from fifty foot catalpa trees brought by Louisiana spring breezes across the Mississippi, wipe out the odor of typhoid and death. The rhythmic slapping of the paddle wheel drowned out the screams from the hold of the Blanche.

They were on their way to Peoria, a town surrounded by rich black earth, pure water from natural springs, a river that provided food and transport, enough grain and livestock to feed and clothe all of Ireland. They wanted the chance to prove their sacrifices worthwhile.

Michael looked for "HELP WANTED" signs, but just beneath every one was another sign, "NINA," "No Irish Need Apply." Michael stopped at every storefront up from the docks onto Main Street. The signs adorned doors and windows as if there had been a town meeting that had condemned a whole race and broadcast the results with banners. Even the bars had decided that enough Irish had stepped off the steam boats from New Orleans.

"Go to the mines, Keystone is hiring you folks. Good wages is what I hear," were the words as the doors slammed in his face. He worked his way south on Jefferson, stopping at each store front, ready to explain his expertise in printing, writing, his knowledge of farming, the best way to rotate crops, the pricing of foodstuffs, which grain should go to the millers and which to the breweries. But no business would even listen to his speech that he had practiced since leaving New Orleans.

"I can start today, make an immediate contribution. I will bring three times the revenue that my wages cost. This is your opportunity to prosper at an even greater rate than I am sure your business is doing at present," he would say if he had the chance. But the closest he could come was holding his cap in his hands with a big smile and uttering the first words in his best American imitation, "My name is Michael Stone." It came out in a brogue as thick as a pint of Irish beer tempered with a French rhythm that he had picked up on the docks of New Orleans.

Established businesses were harder to find the further south he went. He was approaching an open market where farmers brought vegetables, fruits and grains and set them up in temporary stands. Small grocery stores were just beginning to take hold on the recently defined street leading back to the center. But the brick surfaces had given way to dirt packed hard by what seemed to Michael to be hundreds of buggies and wagons all drawn by horses five hands higher and much more muscular than the animals that had taken corpses to the Skibbereen graveyard.

Later there would be street cars running back and forth on a carefully laid out schedule, but today, Michael Stone saw horse drawn wagons following the least resistant path. He avoided wheels, hoofs, horse droppings, and an occasional elbow with a quick step and the last bit of energy his legs had stored. He found himself on the bottom of three wooden steps of a newly constructed two story structure that could have been a brothel or a bar. The owners sign had not gone up, but neither had the hated "NINA" announcement. He stepped up and knocked on the door.

The door swung open. A small compact woman, the top of her head even with Michael's collar bone, wisps of white hair floating around her face, held the door, and said,

"Hello, are you looking for work?"

He stood with his cap in his hands and his mouth open, afraid to speak, wishing he had a pencil and pad that would identify him as a mute.

"Speak up, I can't stand here with the door open, letting in the flies and dirt. You look like a fairly intelligent fellow, *can* you speak? Or should I just close the door?" Her ebony colored eyes stared directly up into Michael's, demanding an answer. Her accent was a strange mix of what he recognized as British, but with a hint of some middle European tone he had never heard.

"Yes ma'am, I mean, no ma'am, I can speak, and I am," he stopped, pulled himself up to his full six foot height,

"My name is Michael Stone, I can start today, make an immediate contribution. I will bring three times the revenue that my wages cost. This is your opportunity to prosper at an even greater rate than I am sure your business is doing at present."

"Well, that wouldn't take much, since we haven't opened. My

husband and I need someone who can work with the farmers that bring their produce to the market. We plan to buy the whole wagon and resell it at a profit. What would take them eight hours to sell, will now take just a few minutes. But we need a good eye and a quick wit. Something you Irish are known for if you can stay out of the bars."

"I don't drink! I know farmers, I know their problems."

"My name is Sara Ann, Sara Ann Goodman," she said as she reached out to shake Michael's hand.

"Come in, come in, I want you to meet my husband Edward."

"Mr. Goodman, meet Mr. Stone, from, where did you say you were from, Mr. Stone?"

"Ireland, Skibbereen, Ireland."

Edward Goodman rubbed his hand from his forehead across bare skin to the crown of his head and brushed up the tufts of white hair just above his ears before he shook Michael's outstretched hand. Michael expected a rough, workman hand, but was surprised when the touch and grip of Mr. Goodman's hand felt the same as his wife's.

"Irish, Irish, what do you think Sara Ann, can we trust this man, he doesn't look too Irish, maybe we just give him a pad and pencil, then the farmers won't know," Edward Goodman talked without tone change, one word flowed into the other without perceptible breathing,

"But then we haven't tried to cover our accents," a slight smile bounced from one side of his mouth to the other,

"We've done ok, if they accept us, they'll accept another persecuted soul."

Michael finally realized that the Goodman's were Jewish, the first Jews he had ever spoken to.

Sara Ann Goodman, and her husband Edward, property speculators while in London, but now green grocers in Peoria, hired Michael Stone as their first employee.

Nora sat across from Michael at a small table in their boarding house room. "Michael, I'm very glad you've found a job, the Goodman's sound like nice people. I'm a little worried about the fact that they weren't in the grocery business in London. What do they know about farmers and dealing with them, let alone the customers they will have that might have some prejudice against them *and* us for that matter?"

"That's why they hired me, Nora. I will be the expert. They

seem to understand the financial side of business, better than I do," Michael said, thinking about how hard it was for him to balance his accounts at the end of every month at the printing shop. "The most important part of this arrangement is that we like each other. I can tell they are good people. If we treat the customers fairly, business will be good."

"I heard you had taken up with the Brits," Emmett Ryan spit out, leaning across the freshly watered lettuce bins from Michael. The last time they had seen each other, Emmett's face was unlined, his eyes had sparkled when he had spoken of going to America that day in Rocky Sullivan's pub. His voice was clear, his eyes filled with dreams of recovery from the death of his father and brother.

"I'll work the mines, get my own piece of land, away from the bastard landlords, maybe open a pub with local beers, Peoria's famous for its grains and breweries. It's a fact. I'll write you as soon as I'm settled, you and Nora will have a friend in the New World."

Today his face was lined, his eyes squinted out from black dust that seemed to have soaked into the skin of his cheeks. The backs of his hands were black, his fingers bent into small sharp hooks, finger nails cracked. His words seemed to be scratched out of his throat. But what struck Michael full force in the stomach was the fact that he was looking *down* at Emmett, not eye to eye as the last time they had spoken. Emmett Ryan's shoulders were now hunched, the back of his neck bulged from under his collarless shirt.

"I've known you've been in town for the last six months, the foremen told me he talked with you in New Orleans, that you decided to skip the mines. Why didn't you come to tell me yourself? I've waited and waited. The doctor told me I have to get out of the shafts, but I've nobody to take my place. I have stayed a year longer than the rest. I thought you were coming. I counted on you. You've got to help me. I have nowhere else to turn now. My lungs are scrap, I can't go back in the hole."

"You son of a bitch, you rotting bastard! How dare you come in here and tell me I am the cause of any of your *deserved* misfortune. I trusted you, followed your direction as if it came from the priest. Then the real motive came out. Go into the mine so you can get out. I lost my child and almost my wife because of your need, your sense of mistimed urgency."

Michael's anger fueled the first few words, words he had been saving until the moment of facing Emmett would come. But now his sense of self righteous superiority slipped into the hole that was always waiting for him around his ankles, waiting to pull him into a black well of suffocating guilt. But this time it wasn't Nora or Mary's hands that he saw reaching up to grab him. Emmett Ryan was dying because of a choice Michael Stone had made.

"I'm sorry Emmett. I'm sorry you're sick. I'm sorry you've lost your dream. I'm sorry I told you I would come. I'm sorry we took the boat. I'm sorry I lost my Mary, I'm sorry Nora married me." These final words came slowly, inaudibly, from Michael, shards of glass he had held in his stomach since reaching Peoria, now hung between he and his friend.

"I will put you to work Emmett. You can deliver to our customers that need deliverin to. But you stay away from the Goodman's *and* Nora. In other words, sit on the corner of the porch until I tell you to come in and get the bags. And, I want you to look for work on the new railroad bridge. How ironic, you'd be thirty feet in the air pounding spikes, not a hundred below ground swinging a pick. "

CHAPTER FOUR
GREEN GROCER

Michael and Nora ran the front of the store. With Michael buying from the farmers and Nora selling to the housewives at prices set by Edward Goodman, the Goodman's turned their attention to their lost London business, property speculation. The store on Merriman Street had been their first investment. Edward and Sarah Ann were able to recoup their down payment in the grocery plus, to their minds, a decent profit. They combined it with a loan from the First Bank of Peoria and bought a hundred acres on the west bluff two miles from the center of town. They set about developing the land for homes, large homes that could be bought by the most successful owners of mines, distilleries, and banks. They moved into their own new home in 1865, just as the victorious regiments were returning from the Civil War.

"Michael, you've proven to be a real asset to the grocery," Edward Goodman stood on the porch to the grocery with his hand reaching up to Michael's shoulder. "You know that we've built a new home and will move into it soon. This grocery has been the start of our recovering what we lost in London. I am grateful to you and Nora for what you've done for us. I honestly don't think I could have handled the business as effectively as you have. I didn't agree with your tactics all the time, especially when you brought that friend of yours, what was his name, Ryan? into the store."

"Yes sir, Emmett Ryan was his name, he needed a job, I know you didn't approve, but you let me make the decision, and I appreciated that confidence."

"He seemed so sickly when you first introduced us, I wasn't sure he could handle even the smallest of tasks you gave him." Edward's attention had already moved on as he made this last observation,

"And you sometimes gave the farmers a little too much for their produce." His voice rose and his hand tightened on Michael's shoulder, before he slapped him on the back.

"But, by then, I trusted you, so what was I to do? "

Michael's heart beat rose with Edward's voice, not sure exactly where his boss was headed. He never quite knew when Mr. Goodman was serious and angry, or sarcastic and happy. Would he and Nora be able to stay on in their jobs, or was Mr. Goodman setting him up for the news that some unknown cousin was showing up the next day to run the grocery? He remembered his father's constant admonition,

"Michael, be happy with what you have, it could always be worse."

It was the last sentence he had heard from his father the day he had left Ireland.

"So, what do you want to do with your life Michael? Does this little business look like it has a future?" Edward asked with an even tone.

"Mr. Goodman, this business is my life, I have learned a lot from you and I'm very grateful." *Here it comes, we'll be out on the street.*

"Here is what I propose. You will buy the business from me at a fair price. You will pay me out of the profits you earn monthly, assuming you make a profit. I will review your accounts with you and decide what the payment will be. We will consider it a mortgage on your new business and home." Edward Goodman's voice then tightened imperceptibly, his eyes narrowed as he glanced down to the street.

"By the way what happened to him? He hasn't been around for awhile." Michael turned slowly and sat down on the step, sure that Mr. Goodman was giving him a chance he would never get again.

"You mean, Emmett Ryan?"

"Yes, your friend, Emmett."

"I, I, of course, of course, I can show a profit, it's a fair offer." He paused, then stood and faced Edward,

"Emmett really didn't like working here, he said he wanted something that required the use of his hands." Michael chose his words carefully, aware of not bringing Emmett's attitudes onto the sun drenched porch.

"He went to work on the railroad bridge as a rigger. He has a skill that is highly prized by foreman looking to fill dangerous jobs. He doesn't care if he dies. I don't know where he is now."

"Better that he's gone," Edward Goodman squinted into the sun, "So, does that mean we have a deal?" he said with a slight smile on his face.

"A deal!" Michael said with a large smile. The two men shook hands and pounded each other on the back. Michael thought of his good fortune in the grocery business, Emmett's lungs, whether he would ever see him again. For a moment, the world seemed out of balance, then righted itself, as evening's first shadows reached the porch.

Michael and Nora moved into 317 Merriman Street. The grocery was entered through large double doors that opened into the bins containing the first lettuce, carrots, tomatoes, broccoli, shallots, potatoes, and rhubarb of the season. Large plate glass windows allowed approaching customers to see the neatly piled displays. Spring Corn encased in sheaths with golden tassels filled a quarter of the front display. A large pot-bellied stove stood in the middle of the room creating a convenient leaning post during the heat of summer and a place to dry gloves and boots during the cold and wet of winter.

Customers were often greeted by the fresh fragrance of cut blossoms from the garden during the growing season and the sweet incense of hot raisin bread, during the drying season. Nora's days were filled with these temporary creations to keep the hours in the present. She thrived in the recognition from the neighborhood,

"What beautiful roses, how do you do it? I can't seem to make grass grow."

"Don't let Willy taste these scones, he'll want them every day."

Michael forced himself to eat the rolls and bread that Nora cooked, knowing why she put so much effort into her kitchen creations.

The first time he went into the garden, he saw Mary's face shimmering from beneath each petal. Nora's fertile hands at work. What was he capable of creating? All he was good at was burying, and selling rhubarb.

Two bedrooms were on the second floor, one back stairway led up from the kitchen. Business blurred the days and nights, their attention focused on solving problems brought in by farmers, housewives, veterans of the Civil War.

Their every minute was filled with baking, flowers, fruits, vegetables, broken only by sporadic and almost unconscious attempts at creating another child. Lovemaking was dutiful, tender, but lacking the passion that had brought them together. Serrated edges of uncovered memories were brought to the surface. Nora's eyes filled with tears in a silent clenching of her teeth and hands. Michael turned slowly away, engulfed by the fear that none of his instincts or intentions would ever fulfill the true intention of sex; the creation of a life.

They fell asleep next to each other, exhausted, the lost child appearing only as a dream, a single image frozen between them, a hand or foot touching, not sure that another opportunity would ever come again.

Six months after moving into the house, Nora called Michael to the front porch. Michael stood with a wet head of lettuce held against the clean white apron he had just changed into. He heard the words he had despaired of ever hearing,

"We are going to have a baby. Doc Murphy says I will have to be very careful. At my age, there are a lot of things that can go wrong." She looked straight into Michael's eyes, put her hand on the side of his face. Her lungs filled with a sweet breath she thought she had lost forever.

"And, Michael, you *will* come to church with me every Sunday. You haven't been for years. Our new child needs a father *and* a God. You will do your part." She pushed the lettuce out of Michael's hands and put them on her stomach. "Feel this body that is now two. *We* did it together. You can forgive yourself. It never was your fault."

Michael shocked Father Kerrigan, the pastor of St. Patrick's, when he appeared the next Saturday morning, asking to go to confession.

"I don't want any sermon, Father, just hear my confession and You will see me every Sunday for the rest of my life. Nora and I are going to have a baby. It's a miracle. You have to promise that she and the baby will be OK. That's the deal."

Father Kerrigan looked at Michael Stone, the man that had eluded him for fifteen years.

"If this is what it takes to get you into church, so be it. Michael, I will do all within my power to influence the Almighty to protect your Nora and child.'

After hearing Michael's confession the priest said,

"Make a good act of contrition, and for your penance, say the rosary fifteen times, once for every year you haven't come into God's home. You do remember how to say the rosary, don't you? Now I expect to see you and Nora tomorrow in the front of the church. *That's* the deal."

"It's a boy."

"Is he breathing?" Nora asked the midwife.

"Of course, he's breathing, aren't you, little man?"

"Count his fingers and toes. Are they all there? Then let me hold him. He is breathing, I see him." Nora pushed the black wet hair away from his forehead. Born on the first of October, 1865, he was an Irish child, the same as if he had been conceived on the island they had left behind.

"We should call him Liam, after his grandfather," she told Michael.

"We need to give him a fighting chance, give him an American name. How about William, it's the same, but he will be American first, Irish next." Michael argued gently, thinking of giving his son a head start. One *he* would have had only by playing the mute.

A month later, he was christened William Edward Stone by Father Kerrigan.

"Welcome to the church, William, we'll see you next Sunday with your mother and father," he said almost sternly to the small group gathered around the baptismal fount at St. Patrick's.

CHAPTER FIVE
LEDGERS

William grew up loving the daily visits from the farmers, the routine of buying the best produce, cleaning it, putting it out for the housewives. He also put a few bunches away for the needs of the rectory and convent. He knew he was serving his family and his church. That's all he ever wanted to do.

His big contribution came in early 1880 when he convinced his dad that they should add meat to the grocery.

"Bad idea, son. Don't forget Friday's, nobody eats meat on Friday. You only get six/sevenths of the week. That will never change. Meat's not as dependable, our customers need fruit, vegetables, bread every day, and where would you put it?"

"You buy too much produce now. I know you do it for the farmers. I hear you telling them, 'I'll take all the carrots, the rhubarb; you need the money more than I, you'll do me a favor some day.' But Dad, we have to store it and then we just throw it away when it starts to smell. Why don't we loan those guys the money they need. If we sell roasts, pork, bacon, a few steaks, we'll have the money to loan out from the profits and even save a little." William finally convinced his father that the price of meat would justify the one lost day.

Michael turned the produce storage area into a meat section. He had a cooler brought in and the largest pine colored chopping block he could find. The block came with two hooks on one side. One for the long narrow sharpening tool and one for the wooden handled meat cleaver.

"Now we have to keep track of the business. I'll use one of those books mom bought last week from the crippled tinker man," William told his father after the meat section had been set up.

William had watched a salesman with a wagon full of everything from knives to laxatives stop in front of Stone's Grocery. The man swung his left leg, rigid as an oak, to the ground, followed by his right leg that bent normally at the knee. He continued the swing of the unbending left leg up the steps into the grocery. He held a ragged dirt stained hat next to his thigh, a sparkling black and red ledger rested on a red handkerchief in his outstretched hand. William hovered behind him in the doorway, ready to offer an opinion or protection. Nora stood behind the recently installed candy counter.

"I would like to see the man of the house, if you please, ma'am."

"You will speak to me or no one. Don't need to see a man to get a decision around here. What's that black book you're holding there?" Nora asked.

"The best accounting ledger around, 10 columns for anything you need."

"Don't you have anything with just lines, no columns?"

The tinker limped back to the wagon and pulled out an identical black and red book.

"Here it is, model 23H. Perfect for recording more words than numbers."

"That's the one I want."

The tinker told Nora that the ledgers were manufactured by Boorum & Pease. The same book had been in their assortment since 1862.

"Each book is hand stitched with 300 lined and numbered pages. People want quality. These books will last longer than we will. That's what our best customers tell us."

"The boy here can use a nice book to write in. It will help him in school, I'll take, lets see, I'll take eleven." Nora winked at her son.

"Great Mom, I can use it to keep track of the meat business. Dad doesn't need a book. He remembers every farmer by name, and what he brought in, and what Dad paid. He says the meat's my business. And maybe the whole store some day. I have to keep track of the numbers."

William sat at the kitchen table every night and listed the day's transactions. He filled the first ledger with information in less than three months. Type, weight, price paid, the name of the farmer that brought in a butchered hog. But it wasn't until the trains started to arrive from Chicago with sides of lamb and beef that the business showed a profit. The Chicago & Rock Island freight's crossed the railroad bridge over the Illinois River and unloaded two blocks away.

William kept the ledgers on a shelf above the kitchen sink. His father watched and laughed as he entered each transaction with a stubby pencil.

"Not much of a memory there William, or maybe you don't trust

the men bringing in the meat. But then it would help us keep track of our cash. You just keep it up, we'll see how your little business thrives. Mr. Goodman might be able to use you some day."

William was shocked when his father asked him if he could use one of the ledgers. "Sure Dad, you can use it for anything you want. It'll be just yours. What are you going to use it for?"

"Not sure, but I'll get you another if you need it. That tinker shows up here every summer at least once or twice."

William thought his father was going to start recording the vegetable accounts. He was proud that he had made a contribution to the family business; a pride that was promptly confessed the next Saturday.

Michael Stone eyed the ledger for a much different reason. He could not bring himself to tear up the pieces of onion skin that held the only record of Mary's death. He and Nora didn't speak of it to William, nor did they speak of the events that brought them to Peoria. They presented to William the façade of America. They were natives that had no past, just the bright hope of a future for their son.

No matter how much Michael wanted to destroy the papers, he could not. Instead, he decided to change their hiding place in the bottom of his trunk. A spot closer to his hand and eye if he ever decided to touch the life he had destroyed. If he was careful, they would exist unnoticed, except by him, until the paper itself crumbled.

William did not see his father carefully place the precious papers into a store envelope, peel the end paper away from the back board of the ledger, slide the envelope in and seal the end paper smoothly against the surface.

The next morning, Michael Stone asked his son,

"Would you mind if I placed my book next to yours?"

"Sure, then you can use it whenever you want. I won't bother it."

Michael Stone walked over to the open shelf above the kitchen sink and placed his blank ledger next to the ten that his son would fill. He let go of Mary, knowing she would be close whenever he needed her. He turned to William and for the first time, hugged him as a man.

William Stone felt a little older, knowing his father loved, and more importantly, trusted him.

THE SINGING BONE
PART TWO 1980

CHAPTER EIGHT
KATHRYN STONE

"Liam, how can you skip so many years? I want to know what happens to these people. And where did Emmett go? He just disappeared. Is he coming back?"

Kathryn sat on the edge of bed in Liam's study, a red pen in her hand.

"That's all I remember," Liam said as he leaned closer to the Selectric, swearing at a misspelled word. "Damn good thing I have this erase and correct thing. Now, the good Miss Brown wants a synopsis or an outline. I can't do that. It will be what it is."

"Dinner's ready and Colin wants to read to you. When will you come down?

"Soon, soon."

STONE AND SON
PART TWO

CHAPTER SIX
JULIA AND WILLIAM STONE
1890

Michael and Nora wanted William to have the companionship, love, and sustenance that only a large family could provide, an Irish family. He didn't seem interested in girls. He was now working in the store six days a week. He didn't talk about friends nor did he bring any home. Michael and Nora assumed that he was too busy with the growing business to have time for friends. They worried about him and decided to do something about it.

Their solution was to arrange a match and hope for nature to take its course. They called Michael into the living room and told him about the Geare family who had five children, two girls and three boys, an ideal Irish family.

"And their oldest daughter, Julia, is gregarious, charming, well read, and your age," Nora told him.

"We have been invited to their house after mass on Sunday. Come and meet them, you could use a few new friends."

They had expected resistance to their idea, suspecting that William lived in a world composed of meat, knives, and brown paper. They were pleasantly surprised when he smiled and said,

"That's a good idea. I could use a little outside distraction."

William had plenty of friends, but he never brought them home. He kept his job and his friends separate. His parents never spoke about the old country. They were much older than the other parents he had met. The only reference they ever made to an Irish outside of the day to day business was someone named Ryan that had disappeared years ago. All in all, he didn't think his parents cared about who he saw outside of the store.

The closest he got to meaningful conversation was when he tried to tell them of a recurrent dream he was having. It was about open bodies of water and violent storms. He wanted to know if it had anything to do with the ships he had heard about. His mother said they were caused by the food he had eaten the night before. His father just shook his head and walked away, as he said,

"That imagination of yours will get you in trouble some day. Dreams don't mean anything."

He found his answers among friends that he met under corner gas lights on the riverfront. They would sit on benches drinking Gipp's beer watching the steam boats pass on their way to and from St. Louis. It was a time that he protected as his own. He loved his parents, but they seemed to him to be occupied with the neighborhood and the church. They didn't talk about Ireland and he felt they didn't want him talking about it either. He resolved not to ask about the old country and not to mention he had Irish friends, some very good Irish friends.

If he couldn't have a close relationship with Michael as a father, he could have a great business partner.

Their smiles and greetings to the customers were identical.

"Mornin to ya, Mrs. Murphy. Is that a new hat? What can we help put on your table today? The carrots and onions are just in from the O'Toole's farm," Michael said,

"And for Saturday's supper, the flank steak, just in from Chicago, would be perfect," William said as he held up a dripping piece of glistening meat.

"They weren't on my list. But what's a woman to do when those two smiles appear at once? Put them on my bill."

Julia Geare was the most important of William's friends. He knew the six Geares. They all had round blue eyes, narrow aquiline noses, cleft chins, broad shoulders. When sitting next to each other they appeared to be three sets of twins spaced a year apart. Julia's twin was her sister Ann, almost identical, until they stood. Ann was tall and slim, angular to her toes, the same as her brothers. It was Julia's curves that had caught William's attention the day he saw her get off the horse drawn trolley in front of Rocky Sullivan's.

"You must be a Geare, at least in the fine detail of your face. But the rest of you suggests something else,"

William stammered the rest of his opening remark.

"I mean, I mean, you don't look like the rest of their bodies, I mean, you have a look of your own."

" And you must be the boy with the meat business, trying to get the good Irish housewives to serve meat on Friday. My brothers have told me about you," Julia replied without hesitation.

William recovered quickly from his show of irreverence, and asked her quite properly,

"Perhaps we could see each other, take a walk over the foot bridge sometime."

"If you promise not to bring me to sin by eating meat on Friday."

"That is an old wives tale, I don't cause sin. I only offer the temptation."

It was a free dialog between the two with irony and undertone that only they heard. Michael knew that if love at first sight did not exist before, it did now. Julia stepped out of that trolley into his path and wouldn't let him pass.

She told him she wanted to be a journalist, but there were no jobs for women writers. They couldn't get the good crime and cowboy stories that appeared in the weekly Peoria Star. Instead, she focused on reading everything she could get her hands on and some day she would write a novel, perhaps under a man's name.

"Maybe, I'll use yours. What do you think? We could call it,

'Adventures of Julia Geare,' by William Stone."

"If that would be the case, I think we should get about creating a few episodes that would guarantee its success," William said squeezing her hand.

He was in love with Julia the reader, Julia the educated woman. She introduced him to Whitman, Twain, Stephen Crane. They walked across the foot bridge and read to each other, held hands and fantasized about ignoring Fr. Kerrigan's admonition,

"We don't need another pregnant young woman sent away to have a baby, now do we." It wasn't a question, it was a demand that went out to the parishioners whenever some unfortunate went away for a few months.

When they were ushered into the Geare's parlor that Sunday afternoon and saw Fr. Kerrigan looking sternly at them, they knew their inner thoughts had been discovered and would have to go to confession right there on the carpet. Instead, Mr. Geare said,

"Julia, Mr. Stone and I want you and William to see each other socially. Father Kerrigan is here to bless your meeting and pray for a future wedding."

They looked into each other's eyes and smiled,

"I would be honored to see this fair young woman on a social basis. And if God intends for us to wed, so be it," Michael said.

The small group applauded. Father Kerrigan raised his right hand and made a sign of the cross over their bowed heads. Later that evening, William said to Julia,

"Good thing we're not Italian. We'd be married and sleeping in The room next to your parents in a week."

They were married six months later and moved into a second floor bedroom in the Geare house, that had belonged to Nora's oldest brother Stephen. William continued to work in the grocery and walked the mile back and forth daily. They wanted six children, but due to lack of privacy in the Geare house and bad timing, Julia didn't get pregnant. She would look at William across the breakfast table and whisper,

"What is wrong with you Stones? I have sixteen nieces and nephews. There are only three names in the Stone bible. Your mom, dad and you. Lucky for you, you're good at night. If I was counting on a baby, you'd be long gone," she kidded him.

William took his responsibility seriously,

"We'll try again tonight, after they're asleep."

CHAPTER SEVEN
THE BRIDGES
1895

Michael Stone was happiest when he and Nora walked across the foot bridge to the grassy knoll encased in elms and pin oaks. It was the narrowest section of the Illinois River, fifty yards from shore to shore, deep and wide enough for the steamboats and packets coming up from St. Louis with their loads of produce and immigrants. Once across they would look back at the crowds at the railroad station and steamboat dock that were within easy walking distance of each other. Many families got off the boat and walked immediately to the train bound for Chicago.

"This is what I remember of Skibbereen, the quiet of the trees, not the noise of the trains or the wheels in the water," Michael often said as they sat among the elms that shut out the heat of the sun.

"It is all I *want* to remember of that place, all I need now is the chance to see our son grow up to be as wonderful as his father. We are lucky he enjoys working with you, a lot of the other boys in the neighborhood are nothing but trouble."

"He must get his good sense from you, Nora. My sense is not always good, or correct."

On a fall evening in 1895, they set out for the ten minute walk to the small picnic area. As they left, Nora turned and saw William waving with his right hand, his left hand rubbing his ear. He looked as if he wanted to say something, then dropped his hands and smiled, waved them on.

"Probably wants to talk about those dreams again, all that violence. Or maybe he wants to know our secret to having a child so late in life," Nora said.

As they reached the final section of the walking bridge, the section that ran under the railroad bridge, they turned to look back at the docked paddle boats just arrived from St. Louis, then up to the underside of the railroad bridge that crossed the wagon bridge on its way to Chicago. The foot and wagon bridge had been built first in 1848 with the depth and width of the river and the height of the steamboat smokestacks that would pass underneath taken into consideration by the engineers. The Peoria and Oquawka Railroad bridge came in 1860 and the location chosen by the engineers was based on the same factors.

It was an easy decision. Start just south of the foot bridge, go across the river high enough to allow the steamboats to pass underneath and at the best angle so that the railroad track would cross the foot bridge close to the East side of the river. It was then an easy link to the track coming southwest from Chicago.

Michael and Nora always stopped and looked up at the train track, wondering what it would be like to be under the track when the steel horse would come across carrying coal from the mines and liquor from the distilleries on its way to Chicago. They shared an odd feeling that they weren't quite safe until they reached the canopy of oaks and pines.

Up until this day, they had never been under the tracks when the train roared by. They had watched from the trees, and could even feel the rumbling under their feet. Today, holding hands and talking about the way their only son made them feel complete, they approached the underside of the symmetrical wooden ties that the parallel iron rails rested on. The rails were held in place by large spikes twisted off as they broke out under the ties. They stopped just for a second to look up as they always did. Their hands tightened as the foot bridge trembled. Michael intended to stand just a second longer, then walk to their favorite spot under the trees, away from the noise that was drawing nearer. He wondered what it would be like to see the engine from underneath, and held Nora in place a second longer.

Thirty five years before, Emmett Ryan had driven spikes into the cross beams as he looked down at the foot bridge fifteen feet below. He marveled at the ability of engineers to sink the struts into the river bottom that held his beams and tracks in place over the existing foot bridge. He sunk his spikes in as surely as he could and bent over and twisted them so that they would never work their way out. Surely, he worried, over the years, the struts would rot with the river constantly swirling about it. He didn't think about the rise of the water level every spring and the constant flow of logs that would be collected from as far away as the Chicago river, that would congeal at the narrowest part of the river at the spot picked by the engineers for easy crossing for the foot bridge and the railroad bridge. He didn't worry about the awful power of the sodden battering ram as it smashed into the bridge struts.

The spring of 1895 had seen severe floods all up and down the Illinois River basin. The Peoria and Oquawka Railroad bridge had suffered daily for two weeks. Cracks had opened on the ten sets of struts that held the track over the foot bridge.

The Engineer of the 6:00 P.M. to Chicago leaned out the left window of the steam engine, and waved at two strollers holding hands and smiling up at him. As the train climbed to its apogee just above the foot bridge, he looked back at the paddle wheeler approaching from the north, thought of his wife and son that waited for him in Chicago. He felt an unusual shiver in the right wheel assembly of his engine as he thought of seeing them later that evening.

His next thought was, "Oh Christ, the struts are shaking." He started to yell, but realized that no one other than his fireman could possibly hear him. The right strut cracked first, forcing the engines's nose to dive at what would have been an angle taking it into the river, but the left strut broke cleanly in two, separating the engine from its tender, twelve freight cars and caboose, hurling it straight down through the footbridge.

William Stone stood behind the police wagon, trying to see who was being pulled from under the locomotive. The engine had come to rest upright on the rivers edge facing Chicago to the north east. The engineer and fireman stood next to a broken iron wheel, their coal darkened faces streaked with tears as the bodies of Michael and Nora Stone were carefully dug out of the compressed moist dirt.

William Stone collapsed to his knees, his ears ringing, knowing that if he had given into the tempation to talk to his parents one more time about his dreams of oceans and babies, they would still be alive.

CHAPTER EIGHT
WILLIAM AND JULIA
1895

"Your father was my first employee in Peoria, in some ways he helped us get back what was ours." Edward Goodman said to William Stone, "so,"

He paused as he looked up at William from behind his large mahogany desk in the downtown First Bank building.

"Do you have this month's payment?"

"That's what I came to see you about Mr. Goodman, I'm not ready to pay this month; the funeral, the graves, the dry spell, we're short this month. I know my father always paid you promptly on the first, and I hate to start out on a bad foot."

"Wait a minute, do you think this deal would go on forever? Hell, it's over as far as I'm concerned."

"Now wait a minute, Mr. Goodman, my family has been paying you for thirty years, now you're going to take advantage of my parents deaths to add to your holdings? Maybe my dad was wrong about you." William's face was red beneath the mustache and mutton chops he had recently grown.

"Hold on young man, you need to listen a little before you speak. It's a good habit to get into. Your dad always listened, then made up his mind. You should learn to do the same. Now, will you let me finish?"

"Go ahead, I'll listen, but I don't have to like it."

"Well, how would you like it if I told you that there won't be any more payments?'

"That's what I mean, it's not right for you to kick us out. Sounds like the reason my dad and mom left Ireland." William turned to leave.

"The grocery is yours, the last mortgage payment was made two weeks ago. I was going to deliver the papers myself, but, well, now you're here."

Edward Goodman opened his desk drawer and pulled out a tan file that had the words "Paid in Full, October 1, 1895" with his Edward Goodman neatly written just below the date.

"I wanted to deliver it myself, but you showed up here this morning."

He handed the file to William, who stammered,

"I didn't know, I never thought much about ever having the place myself. I'm sorry." William took the folder and reached out his hand to Edward Goodman who grasped it with both his.

"I'll do my best to listen from now on. It's just that I didn't know what to expect. I figured it would be a few more years before......I didn't expect that he would, that they would ever be gone. They seemed so happy when I came in every day. I never thought they would be gone."

Edward Goodman walked William to the door,

"You were lucky you were able to work side by side with your parents and know them as you did. Sometimes we don't know the people we love even when we see them every day."

As William walked into the sun on Main Street, it struck him that he had known two people that smiled at him, said that they loved him, but never spoke of where they came from, why they came, what they missed, who they missed.

In the mornings, William got up, buttoned his collar, straightened his tie, and picked up one of the starched aprons Julia prepared every day.

"Why do you dress so well?" Julia would ask, "You dress better than most of the customers, much better than the men bringing in the vegetables and meat. And I'm always starching these aprons."

William looked at Julia, tied the waist of his apron,

"My mother taught me that the way you present yourself hides The pain this life brings. I can smile when I feel the love you put into this cloth."

He used an average of three aprons a day, changed after each of two meat cutting sessions in the morning and midway through the afternoon. If necessary, he would change his shirt. Now that there was privacy, William was convinced he would eventually find the right combination of shirts, aprons, entries in his ledgers, and sex, to bring a child into their house.

CHAPTER NINE
THOMAS STONE
1905

After ten years, the formula worked. Julia told William in March of 1905 that she was pregnant. She told him she was sure it was a boy. William made one last entry in his tenth ledger, just after recording the delivery of a side of beef from a local slaughter house.

My prayers are answered. It was his last entry in the journals. He kept the eleventh and last journal, the one he had given to his father, for his son. William Stone never opened ledger eleven. He never felt the bulge under the back end paper. He never learned of the brief existence of his sister, Mary Stone.

That afternoon, Robert Lucas stopped his wagon in front of Stone's Grocery. His five year old son, Nathan sat next to him. He tied the old roan mare to the hitching rail, lifted Nathan down to the ground damp from the warm spring drizzle, and started to unload dried ears of last years corn. He had been selling exclusively to the Stone's for five years. No matter what he brought, William Stone was ready to buy, or barter, depending on what mood, or what need, was driving the day. Something existed between the two men that neither understood. What they knew was that words weren't always necessary. Just a nod of the head, a slight smile, a thick brogue observation, "top o the morning Robert, how's the head?" from William, a cockney retort from Robert, "up yours mick," confirmed their origins without admitting a feeling of loss. They were Americans, but both know there was more than what they càlled themselves, more that they wouldn't talk about, couldn't because their parents had never spoken. Only today mattered.

Get a good price for the corn, get the best corn for Mrs. O'Donnell and her boys. When Lucas was short on produce and money, Stone would pay for what he called "futures."

"Deliver it next week, call this a down payment."

When William Stone was short on produce and money, Robert

Lucas said,

"Sell this now and pay me later, we're better partners for it."

As Lucas turned to face the grocery front, he heard shouts from inside the store.

"Damn you, you little bastards. Get out of here and don't let me catch you behind my counter again."

The door slammed open and two ten year old scrawny boys, their hair chopped off as if their parents had been searching for lice, raced across the porch and down the steps. As they passed the wagon, they slowed and grabbed two ears of corn from under the tarp as if they could see through the canvas. Robert Lucas smiled at his friends inability to bring the two back for a smack.

"So, William, can't handle the Smith and Harris kids I see. You save a few pennies and I lose a few. Maybe we should call the police. I hear they're looking for baby thieves. Don't take up as much space in the new jail. Hell. There's probably a reward out for those two."

"They're not the only two beggars around, they're just the youngest and the fastest." William said with the beginning of a smile.

"But I know where they'll end up some day and none of us will benefit. So, Robert Lucas, anything left to sell?

"Enough corn for you to sell to half the Peoria housewives and you know what I'll throw in this time William?"

"No, what you going to throw in?"

Lucas reached under the tarp and pulled out a brown jug with a tan cork pushed almost totally into the mouth.

"Careful pulling the cork the first time. It can be explosive," Robert said.

"I know, I know, I've got a patched window out back proving that fact," William replied with a smirk as he walked up the steps with his friend, looked with envy at Nathan's bright blue eyes and shock of pitch black hair.

"One more piece of news, Robert. We can open this and celebrate. I am going to be a father."

Thomas Stone's birth was long and painful. He was born on October 10, 1905, an only child in a neighborhood that had an average of 6 children in each household. After Thomas was born, Doctor Ryan said to William and Julia,

"It was dangerous for you to have this child. You are a lucky couple. But now, no more. You are too old."

"And how do I keep from getting pregnant?" Julia asked him,

"You know what the church allows, Julia, follow the calendar. Or you can abstain."

The responsibility fell on Julia's shoulders to keep herself alive by curbing William's appetites. Thomas Stone was brought up by a mother that was always reading and a father that was always taking baths and going for long walks.

Thomas continued the pattern started by his grandfather, Michael; alone at birth, alone in the crib, alone as a child, no brothers to fight with, no sisters to make fun of.

CHAPTER TEN
GROWING UP THOMAS
1913

Julia and William loved Thomas deeply, but had no idea how to raise him as a child.

William would say,

"Thomas, when I'm busy in the store, you have to help your mother."

Julia would say,

"Thomas, when I'm busy in the house, you have to help your father."

He was the little man in the house, speaking only when spoken to, standing up when an adult came into the room, running errands for Mom, helping Dad with the store.

"Thomas, help your father with the beef, sharpen the knife. Be Sure to scrub the blood off the chopping block when he's done. Bring him his clean apron. Spray the lettuce and take this order over to the Conlin's before you leave for school. And don't get that shirt dirty."

"Right, mom, Jim Conlin could care less what I looked like. All he wants to do is shoot baskets."

"Jimmy Conlin? I'm surprised he finds time for anything outside church. He's always hanging around the priests. And, that game, that *game* will never go anywhere, who ever heard of throwing a ball into a peach basket anyway?"

Thomas came to expect the majority of his education, academic and moral, to come from the priests and nuns. They taught him how to survive, to stay pure. There was no confrontation at home. William taught him how to dress with style and Julia taught him how to appreciate literature.

Later, he would see his life as the confluence of a nun's story, a mother's story, and a father's love. Threads that tightened into a knot he could never undo.

Thomas leaned to the left of the writing shelf on his front row seat and picked a piece of hardened black mud off the toe of his new shoes. This was the first day he had dared to wear them to school. The streets and empty lots were finally dry after the soaking April rains. But he had cut across the school playground in his hurry to get to class on time, and as he jumped for the sidewalk leading to the school door, he had landed in the last piece of moist dirt hidden by long brown grass.

"Oh shit,"

He swore under his breath, and made a mental note for tomorrows first confession.

"Six times swearing. "

He sat back up and started to put the clod of dirt into his pants pocket.

Whap, the nun's pointer hit his desk with a force that set his ears ringing.

"Look here class, Thomas is more concerned with his new shoes than he is in learning how to prepare for his first communion."

His mother told him that morning, "Take care not to get these dirty. I wanted to save them for Sunday and your first communion, but better to break them in a little. You be careful not to get them dirty. Maybe you can stay in from recess and clean the blackboards for sister."

"Yeah, Mom, as if the other guys would let me get away with helping sister during recess," was his first thought. Instead he said,

"Good idea, Mom. I'll be careful."

As he looked up at the nun, he started to say, "I was just taking the mud off my first communion shoes," but thought better of it. He bowed his head as if to apologize. The nun took his chin in her left hand, the wooden pointer held at an angle across her habit.

"I know Thomas, you want to keep those new shoes clean, as well you should, but not in the classroom. We are here for one reason. And what is that reason?"

His head was held rigid looking up at the sharp jaw outlined by the starched habit worn by the Dominican nun.

"To learn what we must do to become worthy to receive the body and blood of Christ," he said between his teeth as her hand held like a vise. She released it as he finished speaking, patted him on the shoulder, and said,

"Very good, Thomas, you're still on the right road."
She turned to the rest of the class and asked,

"Now class, how do we get ready to receive Jesus into the Temple of our bodies?"

The twenty-four eight year olds said in unison,

"We think of Jesus at the Last Supper, how he died for us, and Rose into heaven to be at the right hand of his father."

"Good, and what do we do after we receive communion?"

The nun paced back and forth between her desk and the first row of desks, patting her left hand with the pointer. The class followed her movements with their eyes as they sat straight with their hands folded in front of them. The windows were open for the first time that spring. A soft breeze came in trying to pull their eyes out to the swirling white clouds. All except Thomas resisted the temptation. He wanted to see where the wet spot was that had caused the morning to start out so badly. The nun faced the blackboard briefly, put her left hand on the corner of the desk as she turned to retrace her steps. He couldn't resist and looked out expecting to see robins washing themselves in the murky puddle his shoe had carved out.

Whap. The pointer hit her desk. Somehow she knew he was looking out the window. She turned, looked directly at Thomas and said,

"Thomas, answer my last question."

He hesitated only briefly, confident that he knew what she wanted him to say.

"Be quiet and pray."

"For how long?"
He frowned, lowered his head, and said,

"I don't know Sister."

Nobody knew the answer. If they sat silent for long enough she would go right into one of her stories. This was the favorite part of the day for the class. Nobody told a story like the nun. She didn't seem to be concerned with how long it would stay with them or what impact it would have. That was too distant. She said her goal was to leave an idea with them; something they could perhaps talk about at dinner with their families. Thomas knew it was her favorite part of the day. He paid attention.

"Have I told you the story about the Youngest Martyr?"

"No Sister."

He loved stories about martyrs. Burning, crucifying, flaying of skin, the gorier the better. But they were always about grown ups, far enough away that they really didn't take the early martyr-saints home as friends.

"How young was he, Sister?" Jimmy Conlin asked.

"We don't know his age or his name, just his actions," the nun replied.

"The youth had been at a mass celebrated in secret at his parent's home. After the mass, the priest that could have been one of the apostle's,"

"Wow, one of the apostle's," came out of half of the boys mouths. She waited for quiet and continued.

"The priest asked the youth if he would carry the remaining consecrated hosts to Daniel's family on the other side of the town. He told him that he would have to be very careful because there were Roman soldiers in town.

'Carry the hosts in this small box next to your heart. Do not speak to anyone, do not stop anywhere. Go directly to Daniel's house, hand the box to Daniel and no one else. Then come directly home. I would take them, but the soldiers are looking for me. We cannot risk having the body and blood of Jesus fall into their hands. Communion for Daniel and his family will be safer if you take it.'

The youth was very excited to be chosen to take this small risk for Jesus. He set off immediately. The metal box, containing the pieces of bread turned into the body and blood of Jesus, was held tightly in side his tunic next to his heart. It was almost 3 in the afternoon. The sun shone directly into his eyes as he walked towards Daniel's house. He held his head down, watching the dust swirl around his sandals at each step. He repeated to himself,

Keep walking, don't draw attention to yourself, don't talk to anyone. Jesus must love me very much to give me this task.

He looked up briefly,

I'm almost there, I can see Daniel's house at the end of this street.'

Just then, two Roman soldiers came out of a house directly in Front of him. He immediately looked down at the street and started to walk to the other side.

'Hey boy, where is the tax collector's house? We were told it was

In this neighborhood. If you know we will give you a shekel."

He knew where it was, his parents could use the money. He was tempted, but remembered his mission. He acted as if he did not hear the soldiers and kept on walking.

"Stop," they yelled.

"Answer us when we talk to you. Show respect for your emperor. Or are you one of those Christians that want to start their own empire?"

The youth slowed, tried to show respect by lowering his head even more, but it only made the soldiers angry.

'Come over here boy. You need a lesson.'

His heart was racing, he repeated to himself,

'Don't speak to anyone, protect the hosts.'

By now, people had started to come out of their houses. Many of these people wanted to show the Romans that they were not Christians.

They started to yell at him.

"Yes, show respect. Or are you one of those Christians?"

He clutched the box tighter and tried to go on, eyes still focused on the ground three steps ahead, walking towards Daniel's house.

'Show us what you have in your tunic, or we will take whatever it is you are holding on to so tightly,' yelled a boy about his own age. The soldiers saw what was happening and stepped back. They were willing to let the crowd teach the boy a lesson.

Just then a rock came over the crowd and hit the boy on the side of the head. Blood dripped down his cheek. His stomach was churning, but he kept repeating,

'Don't speak, protect the hosts.'

He felt a hand on his shoulder. A voice said,

'You have won, you have shown that you love Jesus.'

He saw a quiet gray dust rise up around him. Now it was just the voice, himself and the dust. Suddenly, other rocks came out of the crowd, not softly arched to land at his feet, to scare him, but projectiles fired with anger and hate. The first struck him in the stomach, he fell to his knees, still clutching the hosts, his eyes focused on the ground in front of him.

The voice said,

'It is time, come with me.'

More rocks came out of the crowd, each one hitting him as if still in the hand of the hatred that threw it. He fell face down into the street. The crowd backed away, afraid to look at the youth lying in the dust. It was time for the soldiers to come back and finish what they had started. The boy that had yelled at him first, bent down and pulled the youth's arm out from inside his tunic. The boy pried open his fist and found an empty hand."

Thomas was breathing heavily. His heart raced, he wanted to be the youth. Here was a friend, someone that he could take home and talk to. Ask questions and get answers back.

"What happened to the box?" Thomas asked.

"That's the miracle. He wanted so much to protect the body and blood of Jesus, that God gave him courage and took the box before the soldiers could get it."

The nun stopped, she had a concerned look on her face.

"God does not expect you to die to show that you love him. Just follow his commandments and receive the sacraments on a regular basis. That's all, see you Sunday at church. You all have your white outfits, right?"

"Yes, Sister, we do."

Thomas raced home to tell him mother the story. He exploded into the kitchen and grabbed her apron.

"Mom, Mom, do you know about the Youngest Martyr? He Carried the hosts, they killed him, God took the hosts and he went to heaven. He didn't have a name. But Sister said that God gave him the courage and he knew what to do."

He pulled her towards him. He had never been this excited. He had learned the "speak when spoken to" lesson well. Julia looked confused.

"Calm down, it's just a story."

"No, no, he really lived. I know he did."

Thomas sat with his hands in his lap, afraid to touch his mother's face like he did when he was younger, before he learned to be a little man. He was normally quiet around her, no touching. But today his auburn eyes deepened as he told the story, his hands circled and pointed, grabbed her hands, held them tightly.

"Mom, I can be like him. Do what Jesus wants."

"But you don't have to die," she said with a touch of panic.

"Right, right, not die, but be worthy of Jesus."

Thomas wanted the moment to last. The story seemed to bring his mother closer to him.

"I'm like him, Mom. I want to do what Jesus says. Even if I don't fight back, I will get to heaven. Isn't that the right thing to do?"

"If the nuns say so. It must be right. But I'm not sure about not defending yourself. I don't think God wants all his little boys to die before they can grow up. I have a story about courage, would you like to hear it?" Julia replied.

He put his hands on her cheeks and whispered, "It will be our story, right?"

"Yes, Thomas, just ours. But a lot of other young boys already Know the story. It's in one of the books I have."

"Did it really happen?"

"It is like the story Sister told you. Except, the boy has a name."

"What is it?"

"Henry Fleming. He lived during the Civil War, like your uncle Richard."

Thomas pulled back from his mother, sat upright in the kitchen chair, afraid that he had spoken too much, asked too many questions. But she didn't seem to mind. Her face had lost the sharp edges that were there when she gave him directions for the day. Now she seemed softer, eager to hear his questions, hear about what had excited him during the day.

"If I'm careful, she'll smile and love me. This is her favorite room. The best room to talk about my stuff."

The tea kettle whistled.

Julia got up to turn the stove off.

"That's for your dad, we'll send it right out."

Thomas wanted to hear this story. He did not want her to stop to make the tea.

"What about the other boy? What about Henry Fleming?" He said impatiently.

"Julia, Julia, come on out, will you please. Mrs. O'Phelan is here. She would like her order put up," William called out in his politest voice. Julia looked at Thomas, wiped her hands on her apron, smiled and said,

"I will tell you about the boy in the book later. How about tomorrow after school? Just remember, it's OK to fight back if you're right."

Thomas tried to hide his disappointment, his rising anger. His smile hid the words that were in his throat,

"Don't leave... Stay here... Tell me now."

He went through the grocery, said hello to Mrs. O'Phelan, looked at Julia putting the meat and vegetables into a cardboard box.

Decided not to ask if he could carry the box home for her. Anyway, one of her six was outside on the steps waiting to carry it home.

"I'm going over to Coogan's lot to see if the guys are playing football, OK Mom?"

"Sure, Thomas, be home before dinner. And don't get dirty."

As he went down the steps, he thought about the last thing she had said to him in the kitchen.

"If you're right."

"How do I know if I'm right? Maybe the other guy is right."

He stood on the corner and watched the trolley that ran down the middle of Merriman St. stop at the corner. Other boys greeted their dads.

"Hi Pop. How was your day?"

His dad was home all the time. He wondered what it would be like to have his dad gone all day and coming home every night.

CHAPTER ELEVEN
COOGAN'S LOT
1913

Coogan's Lot was half way to St. Patrick's grade school. It wasn't a lot really, old man Coogan's house was the only one on the whole block. The big stone house faced Oak St. and the back yard faced Merriman. In the center of the yard was a rectangular band shell made of rubble stone. Mr. Coogan told Thomas and his friends that they could play football or baseball anytime except November 7th, one day a year when a band actually played there, in memory of the soldiers that fought in the Civil War.

Alexander Coogan had fought with the 82nd Illinois Regiment at Gettysburg. Rumor was that he built the band shell by hand to make up for some guilt he felt from the war. Some said there was a stone for every soldier that died at Gettysburg, North and South. Mr. Coogan walked with a cane, always veering to the left. Watching him walk down the street was like watching a snake move back and forth across the sand. He asked for every sentence spoken to him to be repeated.

"How are you today, Mr. Coogan?"

"Say again."

"How are you today, Mr. Coogan?"

"Fine, just fine, thank you for asking."

The left side of his face seemed frozen. Nobody knew if it was the war or a stroke that gave him the feature from which most kids backed away from. Nobody dared ask.

Thomas saw that the game was over. The last of the boys were leaving the lot.

"Too late, Thomas, we could have used you," yelled Marty McIntyre.

"Maybe we'll play tomorrow morning. Can you get here on time?"

"We'll see," Thomas replied.

Thomas was disappointed. He loved the speed and even the

contact of the game they played. No directions, no adults. It was their game to play any way they wanted. The rules changed daily. Some days throw the ball, other days, just run with it. Some days tackling was OK, others, no tackling. He turned to go home and almost ran into Alexander Coogan. Thomas was full of courage. He looked up, pointed and asked,

"How did your face become like a statue?"

Coogan's answer was immediate, as if he had been storing it, waiting for somebody to ask,

"It was at Gettysburg. I was in the 82nd Illinois. Over a 100 of The boys was gone when it was over. A johnny reb slashed my face with his bayonet."

Thomas jumped back,

"I'm sorry, I didn't mean to ask,"

"Nobody means anything, but all the rest of your friends are too afraid of me to ask. You'd think they could at least ask if they can play their games here. Guess since their fathers played here, they think they can too. Is that what you think?"

"I just thought, I mean we just thought, you didn't care. You never say anything, so we just come and play. My dad says you're a war hero."

"Far from it."

He pulled down his starched collar to reveal a bright red scar that looked as if went straight down into his boots.

"If you'll hold still long enough, I'll tell you about this here scar."

Thomas gulped, wondered if the secret of the band shell would finally be revealed.

"Yes sir, I'll just stay here and listen."

"Good. Let's go sit in the shade, over there, next to the memorial." They walked across the chewed up grass that the boys used for their games. Thomas kept step with the old man, imagined he was carrying a rifle.

"They came across the field like a bunch of locusts, buzzing and munching, we fired and reloaded and fired again. There was so much noise and dust, couldn't see much, but I knew they were getting pretty close. I was trying to reload my rifle when a bayonet came down across my face and stuck in my neck. It must of hit a bone, cuz it broke off. Somebody shot that reb, he fell over on top of me. The next thing I know, I'm in a farmhouse on a table. A man covered with blood was trying to get me to drink some rot gut. Said he didn't have anything else to give me, and he had to dig the tip of the bayonet out of my neck. I told him I didn't need a drink, I couldn't feel my face. He dug around a little more, said, well, if you can't feel it, guess we'll just leave it in there. Then he sewed me up. Wasn't much of a surgeon, took a long time for it to heal over, had to walk with a cane ever since. What you see is the scar that built up around that tip."

"Does it hurt?" Thomas asked,

He reached up to touch the raised flesh.

"Hasn't hurt for some time. Hurt pretty bad after they sewed me up. But gradually, I learned to ignore it. A lot worse happened to a lot more. I thought I was dead at first. But I wasn't. I lived long enough to build this here band shell. Too bad it doesn't get used more. But then we haven't had a good war to celebrate for a long time."

Thomas felt sorry for the old man, then suddenly he felt angry.

"Did you go back to fight those johnny rebs, pay them back?"

"They wouldn't let me go back, I was done. I wasn't mad Thomas, I fought as hard as I could before I got stuck. Lucky for me I got taken out. Guess I would have died if I had stayed in that field. Lucky for you boys too. If I'd died you wouldn't have a place to play football."

Thomas stopped, pulled back from the old man, realized there was no big secret.

"I didn't mean to bother you, Mr. Coogan."

"It's OK Thomas. It was fun talking man to man."

He walked back to the store thinking about courage. *It must be important, people talk about it a lot. Old Mr. Coogan had courage. I wonder if I have any courage.*

CHAPTER TWELVE
ATTACK
1915

"Take his money. I know Stone gets tips from the farmers. No need to hold em down, he's scared shitless."

Pete Harris and Bobby Smith leaned over Tom Stone and Jimmy Conlin. Harris was 5'6" with short dirty blonde hair and a scar that hooked from the side of his mouth to his ear lobe. Smith was taller, lanky, seemed to move in two directions at once when he walked. The two fourteen year olds took pennies and lunches from grade schoolers. Their own classmates were too close to their own size.

"I saw the farmer give him a bill. Could be a fiver," Harris said with his fists clenched and a snarl.

Tom lay with his arms held over his head, thinking of the Youngest Martyr.

"What would he do?"

He tried to stay still, say nothing. But his voice erupted, quivering,

"Why are you doing this? What'd we ever do to you? Why are you doing this?"

Harris and Smith laughed in snorting know it all voices, reinforced by the cowering bodies on the ground. Jimmy lay against the base of the tree. Thomas heard his best friend talking as if he had tripped and fallen against the huge pin oak.

"Something's goin' on here, I can't breathe very well, my ear is warm, wet, my fingers are sticky. Maybe I'll go home and shoot some baskets after I clean my hands."

Harris rammed the toe of his right shoe into Conlin's ribs,

"This one's out, nuthin in his pockets either."

Smith followed Harris's example and ground his toe into Tom's side.

"Yeah, but Stone got a dollar and two quarters. Not for

nothin'. We got our days work done."

Tom kept his head down, looking at the few pieces of grass amidst the dirt and pebbles. A trail of black ants marched past his nose into the base of the pin oak. His arms were held tightly across his chest, a position that would protect him as it had the Youngest Martyr, but a voice he did not recognize betrayed him with a whimper, tears rolled out of the sides of his clenched eyes,

"We didn't do anything to you."

"Oudda here, we're oudda here," Harris said as he and Smith swaggered towards the sidewalk, leaving Tom and Jimmy laying in the dirt.

Tom pulled himself up to his knees, his heart racing like the unengaged engine of the parish priest's model T. He didn't have a word to describe the pain in his stomach and lungs. Not from the kick, but from the fear that engulfed him as he had fallen to the ground, shame at not resisting, anger at seeing his friend kicked and bloodied, doing nothing other than whimper,

"We've never done anything to you."

How could he make the sour water stop rotating between his throat and his stomach? He looked over at Jimmy.

"You OK? You've got blood on your head."

"Tommy, what happened?" Jimmy started to push himself up from the ground, "I thought we were shooting baskets, I remember those two guys yelling, then kind of a blur."

"You hit your head, I tried to stop… I didn't do anything. I was too scared," Thomas said,

"What were you going to do? They're twice our size."

Then it came back to them.

Harris and Smith had asked for money to be allowed across the field. They called it a fee for safe crossing.

Jimmy said,

"I don't have any."

Thomas said nothing,

"What's your problem kid? Can't you hear? Give us your money."

Thomas said nothing.

"Damned Irish," Smith said as he swung at Jimmy, connecting just above his right ear, knocking him against the ragged bark of the tree. Harris had pushed Thomas to the ground, reached into his pocket and pulled out the money. What seemed like hours to Thomas

Stone took thirty seconds.

"You should have just given them the money, Tommy, I wouldn't have this pain in my head if you'd just given it to them."

"I'm sorry Jimmy, I just really got scared."

He did not tell him about the young boy he imagined standing next to him holding his arms tightly across his chest.

"It's OK. Next time, use your head. We'll go another way. Stay clear of those two."

They walked to the grocery and washed James' head with water from the pump behind the house.

"What will we tell everybody? You're bleeding and my pants are torn again," Thomas asked.

"Nothing, we'll just say we were playing football over at Coogan's. I'll see you tomorrow." The small cut above Jimmy's ear had stopped bleeding. He turned to Thomas and said,

"I've got to get home before dark, before Mom gets up. Get cleaned up, fix her dinner, she won't notice.

Thomas leaned against the pump, fingered the hole in the knee of his pants. A cold breeze pushed drops of water from the mouth of the pump against his neck. He felt cold, embarrassed, afraid; each feeling had ragged edges that hooked into the others, he couldn't separate them.

He walked up the steps and into the kitchen and went directly to the shelf above the kitchen sink where his dad's ledgers were. He took down the last one and opened it. He knew his dad had written the words and numbers, but had never seen him with a pen in his hand. Thomas asked his Mother,

"Can I write in one of Dad's books? He doesn't seem to use them."

"I don't see why not, we'll just get him another if he decides to Use them again."

"Write whatever comes to your mind," she told him as she handed him an Esterbrook pen from the drawer.

"Here's a pen and a bottle of ink. Be careful not to spill. Find a quiet spot, away from distractions. Then you'll write well and you won't spill."

"Thanks Mom, you'll tell Dad, right?"

"Don't worry about your Dad," she said sharply. She put her hand on his shoulder.

"Now go change your pants, I'll fix that hole. You were

probably playing football with James, I wish you two would find a game that wasn't so rough."

Thomas went to his room, laid the ledger in the middle of his small writing desk, intent on separating the fear from the cold, the embarrassment from the fear. He measured four inches from the edge of the desk and carefully placed the ink on that spot. He opened the ledger to the first page. He didn't notice the slight rise in the back end paper as he wrote his first entry on page one of the Boorum and Pease ledger.

September 10, 1915

Coogan's Lot

Did I do the right thing? If I fought back, they would have beat us up even worse. Maybe Jimmy would have been killed if I had tried to help. They didn't seem angry, would have been worse if they were angry. Maybe I did the right thing. I couldn't have done anything else. I did just what the Youngest Martyr would do. I thought I saw him. He wouldn't have cried. I'll do better next time.

After the entry, he carefully wrote three initials with sharp corners, "TJS," Thomas Joseph Stone. He closed the book, proud of exploring his feelings without the nuns or priests pulling him by the hand through their extremes of guilt and ecstasy. Control was now in his hand. Recording today, knowing tomorrow, he could predict what was next by writing about the past. He felt a movement in the back of the ledger, something slipping from top to bottom. He worked the top of the paper away from the board and shook out three carefully folded sheets. He spread them on the desk and read his Grandfather's account of the mid-winter crossing of the North Atlantic, then made his second entry.

September 10, 1915

My House

My dad used to write all his customer's names and what they bought in a bunch of journals. Inside my book, I found a story that my grandfather wrote. Learned about death ships, hope, love, why nobody talks about the old country. They didn't want to remember, stopped each other from talking about the worst, and the best, if there was any. I understand why he didn't want to talk about his loss. Their baby. He said that some things can never be forgotten, those that hurt the most and even some you didn't experience yourself. He writes about 'blood memories,' the ones that don't need telling. And a part of his ear that he called the 'singing bone.' He hears a ringing that sometimes leads to blood and then he remembers stories about his mother and father that he is sure they never told him. Maybe it takes courage to hear the 'singing bone.' I'll think more about this later.

Mom loves that I'm writing. I will write down important things when they happen, let her read them, or maybe just save them for later. Then I can go back if I need to remember, see the changes."

Two paragraphs. A ten year old sensing the power of the written word and the unavoidable past.

CHAPTER THIRTEEN
THE OTHER STORY
1915

The next morning, Thomas woke up sweating and cold. The sheets were moist, crumpled, pulled up around his neck.

Maybe I'm sick, no school.

Then he remembered trying to run but not moving. He smoothed the sheet down around his feet, lay quietly, listening for the sounds of morning. An iron skillet moved against the burners on the stove. A meat cleaver splashed against a chopping block. He smelled sausage as it popped and rolled in its own fluids, and the odor of a freshly beheaded chicken.

A feeling of pleasure from the last dream before waking seeped into his consciousness.

I was running like the wind. No effort, hardly touching the cinders. I could pull a thorn from my foot in full stride. Then I saw the pillars.

He thought his hands were bleeding, until he saw sweat running in the furrows of his palms.

Two pillars were on either side of the road in front of him. A bright yellow light encased the distant horizon.

That's the goal, I'm running to the shining river.

A griffin was chained to the top of each pillar, the light shown like a halo on their eagle heads. They were pulling, their beaks open, but no sound came out. Liam was moving his arms and legs, but the ground stayed the same under his feet.

I can't move, I can't get closer. What are they guarding? Are they trying to escape?

The scene faded.

He jumped up quickly, pulled on the clothes from the floor beside the bed, and ran downstairs.

"Did you brush?"

"Mom, after breakfast, OK?"

"OK."

"I just had a bad dream."

"Were you being shot with arrows? Like the last one?"

"No, that was a good dream. I pulled them out. This one scared me."

Julia turned the stove off, put sausages and scrambled eggs in front of Thomas.

"What happened yesterday?"

"Nothin. Jimmy and I just played a little football."

"You're sure nothing happened?"

"Yeah, but Mom, you said you were going to tell me a story about a badge."

The dream slipped back into its hiding place.

"OK, we have a few minutes before you have to go to school. You know, you look a little white, maybe you have a temperature."

She put her left hand on his forehead and picked up the hand not scooping eggs.

"And your hands are cold."

"I'm OK," he said, pulling his hand away and leaning back against the chair.

Julia sat down across the table, wiping her hands on her apron and then pushing the long hair pins down into the bun on the back of her head.

"Don't drink any more milk. One glass is enough."

"It's OK, Mom, milk doesn't bother me as much as it does you. What about the story?"

The nun's story had begun to bother him. What if he wasn't as good as the Youngest Martyr.

God doesn't want cowards in heaven. That's what I am.

"What was his name again?"

"Henry Fleming, but the author call's him "the youth", most of the time."

"Why?"

"Probably to let you know that Henry Fleming is like a lot of young boys. Nothing special about him other than the choices he makes."

"Oh."

This was confusing so far. *Am I supposed to be special or like everybody else? The nun says that pride is a sin. To think that you're better is wrong.*

"Who wrote it?"

"A young man named Stephen Crane, he was 21 when he wrote it."

Julia looked to the side, as if she were speaking to someone else.

"Maybe you could be a writer. You seem so eager to learn, all those questions. But the rest of the men in our family are grocers, farmers, clerks. Not much support for a young writer. Maybe this story is too rough for you, Thomas. Maybe you're too young to understand that people *can* change. I love this book because Henry Fleming changed, he took control. But most people don't change. They stay angry, belligerent, mean. They just go faster in the direction they're already going."

His hands and eyes reached out to her. She turned back to look into his eyes and took his hands and put them on her face, moved her cheeks against his warm soft palms.

At night she sat by his bed and watched him fall asleep. He lay staring at the ceiling with his hands carving arcs and angles in the space above his head. His eyes followed the movements at first than focused on some distant point in the ceiling. His hands would gradually fall gently to the covers and his eyes would close.

She asked him about it.

"What do you do when you draw in the air?"

"C'mon mom, I don't do that."

"It's almost time for school, so I'll just give you a quick idea of what the book is about and then you can read it for yourself, if you're interested." She picked up his dishes and put them in the sink.

"Henry Fleming was a Union soldier, probably had a colt pistol like your grandfather."

"Yea, yea, the one that shoots iron balls and you have to pack each one."

"Yes, and you tried to hammer nails with that gun."

"Shouldn't have done that. He felt pretty bad about the dents."

"Well, when you have something that you cherish like that old gun, and your grandson scars it up… he felt pretty bad. And so should you."

Thomas put his head down, looked at the scrubbed wooden planks beneath his feet. Hoped the lesson was over. Julia started again,

"He enlisted, against his mother's wishes by the way," she said with her chin up and her eyes looking down at an angle.

"C'mon mom, just tell me the story."

"He enlisted, joined a regiment, and they just sat around telling stories. Then the day came when the officers led them into a battle. Henry got scared and decided to run from the fighting. As he ran, he had chances to go back, but he kept telling himself it was better if he could stay alive to fight another day. He saw retreating soldiers and asked one of them why they were running. The soldier was insulted and hit Henry in the head with his rifle. His head bled from the blow and he covered it with a red kerchief his mother had given him. Then he found his way back to his own regiment and he told everyone he had been shot."

"He lied."

"Yes, he lied, but he decided to go back to fight."

"So, what is the red badge of courage?"

"A wound, the blood that says that you have fought in a battle."

"So, his wound was his badge? A red badge?"

"Yes and it helped him decide to return to the battle."

"Was he brave?"

"Oh yes. He was very brave when he returned, he even carried The flag and everybody told him how brave he was."

"So he decided to be brave? Just made up his mind?"

"Yes, Thomas, he just made up his mind."

"Do you think that I'm brave mom?"

"Yes, honey, I do." She reached over to hug him.

"Did you write anything good in your Dad's, I mean *your* ledger?"

"Just a few ideas I had, kinda private."

"You don't have to share them if you don't want to. That's the best part of writing what you really feel. It's just for you. If you decide it will help somebody else, you can share them. Now, off to school with you. And stay away from Coogan's lot for awhile. You'll run out of pants, or I'll run out of thread."

"Right, mom. Thanks for the story."

He let her hug him, felt the bones in his shoulders rise and fall under her firm grasp. He looked up and saw her smile and turn away to the window.

CHAPTER FOURTEEN
ANOTHER ATTACK
1918

Jimmy Conlin took a shortcut across the school playground on his way to the Stone's house, a new basketball under his arm. His mother had given it to him for his birthday and he wanted to see if he and Thomas could shoot this ball better than the lopsided, cracked oval they had been shooting since they first learned of the game.

Harris and Smith were sitting with their backs against the red brick wall of the school sharing a cigarette from a pack they had stolen from O'Neals Tobacco Store that morning. They walked toward Jimmy as if they didn't see him coming, then stopped in the middle of the playground.

"Hey it's the Conlin kid with something under his arm," Harris said to Smith.

"What's that under your arm Conlin?" Harris asked.

"It's called a basketball. My mom gave it to me for my birthday,"
Jimmy said proudly.

"Well, thank her for us," said Smith, as he pulled it out from under Jim's arm.

"We can use this to knock squirrels out of the trees, or maybe practice punching with our fists," joined in Harris.

"Don't," Jim started to say, but Smith shoved him with both hands and he fell backwards onto his left wrist with a loud crack. He knew his wrist was broken.

The crack came at the same time that Tom Stone was throwing himself in a cross body block at the two larger boys. He caught them both from behind at knee level and they went down. Before they could get up in disbelief that that little bastard Stone had gotten the best of them, Thomas grabbed the ball, pulled Jim up off the ground and said, "Let's get out of here."

"Where'd you come from?" Jim asked with a grimace holding

his wrist against his chest as they ran as fast as they could towards Tom's house.

"I saw those two assholes steal a pack of cigarettes this morning.

I was thinking of talking to them about what jerks they are, but then I saw you coming across the playground. Guess nothing I can say will change them."

They raced the three blocks to Stone's grocery. William was standing on the porch wiping his hands on his blood soaked apron.

"Whoa, what's going on here?" He asked.

"Those two bullies were trying to steal Jim's new ball. I guess we got away. But I don't know about going to school Monday." Thomas was shaking. His breath came in short spurts as he tried to fill his lungs, looked past his father, into the grocery. He thought he saw a young man in a Civil War uniform at the chopping block, wiping his bandanna across the moist red surface, smiling and nodding at him.

William continued to wipe his hands on his apron.

"Did anybody else see what happened?"

"I don't think so," It happened pretty fast," Jimmy replied.

"No, no person saw what happened," Thomas said as he continued to look into the grocery.

"Then I don't think you have anything to worry about. The Last thing those cowardly sons of bitches want is for anybody else to know how you stopped them. You two go to school Monday and act like nothing happened. They'll find some other smaller kids to terrorize. Let's put Jimmy's wrist in the Coke cooler. I'll get Doc Ryan to come over. Thomas, go get Jimmy's mom."

Later that evening, Thomas thought of telling his mother of the image in the grocery, but instead wrote in his ledger.

October 15, 1918

Coogan's Lot

I don't believe I did that, I could have been hurt, they would have beat the crap out of me if they had the chance. Then they really would have taken care of Jimmy. Who the hell do I think I am? Some neighborhood good guy? Do I have to confess this act of violence? I did save Jimmy from a worse beating. But what will those two bullies do at school Monday? Maybe dad's right, they won't want anybody to know they got beat. But, what about later, they'll find some excuse to get back. I'm still not sure about this courage thing. And didn't the little martyr have courage? Two kinds of courage, one to accept pain, one to fight pain? Henry Fleming seemed to approve of what I did. His courage was mine today.

CHAPTER FIFTEEN
PROHIBITION
1920

Across the street from Stone's grocery, a model T pulled up to Wallenstein's Haberdashery. Two well dressed 18 year olds with the latest fedoras on their heads got out, looked around, and motioned for the truck to come around the corner and head down the alley. Once behind the haberdashery, six barrels of beer and two cases of liquor were unloaded. Hiram Wallenstein paid $55 for each barrel and $90 a case for the liquor. He threw in another $25 for the kids in the model T. He was willing to risk having the prohibition agents shut him down, but he was not willing to leave his personal safety up to chance. He had walked in on the "kids" pistol whipping his partner, Harry O'Neal, the owner of the tobacco store next to his clothing store, over a box of cheap cigars. Harry wouldn't give them a free box after he had paid his $50 weekly protection fee.

"Now you'll show us some respect. You tell em, Hiram. All We want is a little respect," the youngest had smiled and spoken politely as he grabbed a box of cigars and headed out the door.

Hiram helped Harry up and washed the blood off his temple.

"Harry, we've got to stay ahead of these kids. We've got a pretty good thing going here, a few cigars wouldn't hurt."

Hiram and Harry had planned the speakeasy for months. It would be the first on Merriman Street. In preparation, they knocked out the common wall between their store rooms at the back of the two story brick building. They ordered an oak bar from "Big Jim" Colosimo's furniture company in Cicero, Illinois. The signed contract provided 15 tables and 60 chairs, and a weekly shipment of beer and liquor. The furniture was delivered the day the 18th amendment was passed. The first beer and liquor shipment arrived the next day.

Thomas knew that his Dad paid protection like the rest of the merchants in the neighborhood to the two kids. He knew when they delivered the booze to the speaks, when they collected protection money, how they sent the money to Cicero once a week with detailed accounts of who paid, how much they paid, and which booze they had delivered.

"Harris and Smith are trying to impress Colosimo and his new guy from New York." Thomas told Jimmy, "I hear his name is Capone. And they gave each other nicknames. Bobby Harris is now 'Ty Cobb,' Pete Smith is 'Jack Dempsey,' It's like they think they're a Colosimo farm team. Hit a few homers, get a few knock outs, and on to the big leagues," Thomas told Jimmy.

"Yea, and I hear they shot a guy just for calling them by their old names." Jimmy said in awe.

Cobb and Dempsey hid nothing. They made sure the neighborhood knew the routine. They took liquor and protection money from the merchants, gave a portion to the police, and sent the rest to a contact 20 miles north in Chillicothe. The contact delivered the bag to an address on a business card. The card said,

Alphonse Capone

Second Hand Furniture Dealer

2220 South Wabash Avenue

The driver was given a bag in return that had the kids share of the take. They got 5%. Sometimes a question would be scrawled on the bag.

"Do you need a sawed off shotgun, a Thompson submachine gun?"

Signed, A. Capone

Refusing the kids would be refusing Colosimo and Capone.

Thomas didn't know about Cobb and Dempsey's conversation as they sat in the back of Wallenstein's speakeasy, away from the regulars. They had just divided their take from the previous week..

"Whatda ya think? Should we make a move? We could use Another guy, I almost fell asleep on the trip to Chillicothe last week." Dempsey said.

"Of course, that's what they want to see. That we can handle the big time. I agree we need another guy. Any ideas?" Cobb answered.

Dempsey looked down at his square hands, at the dirt under his fingernails,

"I gotta get a manicure. People expect us to be class now. We can't look like a couple of thugs. What'd you say? Oh yeah, how about the Stone kid. Remember how he took our legs out last year. Saved Conlin's ass. He might be able to do the drivin. I wouldn't trust him with a gun just yet."

Cobb looked at Dempsey and said.

"Jesus, he's only 14 years old. He's not drivin my car. But how about doing some of the collecting. You know, the easy ones, his dad, maybe these two blocks to start. We could work on Aiken alley. None of those guineas want to pay anything."

Cobb and Dempsey looked at each other and smiled. This was their street. The great war was over. 114,000 Americans did not return, but thousands of others came home to buy *their* booze. Maybe they would put some of their money in the market. Baldwin Locomotive was at 110 &3/4. Middle States Oil & steel was doing well at 89 &3/8.

Women were smoking. Maybe they should try to work their way into the tobacco market. And the betting parlors had more and more sports to bet on. Will Wild Bill Tilden win the next French Open, would Bobby Jones continue his winning ways, Will the real Ty Cobb win the batting title next year, or is he too old? Who will the real Jack Dempsey knock out next? Chicago would be their next stop if they kept their own organization lean and productive.

CHAPTER SIXTEEN
BAG MAN
1920

Merriman Street had iron tracks running down the middle of its red brick surface. The trolley ran south into the Irish neighborhood, coming back on its loop from downtown Peoria. Late on a Saturday afternoon, two draft horses pulled the open sided trolley on its oblong route, the driver pulled the reins tight and the trolley rolled to a stop between Wallenstein's Haberdashery on the east and Stone's grocery on the west corner of Merriman St. and 6th Ave. The setting sun shone directly up 6th bouncing off Wallenstein's metal storefront. Its reflection illuminated Stone's grocery in a hazy brightness that gave both sides of the street an eerie sense that there was no such thing as a shadow.

Thomas Stone jumped off the iron step landing on to the mottled gray curb. He had just delivered the last package of meat and vegetables to the O'Donnell's for their Saturday dinner. Fran O'Donnell had asked him to stay for dinner, but he declined, telling her,

"Thanks, Mrs. O'Donnell, I've got to help pop clean up, and anyway, there's not enough for me and your 5. See you next week."

On the way back, he thought of ways to get out of the neighborhood. Maybe he could get his dad to ask Aunt Ann if there was a grocery in another parish. She knew all the priests. He just wanted to get out before those two goons, Cobb and Dempsey, did the same to his dad that they had done to Mr. O'Neil.

As he jumped, he saw them standing in the doorway of the Tobacco store, its maroon and black striped awning, the only shade on the block. Mr. O'Neil was inside, a bandage still on his head from the lesson Cobb and Dempsey had taught him. Thomas thought briefly of turning and grabbing the trolley as it pulled out, but for what end? Too obvious. Pop was right, they didn't want anybody to know how he had beaten them before. They would just ignore him, or maybe they didn't even remember him.

He thought the hazy light that enveloped the street would hide him as he stepped down from the trolley to cross to his house. But they had seen him standing in the trolley through its open side.

"Hey Stone, how's that friend of yours doin' with his basketball? If I remember correctly, he owes us a few lessons."

Thomas was caught off guard. Something inside him said he could change crooks into saints. Could these hoodlums really be interested in basketball? He heard that Capone went to every Loyola game. He was even married to an Irish girl. Maybe these two were looking for a way to get in good with their boss, and he could use their greed to bring them to change them. He ignored his Dad's warning to stay away, cross the street, don't even look at them.

"They'll only bring trouble. Until somebody takes care of them,"

William had said with an anger Thomas had never seen. His father finished the sentence with a swing of the heavy cleaver that started above his right ear and curved down through a lamb's knee joint splattering blood across the chopping block. There was something in his father's arm that never came out in words. A muscle controlling an instant of release.

Thomas squinted up at the two figures standing under the awning.

"Cobb, you could be a pretty good center, maybe Dempsey here could move the ball down the court. It would take a while though. It's not an easy game to pick up."

Thomas was getting excited about the possibility of giving them something to do other than manhandle older people. Maybe he *could* change them a little.

"I don't know if Conlin has time, but I could show you a few things. Father Kerrigan put up a basket on the school wall at St. Patrick's. I could show you there."

Cobb and Dempsey stepped out of the shadow and grabbed Thomas's arms. Cobb did the talking.

"Listen, Stone, we don't give a shit about your basket game.

Our business is growing. We need a tough kid like you to help on the route. You know this neighborhood as well as we do. All you have to do is hand them this empty envelope, wait till they give it back and deliver it to us. Once a week. Hell, we might even have you set up a table in the back of your Dad's store and the money could be delivered to you. You'll start with the easy protection fees. We'll take care of the tough ones and deliver the booze like we always do. We'll pay you one percent of our share. Could be 5-10 bucks a week. Hell, you'll be rich. Whadaya say? We only ask once."

Thomas tried to focus his mind as it spun from one undesirable result to another.

His dad would kill him.

Dempsey would kill him.

Fr. Kerrigan would kill him.

The police would kill him.

Jimmy would say,

"What are you thinking about? It's not *smart*."

All five seemed possible, probable, definite.

Thomas felt a tap on his shoulder. He thought he heard Henry Fleming whisper,

"Now we learn about you, Thomas. Run or fight. Which is it?"

Thomas turned, walked slowly across the street. Two faint images moved with each step; one from the low yellow sun behind him and one from the reflection on Wallenstein's store, moved ahead of him. He sensed Henry Fleming on the edge of the sun's shadow, listening for a response. Cobb's words shot into Thomas's ear.

"You don't get it, do you? You don't have a choice. You start Monday, or we hit your dad, hard."

Both sides of the street retreated into a single gray shadow as the sun sank below the horizon. Thomas heard the words spoken by Cobb but continued to walk with his head down and his hand inside his jacket.

"What's in your pocket?" Asked Henry Fleming. Thomas sped up, looked sideways,

"Go away, I don't need you. I need to talk to somebody real."

"I'm real."

"No you're not, you're just a story my Mom told me."

"Wrong, I'm part of you. How could you hear me otherwise? Your problem is that you shut me out, and that martyr kid doesn't ever talk. You should be more open minded about stuff you don't know anything about. That's why your Mom told you my story. She didn't want you listening just to the nuns and that martyr kid. That's why your hand's in your jacket, you're trying to *be* him, you're trying to ignore the danger."

"I'm going to see Jimmy, he's a real friend. He'll know what to do."

Henry Fleming seemed to slide into the twilight, shaking his head.

Thomas knew he had no choices. Run the route picking up the hard earned cash of his dad's friends. No way his dad didn't find out. Ignore them and leave the grocery and everyone in it vulnerable to their guns. He had seen Mr. O'Neil's face after he refused to give them a lousy cigar. No talking to the two goons. No reasoning would work.

"I'd be an awful bag man. I forget things. I'd never be on time."

They wouldn't believe him. They wouldn't offer him the job if they thought he was an idiot. Walking away calmed him, but he could feel moisture at the edge of his eyes.

"I can't work for them and I can't let them hurt my dad. Henry Fleming would probably stand in front of the store with his rifle and a pistol waiting for the car to pull up, then start yelling and running at them. Scare the hell out of em. Being dead and all.

What would the young boy do? He'd stand in front of the store and somehow stop them from hurting pop, even if it meant taking a bullet or a stick of dynamite before it got to the porch.

He wanted to crawl into his bed and roll into the covers, to block out all the lights and sounds of Merriman Street. He went to his room and made an entry in his ledger before falling briefly into a fitful sleep.

October 12, 1920

Sleep until somebody else fixes it. Or maybe tell dad. Don't let Jimmy know I ran again. Just because I stood up to those guys once, doesn't mean I've changed. I still don't have courage. I'm two people. Brave in a story, needing only a quick turn of the page to find answers and courage. Then in the glare of the day, I curl and wither, cover my eyes, run. Where is the middle seam that holds these two together, or are they doomed to be split forever?

His eyes burned as if he had been up all night sick with the flu. There was no sun, no shadow defining the road, just flat emotion pushing him back and forth as he walked down stairs looking for his Dad.

I'll tell Dad. Please God, let him tell me what to do. I'm not ready to have courage.

William was sitting on the porch steps, smoking a cigarette. The grocery was closed for the day, all he had left to do before dinner was clean the chopping block and sweep the wooden planks with saw dust. He was still wearing his apron stained from the day's vegetables and meats.

"Dad, I've got a problem."

"I'm sure your mother can help. She usually does."

"Dad, that won't do any good, I need *your* help."

William dropped the half smoked cigarette, ground it under his heel. Thomas couldn't tell if he was tired or just not interested. He didn't spend much time with his father. Most of his attention was taken up by school, basketball, his friends, especially Jimmy. He knew he talked a lot more to his Mom. She seemed to really understand what it was like to be fourteen. He was working up to appearing more interested in the grocery business, for his Dad's sake. Now the neighborhood revolved around illegal booze and its side attractions; gambling, girls, and rackets. Thomas wanted out and the grocery store seemed to be what kept them from escaping.

But now he needed his father.

"Tell me about your problem. Maybe we can figure out what to do. My Dad and I used to talk about stuff a lot. We were a real team," William said as he lit another cigarette.

Thomas's eyes were darting back and forth between the haberdashery across the street and the sign over the grocery porch.

"What are you looking for? Christmas to come early? Tell me what's on your mind."

Thomas sat next to William, aware of the strange mix of odors that followed his dad; orange, basil, chicken blood, sweat. He usually found it offensive and stayed a few feet away when they crossed each other's path. But now he found it comforting. He almost reached over to take his father's nicotine stained hand.

"Those two guys, you know, they call themselves Cobb and Dempsey?"

"Yes, the Harris and Smith boys. I know them too well. They Should have been sent to Guardian Angel when they were 5."

"You mean the orphanage? I thought that it was just for kids That didn't have parents."

"They're orphans as if their parents had been dead all these years, for all the help they gave those two. Always hanging out on the corners. Don't know if they ever finished high school. Now the whole neighborhood suffers."

"They want me to work for them. Collect money."

William rubbed his eyes, pushing the orbs deep into the sockets.

"Did you hear me? They want me to work for them." Thomas's voice cracked, "They said five to six bucks a week. I don't know what to do. They said they would hurt you if I didn't do it."

"You'd be collecting from your old man," William said quietly.

"Yea, and all the rest of the old men on the block. I wouldn't have a friend left. I don't want to do it, but what about you and the store, and Mom?" Thomas fought to keep back the tears, his voice rose and lowered with each word.

"When did they want you to start?"

"Monday, after school. I guess." He slumped against the porch railing, then his dad spoke firmly,

"I'll talk to them. Maybe I can reason with them. Get them to Bring somebody else into their little group."

"You'd do that dad? That would be great."

Thomas jumped up as if a large rock had been pulled out of his stomach.

"Then do I need to talk to them again?"

"I don't think so. Let me worry about it. Go in and help Mom with the dinner now."

Instead, Thomas stood on the side of the steps and watched as his father turned and walked into the grocery. He picked up the meat cleaver, hooked it to his belt under his stained apron, turned and walked out the door and down the steps, his eyes straight ahead.

The darkened navy sky rolled eastward pushed by a skillet gray cloud. Drops of rain hit the brick and dust, raising moist petals of dirt into the air.

Thomas watched his father stride deliberately across Merriman St. around the corner, and turn into the alley. Thomas followed, fascinated and afraid at the same time. He did not recognize the man he was following.

Thomas heard the subdued voices of trolley men, miners, bankers, smelled heavy after shave put on immediately after the work day. Women in short loose dresses got out of Model Ts, their hands holding newspapers and lit cigarettes over their heads. Their nylons were rolled just below their knees. A modern world in a dark wet alley.

He saw his father moving along the sides of the buildings, seemingly unnoticed by the crowds nodding hello to each other. Cobb and Dempsey came out of the back of O'Gara's restaurant. One of the few restaurants that chose to honor the Volstead act. Cobb had a toothpick in his mouth and was wiping gravy off the front of his trousers. Dempsey belched loudly in front of two women trying to walk by.

William stepped closer to the two.

Thomas slipped into an alcove next to O'Gara's where the garbage was piled.

"What is it you want with my boy?" He heard his father say.

"Well, look who's here," Cobb said condescendingly,

"What's it to ya? He's old enough to think for himself," Dempsey said.

"I have something for you, but he's not part of it."

"OK, let's hear it," Cobb answered.

"You know Lucas, the vegetable farmer that comes in once a week?"

"Yea, we seen him around," Dempsey answered.

Thomas wondered if they always took turns.

"Still comes in a horse and wagon, when's he going to get himself a decent truck? Maybe we could get him one," Cobb replied.

"Lucas has a still. Best gin in the county," William was smiling, leaning down towards Dempsey.

"How come we never heard of this?" Cobb said.

"Cicero wouldn't like competition. You know what they do With competition," countered Dempsey.

Thomas heard his father switch into a heavy brogue, emitting a charm that he had never seen nor expected.

"That's the point, they don't know about it. Lucas pays with gin, he doesn't sell it. He buys his kids clothes, stuff like that. If you work it right, you could take his production, it's good as Canadian. You two are smart enough to pull it off. Just think, your own liquor on your own route. No more sharing the dough. But then, maybe you're scared of Colosimo's new guy. Not ready for the big leagues yet."

Thomas heard Dempsey's deep hoarse voice,

"We done this long enough. We know the ropes. That's all it takes. They'd never know, we're small potatoes to them."

Then it was Cobb's turn.

"So that's your idea. And your kid stays in school, no bad friends, grows up to be better than you. Better than us."

"Something like that." William said.

Thomas heard a thud and looked around the corner to see Cobb with his hand on William's neck, shoving him against the brick wall.

"You go with us. No bullshit. Just introduce us to Lucas, we'll do the rest. Then you and your kid can stay home. And don't think you won't pay any more. In fact, I just doubled your weekly. And, if Chicago finds out, you, your wife, and your kid, are dead."

Thomas saw his father reach inside his apron, hesitate, then pull his hand out, and say,

"I'll make the arrangements."

CHAPTER SEVENTEEN
WAR STORY

William Stone drove up the gravel driveway and parked his Model T next to the front porch of Robert Lucas's house at 7:30 A.M. on a Monday morning. Lucas had been bringing produce to the Stone Grocery for over 25 years, but neither William Stone nor his father Michael had ever been to see him at his house.

The Lucas house was a one story clapboard with a two step porch. As he stood at the base of the steps, William could see through the tattered screen door into a dimly lit living room. Susan Lucas spoke to her husband as if no one could hear her.

"What does *he* want?" Susan asked.

"Try to be on your good behavior, Susan, I don't want Mr. Stone wondering what's going on here." Robert tried to whisper but only succeeded in enunciating the words clearer.

Robert pushed the screen door open and said, "Come in, come in. This is quite a surprise. What brings you out here William? How about a cup of coffee? Just made. We'll go in the kitchen. Susan, look who's here, it's Bill Stone. All the way from Peoria."

"Hello, Mr. Stone. Sit here. I'll get the coffee."

Susan tried a smile, but only succeeded in making it look like she and Robert had just finished an early morning argument.

"Just call me Bill, OK if I call you Susan?"

"Of course, but Sue would be better. *Robert,*" she said, drawing his name out, "says Susan only when visitors come."

William looked around the house and saw a silent, bloodless battlefield, sensed a pain that hung in the corners and doorways.

As William sat down at a pine harvest table, deeply stained by fluid of some kind, the kitchen door opened with a burst of wind followed by what looked like a ghost. The Lucas's son Nathan limped into the kitchen, holding a gallon jug of clear liquid. He pointed at the jug with a big smile on his face. When he saw the visitor, his shoulders and eyes dropped and his body turned to the side as if to present a narrower target.

"Bill, this is our son Nathan, just got back from France. Didn't You son? Real lucky to get him back in one piece."

Nathan took his cap off, exposing pure white hair from the crown of his head to the nape of his neck . Only a few inches of dark mahogany remained just over his forehead. Without the cap, he appeared to be wearing a white helmet. His skin was the color of the inside of a mature potato, leaving the impression that he was ready for the embalmer.

"Nathan, this is Bill Stone. He buys our corn. His Dad bought it before you were born."

Nathan stared vacantly at Bill Stone, then retreated as he had entered, quickly, no words spoken, just a finger pointing back in the direction of the still, and a banging of the screen door. As Nathan left, Irene appeared in the doorway leading to the second floor. She stood in her school dress, rubbing her eyes. Her dress looked as if she had slept in it.

"What's the noise down here, where's Nathan? I've got to hurry and eat before school. Who's this?" Irene said as she glanced up and to the side at Bill Stone, not looking directly at the stranger in the kitchen.

"It's Mr. Stone. Mr. Stone, meet Irene."

"I've got to go, see you tonight," Irene ignored the introduction and walked to the kitchen door and left without breakfast, saying goodbye to her parents, or acknowledging William Stone. The two men could hear her voice as she left, raised to a pitch meant to be heard.

"Don't need nobody else in this house. Got to keep it safe for Nathan. The others hurt him."

"She's acting a little strange since her brother came back. Not Sure what it is, she doesn't treat him the same, or us for that matter," Robert said with a touch of sarcasm.

"What brings you all the way out here. Somebody need a few Ears of corn, or maybe the stuff from out back?"

William wanted to ask for help in getting rid of the two boys, but changed his mind as he thought about Nathan and Irene. Maybe Cobb and Dempsey would leave his family alone if they could buy Lucas's liquor.

"I have a problem with the kids that call themselves Cobb and Dempsey. They want my son to work for them. I won't have him getting involved with mobsters."

Lucas frowned, looked down at the dirty floor planks, wiped his hands across his overalls. Then looked out to where Nathan had retreated.

"I've already lost Nathan to a war. Don't think he'll ever come back. This appears to be a war, doesn't it, Bill?"

"Guess so, but I only care because it's Thomas, they can do whatever they want as long as it's without him."

"What can I do?" asked Lucas.

"I told them about your still, about how you make the best Gin and if they got you to sell exclusively to them, they wouldn't have to share the money with the guy in Chicago."

Lucas's eyes narrowed and he leaned across the table,

"I never sold to nobody. You know that. The booze is just for trade." He stood and walked to the front porch,

"I don't know Bill, it could put *my* family at risk to save yours. Your plan seems to be to have me sell them my liquor, so you won't be bothered by them. Nathan won't like it. The still's the only place he goes on his own. Acts like he owns it. Guess he likes that there ain't no people there, just pipes and jugs, a little flame and smoke. I don't know what he'll do if a couple a strangers come by. And then tell him we're going to sell just to them. No more tradin. You've put me in a tough position, Bill. I can't say as I like it."

William looked down at the ground, started to walk towards his Model T.

Robert pointed down the single lane running through the corn stalks.

"The liquor is stored down the road a piece. Just before the strip mine. It's full of water, wagons, dead horses, and God knows what else. Some say 100 foot deep in the middle. I've always avoided that hole. Dug out by you Irish. Peeled twenty five feet of top soil away so they could reach the veins. Coal was gone when I got here. Just black water now that don't change from noon to midnight. Kids come to dive in now to show how brave, or stupid, they are. They come out covered with oil slick. My kids don't go near the hole, never taught them to swim. I don't swim, saw no reason for them to learn. Wouldn't help in that god-awful hole."

William had never heard Robert Lucas string more than four words together. Something's changed here, he thought, as he started to open the door of the Ford. Robert grasped his arm and said,

"I suppose it won't hurt to talk to them, see what they have in mind. But don't think we'll be done with them. From what I hear, they don't let go, always going for an extra buck. You're too close, right in the middle of their territory."

"Why change your mind? Why help me?"

"When Nathan first got back, he seemed OK. But it didn't last. Gradually, he became what you saw in the house. More dead than alive."

"A lot of the men won't or can't talk about it. Did he tell you what happened?" William asked.

"He joined those Expeditionary Forces against our wishes. He took his Kodak Box camera with him. Said he'd send snapshots back to us."

"He figured it all out, we had a great time listening to him talk. He'd take pictures with the early morning light before the sun got too high. Said the shadows'd be too harsh on the soldiers. He gave himself an assignment to come back with shots of American soldiers advancing towards the enemy. He said he's show us winning. No dying, just winning."

William sat down on the edge of the grass and leaned against the front bumper. Robert sat next to him and pulled a hand made corn cob pipe out of his overalls. William lit a cigarette and they smoked in silence in the warmth of the morning sun.

"Look at these." Robert pulled a four by six box out of his overall pocket.

"These are the pictures he came back with. Right out of one of those little Kodak boxes."

William dropped his cigarette to the ground and looked at the round images on the stiff paper. The first group showed American soldiers standing, sitting, walking, always smiling. He let out a gasp as he slipped the next to last photo under the pile in his hand. The last was a picture of a mangled body lying against a tree staring blankly at him. Nathan had obviously gotten down on his knees to position the camera lens directly in front of the dead soldier's eyes. On the bottom of the photo he had recorded the soldiers name, serial number, and the date.

"Guess he wanted to keep a record of the dead for their family. All the rest are like this one. Nathan's got them out in the still. He doesn't want these nice ones here. Looks at the dead ones all the time; separated body parts, heads with their eyes open. I keep the one just to remind me how lucky I am to have him back. Doesn't matter he's not the same. He's here."

William handed the pictures back to Robert and asked,

"How did his hair…"

Robert laughed quietly, the kind of laugh that hides the emotion inside.

"A friend of his came by a while ago. We never quite knew what happened, his papers just said, "Medical Discharge. Anyway, his friend said it was a tree."

"A tree?" William asked.

"Lightning hit the tree, and Nathan's helmet. The tree fell on him, he was under the tree for two days before they found him. His finger nails were almost all gone from digging and scraping at the bark. And his hair was like you see it today. Pure white on top, normal brown in the front. At least that's what we was told by his friend."

"It's like somebody washed the color out of him. I go in sometimes and watch him when he's asleep, like when he was little. He's always pulling at his ears, trying to pull something out. I know he's having nightmares, but he won't talk about them, won't talk about the war at all. Maybe a little excitement would be good for all of us. I'll meet with them once and see what they have in mind. You coming with them?"

"Yes, I want to make sure everything works out, for both of us.

CHAPTER EIGHTEEN
SOLUTION

Morning steam rose from the August cornfields, mixed with the dust raised by the Model T Ford to form a dense cloud that defined the narrow gravel road leading to the Lucas house. Cobb and Dempsey turned right off the gravel onto a single dirt track leading through a grove of oaks to the front porch of the Lucas house. William Stone was in the back seat.

"That must be it," Cobb said from the driver's side. He held a wet handkerchief over his mouth and nose.

"I hate it out here, fucking horseflies, fucking cornfields."

Robert Lucas sat on the porch steps, leaning against the rail, a straw hat pulled over his eyes. William could not detect any emotion in Lucas's attitude. Almost too calm.

Cobb and Dempsey got out of the Ford, wiped the dust off their shirts, waved their hats in front of their faces. Cobb started without an introduction.

"We understand that you make a good bottle of gin. Is that right?"

He held Dempsey behind him with his left hand.

"Yup, best in the county since my Nathan got home from the war."

"Why haven't we heard about it before?

"Ain't been selling it, just trading it. Get the money I need from

The corn, sell it in town to the grocers. To Bill Stone here, how you doing Bill?"

"You'll talk to us, Lucas. Stone's here just for directions."

Lucas nodded as if he had been negotiating with thugs all his life.

"So how can I help you two? Bill said you might be interested in some Gin, but like I say, I don't sell it."

Dempsey looked at Cobb with disappointment on his face. He leaned over to Cobb and whispered,

"I thought he was going to sell it to us?"

"Shut up Jack, we just got here. Leave it to me."

He turned to Lucas, moved a step closer so that their chests were almost touching. He seemed to be enjoying himself, a crooked smile on his face.

"Show us the booze, then we'll decide if we can do business. The whole deal revolves around demand and supply. There's plenty of demand since the competition narrowed down, thanks to the government boys. You can help with the supply." Cobb backed a way a step, Robert Lucas hadn't moved.

"One more thing. Nobody, and I mean nobody, can know about any deal we come up with. Your family is part of this now. Am I clear?"

"Anything you say. I'll show you the gin now," Robert said quietly.

"Bill, you can ride with me, if that's OK with your friends."

"We'll be right behind you." Cobb replied.

William drove slowly down the gravel road, the sun was shining directly through the right side of the open car, reflecting off the wind screen into their eyes.

"I told Nathan to stay behind the shed, out of the way. I put three jugs in front of the still. That's what we'll show em."

Bill Stone pulled into the small clearing in front of the shed. Cobb and Dempsey pulled in behind them. The four of them stood around the three jugs sitting on the ground.

'Only one way to tell," Cobb said as he picked up a jug, uncorked it, put it on his shoulder and took a long swallow.

"Well, how is it?" Dempsey asked impatiently.

"Better than Canada."

"Let me see."

Dempsey grabbed the jug from Cobb, wiped off the mouth with his hand, and took a swallow that took a third out of the jug. He held the jug at his waist and said,

"How much can you supply a week?"

"Dunno, never been asked, got a hundred or so jugs buried out back. I'd have to sit down and figure it out. You boys seem to like it so much, take a few home, and next time we meet, I'll have the supply figured out."

Cobb smiled at the mention of supply. Lucas had unintentionally complemented him.

“Demand and Supply, that’s the ticket.” Cobb said proudly as he took one more large swallow.

The sudden slapping of corn stalks caused them to turn towards the sound. Cobb reached inside his jacket, but stopped when he saw a young woman pushing her way out of the cornfield. She was pointing at them.

“Are these Stone’s kids? I thought nobody was to come here Except family and now you bring Stone and these two kids.”

Her dress clung to her body, moist from the sun and the effort to walk through the tightly packed cornfield.

“Go back Irene, I told you to stay in the house. This is none of Your business,” her father demanded sternly.

“Hold on. Who have we got here?” Cobb said, his words slightly slurred.

“Maybe she should stay, get to know us two *kids*.”

He took a step towards Irene, sloshing the contents of the jug as he moved. He grunted as he saw Nathan came around the shed, a shotgun held to his shoulder as if he were advancing towards an enemy line. Nathan let out a scream of anger and pain that seemed to come from deep in his stomach.

“Irene, Irene, get down, drop down.” The barrels were aimed at Cobb’s head momentarily than swung to Dempsey and back.

Cobb and Dempsey stared at the gun held by a ghost with a white helmet, then turned and raced towards the car, their arms and legs flailing in the air, hitting each other. Nathan advanced as if he was in the Argonne, intent on avenging the dead images he kept in the solitude of the still.

William Stone watched, frozen in place, thought briefly of the inanimate Nathan he had seen earlier, now turned into an avenger of the dead, a sister’s protector. He heard the shotgun fire and watched the windscreen and the canvas top on the boy’s Ford explode. They kept running past the car, down the rutted path towards the strip mine. Nathan fired the second barrel, bringing down a maple tree just behind Cobb.

Nathan slowed his pursuit to reload the shotgun, looked down at the sound of the barrels clamping to the frame of the shotgun. When he looked up, the two had disappeared.

William and Robert had followed his constant chorus of,

“You will die, you will die for all of them.”

They found him staring over the edge of the twenty foot

escarpment. They looked down and saw a bubbling black mass as if a giant scar had been opened and closed.

Nathan's face was calm as he said,

"They're gone, Dad, we should give them their car." It was the first full sentence Nathan had spoken since returning from France. Robert and Nathan Lucas drove the Ford to the edge of the clearing, pointed it to the edge of the strip mine, strapped the accelerator to the floor board, and released the clutch. They heard the engine roar above the crunch of dirt and gravel, then whine as it dove, until a crash of water and metal told them the grave had been reached. Finally, they heard a sucking pop, as the coupe's tail disappeared under the shiny black surface.

"Nathan took care of them, and their car, they won't be back. Now they are all safe." Robert had his arm around Nathan's shoulders as he told William Stone.

CHAPTER NINETEEN
MOVE

There were plenty of rumors about the whereabouts of the two kids. William's favorite was that they were executed by Capone when he learned they were trying to set up their own liquor distribution. The police didn't bother to look when an uncle reported the disappearance of Bobby Smith. If the parents didn't care, they weren't spending any time on the case. And the replacements on the bootleg route were already offering more to the police than Harris and Smith.

William Stone wanted to put as much distance between family and the south side neighborhood. He understood his own father a little better each night as he lay awake wondering how to get his wife and son a better place to live. He knew little of his parent's life in Ireland; neither wanted to talk about the famine or the trip across the Atlantic to New Orleans. Even the nuns and priests only taught basic American history. It was as if Michael and Nora Stone, and all their friends on the south side of Peoria, appeared one day with accents and amnesia. But William knew that his parents were just two of many Irish immigrants; that they crossed the Atlantic in mid winter so he could grow up an American. He wanted his own son to have what Michael and Nora came so far for.

When Ann Geare, Julia's sister, offered to have them move into her new house out on the bluff, he said,

"Let me talk this over with Julia."

He meant,

"How soon?"

CHAPTER TWENTY
SISTERS

Ann and Julia Geare were sisters and best friends. Ann was the oldest of the three Geare girls. Julia was second and Emily was the youngest. Ann and Julia looked like twins when they were sitting. Long auburn hair pulled straight back off their foreheads and a long single braid curled at the nape of their necks, oblong faces, wide set deep brown eyes and wide open smiles. When they stood, the resemblance disappeared, Ann was almost six feet tall, all angles, slim with narrow boy's hips. A sharp contrast to Julia's compact curves.

When Julia married William Stone, Ann was the maid of honor, and her future was certain. She would remain single and help their mother take care her youngest sister, Emily. Big Baby, the name given to her by her sisters, seldom got out of bed. She was born with clubfeet and as soon as her parents saw her stumbling and falling when she tried to walk, they did everything for her. Food was brought in three times a day, baths were given every other day or when one of the sisters would say,

"Ugh, time for Big Baby to be aired out," she would be pushed into the bathroom on a crooked wooden chair that her father had attached wheels to, lifted into the tub and bathed. Her education was left to Julia, who read aloud to her from her favorite books. Emily lived as she was treated, with respect, but with no expectations.

After Julia was married, the evening care of Big Baby fell to Ann. She came home at 5:00 from her job at the diocesan office, and took over from her Mother. She would fix the evening meal for the family, eat her dinner and then feed her sister, read to her, be sure Big Baby was comfortable and asleep, then sit down to work on the house accounts.

Ann always seemed to have her arms wrapped around something; a stack of reference books, sheaths of correspondence, or Big Baby. She had worked in an insurance office as a typist until Bishop Ireland asked her to work as a clerical in the chancery office.

He had heard of this devoted daughter and talented typist from her parish priest. She took the job in 1900 just in time to help organize the fund drive for the new high school. All the correspondence between the pastors and the Bishop went through her. She monitored the funds coming back to the Bishop's account at the First Bank and made regular reports. The fund drive gave her access to the parish accounts as well as the archdiocesan books. Nobody knew as much about the diocesan finances as Ann. Her status in the chancery was unusual. She had the position usually held by a priest or brother. But her devotion to the Bishop and knowledge of parish operations made her an invaluable member of the chancery team.

Big Baby died in 1920. Ann talked it over with her parents and decided it was time to strike out on her own, at the age of forty-nine. She bought a house in a new subdivision built adjacent to St. Bernard's church, within walking distance of the Bishop's house and chancery. With the Bishop's word and friends she had made at the bank, the mortgage was obtained quickly and at a very low rate. The new house had front and back porches, a garage in case the new owner would have a car, and a back yard that was suited for a vegetable garden and with the proper fencing, ducks or chickens.

She found the new house lonely after all the years of sharing, would wake up and think she heard Big Baby calling her, get up and walk down the hall to an empty bedroom. Enough of this, she thought, I need somebody to take care of.

Ann went to William and invited the three Stones to live with her, knowing of the issues that her brother-in-law faced on the south side. William told Julia of Ann's invitation and added that he couldn't handle the hours in the grocery store. The same doctor that had told Julia that she was too old for another child, told William his heart couldn't take any more stress, even if Cobb and Dempsey were gone.

William saw the journey from the south side of Peoria to a new house on the bluff as parallel to his parent's journey, an opportunity offered to him by their love and courage. If his father didn't want to explain the depth of emotion that drove them, he would carry that same stoicism and pass it on to his own son.

William leased the grocery to Pytr Kupiecki, an immigrant from Poland who wore a pistol at his waist.

"Mr. Stone, I take good care of your store. Maybe, I even buy it some day."

In the fall of 1920, Julia, William and Thomas, moved in with Ann in time for Thomas to start high school.

CHAPTER TWENTY-ONE
BASKETBALL
1924

Coach Murphy called Tom Stone and Jim Conlin into his cramped office after the Monday four p.m. practice. The office smelled of sweat and rubbing alcohol, and a faint odor that the boys recognized as rye. They stood shoulder to shoulder just inside the door. There was no where else to stand.

Sport Murphy held a freshly lit cigar in a thick callused hand. His collarless white dress shirt was crumpled, the sleeves pushed up over his elbows. The collar band was never buttoned on a neck that rose as a monolith between his muscled shoulders and bald oval head. His only other white shirt was lying on the floor next to the desk, along with an old pair of football pants that barely fit around his ample belly. He wore the same outfit to practice every day. The team speculated that these clothes never saw soap and water. His sneakers were laying on the opposite side of the desk with his bare feet crossed just in front. It was not clear whether he had anything on other than his shirt.

"We're going," was the simple statement that came from behind the stacks of smoke. If the boys could have seen through the smoke, they would have seen a slight smile playing at the corner of his pinched eyes. Sport Murphy coached football and basketball at Spalding Institute. He was the only coach for the sport since basketball had been adopted in 1914.

"Who's going?" was Thomas' immediate question.

"You two, of course, McLaughlin, Coughlin, Larson, and Schmidt. I just got the invitation from the Cook County Diocese. It's been cleared with the Bishop and the Principal. We will be in the first national Catholic High School basketball tournament. Quite an honor based on our record this year."

"That's only six players. What if somebody gets sick, or we get in foul trouble?" Jim asked.

"We can afford six tickets and three rooms for you guys. Two in a room."

"What about Jerry and Matt? Can't we do anything? We could Sure use them."

Thomas hoped that Murphy was holding out, making them feel that he was the only one that could get things done. Maybe this was another of his motivational schemes. Take them down and bring them back up.

"My aunt can ask the Bishop for some help." Thomas ventured.

"Might work, I know your aunt, she's quite persuasive, for a woman," said Coach Murphy.

"Don't let her hear you say that, she doesn't see much difference between men and women when it comes to business," Thomas said, remembering vaguely that Murphy and Ann Stone knew each other.

"I know, I know." Murphy twirled to the side and put his legs up on the desk. He did have pants on. "Stone, you come with me to the bishop's house. Fr. Black and I are meeting with him in an hour to talk about a few things. Maybe having you along will help. I'll do the talking. You just stand there. I'll make the pitch for the other two." He smiled as if he knew the outcome. Another coach technique.

"We'll take the eight A.M. Rocket to Union Station on Thursday. One bag, your uniform, and please, enough clean underwear to get through four days. And a suit and tie. We will appear in public properly dressed. We may win one or two of these games."

"What about a priest? Who's going with us?" Jim asked.

"Flaherty. No one else wanted to go."

"Great, the rest of them can wait for a *football* game to go to."

Thomas jabbed Jim in the ribs, letting his exuberance show for the first time. Fr. Flaherty was the best choice as far as they were concerned. He was more of a friend than a priest. He had already pulled McLaughlin out of a few speakeasies before he could get scooped up in a police raid. Every high school kid needed a priest like Flaherty. And the game was what they had practiced for all their lives. A chance to get to Chicago, play in the new Loyola gym. Walk down Michigan Avenue. Maybe even catch of glimpse of Capone himself.

"Stone. Wait out by my car. Conlin, see you tomorrow at practice. I'll post the traveling roster then."

"Notice how he makes it out so he's always the hero," said Thomas quietly to Jim as they left the locker room.

"This time I don't care, he brought us this far, we have to do the rest," Conlin replied.

Sport Murphy and Father Samuel Black, the Spalding Principal, stood in front of Bishop Ireland's broad mahogany desk. Thomas Stone stood just behind them. The bishop was dressed in the black and red vestments that meant business was being conducted. There was a portrait of Pope Pius XI directly behind the Bishop, flanked by floor to ceiling shelves of books. Doors on opposite walls led to the chancery, which dealt with all the religious issues of the diocese, and Ann Stone's small office, where the financial decisions were made, on the other. Bishop Ireland's office was small by comparison to other bishop's. He liked it that way.

"Power and humility are in the action, not the office," he told his aides. "We will let our actions speak louder than our chairs."

He looked up from his desk.

"Sit down, sit down. Congratulations on being selected for the tournament. That's why you're here, isn't it? To talk about the trip to Chicago? I assume that's why you brought Mr. Stone with you. How are you Thomas? Your aunt speaks highly of you. And more importantly for the coach here, she says you are quite an athlete."

"I'm fine your eminence, thank you." Thomas said with his head down turning his cap over and over in his hands.

"We need to decide on the traveling team," Father Black interjected, before Coach Murphy could speak.

"Who needs to go?"

"The traveling fund has enough for six players, one coach and a priest. We need to take two more players. Tom Stone is here to answer any questions you may have from the boy's point of view. "
The Bishop interrupted Fr. Black.

"Of course, of course, how much can it be anyway? A few dollars? We'll have the parishes take a second collection next week. I'm more worried about how Chicago will affect their morals. A couple of those young men may go into the seminary." The bishop looked up at Thomas,

"Like your friend Conlin, right Thomas?" He continued without waiting for a response. Thomas figured that the bishop knew everything.

"I don't want to give them too many alternatives. Who's minding their after game activities?"

"Flaherty," was the coach's reply.

"Um, good choice, he knows what they'll likely try to get away with."

The bishop leaned forward over the desk, his hands laced together in the middle of the desk in what seemed to Thomas to be almost a praying stance.

"I like the idea of having a Catholic tournament. We'll show those public schools a thing or two. They don't really want to play our boys. That's why Bishop Mundelein started this thing anyway. To showcase the impact our schools are having on urban areas. And it's a chance to show off their new gym. Cost five hundred grand. He actually asked me for money, can you imagine. We'll let the Loyola alumni fund it. OK, OK, anything else?"

Sport Murphy and Father Black looked at each other, marveling at the Bishop's knowledge, and ability to monopolize a conversation.

"No, just the game." Father Black explained to Murphy as they left that he would come back the next week with the request for the biology lab. No sense in pushing his luck. What a shock it would be if they won. The biology lab would be a foregone conclusion.

Eight Catholic boys and a priest stood in the shadow of the black Rock Island steam locomotive. A sharp March wind mixed newspapers and steam belching from the engine around their legs. From a distance, the basketball team appeared to be a large family arriving in the United States for the first time. All dressed alike, four-panel woolen caps pulled down almost over their ears, long tweed coats wrapped around suits of the same weight and fabric. They huddled together for protection from the last winter rain, smelling of wet wool and apprehension about their chances in the tournament. But each player also had reason for elation that they shared trying to outdo the others.

"This will be a chance for the Notre Dame scout to see me."

"Four days away from my Dad, this is going to be great."

"Four days in a hotel, girls on every corner."

"My chance to see the Museum of Natural History."

Each held a small bag with the exact items that Coach Murphy had listed. They knew he would inspect the bags as soon as they got to the hotel.

"You know why we got in, don't you?" Tony McLaughlin asked Thomas. Tony was the tallest of the eight, or the tallest of the midgets as they were referred to by the Peoria Star. At six feet even, he could out jump boys three to four inches taller. The combination of McLaughlin's strength and speed and the finesse of Conlin and Stone left the sports writers looking for new superlatives for this normally ragged, almost dangerous, game.

"What do you mean? We have a decent record, why wouldn't We get in?" Thomas looked down the platform hoping the conductor would be heading their way. The wind blew tears out of his eyes.

"We're the shortest team in the draw. We were the 32nd team picked. I heard Bishop Ireland slipped them a few bucks for their gym. What's the difference. We're in. That's all that counts. Now we have to show them how the game should be played. Maybe we can speed the game up a little. Bring some attention to that stupid center jump rule after each basket," Thomas replied.

Tony looked down at the five foot ten Stone and asked,

"What do you think we should do about the taller teams? You know the Nebraska team hasn't been beaten in four years." Thomas thought of his father, how he handled each problem one at a time, turned to McLaughlin and gave him his game plan.

"We need to focus on the Indiana team. They're first. Use your instinct, move, pass. You need to shoot every time you get a chance. Stop them with constant pressure. Don't let them shoot. It's our speed that'll make the difference, and our courage. We're the ones that decide what to take into each game. Not the sports writers."

The conductor finally walked towards the shivering group, pulled out his leather pad and said,

"You guys the basketball team?" He didn't wait for a response.

"Car one, no booze. If I see any, you're off the train. Got it?"

Father Flaherty stepped forward, stood directly in front of the conductor,

"I'll take care of the boys, you take care of the train."

"You tell 'em Father, don't take any crap!" Tony McLaughlin laughed as he pushed Thomas towards the metal steps, but stopped and said,

"Whoa, who's that?"

"Who's who?" Thomas said as he pushed good naturedly back at the taller McLaughlin.

"The girl getting out of that Buick with the two bags. Maybe she's in our car."

Irene Lucas stood at the door of the car, reached in and said,

"C'mon Nathan, we're here, we've got to hurry."

CHAPTER TWENTY-TWO
TRAIN

The train whistle screeched, then stilled, leaving seconds of blank space suddenly filled by the voice of a father and a daughter.

"Good bye, have a good time. Nathan, take care of Irene," Robert Lucas yelled.

"Who takes care of who here?" Irene yelled back as she handed their tickets to the conductor. The conductor looked at the two tickets, raised three fingers and pointed to the third passenger car. Tony and Thomas were standing at the steps to car one.

"Damn, we'll have to go looking for her," Tony said as Irene pushed Nathan towards the third car.

"I think I know them. I recognize their father, he used to come to the grocery, sold us corn. Dad said he helped get rid of Cobb and Dempsey. But he didn't say much about the kids, just that the son was in the war, he wasn't doing too well. And there was a smart-ass daughter. That must be them. "

"Too bad he didn't tell you more about *her*, but nothing beats a chance like this. Let's go find her after the train takes off," Tony said as he threw his bag into the small baggage area at the front of the car.

"Something strange about the son, he looks so pale," Tom replied as he took off his hat and coat, folded them carefully, and placed them on the rails above their seats.

"Give me your coat Tony, I'll put it up there *under* mine."

"You're too damn neat, Stone. Who cares how the coats look. C'mon, let's go find your friends."

"They're not my friends. But, I wouldn't mind talking to them."

Tony McLaughlin pushed the car door open and stepped onto the metal plate between the swaying cars. He pulled a small steel flask out of his jacket and tipped it to his lips. The wind whipped between the two cars forcing him to hold on to the rail running from the top of the door to the base of the car, with his other hand.

"Jesus, Tony, put that away. You know what would happen if you got caught with booze," Thomas said as he stepped out into the cold between sixty ton boxes of steel trying to break away from each other.

"Flaherty won't say anything, he's one of us. He's asked me where to get the stuff three or four times. He's kinda like the fox guarding the chicken coop, don't you think. Anyway, Tommy, I play better with a drink in my gut. If I lay off too long, I lose my edge."

"Just keep it out of sight. I don't want to know about it. Keep moving. It's colder than a well-diggers ass out here."

Tony put the flask back inside his jacket. They turned to the next car and pushed the heavy metal door open and stepped into a blast of warm air. They walked down the aisle, looked left and right, up and down the aisle. The car was full of a BPOE group on their way to their annual convention in Chicago. Laughter rolled from under thick cigar smoke stinging their ears and eyes. They moved up the aisle looking into each seat. It was all men.

They left the Elks and pushed the door open to the next car. A white haired woman sat on her suitcase in at the end of the aisle almost blocking the path. Nathan Lucas sat quietly next to her on the last overstuffed bench facing Tony and Thomas. They recognized Irene by the strawberry blonde bobbed hair just above the top of the roughly textured burgundy seat across from Nathan.

"There they are. I see the guy with the white tonsure. What a sight," Tony said. As they moved closer they could see bags stacked on the floor between Nathan and Irene. The beaten leather suitcases acted as a table for the war images that Irene was pointing at.

There was a faint scent of vanilla as they drew closer, mixed with the pungent odor of cigar and cigarette smoke coming from the rest of the car.

"Are those Americans?" Tony asked about the images lying on the luggage. Irene ignored the question and continued to talk to Nathan. Thomas stood behind the taller McLaughlin, holding on to the seat one row behind her, smiling and looking as polite as he could.

Nathan listened to Irene, looked out the window, looked back at the pictures, nodded, looked out the window again. He seemed not to notice the inquisitive young man leaning over the pictures with his hand on the back of Irene's seat.

"I said, are those Americans? And what's wrong with his hair?"

Tony almost whispered, motioning his head towards Nathan.

"Yes, and nothing is wrong with his hair. We really don't need any company."

"Would you like a drink? Maybe that would brighten your day a bit?" His hand slipped off the back of the seat onto her shoulder. He could feel warm skin and the sharp edge of her shoulder through the fabric of her dress. Nathan looked slowly towards the bent figure, watching for a sign of distress from Irene. The rhythmic clack, clack, and the roll of the car as the wheels went over each weld in the track, moved them to a slow sensual beat.

Irene pulled forward, away from Tony's hand that had traces of grime from the car doors he had just come through.

"Nathan was in the war, he killed the men in these pictures. He still thinks we are in a war. Take your hand off me and keep going."

"Wait a minute sister, I don't mean anything, I just thought since we're going in the same direction, we could get to know each other a little."

The car jerked, pushing Tony McLaughlin closer to Irene. Nathan stood, stepped over the suitcase, careful not to disturb the order of the pictures that Irene had laid on the suitcases and grabbed the eighteen year olds neck. He pulled him away from Irene and was pushing him back towards Thomas.

"Jesus, McLaughlin, where have you been?" Thomas said hoping that he appeared to be just arriving.

"And what have you started here?" Thomas said to McLaughlin but looked down at Irene. He rubbed his hand back from his forehead to the nape of his neck, trying to make sure his thick black hair was in place.

"Has he been bothering you ma'am? Sometimes the McLaughlin boy here likes to wander around a bit. But he's really an all right guy."

McLaughlin started to cough.

"Could you let him go please?" Thomas asked Nathan. "I'll make sure he doesn't bother you any more." Nathan looked at Irene. She nodded. He released McLaughlin, but kept his position.

Now there were four bodies in a slow dance, rocking to the cars movement, three young men looking down at Irene, waiting for her next reaction.

Irene smiled at Thomas Stone, answered the question that seemed to have asked twenty minutes before.

"No, no, he was just asking my brother and I about the pictures That he took in France. We're taking them to Chicago to show them to Colliers magazine. They are going to buy them."

She tilted her head up towards Thomas without looking straight into his eyes. "Why are you and your friend going to Chicago?"

"We're playing in a basketball tournament at Loyola University. It's the first nation wide tournament of its kind. We're one of thirty-two teams." He didn't say high school , Catholic or thirty second seed.

He wondered what was wrong with telling her the whole. Then realized he was trying to impress her.

"I read about that, you must go to Spalding."

"Um, yeah, that's us."

"Good luck, maybe Nathan and I will come to one of the games if we have time. Although we'll be pretty busy with the magazine."

"Right. Well, you take care of yourselves, maybe we'll see you later."

McLaughlin had been inching towards the door during the conversation between Thomas and Irene, trying to put a whole car between himself and the hand that had almost broken his larynx. Thomas turned to follow him when he realized that he had not asked the young woman's name.

"Listen, what's your name? Mine is Thomas Stone and my Friend here, um, there, is Tony McLaughlin."

"Irene Lucas and brother Nathan," was her quiet response. "I've been taking care of him since the war. This is our, his, first time going to Chicago."

What a considerate, brave, beautiful, girl. Thomas thought as he went after McLaughlin, formulating how he would tell him to stay away from the Lucas family.

CHAPTER TWENTY-THREE
COLLIER'S MAGAZINE

"Why did you use the little Kodak box? I suppose you just didn't want to lug the larger format equipment around," Horace Barnack asked Nathan. He pushed the round images across his desk, marveling at the reaction he was having to them. Each time he pulled the folder out of the metal file cabinet behind his desk and laid it on the table he pulled his handkerchief out of his vest pocket and held it to his nose. He was sure he detected sulfur rising from the paper.

His publication had refused to print the most disturbing of the pictures right after the war. Who would buy the magazine if it made them sick to their stomach? Carnival freak shows were one thing, nobody in the family looked like the attractions. Pictures of severed limbs, entrails, dead eighteen year old eyes staring straight back at the viewer, no matter how revealing of the horrors of war, were too close to every family and too big of a risk to the low margin publishing business. But times change. Everything was going well. There was a brokerage house on every corner. Stories of gas station attendants made millionaires over night were commonplace. It was hardly news anymore. Now was the time to bring the true story to the American public, and pass Life as the number one magazine.

Horace's job was to convince the chief editor of his brilliance as a visual editor. Some hacks wanted illustrators to soften the photos, make them more artistic. Horace wanted realism. He was certain that the camera recorded more than what the eye saw. Nathan Lucas's photos convinced him. War was an abstract concept until the images started to move towards him. He found himself backing away from the table, wiping at his eyes.

"Can you crop these to fit the shape of the pages? I still have to convince the chief editor that we should go in this direction. Perhaps you could stay till Monday when he returns. We will take care of your expenses at the hotel." He realized that Nathan hadn't answered his first question, in fact hadn't spoken at all.

"Tell me Nathan, why did you use the Kodak box, didn't you have a better camera?"

Nathan looked directly at Barnack for the first time, took a deep breath, and said,

"I, I had, um, had, a, another, camera that, that used, glass, glass plates, plates instead, instead of, of film." Irene stared at Nathan, he hadn't spoken this much in her presence since before the war. She pushed herself forward in the chair, placed her arm across Nathan's legs and grabbed the edge of Horace Barnack's desk. She spoke slowly and evenly, making sure that Barnack looked directly at her.

"What he means is that the better camera that he took with him was confiscated by the army intelligence after they saw his first pictures. They did not want what you see on your desk. They wanted sunshine, shiny boots, cigarette smoke, maybe a rifle pointed at a distant tree. Fortunately for you, he took the little box camera with him. I told him to get one hundred good photos just for me. The little box was perfect for that. I sent the whole camera to Rochester, New York. They sent the pictures and a freshly loaded box back."

Nathan smiled, looked out the window, seemed to drift away.

"Let's get together Monday, I will contact you first thing and set a time for the mid afternoon. We can get our business done and get you on the 6:00 P.M. train back to Peoria. What will you do over the weekend?"

Irene reacted immediately.

"Could you get us tickets for the basketball games at Loyola? I Have a friend playing, but he couldn't get tickets."

"I'll see what I can do. I will have them sent to the hotel if I can get them."

Horace Barnack was surprised at how easy it was to get tickets for the first game. He called the Athletic Information office at Loyola and was told he could have as many as he wanted. In fact, if he would distribute one hundred of them, he would be treated to a beer and sandwiches at the hospitality room during all the games.

A mystery Horace did not have time to concern himself with. He was busy figuring a way to get the photographs as cheap as possible. If he owned the photos with minimum financial risk up front, it would be easier to convince the chief editor.

"Hicks from downstate, I'll teach them a thing or two about doing business in Chicago. It'll be a good learning experience. And if this magazine doesn't publish them, I'll take them elsewhere."

CHAPTER TWENTY-FOUR
AL CAPONE

At the age of nineteen, Al Capone felt no emotion as he pulled the trigger on his first murder victim. His only thought was to make sure that the three other men in the crap game knew who he worked for and who he was.

"Perotta owes, owed, Frankie Yale $1,500. I just got it for him. My name is Alphonse Capone." He calmly turned his back on the three blood splattered men shaking on their knees, and stepped out into the Five Point neighborhood on the lower east side of Manhattan. He adjusted his tie, pilled his new fedora down over his eyes as he put the revolver inside his suit coat. He was floating in a zone free of remorse or guilt. *"So, that's what it's like. Just another business transaction. Let them see you in control, no hesitation. Mom would be proud of me now.. So what if I didn't get past sixth grade. Now I'll show them how I can take care of a family."*

Pride, love, loyalty, were deep inside, but reserved for only one house. He loved his brothers, his wife and new son. They were cause and justification for new found success. Street kids that survived on their own determination also deserved his respect, and sometimes his trust.

The strong survived. On the opposite side was everybody else. They deserved what they got; police, politicians, other gangs. The police didn't protect him, the politicians didn't need him yet, the other gangs would soon want him dead.

His business would be better run with only one emotion. A little anger, real or put in as a prop, helped pull triggers, kept people in line. Intimidation worked, fear worked. An internal cult of attitude and action gave him his first sense of strategy. If it works, do it again, but with more force, more attitude. Alphonse Capone had what it took to charm you, scare you, and kill you.

Five years later, Capone was in Chicago. He had been brought out to help consolidate "Big Jim" Colosimo's hold on bootlegging in Chicago. Capone and Johnny Torrio, Colosimo's nephew, took over the multi million dollar bootlegging, numbers, and prostitution business, after "Big Jim" was gunned down at the door to his own restaurant.

Al's feeling of accomplishment and power was salted with a twinge of guilt. The guilt did not come from murder.

His mother wasn't proud enough of him.

He took care of his siblings, his own wife and son. He decided he had to do more for the kids living in the shit that he was brought up in. He would give them the opportunity he had made for himself.

Then his mother would be satisfied. She would know that he understood what she went through, that he understood her pain, her disappointment.

His mother wanted a son that took care of her, his family, respected by the people he worked with, somebody that gave something back to the community he lived in. This would be one side of Al Capone.

This side always had a smile, a slap on the back. This was the side that sent an anonymous $30,000 to Loyola University, matching the $30,000 raised by alumni for the new Alumni Gym. There would be a 3,500 seat basketball auditorium, later to be called "The Big Brown Box that Rocks," bowling alleys, billiard rooms and a pool. A gym that would be used by both the university and the high school on campus. This was the side that sent money to a widow for a son's education after his father had been gunned down by three men with sub machine guns.

No matter how hard he tried to separate his two lives, alternating tongues of anger and compassion leapt freely back and forth. In a meeting to discuss down state money laundering, he found himself thinking,

'I didn't mean to yell at Sophie and Sonny, they didn't do nothin'. I almost raised my hand. "God forgive me."

"Hey Al, what's to forgive? Maybe you should go to confession," His older brother, Ralph, said jokingly. Al stared out the window into the black alley behind the furniture store that served as his office. Al ignored his brother's remark, only slightly aware that he had spoken "God forgive me," aloud.

"We need somebody in that bank in Peoria. We should just deposit the beer money there. It's too risky trying to drive it every week. We've already been hit twice. We need somebody to move the money into the bank, maybe even do a little investing in the market." Ralph said, getting back to the business at hand. He looked around the large oak table for support from the other five members of the gang.

"Yeah, a smart kid working just for us. Somebody that we can trust," said Al. "Who do we know in the bank?."

"The president has the hots for one of the broads at Lil's on Aiken Alley. We could squeeze him pretty good with that habit." Ralph replied. Al stood up, started walking behind each man at the table,

"Isn't there a Peoria team playing this weekend at Loyola? Let's

See what kind of talent they bring up. Remember those two idiots we had running beer a few years back? Whatever happened to them?"

"Some say they drowned, running from a ghost. Some chicken Shits we had there," Ralph said.

Al stopped behind his brother, put his hands on his shoulders, and said, "OK, that's enough. The rest of you guys take off. Ralph, stay with me for a minute."

There was an audible sigh of relief from each of the other five as they filed quickly out of the room. Al had seemed unusually calm during the meeting and this was usually the portent of violence. Ralph sat patiently as Al took his hands off his shoulders and said,

"I want to see how they spent my money. Let's go to the Thursday games. Maybe we'll see the help we need. Turn the lights off. Don't forget your coat and hat, it's cold tonight." He waited for Ralph to darken the empty warehouse, then let him walk out into the damp March night. Ralph was taller than Al, but with the same hat and coat, hunched over against the biting Chicago wind, he could have been easily mistaken for his younger brother.

CHAPTER TWENTY-FIVE
RALPH CAPONE

The gym was half full for the Thursday evening game, two teams nobody had heard of. The Spalding Irish and the Warriors from Vincennes, Indiana were about to play in their first National Catholic Basketball Championship. Spalding was the home team on the scoreboard, but not yet for the Chicago fans. The real home team for Chicago was the Loyola Ramblers, but they had been beaten earlier in the day by Marquette from Milwaukee.

There was no cheering, no cheerleaders, for the two unknown teams, but each bounce of the ball sent echoes from wall to wall driving an unconscious rhythm throughout the gym. This game combined all the senses into an erotic pool not experienced on the baseball and football fields where sounds and odors dissipated into the sky. Barely three feet separated the out of bounds line and the toes of the first row spectators. Squeaking shoes, hands slapped against the ball or another player, coaches and players yelling at each other, flying sweat, and an occasional body, attacked those brave enough to put themselves in the way of a loose ball and the frenzy to recover it. The baskets were attached directly to the wall on either end of the gym, a wrestling mat hung below the baskets as protection for both player and wall.

Ralph and Al Capone arrived at half time. They stood alone on the running track that circled the gym twenty feet above the basketball floor. Al kept his hat and coat on as he looked down on the two teams flowing back and forth. Spalding led ten to two. Conlin had scored three baskets and Stone two. The Vincennes team had shot two free throws and missed the only three shots from the floor.

"Go get us some sandwiches, I'm hungry. I'll wait here." Al told his brother. Ralph ran to the first floor and pushed his way past the two other people waiting to order. "Two dogs, plenty of mustard. Hurry it up. I can't wait all day." Ralph hated running errands. But this was part of the game. Keep Al busy thinking about the business or keep him eating. Both calmed him. He took the steps two at a time.

Handed Al his hot dog. The second half had already started.

"Look at number eight, he runs the show. He's got a plan, pushes the other guys into it. Hardly pays attention to the coach. Jesus, he's the coach. He sees 'em all, all the time. He coaches both sides and the other team doesn't know it. He's the one. Number eight. Get him. We'll set him up at the bank. The other one, the shooter, number twelve, he could be useful too. Find out more about them. They're fast, but not tall enough to beat the other teams. They won't last long. Is Mac outside with the car? Tell him I'll be right down."

"It's only the third quarter, Al. Don't you want to see who wins?"

"I've seen enough. Check on Mac."

Ralph ran to the car, ran back to Al.

"Ready, it's clear to go," Ralph said, puffing slightly. Al turned, pulled the lapels of his wool overcoat up to his chin, walked directly to the car.

Ralph relaxed, pulled out a cigar, bit off the end, spit it onto the concrete floor, and lit it, watched the smoke mingle with the gray-white smoke that seemed to rise from the floor itself. He watched the remainder of the game enjoying the time away from his brother's demands. The final buzzer sounded. Spalding had won the game eighteen to six. He watched the Spalding team maul Conlin and Stone as they made their way to the locker room. He decided to wait until the team was eliminated, they were sure to lose, before he spoke to his brother's targets. No sense in taking their focus off the game. Let them have their moment of glory. He glanced back at the third row of the bleachers to the left of the Spalding bench, wondering if the young girl he had noticed was still there. Instead, he saw a ghost. Nathan Lucas had taken off his cap and was swinging it back and forth in front of his face, clearing the smoke away.

Damn, it's Lucas.

Ralph ran down the steps, crossed the floor under the basket and was confronted by Irene. She had seen him coming and stepped instinctively in front of Nathan.

"Can I help you?"

"I know this man, we were in the war together. I thought he was dead. He saved my life. I thought he was dead." Ralph held his sides, tried to catch his breath.

"So, you know my brother, but I don't know you. Who are you?"

Nathan stopped swinging his cap, raised it to his lips, stared at Ralph about to say something, but remained quiet.

"My name is Ralph Capone."

"You mean Al's…."

"Yes, I mean…..he paused,

Fucking brother, I'll never get away from him and his reputation.

"Capone, my name is Capone, Al is my brother. But he's got nothing

to do with this. Nathan and I were good friends. Is he OK? He looks, you know, not so well." Ralph moved his head up and to the left in Nathan's direction.

"I know, it's been since he got back, I do the best I can, he has Made some progress recently. I think he's really enjoying the game," she said, holding her head up and off to the right, smoothing her loose dress down the front of her thigh.

"But why basketball? I didn't think Nathan even knew what the game was. All he was interested in was his camera, kind of possessed by it. Never talked about girls or sports with the rest of us."

"Nathan's picture editor at the magazine wanted us to stay till Monday and said he could get us into the games. I have a friend that plays for Spalding. He scored eight points tonight."

Ralph's mind was bouncing between his brother's demands, and his own need to speak directly to Nathan. He wanted out of the gang. It was too much like France in 1918, two sides trying to control territory that neither belonged in. Somehow he knew Nathan would help him.

"Who is your friend on the Spalding team?"

"Tom Stone, number eight. He's my best friend,"

"Oh, so you know him well?"

"Sure, his dad and my dad get along swell. They're in business together in Peoria."

He looked past Irene into Nathan's blank face, hoping for some sign of recognition.

Six years before on the edge of the Argonne forest, Ralph Capone knelt on the ground, his hands behind his head. His own rifle was pointed at his chest, held by an eighteen year old conscript from Cologne.

"I surrender, I surrender," Ralph said as loudly and clearly as he could, expecting the mud covered soldier to understand. The German looked like a high school classmate of Ralph's. The same thick hair, square jaw, full lips. But the soldier's eyes appeared to be much larger, staring through Ralph, his voice raspy as a file on the edge of a freshly cut metal pipe.

"No prisoner, you killed my brother, you killed my brother." This was spoken in German, Ralph had no idea what the wild eyed young German was talking about. His own voice had remained calm. He expected to be led off to a prisoner of war camp.

The soldier from Cologne slammed the rifle butt against the side of Ralph's head, took his bayonet out of the sheath strapped to his belt, grasped it in both hands and raised it swiftly over his head. Ralph looked up, dazed and shocked at the vicious blow, saw the blade glisten in the filtered light that left no shadows on the soldier or the sodden ground around him.

This was a light that Nathan Lucas prized for its sharp rendering of every detail from white to black. He entered the small clearing in the stand of Blue Spruce as the soldier reached for his bayonet. The Kodak box was strapped across his chest by two leather boot laces, allowing him to carry his rifle in a ready position as he patrolled the perimeter of the Allied front line. He pushed the camera aside and raised the rifle to his shoulder, pointed it at the German's arm as it swung upwards. He heard an explosion from the end of the rifle, not conscious of pulling the trigger, followed the flight of the black projectile, wishing it to hit the hand holding the shining blade. He saw it enter the back of the German's head and explode out the front, obliterating the face that Ralph had found strangely familiar. The soldier started to fall forward, his arm and body swinging simultaneously downwards in a trajectory towards Ralph Capone's chest. Ralph rolled to the side, his head throbbing with each heart beat, felt a breeze against his cheek as the German's face and blade impaled the ground,

Nathan raced over to the two prone bodies, unsure as to which image to capture first, the German youth or the man whose life he had just saved. He decided quickly, rolled the young soldier over and snapped the two men lying side by side. One's eyes gone, the other's staring directly into the camera. This was the image that Horace Barstad wanted the most.

Nathan pulled Ralph to his feet, said,

"Go, go. We've got to get back to the regiment." He put Ralph's arm over his shoulder and half carried him through the dusk.

Nathan didn't talk about the bullet that had killed the young German. He didn't talk about his rising guilt, his mistake, his bad aim. Instead, he wondered out loud if he had the exposure right.

Ralph didn't admit to his attempted surrender. He couldn't talk about cowardice to a man that took death more nonchalantly than his own brother. Nathan walked Ralph through the death squad, rows of American and German bodies from the day's fighting lined up for identification and quick removal. They walked into the infirmary tent, where Nathan spoke one sentence to the medic,

"He's been hit in the head, quite a fight. The Hun's dead."

The next day, Nathan was felled by the Catalpa tree. Ralph Capone did not see him again until after Spalding's victory over the team from Indiana.

Ralph turned and spoke obliquely to Irene,

"Does Nathan talk at all?" not wanting Nathan to hear his question. Nathan slid down the wall twisting his cap in his hands. He suddenly remembered the eyes of the man standing in front of Irene.

"He is in my picture."

It wasn't the tree, or the lightning that had broken Nathan Lucas. It was the single shot he had fired in the Great War.

"I didn't mean to kill him, I aimed at his arm," Nathan said softly. Ralph moved brusquely past Irene, sat next to Nathan, put his arm around his shoulder.

"You did what you had to do, Nathan, I wouldn't be here otherwise. I wanted to thank you, but you disappeared. You only did what we were all supposed to do. That boy did not deserve to die, but we are here now. That's what counts."

Two students pushed wide dry mops across the floor, removing cigarette and cigar butts, crumpled newspapers and bits of mustard. As they swept out through the door, the gym lights snapped off with a sudden clang. The only illumination came from a red ball that glowed over the exit to the street. Ralph looked up and asked Irene, not sure whether he would ever get through to Nathan,

"Let's get out of here. Would you two like some refreshments? There's a speakeasy next to the Edgewater Hotel."

"Yes, we would like that. We, we, could talk some more," Nathan said nervously as he stood and faced Ralph. He pulled his cap down tightly, almost covered his ears, walked towards the light, said, "Go, go." He was bent forward slightly, his hands closed in loose fists swinging in front of his thighs. Every step carefully placed, one directly in front of the other.

CHAPTER TWENTY-SIX
RALPH MEETS THOMAS

Irene, Nathan and Ralph Capone arrived at the Loyola gym at six P.M. Sunday with 3,500 other basketball fans trying to get into the gym.

"Win or lose, I have to meet with your friend Stone right after the game. I'll find a spot up on the track during the game. You and Nathan sit where you can. It will be confusing after the game, wait until he comes out of the locker room, just pull him aside, meet me outside the main door. It will only take a minute for me to talk to him. You got that?" Capone said sternly as he turned without waiting for an answer, and went up the concrete steps to stand behind two boys holding a hand painted sign. He stood directly above Irene and Nathan.

Over the last three days, Peoria Spalding had become Chicago's home team. "Downstate" was no longer a derogatory term. Even the running track above the gym was filled with fans leaning over the two rails, sure that they had the best seats in the house. The two ten year old boys sat on the edge of the track, their feet dangled in the air, waved their sign, "Go Spalding, beat the shit out of Marquette." The sign drew roars from the crowd below, until a Loyola priest pushed his way around Ralph, and grabbed it.

"What are your names? What school do you go to? I'm going to tell your principal." The crowd standing around the boys started to hiss their disapproval and shouted, "Leave em alone." The priest took the sign, grinned ashamedly, and left without getting their names.

Ralph folded his arms, chuckled at the priest's embarrassment and looked down at the stanchions and ropes that surrounded the playing floor protecting the spectators from the players. More fans than players had been injured in sold out games as overly zealous cagers slammed into the crowd chasing a loose ball.

He saw Nathan smiling, nodding at people as he took Irene by the arm, forced their way to the seats behind the Spalding bench. Saw him mouthing words,

"Excuse me, watch my feet, excuse me, on your left. Thank

you." Nathan had progressed a little each day. Walks along Michigan avenue, throwing rocks into the Lake. But it was the talks with Ralph after the games that affected him the most. Ralph had come to each of the games on Friday, Saturday, and Sunday afternoon. He had stood on the running track during each through the quarter and semi-finals, thinking about moving to Kansas City, Denver, maybe even working for the government as a prohibition agent. Spalding won, no meeting with Thomas Stone. Instead, he met with Nathan and Irene.

She couldn't hear most of what they talked about. Their voices merged until she couldn't tell who was speaking. They shared things that she was not allowed to hear, but she could see Nathan's eyes roam to different lights. Ralph seemed to pull a single shard of broken glass out of Nathan's arm with each meeting, a puzzle piece that he placed in the palm of his own hand and moved carefully until each piece fit in a concatenation of lost pain.

Nathan was alive again, but Irene would no longer be the caretaker. He wasn't interested in going to see Barnack on Monday morning. He had something that interested him more. His obsession with dead bodies and staring eyes slowly dissolved as Ralph described what he wanted Nathan to do. A single glass plate had risen into the air and disappeared as Nathan and Ralph entered Alumni gym on Sunday night.

Ralph Capone replaced Irene as Nathan's caretaker. He listened to Nathan and offered him a plan. Nathan would act as the treasurer for Ralph's used furniture business in Peoria. The branch managers would bring their weekly receipts to Nathan. Ralph explained that the managers had strange hours and needed a location that they could go to at any hour. Nathan would then make a weekly deposit with Thomas Stone at the First Bank during bank hours. Thomas would be given the job based on Ralph's close relationship with Mr. Penn, the president. Nathan knew who Ralph Capone was, what business he and his brother were in. It didn't matter.

Irene turned away from Nathan as they sat down in the fourth row. She looked at the other young women in the crowd. They had on the same loose chemises, nylons rolled just below their knees, the same bobbed hair. She leaned over to Nathan and said loud enough for the surrounding crowd, including Ralph, to hear,

"Don't those older ladies look silly in their long dresses and laced-up boots? I have all the right clothes. The trip has really been worth it. And those hairdos. Where have they been?"

The game started with a center jump between Tony McLaughlin, the Spalding center, and Gus Crithers of Milwaukee Marquette. Players, coaches, scorers, spectators, all moved in unison to the stomping of feet and yelling that marked the scoring of a basket or the delivery of a solid foul. The odor of sweat and nerves rose from the wooden floor to the iron rafters and back, pushed by the sound, without the aid of any comforting breeze. The cacophony of horse carts and model T Fords fighting for the same lane on slippery red bricks was forgotten, replaced by sounds that seemed to come from under the floor. An image of desperately reaching hands entered their subconscious in one singing motion. It was their own hands loosened from their bodies that pushed the ball up and down the court. Often in slow motion, but never out of control as their lives seemed to be outside of the cage. Alone, they could never reach this somnambulant state. In the middle of the crowd, each felt the comforting sting of control.

Spalding 14, Marquette 14, one minute left. Jim Conlin had drilled 3 twenty foot set shots in the last eight minutes to bring the game to a tie.

Marquette won the center jump after Conlin's last basket. Their dribbler looked quickly to the timer. Forty five seconds left. Tom Stone followed the Marquette guard as he brought the ball down the court. The Marquette guard moved towards the right corner hoping for double coverage. Stone waited for the ball to cross the Marquette guard's waist, flicked it with his left hand, grabbed it, and raised the ball to his chest with elbows out. Stone's eyes moved his teammates into a box under the Spalding basket. The crowd leaned in the direction of his eyes, savoring his direction as if it was their own wish.

Irene, bobbed hair wet with sweat, rose from the middle of the crowd, she extended her arm, her finger touching Stone from 50 feet, led a hard pass that settled firmly in Conlin's hands. She raised her arm to the basket as Conlin arched the ball with a two handed set shot. The crowd rose to its feet as the ball descended through the hoop. As it left the net and bounced erratically to the side of the floor, the buzzer sounded and the crowd sat with a shudder, stunned at the final score, Spalding 16, Marquette 14. Then rose, all pointing to the pile of Spalding players in the middle of the floor, and started chanting, "Spald—ing, Spald—ing."

After the award ceremony, Coach Murphy held the tournament trophy in the air and started for the locker room, motioning for the players to follow him.

Thomas was the last to leave the cheering crowd. His step was firm, with a slight bounce that could have been called a swagger. A new found confidence shown in his wide set brown eyes. He held the silver pocket watch that each player had received, over his head, showing it to the cheering crowd, as he had seen Coach Murphy do with the big trophy. But something hit his elbow and it started to fall to the gym floor.

"Oh God," he muttered, as a slim hand reached out from the crowd and caught it just as it passed his waist. He looked into the round green eyes of Irene Lucas. Her bobbed hair and make up sent an initial warning, but as she smiled and handed him the watch, and said,

"You almost dropped this," the slight guilt stirring in his stomach turned to a rumbling.

"Good hands," he started to say, as the crowd continued its movement into the Chicago night. His hand touched hers as they exchanged the watch and stared at each other. Moving to the side away from the crowd, he said,

"Irene?"

"Yes."

"I thought you and your brother might have gone back."

"You mean, you looked for us?"

"Well, I looked for *you*. Listen, can you wait a few minutes," he said.

"If you hurry, I'll wait outside. There's someone I want you to meet," Irene replied.

CHAPTER TWENTY-SEVEN
JOB OFFER

Tony McLaughlin had made the rounds of the neighborhood on Saturday and brought a bottle of Canadian champagne back in his gym bag. He was pouring it into the paper cups from the sandwich room. Coach Murphy and Father Flaherty pounded each other on the back, ignoring the smiling McLaughlin.

"OK, OK," Murphy held his stubby hand in the air. "Back to earth. McLaughlin, get that bottle out of here before the chief of police shows up. He's a cousin of the bishop, our bishop. Great job; as I promised, you're on your own till midnight. Then Father Flaherty and I will check each room. The train is at 8:00 A. M. We leave here at 7:00 A.M. Is all that clear?"

The room quieted and each of the high school seniors nodded his head seriously and said in unison,

"Right, coach, you got it. See you at twelve."

Thomas turned to Jimmy Conlin and said,

"What are you going to do?"

"I'm going with Flaherty, look out for the rest of you."

"Jesus, you're serious about this priest stuff, aren't you."

"Yeah, tonight made my mind up. It makes sense that I try to help other people.

We worked hard together as a team, it paid off. I like that feeling of working hard for other people, maybe I can make a difference in a few lives. I can't explain the rest, the vocation stuff. I'm not sure I even like the bishop. But he thinks I would make a good priest. Enough already, what are you going to do?"

"I wanted you to come with me. Remember the girl and her brother I told you

about. They're here. She wants to see me and introduce me to someone. She's amazing, but I'm not sure about this meeting. It seems too complicated. Unless she knows the Notre Dame scout."

"He was here, I saw him up on the track."

"Yeah, maybe that's it, it'll probably be OK."

"If you're not back by midnight, we'll send out a search party.
I've got to go.
See you later, McLaughlin just left." Jimmy Conlin ran out the door behind Father Flaherty.

"Well, now where's your courage?" Henry Fleming stood in the arch leading to the showers, bouncing the game basketball.

"I thought you had disappeared forever," Thomas said under his breath, as he started to pull his overcoat out of the locker.

"You sure nobody else can see you? You drive me nuts."

"Yes, I'm sure. I was proud of you tonight. I don't know the
rules very well yet,
but you seemed to play well. It's not easy keeeping a bunch of kids from killing themselves in this game. Now what are you up to? You better be careful. No telling what she wants." Henry Fleming stopped bouncing the ball and held it under his arm.

"You really need to get a life of your own. Hell, you already had one. It's my turn. Go away for awhile, I'll call if I need you." Thomas turned as he went out the door, expecting to see Henry Fleming waving to him. Instead he saw the final bits of steam washing along the tile floor.

Irene, Nathan and Ralph Capone stood next to a large black enclosed car, the motor running. Irene saw Thomas and ran to him, pulled him by the arm towards the car.

"Thomas, this is Ralph, he was in the war with Nathan."

Thomas was sure this wasn't the Notre Dame scout, but who was he?

"I've heard a lot about you Thomas. I have seen all the games this week. You have a real talent. If you don't mind, I'll get right to it. I have a used furniture business that is doing quite well in Peoria. And if I can put a few trustworthy men into position, I can focus on the rest of the state. Nathan here will be the treasurer, but he needs a contact in the First Bank. I know the president personally, and with a few words, I can get you that job right after graduation. The way the economy is going, you could do quite well very quickly. And I could probably do something for the Conlin kid too. What do you think?"

He looked at Irene, wished he was in an elevator stuck between floors, pressing her against the door. She now had her other arm through Nathan's and looked angellically up at Ralph, then to Thomas and back again.

"I don't know, I've thought about going to college. But you're right, there's a lot of money out there." His disappointment at not meeting the Notre Dame scout slipped away, replaced by images of clothes, cars, Irene. They had beat the best in the country. Already there was an offer in front of him. He had no idea what went on in a bank, but he'd learn fast. It couldn't be that hard. He'd heard stories of gas station attendants making thousands of dollars in the stock market. The bank was an essential part of the whole process, probably safer than the brokerage houses popping up in almost every city neighborhood.

"What would I do at the bank?" Thomas asked. Ralph paused.

"We'd work that out. Just say the word, and we'll put it in motion. What about Conlin?"

"I"ll talk to him, but he's pretty set about becoming a priest. He doesn't care much about money."

Ralph seemed impatient,

"The main thing is for you to handle the transactions, make sure the money gets deposited and the President or the bank takes care of the rest, just like he does everything else. Then, I can tell my boss that everything is smooth. And," a smile crossed his lips, "I can repay Nathan for saving my life." Thomas thought there was something unsaid, but before he could ask,

"Tommy, Tommy," Jimmy Conlin was yelling at Thomas Stone, calling him by the name he only used to get his friend's full attention. Thomas hated being called 'Tommy.'

"McLaughlin's into it again, you've got to help. Come on, Father Flaherty needs us." Conlin had Stone by the arm and was pulling him in the direction of the Edgewater Hotel.

"I've got to say good bye to Irene."

"There's no time. Call her when you get home."

"I'll call my friend in Peoria," Ralph yelled after Thomas.

Thomas looked back over his shoulder, torn between the obvious needs of his friends and the unsure future that Irene, Nathan and Ralph represented.

"Great, give him a call," he yelled back at Ralph Capone, still not knowing who he was, and in the same breath,

"Irene, I'll call you."

CHAPTER TWENTY-EIGHT
THE JOB
1924

Thomas Stone boarded the number three streetcar at the corner of Illinois and Indiana wearing his best black suit. His hair, slicked back with Murray's pomade, shone in the unusually warm May sun. He had practiced the swagger he had seen on the Chicago streets as he walked from his house, waving at his mother who stood on the porch with her arms folded tightly over her chest. He knew what he looked like, but it didn't keep his hands dry.

Two elderly women, dressed in identical black shirtwaist dresses, tan wrinkled hose, and black tie pumps, smiled at him as he took a seat in the middle of the car on the left side. He nodded and said,

"Good morning, how are you," He knew them from St. Bernard's. They made breakfast for the priests, cleaned the rectory, and sometimes the church itself.

"How you doing, Master Stone, quite a game. You made us right proud."

His stomach quieted with the recognition. Even after two months, they remembered the game. He recited a Hail Mary as he opened the window and took his jacket off. He hung his hands over the window frame.

"I don't sweat this much during a game."

The trolley made stops at every other corner alternating on odd and even days. There were three stops to the bishop's house where the two women got off for their second assignment of the day. Ann Stone had found the job for them. They started the day at five thirty, leaving their south side tenement and arrived at St. Bernard's church at six fifteen. Then on to the bishop's house by 9:30 A.M. to follow Ann's daily directions.

As the trolley pulled away from the bishop's house, Thomas thought of the interior office his aunt Ann occupied and wondered who had set up the interview at the bank. He didn't think it was

Irene's friend. He hadn't seen or heard from either of them since the game. Maybe it was Ann, maybe she told the bishop that he needed a job and then the bishop called the bank. But she would have told him if she did something like that.

The tracks traced a path down the middle of the brick streets. Past St. Francis hospital, Hunter's hot dog stand, the Standard oil station, turned left onto Main St. as Peoria's business section came into view. He could see the bank, and past it to the terminus of the trolley line at the Rock Island railroad station.

Thomas stepped off the car in front of the Brown Sugar restaurant. He turned, waited for the trolley to lurch forward on its way to the train depot. He walked back across the tracks to the First Bank Building and stood in front of the ten story office building, the hub of all activity for downtown Peoria.

The phone call had come the day before from the office of the president of the bank.

"This is Shirley, Mr. Penn's personal secretary. Could you be in His office tomorrow at ten A.M.?" That was it, no other explanation. She expected him to know who she was and who Mr. Penn was.

"Of course, I can be there at ten." He knew who they were. Everybody in Peoria knew the name of Andrew Penn. President of the largest and most successful bank in central Illinois.

Thomas looked up at the granite façade and saw the height of his career ambitions. Even better than going to Notre Dame. The day before he had told his mom,

"I may take that job at Keystone. I thought the job offers would come rolling in after we won. But this is the only one. They asked every guy on the team. The pay is pretty good and I could help with the bills."

"There you go, selling yourself short again. Where's all that Swagger you had when you came home from Chicago? What about Notre Dame? Or some other college? That's not the only one."

"You know as well as I do that my grades aren't good enough, no matter how much they would have wanted me. I have to think of how best to help here."

"Honey, you can't fix everything. Although I love the idea of Having you around a little longer."

Keystone was a steel mill specializing in rails and wire. Business was booming in 1924 and the company wanted to expand its management team from the ground up. Thomas would start like the other hopeful managers, in the soaking pits where the molten steel began its journey to the expanding railroads and highways. He wouldn't be wearing the wool suits his mother had been putting in his closet since he was sixteen.

Today, standing in front of the bank, the future looked closer to his own vision of Thomas Stone. This is what he could be. The president of the bank wanted to see him, alone. Not like the Keystone meeting when even Tony McLaughlin showed up for a lecture on the future of railroads and chicken wire. His coach told him he had a bright future, the priests told him he could do what ever he wanted to.

"Just put your mind to it, Thomas, make us proud."

The hand carved mahogany door opened and he was welcomed into the domed lobby by a sharply dressed black man.

"Good morning sir, where may I direct you this fine morning?"

"I have an appointment with your president at ten o'clock. He said to be on time. I am."

"Right you are, just step over to the receptionist desk." He pointed to a desk, the first in a line that ran down the middle of the lobby. Teller windows lined either side of the row of mahogany desks.

People hurried back and forth criss-crossing between the barred windows, past the neatly lined desks, in what seemed to Thomas to be a game plan dreamed up by some financial coach. He heard snatches of sentences that said this was the place to be;

"Anaconda up three fourths, buy it before it gets to the top. Keystone down one eighth, sell it before it bottoms out. Then buy it again."

Behind the first desk sat a smiling woman, her yellow teeth a sharp contrast to black hair mixed with gray piled on top of her head. Her face was smooth, each cheek a frozen plane. Thomas guessed her age initially at twenty-five, but changed it to sixty when he saw her hands, veined and spotted with the fingers permanently bent. Neat piles of papers and envelopes were spread before her. A small rectangular sign said "Information" in what surely was gold lettering.

"Mr. Penn please, I have an appointment at ten. He said to be sure to be on time."

"Your name?"

"My name? Stone, Thomas Stone."

"Oh, I thought you looked familiar, you're one of the Spalding boys," she said as she looked at the sheet of handwritten instructions in front of her.

"Are there others?" Thomas said with a noticeable droop in his shoulders. He could feel the edges of his suit loosen and fall into folds around his arms and legs.

"No, there's just been a lot of talk about the team. Even the Public school guys were excited." She hesitated, "I don't remember any glasses in the pictures though."

"Yeah, well, we take them off during the games and for pictures.

I really couldn't see how pretty you were without them." His suit regained its press, confidence had been restored.

"Take the elevator up to ten, you'll step into his office."

"Thank you, Miss, ah, Miss?"

"Schwann. But just call me Pearl, and thanks for the blarney."

He waited in front of the plain wooden elevator door and heard the iron gate behind it jerk open with a loud bang. As the door slid to the side, he saw that the gate had been wrestled open by Pearl Schwann, except that she had white gloves and a pillbox hat on. Her face was set in a permanent scowl.

"Get in, I can't hold this much longer."

"Ten please, Mr. Penn's office. Are you…."

"Yeah, we're sisters, I'm Ruby. We're two jewels. At least that's what mom thought. You got an appointment? Mr. Penn doesn't like surprises. You wouldn't get by the goat anyway. So you better have an appointment. I told them to give me a list every day, but no, no list."

Thomas started to say yes, but the door was banging open on three, allowing two balding, hunched over men with green eye shades and rubber garters above their elbows to get in. They had been talking very loudly, but as they entered the elevator, they looked at each other knowingly, went to the back and stood quietly facing the door.

"Well, what floor?" Ruby said as the door slammed shut.

"Can't go anywhere unless you tell me."

"Ruby, we only go to three or nine. We got on on three, what's left?"

"Some day you will go to seven or eight. Better to ask."

"Ruby, would you take us to nine, please."

"Nine, then ten. Coming up."

The two clerks looked at Thomas, nodded hello, then waited silently until they got out on nine.

"You're next, good luck." Ruby said to Thomas as he stepped

into the foyer of the President's office.

Shirley Edson looked up from her desk with neat piles of envelopes and typed sheets of paper. Her hair was tufted on the sides just above her ears. Her eyebrows were caterpillars marching to the bridge of her nose, which was square on the end. Thomas knew this was the woman Ruby referred to as the goat

"Right on time, Mr. Penn likes that. Have a seat, he will be Right with you. He's in a meeting right now, but it won't be long."

Thomas pulled his championship watch out of his vest pocket, made sure that Shirley saw it, it was two minutes past ten. The next time he looked, it was ten thirty. He stood up and walked past Shirley to the window overlooking Main St.. She was busy folding each piece of paper into three. He could see the scripted First Bank logo on the upper left hand corner of each creamy white envelope as she ran it over a small sponge sitting in a glass container of water. Then placed it in the ever growing pile of envelopes needing three-cent stamps.

He could see smoke rising to the south of downtown. It must be Keystone. Steam from molten iron pouring out of the blast furnace into molds in the first step on the journey to create links from one city to another. He saw a romance in the links between steel mills, railroads, big cities, a way to contribute to the country's growth. He could be part of bringing people closer together. That was the speech the team had heard about the future of the steel industry. They needed devoted, passionate leaders. Some would come from the ranks of the universities, but what they needed most were young men that made it with their hands, their wits. Young men just like the Fighting Irish of Spalding. Just like the new champions. His grandfather and father had been part of the agrarian age. Watching the man from the steel mill he saw himself as part of the changes that industry was bringing to the world.

But the bank gave him another option. He felt more in control. Everything he wanted to accomplish in his life lay ahead. Take care of his mother, his father, his aunt. Help with the parish work, join the Knights of Columbus, carry the ceremonial sword, even local politics could get a few minutes of his busy schedule. Then there was Irene, find her, start his own family. Anything was possible.

"You can go in now."

He shifted back into the office, said a quick Hail Mary, straightened his tie and turned from the window to walk through another carved door into the largest room he had ever seen. The

Loyola gym would fit in Mr. Penn's office. Three solid walls of books, one wall with two casement windows as tall as he was. The desk was the size of their new dining room table. There were three phones on the right side, a ticker tape under a dome on the left. In the middle was a three by three leather desk mat. A large curved ink blotter sat next to a black pen. Mr. Penn sat in a high back leather arm chair that rocked when he greeted Thomas.

"Mr. Stone, you do Peoria proud," as he reached over the desk, actually leaning a bit to reach Thomas's outstretched hand, shaking it vigorously.

"Sit, sit. That was some performance you put on in Chicago."

"Thank you sir. It was a very exciting four days."

"I'll get right to it. What are your plans now that you have graduated?"

"I had wanted to go to college, but my Dad isn't well, neither is My Mom, we live with my Aunt and she's going to retire soon. I would like to stay here in Peoria, start a career."

"Good answer. Ever think about banking? The finance world is exploding. The bank needs sharp young men. I would like you to talk to a few people here. See what you think about the operation. Then we'll get together again. See Shirley out front, she'll set up the meetings. That's it. Any questions?"

Thomas shook his head "no."

Mr. Penn rocked back in his chair and turned to the first phone.

Thomas rose, put his hand out, then lowered it as he turned and returned to Shirley's desk. He had been in the office three and one half minutes. "*Was it the bishop? Was it Ralph and the used furniture business? What would he do? Who would he meet with? Who cares?*"

CHAPTER TWENTY-NINE
DEATH

"Every time you come home from a game, you tell me how well you did. Two hits, a great catch, a touchdown, four points. Is this going to be different? Don't keep me waiting. Will I be proud of you?"

Julia sat in her rocking chair looking out at the street car tracks. Her prematurely white hair was pulled back in a bun, wisps floating gently around her wire rimmed glasses. Each phrase ended with a low creak from the curved wooden rockers.

"Don't keep me waiting," she repeated as Thomas knelt to the side of the rocker, reached out and took her left hand, rubbed her gold band between his fingers.

"Your father will be home any minute now. Do you want to wait and tell us both at the same time? Maybe he would enjoy being part of your revelation," she said as she looked worriedly out the window.

"Let's wait till he comes home. I'll give you a clue. I will be able, no, required, to wear a suit," Thomas said. Julia smiled, rubbed her hand across his shoulders.

"I can wait."

Thomas still did not have the words worked out. He did not know where the job came from. He was jubilant at the thought of a job at the bank and a second later scared that the job came from Chicago. He knew that his father would never let him take the job at the bank if he even suspected involvement with the Chicago mob. Ralph must be connected in some way. This time Thomas *wanted* the job, but his father wouldn't see the difference. Penn would be the same as Dempsey and Cobb to him. Involving him in the work of the devil. Thomas did not want to find out if the rumors about Dempsey and Cobb were true, that they were driven to their death in boiling oil by a white faced horseman.

There must be another reason why he was being offered the job. Penn did mention the bishop, no, that was his secretary that mentioned the bishop. Penn didn't mention anybody. Maybe Thomas could say that Ann got the bishop to call the bank. But that would be a lie. Basketball hero must be it. After all, Keystone had made him an offer. But maybe they were just trying to soften their image. The steel workers had been on strike for a month demanding safer working conditions and higher wages. The community support, what there was of it, was for the strikers. If the management of Keystone offered the whole team jobs, the city would see their sincerity.

"I wish he hadn't gone to the steel worker's rally. You know there will be problems. The newspaper is calling the strikers Communists. Striking for safety and a living wage, how can that be Communism? I told him to stay home," Julia's voice and face hardened as she spoke of William's desire to support his friends at the steel mill. These were men that he had sold meat and vegetables to for years. Not charged them when times were tough. Commiserated with them when their sons did not return from Europe. They eventually paid everything they owed, and in some cases, more than the original bill called for.

Now the pendulum of need was back on their side. The steel workers union had asked for his support. All he had to do was stand with them, chant their slogans on the corner of Main and Adams. He agreed immediately. He did not know the strike breakers, bused in from southern Illinois. They were strangers, his loyalty was to the men that he knew, as much family to him as Julia, Ann and Thomas.

A line of five street cars rolled down Main. Police walked on either side of the cars, sometimes putting their arms up to fend off heads of lettuce and tomatoes. But the crowds were generally quiet on this Monday in May of 1924. The steel workers cause was not enough to bring the ordinary citizen out in support of either side.

"They should just figure it out and let us go on our business," was the prevalent attitude. The strikers stood arm in arm, ten men across, five deep. William was in the middle of the last row, straddling the trolley rail, one of ten men with a sledgehammer in his hands, given to them by organizer, Tommy Hartness.

"I hear you have a solid swing," he said smiling at William,

"Just Stay with the beat."

The strikers chants gradually engulfed the police and the strike breakers,

"No safety, no rails. No fair wage, no wire," was accompanied by ten hammers smashing into the trolley rails in unison. Each orchestrated swing seemed to make the cars jump and vibrate violently. The police jumped into the open cars. In the first car a man in a dark pin striped suit told the strike breakers to get down on the floor. He held onto the door of the car with his left hand. His right hand was in his suit pocket. He turned to the trainman and said,

"Speed up."

"What? I thought we were going to stop if we had to." The man in the suit pulled out a 38 revolver and pointed it at the floor.

"Do as I say."

The police said nothing.

The trainman pushed the lever forward and the trolley picked up speed as it crossed the mid point between Jefferson and Adams.

"Move, move, it's not going to stop," yelled the men in the first few rows, as they stared in disbelief at the oncoming steel car. Each row was far enough behind the one in front of it to allow for the swinging of the hammers. The first rows dropped their hammers as they jumped, pushed, pulled each other towards the curb. The fifth row couldn't see the cars, or hear the warning. They were focused on the rhythm of the striking hammers, enjoying their chorus. The two men straddling the track were caught by the catcher on the front of the street car with their hammers at the apex of their swing. On the right, Goran Ivanovich was flipped over, still holding the sledgehammer. His head smashed into the curb, killing him instantly. On the left William Stone had felt a tingling in his left arm with each swing of his hammer. Just as the men in the front row were yelling, "Move, Move," the tingling moved up through his shoulders, down across his collar bone into his chest , squeezing, stopping his breath. His mouth opened to utter a protest,

Not now, God, not now, Julia, Julia. He looked down and saw his legs swiped by the catcher, much as it had done to Ivanovich, but the impact whipped him around under the car between the front and rear wheels. His right arm was severed at the instant that his head was caught by the rear axle. The trainman had put all his weight into the brake lever, but the train continued for one full block before it came to a stop with William Stone resting on the rear axle.

The man in the dark suit stepped off the car and disappeared into the crowd.

CHAPTER THIRTY
JULIA STONE
1924

Four months later, Julia sat in her bedroom rocking chair looking out at serrated leaves marching in circles across the brick street. The bare peaks of the elm trees that William had planted when they moved in with Ann just reached the front porch roof. Their skinny afternoon shadows skidded just below Julia's face as she looked for William to cross Indiana Ave.

"Ann, what time will William be home? We've got a roast and potatoes to put in.

And Thomas, is he going to be home from practice? I wish he would take a season off from one of those sports he plays. Maybe he would get home for dinner at a decent hour. I love you Ann, but I miss having a man at the table. The conversation is much more interesting, don't you think? But then, all I have to do is listen. Much easier to listen. Let them do the talking. Ann, where are you? Oh, there you are. It's so nice having you here in the house. How long have we had this house? It was nice of William to ask you to live with us. He is so considerate of family. Thomas is the same, isn't he? Just like his father. Ann, what time will William be home? We've got a roast and potatoes to put in."

CHAPTER THIRTY-ONE
ANN GEARE
1924

Thomas placed his father on a catafalque deep inside his consciousness. Each day was too full of learning the bank business and caring for his mother to allow the bubbling fountain of grief and guilt to squirm its way into his consciousness. He thought about getting home before Ann, checking on Julia, starting dinner. He knew this was an opportunity that would never come again. A chance to prove his strength *and* courage. He liked being the last one out the bank door at night. Maybe he would be the youngest vice president. Maybe he would get another client besides his friend Nathan Lucas.

Once home, he would eat dinner with Julia and Aunt Ann, tell them about his day at the bank, making up most of it. He now knew where Nathan's money was coming from, how he got the job. He'd feel a slight rustle of illegal air swirl through his office as Nathan made his daily deposit. But if he didn't take it, some other bank would. Nobody was hurt. A clean, profitable business. To Julia and Ann, he was helping a used furniture business get started on the south side, in their old neighborhood. He told them how he counted the cash, gave the receipt to Nathan, then took the elevator to the ninth floor and personally handed it to Albert Bredahl, the bank treasurer. Mr. Bredahl, a short, round, man in his mid fifties, counted the money with his shiny manicured hands. He compared his number to the one handed to him, nodded, muttered,

"Right again young man," then handed Thomas a deposit slip made out to the Lucas Used Furniture Emporium. From there, the money went into the bank's general funds to be invested in the booming stock market.

Julia and Ann loved hearing the same story every day. They would ask what Nathan was wearing when he came in. Was the money in a brief case, in a paper bag, was it in fives, tens, fiftys? What did

Mr. Bredhal smell like again? Too much after shave? What suit did he have on? Did he treat you OK? Do you ever see Mr. Penn?

On a cold November Friday night, Thomas arrived home from the bank at his usual hour, seven P.M.

"Mom, Mom, where are you? I'm home," Thomas yelled up the stairs expecting to see Julia standing at the top in her housedress, smiling down at him. As he stood in the front hall way, taking off his hat, silk muffler and long wool wrap overcoat, hanging them carefully under the front stairs, he heard his own frigid breath, his coat settling against the wall, and the wind picking its way down the fireplace chimney. Nothing else. Suddenly the front door slammed open against the wall.

"Here she is. I found her up on Knoxville, waiting for William. She has it in her head that he's at the grocery and is coming home on the number six."

Julia was in her light gabardine rain coat, Sunday church dress, lace gloves, hat and veil perched on the side of her head, oxford shoes, and a black leather pocketbook with two extra-large rubber binders tight around the clasp. She had been at the trolley stop since four that afternoon. Ann had come home at five thirty and knew immediately where to look.

"Come home Julia, he's not coming home. Remember, he died in May." Ann wrapped her arm around Julia's shoulder. "Let's go home now, Thomas will be home soon."

"Was I married long Ann? Was he sick?" Julia leaned into her older sister's angular body.

"Why can't I remember? Am I forgetting things too painful to remember? Am I becoming a strange person? Why can't I remember? What's wrong with me? You will always come after me, won't you Ann? I don't know how to stop forgetting."

Thomas and Ann sat at the kitchen table drinking coffee after eating dinner with Julia and being sure that she was safe in bed. He wanted to bring up Ann's retirement, but each time he looked over at her, he hesitated.

"It's not safe for her to take off like that. It's also not good for us worrying about what she'll do next."

Ann listened quietly, pulled the hairpins from the back of her down turned head and let the long white braid fall over her shoulder to rest in her hands. She slowly twisted it into three concentric circles. The outer circle carried Big Baby from the bathroom into her bed.

The next circle had priests walking along its edge, their hands held behind their backs, waiting for instructions. The inner most circle, the one that Ann dropped into her lap, was looped around Julia's waist.

"I will talk to the bishop tomorrow." Thomas saw tears in the corners of her eyes.

"Listen Ann, maybe she will be OK a while longer. I can come home earlier, maybe even come home at lunch once in a while."

"She's not going to get better, I know that Thomas. It's better with me here full time. I can retire with a small pension that the bishop has promised me. You can focus on your job then. Maybe you can look for that girl you talk about. Irene, is it? I really don't mind. I will just miss telling those men what to do with their money. They are such idiots sometimes." She stood, wiped her cheeks with a cotton hanky and looked out the kitchen window at the clouds whipping darkness into the kitchen. The room seemed to close around her as she stepped onto the back staircase. She turned, smiled at Thomas, who had both hands wrapped around his coffee cup, staring into the grounds. She realized that when time surprised her, she could easily predict her reactions. So many years of serving, waiting on others, nothing changed. In some quiet way, she welcomed the return of monotonous days.

Thomas looked up at the retreating Ann and thought he saw his mother's stooped shadow cast back by the bare bulb on the landing.

CHAPTER THIRTY-TWO THOMAS STONE

Thomas left the house full of thoughts about the upcoming day. His father was gone, Ann was home taking care of Julia. Nathan's furniture business delivered a steady cash flow to the bank. It stayed there long enough for the bank to float the buying and selling of a few select stocks at a profit. Today he had a second project, a chance to prove his worth to the bank officers.

A man his father's age had been sent to his office by Pearl Schwann from her position as receptionist to all coming into the bank.

"I want to talk to a loan officer about a business loan," Peter Stoll had told her.

"And what would the type of business be?" she asked cheerily. "It's a new venture. I have an idea on how to eliminate the mercury that steel mills generate in their smelting process."

"Um, sounds pretty technical. You can talk to Thomas Stone. He's one of our new managers. He can answer all your questions about the loan process. " Pearl had been with the bank for fifteen years and knew that they wouldn't give an idea like this ten minutes in a loan meeting. They spent all their time discussing the bank's investments in the stock market. She could have sent him to the Jefferson Bank, but she thought instead of the strange young man that was Thomas Stone's only visitor. He would certainly have time to give Mr. Stoll's request a well thought out answer.

Thomas met with Peter Stoll, listened to his request for money to fund his research. He sat across from Thomas, amazed that they both fit in the room with a desk, two chairs, a small book case full of text books: "Basics of Cash Flow," "Appraising the Risks of a Loan," "Accounting 101." The only other piece of furniture was a wire waste basket in the corner just behind Stoll's left shoulder. A small amount of reflected light came in from the shiny brick wall outside the lone window behind Thomas. Stoll squinted and thought briefly of the age of the man sitting across the desk who seemed to listen attentively, wondered, *how the hell is this kid going to help me?* But the fact that anyone was listening at all swept his doubts away. His hands opened and closed on what would have been a lap, but his thighs were a continuation of his stomach. He ran his right hand nervously across his thinning pate onto the back of his neck, through the loosely populated curly strands of white hair. Thomas told him that he didn't know much about the steel business, other than that they were in an expansion mode. But with the proper testing of his idea, a company such as Keystone might be interested.

"What we have to consider is the impact on their cash flow. How much do they have set aside for research? What would the cost be to implement a change in the smelting process? Do they really care about the impact that mercury has on the rivers? By the way, what impact does mercury have on rivers?"

Peter Stoll spoke in short bursts, noisy exhales of breath through his mouth, breaking the rhythm.

"I would be happy to take you to the inlet,"….."where waste is dumped from Keystones furnaces,"….."into the Illinois River."….. "There are no fish, no frogs, no lilly pads, no foliage, period."….. "There is a reddish white scum bubbling along the shore where the pipes enter the water."….. Peter Stoll's voice rose as he ended, breathed deeply, face reddened and his hands clenched as he described the river. Thomas sat back, amused and afraid at the same time for this slightly deranged man.

"And, Mr. Stoll, the most important question for myself and the bank is your ability to repay the loan. Do you have any collateral, any relatives that could co-sign for the loan?"

Peter Stoll looked at his still clenched hands, sat back in his chair,

"I've never thought about that. Isn't that what a bank is for, loan the money to me because I don't have it?"

"The bank needs some guarantee that if the process doesn't pay off, the original funds will be repaid. The riskier the loan, the more guarantees we need. You see that, don't you?"

"Sure, sure. Give me a few days, I'll see what I can come up with." Thomas thought about how the success of one venture like this would solidify his future at the bank.

"Sometimes, if we really believe in a venture, we can reduce or waive the collateral, but that only happens in rare cases. You see what you can do on the collateral issue. Come back next week and I'll see what I can do."

Peter Stoll hated the bank for putting him in the position of asking his son and daughter for help, but he believed this young man would do what he said.

"Mr. Stone, I appreciate your time. I will see what I can do about collateral."

Today would be their second meeting. Thomas jumped off the trolley eager to get to his office. He waited for the car to roll away to its next stop, turned to look down the street, still moist from an early morning rain, at the spot where his father had died. He did this every day, knew that the look was automatic, he could not stop his head from turning and saying to himself,

"He's gone, I'm on my own now." It set his resolve for the day, tearing a piece of anger from his stomach and waving it in front of his eyes.

"This is how I get through the day."

William's friends had told him of how his father died, calling for Julia. He had buried that story along with other pain inside a growing mountain that had turned into magma flowing down Main St., headed for the brick that William had stood on as the trolley smashed into his legs.

"Why didn't he stay home? Julia needed him, now she's slipped into her own prison. She won't come back. She's too old to come back. Thank God for Ann. Always there to take care of somebody else. Never thinking of what's best for her. People are one or the other. Just for themselves or just for others. The pendulum sticks on one side. No balance, no gradual swing to balance the moments. You're born with a side. Ann is a helper, Dad was a helper. Plenty of people in the bank are on the other side, looking out for themselves. He cared more about mom than anything, but he still went. How could he know his heart would give out? How do I know his heart gave out?'

Tinnitus started in each ear and drove wavy lights across his eyes. He stood paralyzed as the morning crowds moved slowly by him.

"Honor, courage, both unknown until he saw a break in the wall he walked behind all his life. He saw the hole, stepped through it, grasping and squeezing until Julia's name formed on his lips as his chest froze and the trolley smashed into him. Where is my courage? Where is my honor?'

He started across the street, but was slapped in the face by a returning wind carrying his father's blood and orange odor. His foot felt like cement and fell heavily onto the dark silver rail that he had purposefully stepped over for the past two years. He turned to the right and saw the departing trolley pass through the image of his father. William held the hammer high over his head with one hand and clutched his chest with the other. His eyes were moving rapidly from side to side until they settled in a line directly into his son's bewildered eyes.

"I'm not gone, I'm dead. You're the one now. You take over. I've done my best. It's your turn. Listen for the words."

Suddenly, Thomas felt himself being pulled by a grip on the neck of his suit jacket. His feet automatically started to back pedal and his arms swung out as they often did when guarding an opponent on the basketball floor. He began to fall backwards as the #4 trolley pulled to a stop in the spot he had just vacated. He was afraid to look around to see who had pulled him off the track.

"It can't be him, it can't."

CHAPTER THIRTY-THREE
SAFETY

Thomas looked back up into the sun and saw a dark figure holding his coat, pulling him across the bricks to the sidewalk.

"You were going to die," a voice said, coming out of the sun, shaking his head as he stepped up on the sidewalk, brushing Thomas's coat back into place on his shoulders. A small crowd started to applaud.

"Good thinking," "Great hands," "Way to go."

Thomas was rocking between the vision of his father, a cold silent energy, and the cacophony of the morning rush with trolleys, horses, Model T's, squealing and belching into the morning mist that hung over the street. Out of this confusion stepped Ralph Capone.

"I came to see you. Nathan said you would be here. I didn't expect to be back in a battle, especially with something as big and dangerous as that damn trolley. Are you OK? We should go into the Brown Sugar and get a cup of coffee." Thomas didn't say anything, nodded his head, and followed Ralph through the diner's door to the booth that Ralph had just left.

"Back again, guess you couldn't stay away," a blonde waitress said to Ralph between smacks of gum.

"What will it be? Coffee, black with two sugars, right? And your rumpled friend here? Looks like he needs more than coffee."

Thomas forced his response, "Coffee please, cream and sugar."

He took his glasses off and wiped them with his pocket handkerchief.

"Shouldn't wipe glass with a dry cloth, you'll scratch the surface," Ralph said with a touch of sarcasm.

"Thanks for the tip, and thanks for saving my life. I was thinking about what I have to do today, guess I got too involved," Thomas lied, stopped wiping his glasses, put them back on his head, one ear at a time.

"This is a little weird, now that I saved your life, I have to warn you about saving your own," Ralph continued.

The Waitress delivered two cups of coffee, Thomas picked his up, twirled it slowly between his hands, half listening to the words coming from across the table, hearing instead his own internal monologue:

"I guess it was you that set me up in the bank. I didn't want to admit I was working with Chicago. Even indirectly through Nathan. Now you're here to put the squeeze on, ask me to kill somebody, right? I knew it was too good to last. I'll never be a banker. It's over now, I'll never kill. I'll just resign, go to the steel mill. "

"Stone, Stone, are you listening? Did you hit your head when I jerked you away from the trolley? Christ, kid, pay attention. Here's the deal. I'm leaving the furniture business, so to speak. I'm on my way west from here. New opportunities."

Thomas stared out the window to the sidewalk, lost amongst the bank, his father's glare, the steel mill, and this man sitting across the table that Thomas would be happy never to see again.

"Ah," was all he could say as he looked into the black grounds receding into the bottom of the coffee cup.

"I just wanted to tell you that Nathan is continuing as my man here, and as long as the money keeps going through the bank, you'll both be fine. My brother has forgotten you two, other things are on his mind. Once he discovers that I've gone, he'll look for me for a while and then forget that I was ever around. That's the dangerous time. Just be sure everything runs smoothly for the next few months."

"Why are you leaving?" Thomas asked but really didn't care, he felt relief that this man would be gone from his life. The question was meant to show that it really didn't matter to him one way or the other.

"Nathan's not the only one that came back from France with a problem. The war isn't over for me. It may never be. Bullets sound like hornets. When I hear a gun, or a car start, or backfire, I feel them crawling on my face. Next thing I know, I'm in a corner shivering, even in the summer. Helping you and Nathan was good for me. I understood for the first time what doing something for somebody else could do. Maybe I should have kept you out of it entirely, but I didn't know how. My brother would have found some other way to bring you in if I had refused."

Thomas nodded his head after every sentence, not really understanding how difficult it was for Ralph to break the co-dependant relationship he had with his brother.

"Now," Ralph paused and sighed,

"Remember Nathan's sister, Irene?"

"Yes, I remember." Thomas's heart froze.

"She's back home."

"Oh, where has she been?" Thomas asked quietly as if Irene was the furthest person from his mind.

"She's been in Chicago with a magazine, but it didn't work out. She came on the train with me last night. Nice girl. Talked a little about you and the basketball game. You should look her up."

"Right, right, maybe I'll do that. Did you say she's at home? Maybe I'll do that. Listen, Ralph, It's been real good talking to you, but I have to go, I have a meeting in a few minutes. Thanks for the tip, or maybe I should say warning. And thanks for saving my life. And good luck wherever you go."

They shook hands.

"Good bye."

"Good bye."

Neither of them knew what was going to happen next. With each step out the door of the Brown Sugar, they felt the void of freedom chipping at the masoned walls of fear that they had built to survive in their own worlds. Ralph jumped into a model A and disappeared around the corner. Thomas stepped carefully out into the street, looked to the right, saw nothing, ran across the street into the bank building.

Mr. Stoll stood outside his door.

"Morning, sorry I'm late, c'mon in. Have a seat."

Thomas looked at his watch, 9:15, Nathan would be in at 11. He might have to wait.

"I have what you want. I hated asking, but my son will use his stock portfolio to back me. A year ago, he was asking me for rent money. Now I go to him. He says there is plenty to cover me in case we don't sell the process. Of course, he wants a percentage. A real businessman. Quite a change from working in a haberdashery. He goes to the broker every day. I tell him to put some of his money in real estate, but he says he does fine with the market. Doesn't pay attention to me any more. I think the only reason he's doing this is because he thinks he'll make some money."

Thomas half listened, nodded periodically, and realized that Mr. Stoll was speaking without huffing. Amazing what a little money will do. The rest of his thoughts were on Nathan's visit, what about Irene? Was she OK? How soon would he see her?

"That's great Mr. Stoll. Here are the papers you need to have your son sign and have notarized. They basically say that in case you default on the loan, your son will sign over enough of his portfolio to cover your default amount. I will go to the committee as soon as you bring them back."

Ruby Schwann opened the elevator door on the main floor. Nathan Lucas nodded and pinched his fedora as he stepped up into the elevator, not sure if she would close the gate on him.

"Morning, Ruby."

"Morning. That you Mr. Lucas? Sometimes I can't tell with that stupid hat pulled down on your head so tight. Early today, aren't you?" as she slid the gate into place and started the elevator on its journey to the second floor.

"Where's your satchel? It's usually tight to your body like it was about to run away all by itself."

"Yes, Ruby, I am early, news for Thomas." He replied with a slight smile, aware that the repartee with Ruby was the highlight of her day.

"Hope it's good. He looked pretty distracted when he came in. Late too. You're early, he's late, must be a full moon."

"We're, here, Ruby, you can open the door."

"So we are, so we are. Very observant, Mr. Lucas."

She slammed the metal gate to the side, and pulled the wooden door open with a very un-lady like grunt. Nathan stepped out into the dark corridor onto Peter Stoll's foot.

"Sorry, mister, didn't see you there," Nathan apologized and brushed past the agitated Peter Stoll.

"If you looked up from the ground, it would help," Stoll said to the swiftly moving figure.

"Damn young people," he muttered under his breath, "no respect."

Nathan rushed through the door without knocking, almost sliding into the chair in front of Thomas' desk. Half rising, Thomas said,

"Nathan, you're early. That's OK, no other appointments this morning. Glad you're here."

Nathan reached over his shoulder and pushed the door shut.

He turned and looked out the small window just over Thomas' shoulder. The window was in line with nine others rising directly to the tenth floor where the windows increased dramatically in size. His view was a brick wall with identical windows twenty feet away.

When the sun shone, Thomas could tell the time of day and year by the amount of light coming through the window. Today was October 5, his birthday, he was twenty-one years old. The sun was at ten o'clock, just above the spire on top of the bank building, shining directly into the window across the courtyard. The quivering golden light reflected back onto Thomas's desk, and moved slowly from Thomas' side in a line that would end in Nathan's lap before it disappeared. Nathan had watched the march before, always felt compelled to finish his business before the room lost its only source of natural light. His own love of photography came back on those days when the light loosened the shadows and depth of pattern in the wood on the desk. It was in those brief moments that he knew his war had not ended. It was dormant somewhere in his soul waiting for the frantic pace of working for the mob in Chicago to come to an end. Then he would find his way again through the revelations of images given up only through his understanding of light.

Neither spoke, waiting for the other to start. Thomas clenched and unclenched his hands, rolling a wad of paper and finally throwing it over Nathan's shoulder into the wire waste basket in the corner,

"You're the only one that moves the chair in the right direction. Everybody else blocks my shot to the corner," Thomas said with a shrug.

"I'm glad I can be of help keeping your hand-eye co-ordination sharp," Nathan shot back. He was wearing a new three piece pinstripe suit and his hair was slicked back.

"All you'd need is a pair of glasses and I would ask your opinion about a new loan strategy," Thomas smiled, avoiding his real question.

"Wouldn't give him a cent, if you're talking about the old man that just left here. He can't move to the left very well. How is it we always end up talking about basketball?" Nathan was getting visibly agitated with the small talk.

Thomas said, "What about…" and stopped, not sure what he should ask about first; the missing bag or Irene. Nathan stood up, started walking back and forth.

"Irene came home last night. We knew she was in Chicago,

working for that magazine. But she never wrote, didn't seem to care if we knew she was OK or not. You know, it's almost killed dad, 'first you, now Irene," he would say. Mom just complained more about men, 'she's probably run into some controlling man, won't let her write or call us.' Then she shows up after two years. Ralph Capone was with her. Says he met her on the train and was just giving her a ride home from the station. He pulled me outside and said he was through with his brother and the business. Said we had to keep things smooth, and then we'd be OK. Then he takes off, didn't even come in. Probably better, cause Mom really lit into Irene. Called her a whore, a slut, a few words I had never heard before. Dad just sat there, didn't say a word. He's just about had it. I don't know who she hates more, me, Dad, Irene, or men in general. It's almost like Irene had stayed in Chicago just to get away from her. Irene didn't say a word the whole time. Sat there like Dad. He's just glad she's home. I can't say I much care one way or the other. Except she knows about the business, almost as much as we do. " Nathan slumped into the chair, slid it to the left and watched the sun's reflected light hit the door.

"Well, how is she? Is she OK? Did she say anything about me?" Thomas blurted out his own concerns.

"She's twenty one going on forty one. I don't know if she's OK. Hasn't changed much as far as I can tell. Yes, she asked how my 'banker friend,' was doing. I think that's you. But here's the deal, Thomas, my banker friend," Nathan's voice lowered and he grasped the edge of the desk.

"She wants to be part of the game. 'I can help,' she says. 'Help deliver the money, you pick it up, I'll take it to the bank. When can I start?' Takes it for granted that I'll do as she says. I told her I would talk to you first. That you and I would decide if she fits in. You and I both know that this works because the cops look the other way. The runners give the beat guys a few bucks and all is well. We don't have the big payoffs like Chicago, but who knows if that will continue. It's clean and safe so far. With Ralph gone to start a new life though, it could get rough. Maybe we should get out."

"Nathan, the reason I have this job is because of the booze, I'm just to the point that I may be able to contribute something of my own to the bank. I'm just a guy hidden away on the second floor. Ruby sees me more than anybody and she's the god damned elevator operator. We have to hold on to this a while longer. Prohibition can't last forever. This "job" you have won't last forever. What we need is time and a little luck. And I sure don't want Irene involved in any way with this business. Why don't I talk to her. She just wants to be part of a family again. Make some contribution."

Nathan looked at his friend, *I wonder if he knows what he's in for?*

"Ask her if she will meet me at the Rialto theatre tonight at seven. There is a new F.W. Murnau movie she might like. Will you do that?" Thomas asked.

"Fine, let's see what you can do with her. Sure doesn't seem to matter what I do," Nathan replied.

CHAPTER THIRTY-FOUR
SUNRISE
1927

Thomas arrived at the Rialto theatre at six forty-five, fifteen minutes before the main attraction, F. W. Murnau's new film, "*Sunrise,*" was to start. Nathan had taken him to see "*Nosferatu*" to show him the lighting techniques used to depict fear and superstition. But he remembered nothing of the dramatic shadows, only the long bony fingers of the Vampire clasping Greta as he suckled her neck.

Perhaps "*Sunrise,*" a story of love shared, love taken away by a wicked third person, and love finally returned after a severe testing, would hold the same erotic undertones as the rest of his films. Irene would certainly see the parallels between the artistry of this great director and their own brief relationship. And she certainly would be flattered by his comparison of her to the lead character played by Janet Gaynor.

"Where are you going tonight?" Ann asked as he combed his hair in front of the mirror in the dining room.

"I'm going to meet Irene Lucas at the new Murnau film," he said with a smile and a quick glance to see how Ann would react.

"Someday, I would like to see a movie. But I'll bet they're not as exciting as my books. I think it's great that she's come back. Maybe you could bring her over sometime. I'd love to meet her, and so would Julia. We could have a little picnic in the back yard, it would do your mother good." Ann leaned on the screen door as Thomas walked to the garage and backed the Ford out to the street. She moved back into the kitchen and slowly started to set the table for two.

CHAPTER THIRTY-FIVE
IRENE LUCAS

A large crowd surrounded the ticket kiosk under the flashing red, white and blue bulbs that illuminated the plastic letters, "Sunrise." The street was full of horse drawn carts moving in an adversarial dance with Model A's and every now and then, a new Cadillac. Irene wondered when the horses would disappear from the city, finally eradicated by fire and smoke belching exhausts. So many changes in the last few years. It was truly a modern age born of industrial power.

She stood motionless in the middle of a group, unsure as to whether she was in the ticket buyer's line or the ticket holder's line.

"I don't know. I want to buy a ticket. It's not very well marked. They obviously aren't used to big crowds," a matronly woman said sarcastically to Irene.

"I could certainly give them a few tips on organization, what a waste."

Irene ignored the swirling banter, confident that Thomas would spot her. She wore the same silk dress and cloche hat pulled down over her ears that she had worn in Chicago on the night of the championship game. On this morning she had her mother trim her hair to look just as it did at the basketball game.

She had entered the house last night to the same darkness that she had left. No voices. Breezes blew at odd angles between rooms never intersecting. Bodies within touching distance excluded intimacy. Even Nathan's recovery of his voice did nothing to warm the eyes of his parents. To Robert and Susan Lucas, his recovery had come at too great a loss. Even now with Irene's return, their frozen anger at each other would not thaw.

"Same length as my boy friends," Irene told her mother. "Mine's a little wavier in the front, but it's the same in the back."

"He's hardly your boyfriend, honey. You certainly don't think he's waited for you to come back, do you? Nathan says he's doing quite well at the bank, probably has a dozen girls like you waiting for him on the corner every morning."

"Nathan says he wants to see me. That's all I need," Irene spat back at her mother.

"Sounds like he's a lot happier to have me back than you are."

"Listen, Irene, I'm glad you're back. Sorry I yelled at you, I just blamed you for making me feel bad. "

"Yeah, something you usually reserve for Dad."

A cold quiet spread through the room. Then, Susan Lucas said,

"Keep your wits. He may be good for you in some ways."

Irene stood in front of the theatre thinking of her mother's words as she imagined what could come from a marriage to a successful young banker. Chicago hadn't worked the way she wanted. She wasn't in control. Better that she got out of there when she did. Get a new start.

She heard Thomas pushing himself through the noisy crowd.

"Excuse me, sorry, I'm joining my friend."

Irene turned in the direction of Thomas's voice and looked into the eyes of a slightly taller woman. Something about her was familiar, but the effort to remember was pushed aside as Thomas came into view. Irene did not notice the woman reach up under her hat.

She pulled out a single edged barber's razor, opened it with a single flick of her wrist as if she had been using it for years. Thomas had his hand up to reach for Irene, but pulled it back as he saw the blade start an arc towards Irene's neck. He rammed his fist into the bone and soft flesh of the woman's temple. The blade altered its line and caught Irene at the corner of her left eye and traced a fine red line down her cheek, leaving the skin at the corner of her jaw just below her ear lobe. The woman fell against Irene, dropping them into a pile of tangled silk and cotton. The woman's two hats flew off her head and settled in the dirt brushed up against the ticket kiosk. Irene opened her mouth, but no sound came out as Thomas jammed one hand against the attacker's throat, while the other hand carefully pulled the razor from the woman's hand, closed the blade into its bone sheath, and slid it into his pocket. He pulled a white handkerchief from the breast pocket of his suit coat and gently placed it against the line on Irene's cheek from which a dark red fluid dripped onto the ground. She looked up at Thomas, her head tilted to the side. Her words were barely audible as if they were escaping from a grave that had just been opened.

"She hit me, I didn't do anything to her. He left on his own, I didn't make him leave."

"Shh, it's OK, I'm here," Thomas whispered, then looked up to see the crowd back away in a tight waltz, caught in a silken web spun by the lady with two hats, waiting to see the next move of the conjoined figures on the ground.

He looked up and pleaded with his eyes for another hand as the attacker struggled against the hold on her neck.

"Damn it, somebody help me with this woman. Call the police."

Nobody in the crowd moved or spoke as if they were afraid they would be the next victim. Suddenly the theatre manager appeared from behind the ticket kiosk.

"The police and an ambulance are coming. Bring the young woman into my office. I've got this one."

The crowd broke apart, focused quickly on improving their place in line.

"Will the movie start on time? We have to be home by ten."

The manager looked up to the sarcastic woman as he pulled the attacker towards his office, and said, "Of course, we are always on time. Do you have your ticket? The seven o clock show is sold out."

CHAPTER THIRTY-SIX
JAMES CONLIN

"Then what did you do?" Jimmy Conlin sat in the corner of the heavy velvet couch, pulled at the edge of the beige doily under his hand. He was home from the seminary in St. Paul for the Thanksgiving holiday. Thomas had told him how Ralph Capone had saved his life, his plan to disappear, how Capone had accidentally met Irene on the train.

"Did the police come?"

"They came, took that deranged woman to the station, but didn't do anything." Thomas answered. "Irene wouldn't sign a complaint. She said the woman obviously needed help and wouldn't get it at the police station. Irene knew who she was. I think she felt sorry for her. It was Ralph Capone's wife. Somehow, she figured Irene was to blame for all her troubles. She followed Ralph to the train station, saw them together, and assumed it was Irene that was taking her husband away. She must have followed Irene to the theatre. The woman's nuts. And get this, the police drove her back to Chicago."

"Maybe Mrs. Capone was right. Maybe Irene was shacked up with her husband. How else would Irene know that Ralph was fooling around?" Jimmy asked.

"Irene says she hadn't seen Ralph since the game."

"Do you really believe that?" Jimmy asked incredulously.

"I believe what she tells me."

"You are a fool."

"It's really none of your business. Don't you care about how Irene is? She's the one that was attacked. I'll tell you. She had ten stitches in the side of her face. She will have a scar, but it won't be obvious with the way that she wears her hair. Do you want a drink? You can still have a drink? Can't you?"

"I'm in the seminary, not a prison. Yes, I will have a drink." Thomas went to the kitchen, poured two glasses half full of Canadian whiskey, put two ice cubes into each glass, and returned to face his interrogator.

"How long will you be home?"

"I'm taking the train back to St. Paul tomorrow. Want to come? I think I can talk the chancellor into giving you a chance at the priesthood if you change your sinful ways."

"Fuck you. What's this I hear about Rome? I hear from Tony that they may be sending you there. What would you do? Sweep the catacombs?"

"No, that job is taken. I would go to Canon Law school."

"You mean, become a lawyer priest? What a great combination." Thomas said swirling the melting ice to distribute the water evenly through his whiskey.

"They want me to focus on canon law, especially annulment. It's the next big parish issue, right after murder and bootlegging. What are you going to do next? You've got a lot going on right now. Most of which sounds a little illegal and more than a little dangerous. And I'm not here to keep you out of trouble."

"Who kept who out of trouble? I don't remember you knocking the shit out of Dempsey and Cobb. That was me."

"Tommy, what do you want? A wife, a job, a house?"

"I want my freedom. Irene's my chance. I am sick of all the rules, don't do this, don't do that. A lot of the rules you'll be enforcing in a few years, along with refusing annulments."

"If I said that you were free to dive to the bottom of the Illinois river, win a hundred dollars for bringing up a clam shell, do you know what would happen? Don't guess. You would drown, you don't know how to swim. Being free doesn't mean doing what you want without paying for it. It means taking responsibility for what you do, and sometimes what other people do. Irene and a lot of other girls her age, say "modern," "free."

Thomas interrupted, "Our age, Conlin, it's our age."

The future priest pressed on. "What she means is that it doesn't matter. If she can get away with it, there are no consequences. She wants to wear loose clothes, smoke in public, drink with you, have sex, without paying. But you know who'll pay? You Tommy, you'll pay."

"You sound awfully old, Jimmy. You'll give some great sermons. I'm going to have another drink, want one?"

"Fill it up, I've got nowhere to go."

The house was quiet. Julia was asleep in her bedroom, Ann was visiting a friend. Jimmy Conlin and Tommy Stone were having a quiet struggle to show each other that they were both right. They only needed to explain it to each other as best they could and they would leave confident that each had left the other impressed with his resolve.

"I'm going to marry her," Tommy said as he returned with two full whiskey glasses.

"Do you really think you can satisfy this woman?"

"First time you've called her a woman."

"Listen Tommy, I know more about sex than you do and I'm in the seminary. Somehow, your Mom and Dad, God rest their souls, kept you from the shit in the streets, but you missed some of the good lessons. I grew up on the street, watched my Mom and her paying customers. I'm going to be a priest because of what I saw. I'm going to help people that can't control their own destructive desires. I've seen too many cuts and ugly bruises in my own house. I want to help people past their physical pain to reach their souls. You missed all that, but it meant you missed learning how to take care of yourself with women."

"You'll make a good priest, Jimmy, all that practical experience will make you meaningful in a parish."

"Don't get smart, I still have Irish guilt, I'm not immune to thoughts, but I know where to stop. You've got guilt too, but you haven't started learning how to handle it. If she doesn't get what she wants, she'll find it someplace else."

"I can give her a home, the latest clothes, the chance to play the market. What else could she want?"

"You're a smart guy Tommy," Jimmy paused, "In some ways. In others, you're just plain stupid."

The sound of old gray bones filled the room as they looked past each other for the truth in their choices. Nothing appeared. No ghosts, no spirits, no signs.

CHAPTER THIRTY-SEVEN
LEDGER ENTRY

Thomas walked out to the garage, waved to the Walker's five year old boy who was hanging from the lowest limb of a crab apple tree.

"Careful there bub, don't fall."

"I won't Mr. Stone. I'm pretty strong for my age."

Thomas liked being called "Mr. Stone." Even if it was from a five year old. But today, it went unnoticed. His mind was on the conversation he had just had with Jimmy Conlin.

"Nothing makes sense. Jimmy says I'm a fool. Can't blame him. He's off sitting in a dorm room, idealizing his life, thinking about other people. Knows exactly who he is."

He looked to the right at the clapboard garage butted up to his backyard. Red and green rhubarb stalks lined the base of the garage from the front edge all the way to the cinder alley. He wondered who planted it. Maybe it was wild. Like Irene, just there. *"I know I want to marry her, nothing else matters. We can live here, in the back bedroom. Mom can stay in the front looking for Dad to come home. Ann can move to the middle room. Then we can have a little privacy."*

The door to the garage was stuck. He forced it open and walked over the freshly swept wood floor.

"Ann's been here."

He opened the wood box under the Gipp's beer case, and lifted the top ledger out. He rubbed his hand across the front cover, around the spine. He thought he felt two other sets of hands squirming under the back cover. He had placed his grandfather's story of the Atlantic crossing and one of his father's distinctive pages of grocery transactions carefully behind the end paper when he started recording his own thoughts. He pulled them out and read them as he did every time he wanted to write about his own life.

This was all he knew about his grandfather. Too bad his Dad didn't tell him more about his family in Ireland. They were Americans now. No sense talking about the past. Got to work hard here.

Thomas sat down and started to write.

October 10, 1927

"I have my own life. Feels good to put it down on a piece of paper. Put it away, come back later to see what I wrote. Sort of seals the actual event under the weight of the words. Then I don't worry about it. Got rid of Dempsey and Cobb that way. I know I had as much to do with their disappearance as Dad did. I wrote it and they went away. Doesn't always work though. Says on July 8, 1927, 'Dad come home tonight from the steel rally.' He didn't. On September 1, 1927, I wrote, 'Mom's back.' She's not. She's still waiting for him. Sometimes she doesn't even know who I am. Maybe I can make things happen. Sure can't change what's past. Now I have choices. The job's OK, I like working in the bank, wearing a suit. The formality of it all gives me a sense of security, but it could be a thin layer. I see men leave once in a while that never come back. Rumor is that they were caught stealing or fooling around with a secretary in the washroom. Thing is, they just disappear. No security there. My job is a half job. One client. One possible new client. I study but they don't seem interested in giving me new responsibility. But I can handle this, it's a steady income, and the way the market is, I may be able to make a few investments of my own pay off. The real fear I have is Irene. That's right, I love her and I am afraid of her. Something in that sideways look of hers says, 'Be careful mister, I love you, but I'll do what's best for me.' She doesn't say it out loud, but I feel it. Nathan tolerates her. Her Mom and Dad don't talk to her. If I get her out of that house, she'll see how much I love her and she will change. Not so suspicious. Trust me, that's what I want. I want her to trust me. Better tell Jimmy that's what I want. Irene's trust. I can take care of her. She'll see that in this house. People trust each other here. They love each other and don't ask for reasons or anything in return. Once she meets Ann, she will see real devotion and caring. She may even want to help out with Mom. This could be her chance.

Thomas had written his prediction, his hope. It had worked before. He believed it would happen again.

The sound of old gray bones came for the second time that day in the leaves of the pin oak as they leaned against each other in the early fall wind. He could hear the faint whistle of a freight train leaving its river stop on the way to the steel mill that he blamed for his father's death. Writing it down hadn't stopped the killing. He recorded these thoughts not thinking of another ever reading them. They were his, no one else's.

CHAPTER THIRTY-EIGHT
AL CAPONE
1927

He stood, turned to the man on his right, and slammed his fist on the table. Spit flew from his mouth as he spoke.

"I know he's gone. I won't do anything about that. But I'm not going to let the scheme he set up in Peoria go on. Send a few guys down there. Take out the runner. Lucas, that's his name. Leave the kid in the bank. We can still use him."

"What about the girl?" Asked Malone, wiping his face with the back of his hand.

"Leave her alone. Let her watch him die."

CHAPTER THIRTY-NINE
NATHAN LUCAS

The Model T Ford roared down the middle of the newly poured macadam two lane road. Thomas drove on the crown of the road careful not to stray to either side. Inflorescent corn hung over the edges of the two lanes striking the sides of the car if he strayed from the imaginary middle line that he tried to follow. Dust was laid on the dashboard each time the car moved left or right in the early morning wind. His mind was made up. That morning he would ask Robert Lucas for Irene's hand in marriage. He drove down the hill past Bradley park, looked at the sliding hill that his father had brought him to in past winters. A good run was down the hill, across left field, and ending on the pitcher's mound.

It was easy now. Get married, but in what church? Irene said she was Catholic. But the Lucas family didn't belong to a parish, didn't go to church as far as he knew. Maybe St. Bernard's. Yes. That would be it. Father Salmon would marry them. Maybe Nathan would be the best man since Jimmy would probably be on his way, if not already in Rome. It seemed easier without Conlin.

The slow beat of cricket wings bounced through the air, reached his ears at the same time that dragon flies splattered against the wind screen. Hope was in the corn tassels ready to fall to the dark clods of moist dirt. He remembered his father telling him that if went out on a hot August night and watched carefully, he would see the corn grow. But the sound of the insects battered his sense of confidence as he focused on finding the road leading to Irene's house.

A sound of hornet's climbing and diving came from the road as it wound through the forest of corn. He took his foot off the gas and shifted into second gear, feeling the grinding that said he hadn't waited long enough before moving the gear shift. Dust rose over the corn on the left as an enclosed black Ford burst out of the fields, swerving back towards downtown Peoria. Thomas jerked the wheel to the right and collapsed four rows of corn stalks before he came to a stop. Between the shifting gears of the speeding Ford, he thought he hear the sound of laughter. He pulled the car carefully out of the field and turned into the road that led to the Lucas house. His heart was flying ten feet in front of the Ford emitting a steady beat that drowned out the sound of the scraping gears. His own dust surrounded the car as he pulled to a stop in front of the Lucas porch. He was relieved and horrified at the same time by the vision of Irene holding Nathan in her lap, rocking back and forth trying to stop the blood that flowed from his chest. Nathan's mouth was open at an odd angle, his eyes staring at the sun. Robert and Susan stood over them, not moving. Their son was gone for the second time.

Mosquito's swarmed around Nathan's body then alighted on Irene's bare feet.

"He's dead, he's dead," Irene repeated slowly as she as she slapped her ankles with blood soaked hands. Thomas reached out to her and she said,

"No, don't touch us, he's dead. I didn't stop them. I was too late. It's all my fault. I should never have gone to Chicago. It's all my fault."

Thomas and Irene were married one month later at St. Bernard's Church. Monsignor John Salmon presided over the ceremony. Robert Lucas gave the bride away and acted as the best man. Ann Stone was the maid of honor. Thomas and Irene moved into the back bedroom at 606 East Illinois Avenue.

CHAPTER FORTY
IRENE STONE
SEPTEMBER 1929

Indian summer lingered under the red sugar maple leaves in the spaces between the bricks on Illinois Avenue. Irene could feel the dry heat rising from under the leaves sweep up through her skirt and down the backs of her legs. The slight breeze against her cheek blew from New Orleans carrying droplets of gulf moisture. She reached up to wipe her forehead with a lace handkerchief.

"A few more days of this and I can switch to my new fox collared jacket," she thought as she considered how long she had before Thomas came home from work. Was there time to get to the brokers office on Knoxville and Main and back again?

She was the proud owner of a growing stock portfolio, all bought on loans from her broker. On her way to independence. Resourceful, willing to put up with the two old women that shared her house and husband. Her own mother had died in the spring of 1929 when her lungs collapsed from tuberculosis.

"Make sure you have money," were the last words coughed into Irene's ear as she lay dying in the Ottawa sanatorium. She guessed at how her father felt about his wife's death. *"He's probably glad to have her off his back. No more icicle stares in the morning, bitching about the lack of money."* She heard her mother say to her father, just before she died,

"You should have stopped them, put your body in front of his. We'd all be better off." She visited her father and saw him avoid the empty shadows filling the house. Gradually he started avoiding the chairs that Nathan and Susan had sat in. Then he stepped over rugs that he had seen them stand on. Rooms that held their voices were closed off. Within a few weeks of his wife's death, Robert was relegated to walking in sweeping curves through his house, sitting on a lone chair and sleeping in the kitchen on a cot brought in from the still. It was then that he started visiting Irene and the Stone's every Sunday after they had attended mass, bringing a single bottle of clear liquid inside a brown paper sack. He would hand it quickly to Thomas with a wink, "I'll just have a little glass in the living room. Will you join me?"

Every Sunday, after they had swallowed the hot liquid and Robert had left, Thomas took the bottle to the basement and put it in a box under the steps to the kitchen with a growing collection that would stay undisturbed for over thirty years. The two men would sit on the couch through the afternoon, drinking coffee laced with the gin, telling stories about the grocery on Second Avenue. The three women seemed to disappear into some hidden corner of the house. Robert and Thomas spoke of Dempsey and Cobb who were evil with no qualities worth mentioning. William Stone was a hero, wiser and braver each Sunday. Nathan was the war hero that never recovered and was assassinated by hoodlums at the peak of his life. Robert never mentioned his deceased wife and Thomas never asked about her. He respected Robert for the way he handled his grief inside, never showing pain or expressing concern about his difficult life. The last question every Sunday was,

"Time to start a family, don't you think, Thomas? Make me a proud grandfather. I'll spoil the heck out of the kid. See you next week."

These last words were said as he walked down the steps to his car, always before the priests and nuns arrived for their coffee and pie that Ann had prepared.

As Irene put her handkerchief back in her purse, she decided she had time to get to the broker and back again. She was sure that Thomas would never find out about the size of her separate account. After all, it was he that *gave* her the shares of Anaconda that he bought just after their wedding. She could do what she wanted with them. She had spread her portfolio by borrowing against the Anaconda, buying stocks that had strong names, Bethlehem Steel, American Locomotive, and selling them before the loans came due. Risky, but Mr. Barrett encouraged her to be aggressive, sure that her husband would cover any mistakes she might make. And she still had access to their joint account at the First Bank, where Thomas kept more conservative stocks.

The trips to the brokers office were made under the pretext of going to the beauty parlor, shopping at Bergner's, going to see her father, or just going for a walk. The walks were used only when she was sure that Ann and Julia wouldn't want to go. Having to share the single bathroom was bad enough, let alone the suggestion of spending time with them outside the house. Dinners were spent in silence. Julia looking out the kitchen window, Ann waiting patiently for Irene to say anything, Irene glancing at Thomas, then back at her food, and Thomas talking about how boring his job was.

"Mr. Stoll's been written off by the loan committee. Something about 'focus,' is what Mr. Penn said. I went right up to him after the loan committee rejected my proposal. He told me he wanted me to stay focused, make sure the cash continued to flow in. He's probably right, there's a new guy every month bringing in the dough. I spend my time training them how to bring the money into the bank. It's like teaching somebody how to tie their shoes when they wear loafers."

Irene walked down the steps without saying goodbye to Julia or Ann.

There was less and less conversation between Irene and the two sisters. Ann left her alone, hoping that she would slowly open up, maybe even offer to help around the house. Irene figured the old women had given in. That they realized she had won. Thomas was hers now. Soon they would move out of this three bedroom, one bathroom house, out to banker's row on Grandview drive overlooking the Illinois River Valley. Then the old women would have a wing to themselves. If Irene was lucky, she would nod to them as they passed each other in the halls.

She knew that Thomas saw nothing of this. As far as he was concerned, the women in his life were getting along fine. He seemed oblivious to the way Irene ignored the two older women. He didn't even seem concerned about the recent lack of sex.

At first, Irene had seemed eager to put a towel under the door, cover the floor vents with thick rugs, turn up the radio, and enjoy the warm moist caresses of his hands and tongue, but he never seemed to last long enough for her. She wanted him to follow different angles, move to another part of the room, but he wouldn't leave the single bed and was very careful of noises that might rise over the music from the radio on the night stand, on the way to the other bedrooms in the house. He was quickly satisfied, but she never reached the edge of the abyss that she knew was there.

Finally one night after he had made all the preparations with the towels, rugs, radio, she said,

"Not tonight. I'm tired. Maybe tomorrow." That was two months ago. Her visits to the brokers office had increased and her stock transactions became riskier.

Irene walked up the hill towards Knoxville. The elms that canopied the street suddenly quieted. Their stiff deeply colored leaves hung as suspended dry paper. Male cicadas that had been proudly roaring their resonating drone had stopped in mid note. She could hear the trolley's vacant rattle and moved quickly over the shining bricks to reach the familiar stop. But her ears could still hear the invading cicadas even after the horde had broken their sensual song.

She stepped up to the conductor and deposited one small round token. The trolley's lurch created a breeze that touched her neck and slid down her back under the loose cotton shift. Her arms shivered into tiny bumps.

Last night, at dinner, Thomas had said, "Montana Oil is merging with Missouri Gas, could be worth 10 points." She knew she had to be careful his friends don't see her at the brokers. It would be too obvious that she was trading on inside tips.

As the trolley went by the bishop's house , she wondered what the priests and nuns would think of what she was planning. Her new house would be bigger than that pretentious bishop's residence paid for out of the pockets of poor Irish, Germans, Poles. If she played the market correctly, she would be the one to invite them, instead of having them just show up every Sunday evening, uninvited. How she hated Sundays.

Today, she would borrow against her whole portfolio, buy the Montana and Missouri stock, make her big killing. Today would be the day.

CHAPTER FORTY-ONE
CRASH
OCTOBER 1929

That night, Thomas described how he had stepped into the hall outside of his office, aware of a silence, no clanging elevator, no sharp words from Ruby. Turning back to his desk, he saw his window blacken for an instant as if a great bird had swooped down to grab an unseen prey in the courtyard. He raced to the window, opened it in time to hear the sickening splat of the bank president's body on a concrete bench.

Irene sat at the kitchen table, toyed in the mashed potatoes with her fork. Thomas' description of the smashed body parts didn't bother her as much as the reason for the apparent suicide.

"He had bought a lot of stock on margin, borrowed against the stock itself, assuming it would rise in price and then sell it before the loan came due. It came due and the stock had fallen 20 points. He owed $2,000,000 of the bank's money on his own account. At least that's what Ruby and Pearl say. They say the same thing is happening all over the country. I may be out of a job."

The kitchen was quiet, all eyes except Julia's were focused on their plates. She smiled and nodded as she sat quietly staring out the window into the back yard, still waiting, still hoping.

Ann wondered if the bishop would take her back if Thomas did lose his job. Somebody would have to bring some money in and Irene gave no indication of ever helping with anything around the house, let alone contribute financially.

Thomas thought of calling all his high school friends.

Irene thought of the trade she had made two days before. Mr. Barrett seemed nervous about something. But he still advanced her $5,000 to buy Montana Oil at $10 a share, using her Anaconda as collateral.

"With the merger tip, we can safely say it will go to $15. Then sell. Pretty soon Irene, you'll have enough for that family you want to start."

But what if her stocks didn't move ahead, what if they fell

below the
value of the loans she had outstanding? She certainly wouldn't take the cowardly leap of President Penn. Her mother's words "You're all alone, Irene. No one stays with you. They leave sooner or later. You have to fight for what's yours. If you can get it, that's all that counts, not how you got it," gave her the beginning of a plan.

On Monday morning, October 28, 1929, at 5:30 A.M., Irene's eyes snapped open. The bathroom light shone through the transom over the bedroom door. It looked like Iowa, squared into a corner. From their first night in the back bedroom, she had insisted that the light be left on all night. Thomas slept with his head under a pillow, face down, resting on his nose.

She had lingered on the edge of sleep throughout the night, aware of brief minutes of quiet followed by Thomas's snagging snores when he rolled from one side of his face to the other. She lay there, planned the steps that would protect her future. She swung her legs over the edge of the bed, felt the cold pine floorboards press against her feet, wrapped herself tightly in a terry cloth robe and tiptoed out the bedroom door. Commandeering the bathroom before Thomas or the two old women woke, her mind focused on Monday's plan. Nothing would get in her way. She bathed, put her make-up on, and went to the kitchen.

She was standing at the kitchen sink drinking coffee, smoking a Camel, when Thomas came down the stairs in a white dress shirt, silk tie and navy pinstripe suit that he had just taken out of the winter storage box. His arms hugged his chest to fight off the sudden October chill.

"Thought I'd lost you for a minute, till I heard the water running down here. What's up? Got a big plan today? Guess I better drink a cup of that before I head to the bank." Irene poured the coffee out of the mottled coffee pot into Thomas's cup.

"I just spoke to Dad. He wants me to come out for a few days, help him rearrange the house. He needs a change."

"I didn't hear the phone ring."

"He called while you had the bath running."

"Well, it's a good idea to help him out. I can get the house ready for winter while you're gone. Adam's delivering a load of coal Wednesday. I need to make sure the coal bin and furnace are ready. Lots of stuff to do."

"Dad said he would pick me up around nine. You go on to work."

"How long?"

"How long what?"

"At your Dads, how long will you stay?"

"I'm not sure, I think he's starting to forget things, I want to make sure he can get along OK. Maybe a few days." Thomas finished his coffee, pulled on his gabardine overcoat, put his gray fedora on his head, careful not to disturb the line of his combed back hair, reached over and pulled her to his chest.

"Don't be gone long," he said, thinking that a few days away would be good for them, maybe the whole stock thing was exaggerated, maybe her sex drive would be back.

"Call me tonight."

"OK."

Irene went back to the bedroom, packed her wool and heavy cotton dresses and skirts, all her nylons, pumps and best underwear. She took one of Thomas's razors, two bars of soap, and a set of towels and washcloths. She knew there wouldn't be a clean piece of fabric in her father's house. A door in the middle bedroom rattled. She envisioned Ann reaching into her closet and taking her robe out.

She put on her fox trimmed wool coat, picked up her suitcase with two hands, walked as quietly as she could to the front hall steps. Julia's bedroom door opened. She stepped out, her nightgown hung off her left shoulder, exposing a sagging breast.

"Hi honey," she said, as she pulled the gown up and smiled her best smile.

"You look nice in that coat. Off on a vacation? Is Thomas going too? I think he needs to stay here and help his Dad with the furnace."

Irene ignored Julia, went down the front stairs, set her suitcase on the floor in the hallway and took all the stock certificates and the bank passbook out of the dining room buffet.

At 9:00 A.M. Irene put in a sell order at the brokerage house that handled their joint stock account. Both names were on the account, Thomas *or* Irene Stone. Only one signature required. The proceeds were then transferred to their joint checking account at the First Bank next door. She had arrived at 7:30 A.M. There were fourteen people in line waiting for the 8:00 A.M. opening. It took an hour for the broker to take her order in between furtive glances at the ticker tape that was now one and one half hours late. The board that held information on the *New York Times* list of fifty leading stocks had been abandoned by the young clerk whose job it was to hang the numbers next to the stock symbol. Prices were changing too fast to keep up. Instead, on a lark, he spent his time putting in buy orders at $1 on all the Dow Jones industrials. The rumor circulated immediately that he had bought five shares of Anaconda Copper.

Irene's trader put her order in front of five other old customers of his. He had reacted to her sideways glance as she licked her lips and said,

"My aunt and mother-in-law are both very ill, I would be most grateful if you could be sure to follow my paperwork through." He fought his

way to a phone and got a line through to the New York office. In his mind, this was an omen. His reward would be more than a commission on trading ten stocks.

"Lucky for you ma'am, I got a line in and sold your stocks, the money's being transferred as per your instructions. Now, how about the two of us getting together sometime?" He said with an exact copy of her teasing look.

"Here's a number you can call. Leave a message for Irene."

"Right, right." He called that night and got the receptionist at St. Francis Hospital. "Sorry sir, nobody by that name works here."

Irene went across the street, her hat pulled down over her forehead, glancing constantly to see if Thomas would appear. She stepped into the Brown Sugar, sat in the booth furthest from the door, ordered coffee and apple pie. The waitress looked down at her and said,

"Aren't you Tom Stone's wife?"

"Yes, we were supposed to meet for coffee, but he probably got caught in a meeting. It's a little nuts over there."

"Yeah, the conversations from the early morning crowd were downright depressing. Haven't seen droopy mugs like that since before the big war."

Irene paid the check, wrapped herself snugly in her coat and walked back across Main Street. It was 12:30 P. M. Bits of paper hung patiently in the air, never reaching the ground as the first cold wind from the north marched into the heart of Peoria. She went with her head down to the teller's window at the far right of the main floor of the bank, avoiding Pearl Schwann at the reception desk.

Pearl's desk was surrounded by lunch hour customers yelling at each other. She sat calmly at her desk.

"Patience, that's all we need, just a little patience. Somebody will be with you shortly." The crowd ignored Pearl's exhortations, pointed fingers at each other, nodded their heads as they spoke loud enough for the whole lobby to hear.

"What's this about the President? Actually jumped out of his window?"

"Probably some marriage problem."

"No, I heard he had a big loan against some oil stocks that he couldn't pay off. Ruined him."

"I heard Capone came down and threw him out the window. Owed him money."

"Doesn't say much for the bank, does it?

"Are you going to take all your money out?"

"Damn right. Can't trust a bank with a president dead from his own hand, or somebody else's."

Irene slid her withdrawal slip under the teller's bar.

"All but $100, Mrs. Stone. Are you sure? There's quite a bit in here."

"Yes, and it's really none of your business."

Irene put the cash in her purse, turned and walked quickly out the

door, got on the trolley and returned to the Stone house. Her father was on the porch, talking to Ann.

"Do you think Tom will lose his job?" He asked.

"I don't know," Ann replied.

"God willing, he'll be O.K. and the rest of us too."

"Right you are, right you are." Robert Lucas turned to see Irene walking up the sidewalk.

"Hi honey, glad to see your old man?"

"Sure daddy, I'll just get my bag, be right out."

She walked by Ann, nodded, and said quietly,

"Aren't you going to ask him in? That's the polite thing to do."

Irene left the house not caring whether she ever saw it again. She didn't care if she ever saw Thomas again. She was leaving with more than she had arrived with.

CHAPTER FORTY-TWO
GONE
NOVEMBER 1929

"Thomas, she's gone. I don't think she's coming back." Ann spoke slowly to her nephew as they sat next to each other at the kitchen table set for four. The oven door was parallel to the floor, radiating a welcome heat against their backs.

"It's insane Ann, my life is insane. I lose my job, the bank probably will fold in a few weeks. My wife disappears with the few dollars left in our bank account. We could have gotten through it if she had talked to me. It looked so right. I know I would have been promoted at the bank. I missed the signs, all that margin buying. She didn't tell me about any of it. Maybe she wanted to surprise me. The broker says she owes $5,000 on the stocks she bought. It'll take me years to pay that off. There are no jobs. It's insane." Thomas's head sank to his folded arms. Ann moved her chair closer, took his hands and folded them on her lap. She felt his heart beat through her fingertips, saw a child slide off the rail of a rolling ship and fall towards a flat black sea. She gently put her hand under his chin, turned his head to look into his eyes.

"Look at me Thomas. You have a choice. Try to change her and fail, or take control of your own life. I make a choice every day to live my life the best that I can. I don't think about what's glamorous, what would be fun. I think about doing something for my family, something that will help them grow. I had my time with the business world. I enjoyed telling those men what to do. But when my sister needed me, I made a choice." Thomas sat back and took a deep breath.

"You think too much about other people Ann. I probably don't think enough. Except about Irene. I need her. I felt satisfied with my life for a while. I don't know where I lost it. She always looked at me sideways like she was getting ready to leave. A step just to the right of where I was going. I couldn't lead her back. The pressure was hers, always pulling away from my love. I don't think that it ever mattered to her that I loved her. She thought she deserved whatever she could get from me. I know she lied, about the stocks, about loving me. Sometimes she would cry at night," he hesitated to go on, but it was the only way to describe his new understanding of the woman he loved.

"She would cry after we made love. I thought I had hurt her, or she missed her family, I don't know, but I never asked her about it. I still don't know where the tears came from, maybe she felt the world wasn't being fair to her, and worse, I wasn't being fair. Then I would try to give her things, like stock tips. I knew what I was doing, but it didn't seem wrong. But she never told me what she was so afraid of. I should have tried harder, maybe she would have stayed," Thomas paused, "the night before she left was horrible. She said some things," his voice trailed off as he turned to stare out the window.

"She told me that I should have seen the market crash coming and found another job. She said that if she left, nobody would miss her, not my senile mother, not my smiling aunt. What do they expect from me?' she said, 'be their maid? I did the best I could with what you gave me, Thomas.' I wanted to scream at her but I couldn't yell at my little girl." He wrenched forward, scraping the chair on the bare wood, amazed at what he had just said. "I called her my little girl. I was trying to be a husband and help her grow up. I couldn't change her and I was ashamed that I couldn't satisfy her." He pushed the chair against the wall, again took a deep breath. His voice lowered, "And we lacked the most important element. Trust, she didn't trust me. She won't trust any man."

Ann had sat back as Thomas leaned forward. She saw a change in his face that aged him. Each of his words emerged with blackened edges, as if they had yanked from inside a burning tree. Her heart ached at his sadness, yet she knew that his life was not free, not while Irene controlled him.

"She's not coming back, if she does, it will only be to get something from you." Ann sat back, wondered if this is what a priest did in the confessional, or did they have it much easier;

"Say three Our Fathers, three Hail Mary's, now go son, live a good life."

Thomas stood and walked to the stove, ran his hand inches over the cold burner. Ann rose from her chair, put her hand on

Thomas's shoulder. They looked out the window at the familiar gray garage, the hedges that lined the alley, and the metal garbage cans that Thomas had carried down the sidewalk for pick up the next morning.

CHAPTER FORTY-THREE
THOMAS STONE
1929-1932

Ann helped Thomas find a job in Schradzki's, a department store on the south side. He worked behind wood and glass counters that held the best shirts and ties for men lucky enough to need them.

He woke every morning, grabbed his cigarettes, and went into the bathroom to get ready for the day. Shaved, brushed his teeth, had his first cigarette, slicked back his hair, sure that there were no stray strands. Went back to his closet, put on the starched white shirt that Ann had ironed the night before, tied the dark burgundy tie in a four in hand knot. There were five slightly different dark patterned ties hanging on the closet door, all burgundy. Then he put on one of the elegant black suits that Julia had bought for him over the years. He selected the one on the right each morning, and replaced it on the left at night, keeping three fingers between the hangers, guaranteeing the longest life for each of the identical five suits.

Thomas's life had been ordered and predictable before he met Irene. His marriage had the same qualities on the surface, but the small sacrifices he made, the gifts he gave her, were never reciprocated. His misgivings were covered by his own willingness to compromise, give in when it would make things easier. At the end it was chaos. Sex and money, roots of pleasure and evil, became the only factors that made a difference to her. Now he had a job selling shirts and ties.

His best customer was Everett C. May, one of the bank officers that had sat on the loan committee. His had been the only affirmative vote on the Stoll application for a loan. He voted yes to show confidence in Thomas, not confidence in Stoll's idea. He was always a step behind Penn and the other officers in their race to feed speculative stocks and had quietly reduced his equity positions a month before Black Thursday. He had cash accounts in ten Midwestern banks where he personally knew the president and his investing strategies. These accounts offset what he lost when the First Bank went under. He used his cash to buy into the Illinois Life Insurance Co. as a partner.

Mr. May's conservative investment strategies had a corresponding indulgence in shirts and ties. His assistant bought five shirts and ties every two weeks. The same straight collar Arrow shirt and dark stripe tie.

"What does he do with all these shirts and ties, he can't wear all of them." Thomas asked Albert Bredahl, ex bank treasurer, now assistant to a man that was once a peer.

"I have no idea what the hell he does with this crap. Lines his waste baskets at home for all I know. Shit job coming down here to get his God damned shirts and ties."

"Cash or charge, Mr. Bredahl, that'll be $35."

"At least you still call me Mr. Bredahl. Thanks Tommy, cash."

Late on a Friday afternoon in August of 1932, Everett C. May walked up to Thomas's counter.

"Hi, Mr. May, where's Mr. Bredahl?" Thomas asked as he wiped off the top of the glass counter, a surprised look on his face. He hadn't seen Everett May for at least four years.

"No longer with us, Tommy. Retired early. That's why I'm here. Let me see that 15 ½, 34, the white Arrow with the straight collar."

Mr. May wanted a discreet, loyal employee. One that wouldn't bad mouth him all over town. One that would show some enthusiasm for whatever task he was assigned. He wanted Thomas Stone.

"Can you come over to see me Monday morning? I'd like to talk to you about the insurance business."

Thomas stifled the urge to jump over the counter and shake Mr. May's hand.

"Sure Mr. May, what time on Monday?"

Everett May picked up his parcel, put his hand out to Thomas,

"Early, if it's OK with you, about 8:00?"

"I look forward to talking to you, next Monday at 8:00."

CHAPTER FORTY-FOUR
DIVORCE
1932

"The right thing to do is get a divorce, now, get her out of my life. We can talk about an annulment later. The only reason I would need an annulment is if I wanted to get married again. Uh-uh, not for me. I've learned my lesson," Thomas said as he turned and scrambled up the caramel colored ridges of the vertical hill, getting a head start on Father Conlin. Hand and footholds crumbled at each attempt to find firm resistance. Father Conlin caught him at the top, both exhausted. A tie.

The fissure lines on the hill were changed every year by the April rains. No two routes were ever the same. The best time to climb was June when the wall was newly dried and deepened to chocolate, hand and footholds secure. This was August, the month of erosion. The race would be won by the fastest descent, by the one with the most abrasions and ripped clothing.

They sat on moist grass at the top of the hill, wet from a sprinkler running in the back yard of the closest house, catching their breath, mustering the courage to face the descent. This race was the first in eight years, not yet below their status as a priest and future employee of a respected insurance company.

"No talking, I can't think, let alone give you the advice you obviously need. Who's idea was this anyway?" Fr. Conlin said as he faked breathing hard. Suddenly, he jumped to his feet and yelled,

"Go!"

They ran, stumbled, rolled, screamed, laughed, until they hit the flat leading to the tree lined creek.

"Tie?" asked Tommy, one pant leg almost shredded.

"Tie," replied Jimmy.

They sat on the edge of a thin stream of water that carried enough of a breeze to evaporate the sweat and cool their bodies. Dragonflies hovered over them, linked like an engine and its' tender,

Thomas said,

"I start Monday with the Illinois National Insurance Company. A new beginning. I'm going to get a divorce. She's been gone almost three years. I don't want her coming back asking for money or anything else."

"If you want my advice, you should have listened a long time ago. I don't have much to say about a divorce. It's a civil issue. Between you and your government. Talk to me when I get back and you want to get the thing dissolved properly. Don't do anything rash while I'm gone."

Jimmy said to Thomas as they shook hands,

"See you in three years."

"No vacation, huh."

"Right, no vacation."

Robert Kavanaugh handed the Bill For Divorce to George Sturch, the Circuit Court Clerk for Peoria County. Sturch, a devout Catholic, had been clerk for thirty-two years. He hunched over his desk, pushed his sleeves up, placed the brown document holder in a wire basket with ten others of the same size.

"Never seen so many divorces. If Hoover doesn't put more men to work, won't be anybody left married. The bishop called me. Asked if I could do anything to stop em. Divorces, I mean. I told him that was his job." He sat back and loosened his belt.

"What's the deal here, Bobby?"

"None of your business George, but I'll give you a clue, money and desertion."

Sturch pushed away from the desk, stretching his arms over his head, and yawned. The desk moved two inches towards Kavanaugh, propelled by Sturch's loosened stomach. George looked up at the lawyer and said,

"This will be the batch for today. Is it signed by the complainant?"

"Of course," replied Kavanaugh, irritated at the nonchalant attitude of the oldest clerk in Peoria. Kavanaugh wasn't getting the respect he thought he deserved.

"Now I need the summons for the wife to appear in court. We've tracked her to Ottawa, so we need it to be served in La Salle county." Sturch crossed out the word 'Peoria County,' wrote in 'LaSalle County.

"That'll be a buck seventy, date set for the second Monday in September. Good luck." Sturch pushed the summons across the desk into Kavanaugh's hand.

"Now what?" Thomas asked his lawyer the week after he had submitted the Bill for Divorce.

"We wait, see what she says. She'll get a lawyer, make it out that she didn't desert you, just needed to be in the TB sanatorium for awhile. She'll try to get more money."

Thomas looked at the floor, rubbed his hands together,

"She may have been sick, but I didn't know about it, I would have helped. You are right about trying for more money. It seems to be her only real passion."

Kavanaugh reached into his drawer and pulled out a silver flask.

"Want a swig?

"No, and I'd appreciate it if you wouldn't either. I would like you to keep a sober face during this process."

"Don't give me any crap, Tommy, I know how you got through the twenties, the liquor business was pretty good to you."

"And look where I am now. An insurance agent. I could have been a bank officer if it hadn't been for Hoover. All I ask is that you don't screw this up. Let's just get it over with."

Kavanaugh put the flask back in the drawer. His own approach would have been to leave the bitch out in the cold. But he wasn't going to argue with his young client, whom he considered to be totally naïve. He'd have a drink after the meeting was finished.

"It might cost you a few dollars to buy her off. She's got a pretty good lawyer, Harry Heyl. He will know how much you make and ask for a chunk of it."

Thomas thought about the bank account that he had built to $200 in the last year.

"How the hell is he going to find out that I make a lousy $175 a month?"

"It doesn't matter how they find out, Tom. It's more important that we be ready with a dollar amount you can come up with. We'll get them to sign off and you'll be free."

"Thanks, Bob, I pay her and I pay you, and go home broke."

"You've got your life back, Tommy. And she can do whatever she wants. It's the most you can hope for."

Thomas walked out of his lawyer's office, torn as he often was between the humble act and the courageous. The divorce was his way of forgiving Irene. He looked to the corner and saw the Youngest Martyr nod in approval. Thomas had chosen the honorable course of action. Henry Fleming stood just to the boy's right, swinging a piece of lead pipe against his thigh. Thomas wondered if they ever saw each other.

The Bill Of Divorce filed on August 15, 1932, by a sober Robert Kavanaugh for Thomas Stone, stated;

TO THE HONORABLE JUDGES OF THE CIRCUIT COURT OF THE COUNTY OF PEORIA, IN THE STATE OF ILLINOIS, IN CHANCERY SITTING:

....your orator further represents, that the said Irene A. Stone, wholly regardless of her marriage covenants and duty, and afterwards on October 30, 1929, willfully deserted and absented herself from your orator, without any reasonable cause, for the space of one year and upwards, and has persisted in such desertion, and yet continues to absent herself from your orator.

Forasmuch, therefore, as your orator is without remedy in the premises, except in a court of equity, and to the end that the said Irene A. Stone who is made party defendant to this bill, may be required to make full and direct answer to the same, and that the marriage between your orator and the said Irene A. Stone may be dissolved and declared null and void by the decree of this court, according to the statute in such case made and provided: and that your orator may have such other and further relief in the premises as equity may require, and to your Honor shall seem meet.

Irene and Thomas met on a downtown street corner in November, without their attorneys. The late afternoon sun cast their lone shadows across the sidewalk and up two floors of the Peoria Life Insurance Co.

"We can work this out between us, we don't need those two idiots getting between us," she told him. "I don't want anything of yours, I just want you to pay my bills at the sanitarium."

"How much?" he asked her, as he lit a cigarette.

"Thanks, I'll have one too." She reached up and took the lit cigarette.

A photographer from the Peoria Star stood across the street, fascinated by the long shadows . He waited for the traffic to clear, and shot one exposure that appeared in the next morning edition with the caption, "Couple shares secrets and cigarettes in last sun of the day."

"$650," was her clipped response.

He told Kavanaugh that he could go up to $650, but no more. How did she know?

"Agreed. Is that all?"

"Yes." She turned and walked up Main St. Thomas noticed a difference in her stride that he could not identify.

The Decree was handed down by the circuit court of Peoria County:

…having heard the arguments of counsel, and being fully advised in the premises, and on consideration thereof finds that the defendant has been guilty of willful desertion for a period of more than one year.

IT IS THEREFORE ORDERED, ADJUDGED AND DECREED, by the Court, that the marriage between the plaintiff and the defendant be dissolved, and the same is hereby dissolved accordingly; and the said parties are, and each of them is freed from the obligations thereof.

IT IS THEREFORE ORDERED, ADJUDGED AND DECREED, by the Court, that the said plaintiff, Thomas Stone, shall pay to the said defendant, Irene Stone, the sum of Six Hundred Fifty ($650) Dollars, which sum shall be in full settlement and accord of any and all claims for maintenance and support from the said plaintiff; and that by the payment of the said sum, and the acceptance of the same, the said defendant, Irene Stone, is and shall be forever barred from any and all rights of maintenance and support, and from any and all interest in and to the property of the said plaintiff, the same as if said marriage had never taken place.

CHAPTER FORTY-FIVE
SATURDAY NIGHT
1932

It was Saturday night. The yard was empty. The neighbors had all drifted back to their homes, full of ham, roast beef, potato salad, rhubarb pie, and, whatever liquid they had chosen from the beer, whiskey and soft drinks. The priests and nuns had gone back to their rectory and convent to prepare for tomorrow's masses. All the tables and chairs had been put away.

His mother and aunt had gone upstairs hours ago. Thomas knew they were asleep and he didn't worry about the noise of the collapsing tables and chairs. They slept through the worst of thunder storms. He was the only one who got up to close the windows. He picked up the linens folded by the nuns and carried them through the two wooden doors angled over the wooden steps, walked down to the screen door, pushed it open with his shoulder, made a mental note to oil the spring that kept the door closed, and stepped into the basement laundry room.

Two metal edged sinks were on the right wall with the new electric washing machine and mangle sitting to the left. Thomas placed the tablecloths in the tub he had filled with cold water and bleach. He would give them an Irish soak overnight and Ann would finish them in the morning before Sunday mass. He yawned, glad he only had the beginnings of a headache from mixing beer and whiskey and reminded himself to take two aspirin before going to bed. He walked back to the screen door, pulled it open, looked up and saw Irene's slim legs placed firmly on the top step.

His eyes followed the curve of the calf to her knee caressed by a silk chemise. He moved slowly up the stairs and fought the urge to pull her into the basement for his own pleasure or drop-kick her back to wherever she had come from.

Thomas looked up into Irene's face, noticed a slight puffiness around the eyes, or maybe it was just too much mascara. He said in a controlled voice,

"I thought you weren't coming back."

She replied with a demure glance to the side. Thomas had to lean close to hear her words, smelled her fragrance, the one she wore before she stopped putting towels under their bedroom door for privacy.

"Dad died, just like Mom, of T.B. I sold the house, that money's gone. I need help. You're the only one I can turn to."

"Money, you want money?" He replied quietly into her ear. He pulled her by the hand into the dark coolness of the stone walled basement room next to the coal burning furnace. Her dress slid easily up the angle of her thighs as he sat her on the edge of his father's work bench. There was no sound, no change in facial expression from either of them. Their eyes locked as if on a battle field waiting for the other to surrender.

Thomas broke the silence as he climaxed.

"I have no money."

He saw her bite her lower lip as a low moan escaped, a sound that he had never heard in the two years she had lived in the house on Illinois.

He pulled away, straightened his clothing, walked past the sink and looked into the old cracked mirror next to the screen door. There were two images. On the right he recognized the control he felt in his act of sex, but was startled by the flash in the corner of the mirror that came from his pain and anger turned into hatred.

The screen door stayed open as he went through and walked up the steps into the moist air, breathing heavily. He stood for a moment, listened to the beginning of the cicada cacophony when he felt a movement in the air and turned to the left as a lead pipe hit him across the shoulder. He swung out with his left arm, knocked the pipe from Irene's hand, his right hand reaching for her shoulder, but she fell backward in an arc anchored by the left heel that had sunk into the groove between the cement wall and the top step.

Her arms reached out for him, something Thomas had never seen. The pipe

bounced down the stairs as he looked into her eyes, saw them roll slowly backwards, then heard a crunch as her head lodged momentarily between the first step and the wall. Her foot came loose from her pump and her legs followed the arc started by her head and swept past her shoulders and she landed in front of the sink that held the soaking linens.

He expected her to get up and wipe her hand through her hair, sneer as she left him again. She didn't move. He picked up the pipe and placed it in the corner. Then grasped her hand and rubbed it between his. She still didn't move. The chirping of the basement crickets was gone, the only sound was his own heart pounding. He put his hand under her neck, expecting to feel a pulse, but only felt a swelling hot to the touch.

There was no blood, only the sticky fluid that he noticed as he smoothed her dress down over her exposed thighs. He pulled his handkerchief out and wiped her dry, arranged her hands over her breasts, and put her shoe back on her left foot. She looked at peace for the first time. The only signs of impact were a few strands of hair left wedged between the stair and the wall where her head had stuck momentarily. He pulled them out and put them in the middle of his handkerchief, folded it and put it in his back pocket.

Thomas walked up to the stairs leading to the second floor and listened. The air was broken by a regular exhale through his aunt's open lips. No sound came from the front bedroom where his mother slept dreamless.

Irene had no relatives.

No one would miss her. The only people to suffer if he called the police would be the two women that he loved. The guilt came from the calm violence of the sex act. He soothed this over with the thought that that they were still man and wife in the eyes of the church. There is no sin. No priest need hear the story. He could live with the guilt to save the people that he cared about.

His mind raced through the chaos, call the police?

No.

Bury her in the coal room?

No.

Take her to the river.

Yes.

He shook last winter's coal dust out of the canvas tarpaulin that was used to line the coal room floor and returned to the laundry room, carefully rolled Irene onto the blackened surface and tightened the ends with pieces of twine. Once more he went to the door leading to the second floor, heard the alternating sounds of expelled breath coming from his Mother and Aunt. He turned, walked down the basement steps and carefully placed Irene's shroud over his shoulder.

The drone of basement crickets returned, combined with the booming chorus of summer cicadas, to cover the sound of the house doors being locked before he walked slowly to the garage. He put the body in the back seat of the Ford, backed out into the dimly lit street, stopped and returned to close the garage door. His only thought was that Julia and Ann could still get a good night's sleep. Hidden beneath the night sounds as he drove, was the rolling of the body in the back seat of the Ford, a ship trying to cross a stormy sea.

A crescent moon stared vacantly at the lone car travelling down a hardtop road parallel to the Illinois River. Thomas felt that he was tracing a strand of yarn in an intricate piece of woven fabric, unsure of where he would turn next. Then on his right was a gravel road that he recognized as leading to a seldom used beach of dirt and sand. It was posted,

"No Swimming, Treacherous Currents."

He backed the Ford as close to the water as he dared. Untied the twine and pulled Irene's body out of the tarpaulin. He walked into the black water until he was chest deep, felt the current pulling at his legs. He pushed her out as far as his arms would extend. She bobbed momentarily like a cork on a fish line and then disappeared under the oily surface. Thomas turned and walked back to the car with one thought, get back to the house before his mother and aunt woke up.

"Thomas, Tony's here to see you." Ann yelled from the front door. Sheriff Tony McLaughlin stood in the entry-way, turning his hat over and over.

"Come on in Tony, can I get you a beer?" Thomas asked in a subdued voice.

"No Tom, I can't stay, it's official. We have a missing person report on your ex. Her doctor in Ottawa called it in. She's turned up missing. He said it was nothing unusual that she hadn't shown up for her treatments, but this time, it was a few weeks longer than usual. I thought she might have come here."

"Let's go out on the porch. I did see her." Thomas felt that it was time to tell someone. May as well be the sheriff.

"She came over about a month ago. Wanted money. I told her I didn't have any. She got mad and came at me with a pipe. I pushed her away and she fell, hit her head pretty hard. I thought she was dead."

"Was she?" Tony asked.

"No, she got up and took off. I asked her if she wanted to go To the hospital. She said no. She just wanted to get away from me."

"You sure that's all that happened? I know what she did to you. If it was self defense.....," McLaughlin turned and looked out to the street, put his hat back on.

"Listen, I'll keep it a missing person report, file it tomorrow. I won't mention that she stopped here, just that I checked. You and your Mom have had enough the last few years. We'll tell the doctor in Ottawa to keep looking. If you think of anything else, you call me *first,* OK?"

Thomas was ready to put his hand on Tony's shoulder and hold him back, when he heard,

"Thomas, is your dad home yet? It's almost dinner time?" He pulled his hand back and said, "Thanks, Tony, I'll certainly do that."

Tony looked up at Thomas from the bottom step as he moved towards his car, raised his eyebrows as dramatically as he could.

"Have you seen Jimmy yet? He's back from Rome."

"Tomorrow, I'm seeing him tomorrow. Thanks again."

"I'm not upset," Father Conlin told Thomas, as they sat in the first pew of St. Bernard's church.

Mrs. Olson, hands moving a rosary along its path, lips pulled back with a silent "Hail," and pursed forward with "Mary," was already lined up at Fr. Conlin's station even though he was not scheduled to go in the confessional box for another thirty minutes.

"Bishop Ireland put me here. Three years of studying Canon Law in Rome wasn't enough to get me into the chancery. I guess priest lawyers were as plentiful as lay lawyers. He said he needed parish workers, help with the relief work, counsel for the unemployed, keep the family structure together. He said," James Conlin did his best Irish brogue, 'Conlin, your street education on the south side will make you a very effective parish priest. St. Bernard's, with Monsignor Salmon, that's the assignment. You'll spot the problems early and show the parishioners the right path on Sunday.'"

Fr. Conlin spoke quietly, each word measured carefully,

"It's what the Bishop wants, and in reality it's what I always wanted. I don't need to be a litigator, arguing the moral points of passion and failure. I saw enough aristocrats and their sniveling prayers in the Vatican. I had to get out once in a while to see the streets. Some days I would wander around the slums, pick my way through cats and beggars. One woman sat on a street corner, you and I would call it an alley, held a newborn in one arm and reached out and grabbed my robe with the other. She didn't speak, just used her eyes. I tried to talk to her in Italian, but she wouldn't respond. I thought she was Roman, or from somewhere south of Rome. Until I felt my wallet being pulled out of my back pocket. It was the third member of this little gang of Gypsies. She and the newborn were the distraction, her eight year son was the pickpocket. I grabbed my wallet and the boy."

"Then asked them to go to confession?" Thomas asked with a slight smile.

"No, I gave her all the money I had with me."

"Soft touch. No wonder your confessional line is always so long."

"That's not the point. She worked hard for her money. I don't condone it, but she wasn't much different from my mother, except that my mother worked alone on her back."

"I know Jimmy, you had it tougher than most of us. But look at you now, associate pastor, a great education, you've still got me as a friend. A real lucky guy, too bad you won't get to use that education. Bishop Ireland should have put you in the chancery. Mrs. Olson needs you, better get in the box. See you later."

Fr. Conlin walked to the confessional, thinking that his friend was trying to tell him something, and he hadn't listened very well. He resolved to ask him the next time that they spoke.

Two hours later, Thomas knelt in the confessional,

"Bless me Father, for I have sinned."

"Tommy, is that you?" Fr. Conlin turned to the mesh separating the confessor from the penitent.

"Yes. You are a priest? Aren't you? Ready to hear confessions from whomever is kneeling here?"

"Of course, go on."

"My last confession was two months ago."

"Get to the point. What are you doing here? Are there very many behind you?"

"I'm the last one." Thomas paused, shifted from one knee to the other, sweat started down his back. "I don't know if what I did is a sin or not. I think it was illegal, but I don't know if it was a sin."

"Tommy, what you did during prohibition is not a matter for the confessional. We've talked about that already."

"It's not that, it's Irene. She came back, just before you got back from Rome. It was after one of the Saturday picnics in our back yard. I'm in the basement washing the dishes, soaking the tablecloths in the sink. I looked up and she was standing at the top of the basement steps. Smiling, beautiful…..Said she needed money. She told me her father died of T.B. Same as her mom. She sold the house, that money was gone."

Fr. Conlin wiped the sweat off his upper lip. "How long had she been gone?"

"Six, six years. She didn't tell me where she'd been, just that she missed me, maybe we could get back together. Anyway, I really did something stupid. It just happened. We were in the basement, it was cool, she had this dress that sort of clung to her, it was real loose, she didn't have any und…" The pit of Tommy's stomach tightened, the same as it did during every confession.

"We had sex."

"There's nothing wrong with that, Tommy, you're still married as far as the church is concerned."

"I know that, that's not why I'm here." Thomas's voice deepened and rose in pitch at the same time. "I told her I didn't have any money, couldn't borrow against the house, it wasn't mine. She got mad as hell then, came at me with a pipe. The rest is a blur. I put my hand up, she fell. Hit her head."

Jimmy Conlin dropped his hand from his chin, tried to see through the mesh into his friend's eyes.

"What are you trying to tell me? That you killed your wife?"

The next words were spoken as fast as Thomas could get them out.

"No, I'm telling you that we, she, had a terrible accident and I panicked. I wrapped her up and took her to the river, to the dirt beach by Keystone. The current took her away." He paused,

"And I lied about it to Tony. I told him she left alive. I am sorry for these sins and the sins of my past life."

Thomas spoke in a quiet whisper, but it felt as if the words exploded out of his mouth. He dropped back on his heels, felt his face, it was still in one piece. He had survived. He was ready for the priest's response.

"It was an accident." Fr. Conlin started slowly. "You didn't commit a murder or intend to commit a murder. Your sin *and* your error was in disposing of the body and lying about it. The question is whether you are truly sorry for those sins? If they find her body and connect the two of you, you'll go to jail for a long time. I can't give you absolution for something you didn't do." His voice was now steady and monotone.

"Say a good act of contrition, and for your penance, say the Rosary three times. I absolve you in the name of the Father, the Son and the Holy Ghost."

THE SINGING BONE

PART THREE

CHAPTER NINE
LIAM STONE
AUGUST 1981

"It's Amy Brown from White Cloud. I told her you were working on the novel, that you weren't to be disturbed. She said something about your current obligations, wants you to call her back as soon as you can, and your lunch is ready." Kathryn called to Liam in a loud voice.

"Right, thanks. Tell her, um, tell her, I'll call her back Monday." Liam kept writing, wondered why the hell she was calling him on Saturday, wasn't a day with the family sacred anymore? His fingers moved quickly across the Selectric, recording the four hand written pages he had just finished.

Fifteen minutes later, Kathryn called from the steps, "C'mon, Liam, your lunch is ready, and y ou have to take Colin to his guitar lesson at two."

"Can't, not now, I'm really movin. Can't we send Colin on the bus?

MacPhail's right on the line."

Kathryn threw his sandwich against the kitchen door and said in a loud but controlled voice,

"No, he's ten years old, I'm not sending him on a city bus so you can stay in your room."

Colin poked his head around the kitchen door and said,

"Mom, Mom, I can ride the bus, the other guys do it all the time."

Liam heard the anger in Kathryn's voice and reluctantly turned off the Selectric, grabbed his jacket and walked past the full length hall mirror towards the steps. The reflection shocked him. His hair was sticking out in clumps, as if he had just gotten up. He hadn't shaved or changed his t-shirt and jeans for four days. He had one black sock under a tassel loafer and one white sock under a penny loafer. He turned back to his study to change his shoes and socks, stumbled over the sleeper that he hadn't made up for a week.

His father sat on a straight back chair in the corner, eating a Haralson apple. Thomas Stone leaned forward, twirled the apple in his hand, waited until he had swallowed the last of the soft white fruit.

"Now you're really in trouble. Your family needs you, your editor hates being put off, especially by procrastinators like you." Liam turned his head slightly in the direction of the words, decided to go along with the charade one more time.

"Lay off, can't you see I've finally figured out how to get inside and write what I know. There's a lot to be said for this Singing Bone, especially if you want to write a novel. All I have to do is fill in the empty spaces. I'm just not very good at turning it on and off. Other stuff gets in the way."

"Is that what you're going to tell Kathryn, and the book broad from White Cloud? That you've discovered religion, the route to your creative muse? Won't work. Your family needs you, otherwise they won't be around when you finish your book. Your editor's committed cash to you for 5,000 copies of another unsaleable book of your over wrought poems. She's already given you three extra months. But," Thomas' voice softened,

"The stuff you're writing now is a touch above anything else you've ever done. That part about Irene in the basement, you got the emotions right. I was mad as hell, It's not my proudest moment….. I was another person driving to the river. It was easy letting her go. Like giving peace. But you missed a couple of things."

"What did I miss?" Liam asked as he pulled on a clean t shirt. The jeans weren't *that* dirty.

"I ruined my shoes, had a helluva time explaining that to Ann. And driving to the river was not like 'following a thread.' I knew I was going to the river. It was like driving in a tunnel of clouds, black as the strip mine behind the Lucas house at first, then a lighter gray, the color of Jimmy Conlin's face when I told him about that night. I drove towards this white haze on the horizon, almost went into the river. Another thing you missed. She turned over."

"What? What do you mean?" Liam's voice rose as he tucked in his clean t shirt.

"I pushed her out towards a white haze that hung over the river, but the current took her downstream, fast as I ever saw it. Towards a red light; the city, a fire, I don't know. She turned over, face up, stayed that way till I couldn't see her."

Thomas Stone's voice quivered slightly and started to fade,

"You know, we never talked about much besides sports and school when I was around. It's good to talk about stuff that matters."

Liam stared into the corner, couldn't stop his next words,

"You were gone all the time, how were we supposed to get close enough to talk about living, dying." Liam reached up to wipe his eyes.

"I watched you leave every Tuesday, I hated you for that. You left me,,,,,, you bastard,,,,, you left me."

"We did the best we could, Liam, we tried so hard to protect you. Sometimes it was like you were in a cave and came out only when it suited you. I was never sure where your head was. You had incredible imagination. Somewhere along the line, it dried up. Now I see you care very deeply, otherwise you wouldn't have gotten this far. There is no other way for you."

Liam reached out to the chair. He saw a brown apple core fall onto the floor. It was the last time he would see his father. Later, he would think he heard him say something like, "good," or "slow down," but when he turned, there was never any one there.

"Liam, we can't wait, you stay there. I'll take care of the kids. You'll have to make your own lunch," Kathryn yelled up the stairs.

Liam walked down the steps to see Kathryn going out the back door with Colin. He heard Colin,

"What's wrong Mom, can we help? I can help for sure."

Kathryn wiped her eyes and said,

"Nothing honey, I've just got a sinus head ache, must be something blooming in the yard."

Liam grabbed the bologna sandwich off the floor, wiped up a bit of ketchup, took a large bite, and went back to his study.

He had to finish the story, he wasn't going to take it to his grave. Too many things in his life had been cut short by his own mistakes, or the stupidity of others.

He would make this up to Kathryn and the kids.

They would see, yes, they would see.

STONE AND SON

PART THREE - 1935

CHAPTER FORTY-SIX
SWIMMER

"We need a good auto and casualty agent in Hamilton, Thomas, the Iowa farmers will come across the Mississippi for our policies. What do you think? You'll need a car. Take my 34 Ford, you pay gas and maintenance, until you buy your own, then I'll pay expenses. Spend a few days, interview a few hungry men?" Everett May smiled at his assistant and didn't wait for an answer.

"Tomorrow, go tomorrow. Call me when you have two or three candidates."

"I'll only need one day. I've heard of a few guys with their own agencies. I'll need money for a hotel and food." Thomas tried to sound confident and professional. This would be his first chance to prove to Mr. May that he could do the work of a special agent for the Illinois Casualty Insurance Co.

"Get it from Pearl, or is it Ruby we hired? I never could keep those twins straight." Mr. May turned back to his desk, picked up the phone and rested it between his ear and shoulder. "Sometimes I think we hired them both, and they just take turns at the desk. You just make sure they get one check."

Thomas wasn't sure if Everett May had a very dry sense of humor or none at all. It had been Thomas's idea to hire Pearl to handle the reception desk and petty cash. He was sure that she and her sister Ruby alternated days answering the phone.

On Friday evening, he pulled into the "Roadway Motel," in Hamilton, Illinois. His left arm was burned from the sun. The heat blowing past the windscreen brought a mixed odor of pig and cattle manure into the cab of the Model A. His head throbbed from the ammonia odor. The first thing he would do was get into the bath-tub and scrub the advancing odor of Iowa off his skin. Then he would take a look at the Mississippi, reputed to be at least one mile across to

Keokuk, Iowa. He thought it would look just like the Illinois River; gradual hills lined with full stands of maple and aspen, leading down to shallow dirt and sand beaches.

He finished his bath, slicked his hair back, put on a clean white shirt, and drove up Highway 28 to a small roadside restaurant where he had a meal of catfish and fried potatoes. He washed it down with an ice cold beer of unknown origin left over from prohibition.

Curious to see the Mississippi, he asked directions from Maud Winters, the waitress, chef, and owner, of the "Hamilton Fish Fry Restaurant."

"Where's a good place to get a view of Iowa? Preferably without the smell?" He said good naturedly.

"You mean, see my hometown?" Maud smiled, trying not to act offended by the smartalec from the city.

"Drive north a ways up the road, keep looking left till you see a break in the corn, going left, turn and head straight to the river. Some people use that as a picnic spot. We call it Hamilton Park. Roosevelt had it cleared this summer, government paid for all the labor. A real windfall for my husband. Hope you enjoy it."

Thomas drove with his left sleeve rolled down, his arm well inside the cab of the car. For the first time in months, the memory of Irene's head hitting the step, the sight of her body disappearing into the Illinois River, drifted out of his mind.

It felt good to be out of Peoria, away from the daily visits to the same agents, trips to the grocery store for Ann and Julia, calls from the priests to see how he was holding up, the only divorced man in the parish.

He felt like a monk, locked up inside a monastery, chained to a vow of chastity, but not wearing the robes that brought respect. He saw people look at him with pity, not sure what else he would do with his life. He wasn't the only man that had lost a future with the crash, but his lack of vision into the future about Irene doubled the pain and the sense that he was a failure. He had fallen a great distance since the championship game of 1924.

One Sunday, he heard two old maids talking as he walked out of church, "He'll end up like Ann, taking care of his mother, never married again, no kids of his own. Too bad, he's such a handsome young man."

Thomas pulled onto a gravel road as Maud had instructed.

The sun shone directly into his eyes, he pulled the visor down, put his left hand up to his forehead, and drove slowly into Hamilton Park. He could see the river as he parked the car in a small clearing. The thought of just sitting in the glare of the sun was comforting. He pulled his ledger out of the glove box and sat on the edge of the grass.

September 25, 1935
Hamilton Park, Hamilton, Illinois

There is a clearing the size of Coogan's Lot with two oak picnic tables. The tables are set back from a dirt and black sand beach. Instead of a canopy of shade trees, six foot corn stalks surround the clearing. The first sound comes from minute white capped waves that lick at the sand and dirt mix. The waves spit back the unwanted sand and carry the rich soil out to the almost silent roar of a current that ends in the New Orleans delta. The Mississippi has power that no small tributary like the Illinois can match.

Thomas put his pen inside the ledger as he lay on the edge of the grass, yawned, and looked out at the river at eye level. He raised his hand to shield his eyes from the glaring sun.

He saw an arm rise out of the black water, then another. He expected the form to be pulled toward the Hamilton-Keokuk bridge by the current. Instead, the powerful strokes held the Mississippi in check and advanced slowly in a straight line from Iowa to Hamilton Park.

She stepped out of the river, turned to look back at Iowa, pulled her cap off and shook the water out of her short black hair. Thomas held his breath to keep from scaring her, but also out of awe. He had never seen shoulder muscles ripple or thigh muscles flex side to side on a woman.

She turned towards him, smiled, and said,

"I didn't mean to disturb your nap, I'm going back in just a minute. I must be across before dark, otherwise I can't see the logs in the current. My sister is watching on the other side, yells if she sees something, but I don't always hear her."

Thomas had an idea, surprised that he could think in the presence of such a creature. How had she made it across? And now she wanted to go back?

"Listen, maybe I can watch and yell from this side. Then why don't I meet you
on the other side, get a cup of coffee, or a towel?"

She shoved her hair back under her cap, said,

"Java Town, just off the bridge to the right." She walked out into the murky water, dove gracefully into the Mississippi.

Thomas stood on the shore until he couldn't see the swimmer. He didn't see or hear the sister that he imagined was yelling at the top of her lungs to protect what must be the first woman to swim in a straight line from Keokuk to Hamilton. As he walked back to the car he noticed that his feet were soaked.

He took his shoes and socks off and tied them to the windscreen, then drove across the bridge to Main St., Keokuk, Iowa, turned right and saw the "Java Town" sign at the end of the block. He parked, put his half dry shoes and socks back on, pushed his hair back, and walked into the coffee shop.

The chairs were upside down on all the tables except one. Two women sat with their backs to Thomas. They appeared to be laughing at something the waitress had said. He spoke to the waitress as she went behind the soda counter.

"Are you still open? I could sure use a cup of coffee."

She looked him up and down, glanced to the occupied table, and said,

"Depends on who you are. Ever been to Hamilton Park?" As if on cue, the swimmer stood up, said,

"He sure has. He helped guide me back home. He deserves a cup."

She walked over to Thomas shook his hand, and said,

"Won't you join us. I'm Margaret, this is my sister Grace Lee." They were sisters in their jaw and nose structure only. Margaret was taller and more muscular than her petite sister.

"Great, I'm Thomas Stone, from Peoria. I didn't get your last name."

"Nelson, our name is Nelson"

"Ah, um, I'll be a here for a day or two on business." Thomas looked down at the floor. He was sure he was making an ass of himself, his shoes made sucking sounds with each step.

"What were you thinking about, swimming in that river? It looks dangerous. But maybe that's just my point of view. You sure don't seem scared by "Ol man river."

Grace Lee pushed forward and said,

"She's thinking about the Berlin Olympics in two years. She Could have gone to Los Angeles in 32, if I'd been coaching her and she didn't have that dumb library job."

"Shush, I'm not thinking any such thing, that's all in your head. How can you think that far ahead? I'm not anywhere good enough to go to Berlin, and they don't have a river event as far as I know. Why, they stop at 400 meters for women, not even a 1500. And, we *have* talked about going to Peoria looking for jobs," Margaret said as she frowned at her younger sister.

"Shush yourself, you'd be another Babe Didrikson. You were born on the same day, but you're better looking." Grace smiled at Thomas as she compared her sister to the best female athlete in the world.

Thomas felt a sting in his throat. It wasn't the thick black coffee,

it was his own conscience saying,

Careful bud, you're still married, according to the Church. He cleared his throat, and said directly to Margaret,

"If you do decide to come to Peoria, I can help get you a rooming house, and maybe line up a few interviews."

"Sit down, have your coffee," Margaret said, "We'll think about your offer."

"Have a lot of your friends gotten across and back?" Thomas asked.

"Not my route. I'm the first, that's why I did it," Margaret replied.

"Didn't you tell your friends you were going to try?"

"I don't need a crowd, I just wanted to prove that I could do it."

"I personally know four people that drowned trying the Hamilton Park route," Grace said. "Lots of kids make it following the bridge, but that's only a quarter mile, with bridge pilings to hang on to. Not much of a challenge. Margaret swam the longest distance and the most dangerous."

Thomas stood, looked at Margaret. His hand shook as he handed her his new business card,

"If you get to Peoria, this is my number. Remember my offer, I could help get you settled."

His shoes squished as he left the coffee shop. He was sure he would never see the swimmer again.

Everett May was pleased with the progress Thomas had made.

"Hamilton has worked out nicely," he said to Thomas a few

months after his trip to the Iowa border.

"That new agent is proving to be a real cash generator. Sent in $500 of new applications this week alone. We need to keep in touch with him. Make sure he has all our products and knows how they are better than the other companies he represents. I'd like you to go back there once a month. Be sort of a 'Special Agent' for the company."

"Good idea," Thomas responded with a smile that he controlled by pinching his leg.

"Mr. Horton isn't going to come here to see the new products we're developing. And the personal touch is very important."

Thomas didn't want to be a salesman with income dependent on making the right deal, twisting an arm at just the right time. This idea of being a 'Special Agent,' was intriguing. He liked the status that the name carried. Not the same as a 'VP, First National Bank, but a step up, never the less.

Mr. May threw out a seed and Thomas planted it in every little town that had an insurance agent in central Illinois, from Indiana to Iowa. The sense of freedom was overwhelming as he drove along two lane black top highways, waving at farmers and honking at other troubadours reaching out for business in mid depression Illinois. Just having a car was a sign of survival, even success. His hands held the wheel of the car and his own destiny. The towns he visited, the people he met with, were his own creation, not the regimen that the bank had imposed. There were no quotas, no dollar goals he had to achieve. It was relationships he was after and nobody was better at establishing and nurturing the small town business men. The agents in Galesburg sold the Illinois Insurance policies because Tom Stone had been there the day before.

Life had a new order with the establishment of his own territory.
Work the Peoria agents on Monday, leave Tuesday, come home Friday, repeating the route so that his agents never went more than three weeks without seeing him.

At each stop he recorded a piece of his day that set a brick of the pattern in place. He wrote at night sitting on the edge of a motel bed, a bare 300 words each day, just enough to capture an event away from the house on Illinois Avenue.

Writing about Dempsey and Cobb, the bank, his father's death, Nathan, Irene, the words were soft and round, ready to be replaced at any time. He had wanted to change the way things were. Now he wanted only to keep the world as it was. The letters were angled sharply, as if their edges were digging into the paper. But something was missing. He knew it was the swimmer.

THE SINGING BONE
PART FOUR

CHAPTER TEN
KATHRYN STONE
1981

"I'm taking Colin, going to Mom and Dad's." Kathryn said quietly as she stood in the doorway of Liam's study. He sat hunched over his desk, punching away at his typewriter. She looked around the room that had swallowed him since Fr. Conlin had died and he had brought those awful books home. She saw the ledgers as the cause of his obsession. If they weren't the cause, then certainly the catalyst, and worthy of her thoughts of intervention by fumigation, with Liam at his desk. Too violent? Then just send Colin into the room with peanut butter and jelly and a couple of Grape Fruit Juice containers. Instead, she had decided to act for herself, not for her husband. He was responsible for changing himself. She wasn't.

Her mother and father offered to pay for graduate school and gladly accepted the task of feeding and driving Colin. She would finish out the school year as the second grade teacher at Glowing Earth alternative school. Then start on her master's in elementary administration at the U. Her principal had been trying to get her to start the program since she started at his school two years ago. Now was the time to do something for herself. Stop taking care of Liam. He kept saying,

"You'll see Kathryn, you'll see, as soon as I finish this project, you can get your Master's. I'll have enough money coming in to pay for graduate school and enough time to take care of Colin."

"Be back by Saturday?" He asked as he continued to peck away at his Selectric.

"No. Longer. Good bye."

"OK," see you lat… what do you mean, 'longer?'" He said as he swirled, the cord from the typewriter popped out of the electrical socket, and wrapped around his ankle. He fell forward, landed prone at her feet.

Kathryn reached her hand out to Liam, then pulled it back,

"Just keep typing, you'll figure it out all by yourself. I can put up with your poetry, even encourage it, but this book, it's obsessed you. There's no time for us. You don't talk to Colin. It's not worth it to me to see you ignore him. You'll never have another chance. He'll be gone soon, and you won't even know him. I'm starting grad school this summer. You keep working on the book, figure out who your dad was, figure out who you are, and maybe, who the other two people in your life are. I'll call you later if I need anything from the house."

She turned and walked down the stairs and out the back door to the car where Colin was waiting.

STONE AND SON

PART FOUR

CHAPTER FORTY-SEVEN
THOMAS STONE
OCTOBER 1935

After the third trip to Hamilton, Thomas got rooms in Peoria for the Nelson sisters, with Ruby and Pearl Schwann. The sisters from Iowa moved into two third floor bedrooms on the north side of town. He knew the rental income of thirty dollars a month took the pressure off the twins to find another job for themselves. Instead they put their energy into finding jobs for their new wards. The girls started as waitresses at the Brown Sugar in December 1935, just in time for the holiday rush.

The next months were the happiest the Schwann twins had had for years. The noises and smells cascading through the house brought their own lives into balance. They had a family that each had given up on years before. Pearl watched over Margaret, Ruby guided Grace. Each tried to impose their own personality on what they considered fresh and open minds.

Pearl gave Margaret projects to keep her busy in the house.

"I have the crochet club coming over Friday night, would you care to join us? You'll learn how to make afghans in no time. Then move on to sweaters." Margaret wanted to show her gratitude for the house and food, always said yes, even if she had a date.

Ruby loved watching Grace get ready to go dancing.

"Tell me all about it when you get home. Just wake me, anytime is fine."

When the girl's mother, Mae Nelson, came for her first visit in early 1936, she was more like a visiting Aunt. Pearl shared Margaret's life as if she were the proud parent.

"Margaret has a great friend that we know personally, he's got a job at the insurance company that we, I, work at, so I know all about him. A good Catholic boy." Mae Nelson frowned a little, and said,

"We're Lutheran, but Catholic is good too. As long as he's a Good boy."

"Not really a boy, he's a little north of thirty, been married once, but he is a wonderful person." Pearl wanted Mae's approval for the romance she had been working on since the girls moved in. It would be the final stamp of approval for her own family project.

"I know Mary loves it here, and how's my Grace doing?" Mae asked. Ruby answered.

"Why, she's the most popular waitress at the Sugar. All the men ask to be put in her station. She's so vivacious. The Dolans, you know, the owners of the restaurant, say that Grace is great for business. You should be real proud of her."

Every Friday afternoon, on the way home, Thomas tested the speed limit, driving sixty- five on roads posted fifty-five. He saw her at an intersection, waving as he went by, then saw her again at the next intersection, waving him on, until he pulled into a parking place next to the Brown Sugar. There she was, taking an order for coffee and the soup of the day from County Sheriff Tony McLaughlin. He waited for her to walk back to the order counter before pushing through the front doors, then went directly to McLaughlin's booth.

"Hey Tony, did you leave anything for us law abiding citizens?" Thomas said as he reached over the banquette table and shook hands with his ex-Spalding teammate.

"I wouldn't waste time eating if I was serious about Miss Nelson here, Tommy. She talks about you all the time when you're gone. If you wait any longer, she won't be here on Friday nights."

"I've decided, Tony, I'm *not* waiting any longer."

McLaughlin smiled than frowned, as he thought about the last time he had seen Thomas.

"Never heard any more about your ex, how about you, Tommy, heard any more from her?"

"Nope, not a word."

Sheriff McLaughlin drank the last bit of coffee, put his cup back on the saucer with a little extra noise.

"Talk to Conlin about Margaret yet? I'm sure he'll have a thing or two to say. He's gotten real smart since he got back from Rome. Have you noticed?"

"Yeah, I've noticed, and no, I haven't told him yet."

Tony slid out of the banquette, pulled his Peoria Sheriff's hat on and said,

"Better see Jimmy, he knows all the important marriage stuff. Don't wait, she's a terrific gal."

"Thanks, see ya Tony."

Margaret waved at Tony McLaughlin as he left and brought Thomas black coffee and apple pie ala mode. He looked up at her and said,

"Margaret, it's time you meet the other Stones and a few of our friends. Next Saturday, would you come to my house for a back yard picnic. Bring Grace and the twins."

CHAPTER FORTY-EIGHT
BACKYARD PARTY

As soon as Irene had moved out, the parish had rallied around Thomas, offering what they thought were consoling comments.

"You deserved better," yelled Bev Sigley from across the alley.

"It was only a matter of time, Tom. You did the best you could with her," Wayne Lester told him. Sister St. John said,

"God watched over you, Thomas, it will all turn out for the better."

Monsignor Salmon coughed into his handkerchief, shoved it inside his sleeve and said,

"Now, maybe you'll believe me when I tell you what's best. I knew from the moment you said 'I do,' that it wouldn't work."

On this Saturday the long tables were set on the driveway as usual with ham, roast beef, tuna casseroles, home made bread, fruit salad, Jell-O salad, apple pie, cherry pie and rhubarb pie piled on the best linen table cloths. Beer and soft drinks were immersed in large metal buckets of ice. A small table sat in the garage doorway with rye, whiskey, a small ice bucket and water. Ralph Whelan stood behind the liquor, mixing highballs and telling crime stories. Bishop Spalding and Father Conlin insisted they wanted a soft drink. Ralph poured them reluctantly,

"Personally, I don't drink till after six, except on Sundays, then it's noon. But I can't see not drinking at all. How you gonna relax?" Card tables and chairs were set up in clusters throughout the backyard. Pearl and Margaret served the meat, Ruby and Grace served the desserts. At first, Margaret fielded a gauntlet of questions,

"How do you like Peoria?"

"When did you move here?"

"Where do you work?"

"How did you meet Tom?" She answered them all with a smile and "Be sure to come back for seconds." Bev Sigley was the first to tell Margaret, "You're doing great, honey, let me take over here. You go talk with the other ladies. We live just across the alley, you come over any time you need anything."

The men came in their best casual attire; suit pants, white dress shirts with the sleeves rolled up, some with ties, no jackets. They stood with drinks in their hands, discussed Roosevelt's latest plan for revitalizing the economy. Father Conlin moved over to toss a baseball with Wayne Lester; would the Cubs or White Sox get to the end of the season over 500. The bishop moved in, took Wayne's glove, and said to Father Conlin,

"Now I'll show you the curve that almost kept me out of the seminary."

Wayne walked over to Thomas and said,

"Looks to me like you learned a thing or two since Irene. Margaret is pretty special. But what about the Monsignor? He put in his two cents yet?"

"Nope. What do you think he'll say?" Replied Thomas rubbing out a cigarette in the grass.

"He'll wait to see what you do. He doesn't say much ahead of time. What about Jimmy, any advice from him?"

"Annulment."

"That could take years. Hell, just getting the diocese to consider

it could take years. Let alone sending a letter to Rome," Wayne replied as he picked up the ball, tossed it to the Walker's fourteen year-old and said,

"Don't wait."

The highlight of the afternoon came when Pearl and Ruby, already in identical hats, gloves, dresses, and aprons, changed into black tap shoes.

"Attention, attention," Ann Stone waved her arms and announced,

"The famous Schwann sisters will now do their patented vaudeville routine that has captivated audiences for years. Girls, do your stuff." Pearl and Ruby did a buck and wing down the driveway, to the street and back. The yard roared their approval, and demanded more.

"We need help this time. Margaret, you and Grace get over here." Margaret went to each child and said, "We'll do it together." The next line was led by Margaret, followed by a line of nine grade school kids, with Grace bringing up the rear, all doing their best to imitate Pearl and Ruby with flapping arms and strutting feet.

Margaret held her sides with laughter as they finished the performance to applause, hoots and whistles of approval. She sat between Ann and Julia, they each took a hand. Nothing was said, they just took her hands, held them in their laps. Julia finally said,

"Thomas needs you."

Ann looked over, her jaw lowered in shock to hear her sister speak directly to this young woman that they had just met. She knew then that it would work. Even Monsignor Salmon and Fr. Conlin seemed to be impressed. But an extra rosary would help that night before she went to sleep.

The Nelson and Schwann sisters left in Pearl's car at nine,

"We have to get going, mustn't overstay our welcome," Pearl started saying at seven. As they left, she waved at Thomas and said,

"You come over tomorrow. We'll show you our whole routine."

The yard was empty except for Fr. Conlin and Thomas Stone. Julia and Ann were asleep, exhausted from the long day. Both had let their braids down, said a prayer of thanks for having their Thomas, and got into bed feeling good about Margaret. Thomas whistled quietly as he picked up newspapers, plates, knifes, forks, empty beer bottles, and put them in the trash. He went inside and got his ledger, came back and sat on the porch steps. Fr. Conlin finished putting the tables and chairs into the garage and sat next to him on the steps.

"Still writing in those books?" the priest asked as he took the Camel offered by Tommy.

"A little bit every day, kind of a habit, like you saying Mass every day." Thomas

lit what he hoped would be *his* last cigarette of the day. He had written one line,

"She is my life."

"May I see what you wrote today?"

"No, I don't intend other people to read these, ever. I've told You that a hundred times."

"Doesn't hurt to try, I'm never sure when you want to share something with me." He crossed his legs and drew the first puff on his cigarette and blew it towards the kitchen window.

"Now, I want to talk to you seriously about your intentions."

"Honorable, totally honorable, I assure you. I am a single man in the eyes of the state. I'm going to marry her."

Fr. Conlin took out his championship watch, opened the case to check the time, ignored his friends' remarks.

"I can still practice in Rome. I can present your case to the Rota. I'm not sure if they will hear it though. The priorities are set by a committee and they, I hate to say it, are influenced by donations to the Vatican charities. It's not a matter of buying an annulment outright, it's a matter of paying to get on the docket in a timely fashion. I saw petitions that were five years old. The good news is that each case is decided on its merits. You have a very good chance if I can get you a hearing. It's worth a try, then you and Margaret *can* get married."

Fr. Conlin paused, not sure if he was getting through.

"Irene's still controlling you. You can't marry Miss Nelson without an annulment."

Thomas stood, walked a few steps towards the alley, and turned, spoke in *his* sermon voice, softly, but with punched verbs.

"So, I pay the Vatican and you practice being a priest-lawyer. Stay here Jimmy, hear confessions, other people need you a lot more than I need an annulment. An annulment means there never was a marriage. That's not the honorable solution. It could take years. I can live with my decisions, I still have my family at home, and," he paused, lowered his voice,

"You'll still be my friend and I can still help out at fund raisers. If I do marry again, I know the consequences, no sacraments. That's it. Right? I can still go to mass, raise the kids Catholic, help out with bingo, right? Downside is, no communion, and you won't ever get to hear my confession again."

For the first time, Fr. Conlin's tone was that of a Sunday sermon, as if he had taken a cue from Thomas.

"I am your friend, but, if you go ahead and marry her, it won't be in a church, at least not Catholic. I don't know how mortal your sin would be if you marry outside the church, maybe not at all. It is a choice you have to make."

Fr. Conlin stood, crushed his cigarette in the grass. He did not have an answer. He couldn't force him to go to the police, couldn't force him to wait for an annulment.

"If you do marry her, I would expect to see you in church every Sunday. And, you and the swimmer will raise the kids Catholic, even if *you* end up in hell." He rolled his sleeves down, put on his Roman Collar and black suit jacket.

"See you in the morning, at mass."

"Thanks, Jimmy, I know you're thinking of what's best, for all of us."

August 27, 1936

My conflict has a physical presence.
Live as a celibate bachelor, like Jimmy, for the rest of my life.
Or, try for an annulment and risk never getting it. I'm not even going to ask what the "fee" would amount to.
Or, share the rest of my life with the woman I love and trust. Live with the church's sanctions.

CHAPTER FORTY-NINE
THE FUTURE
October 1936

Thomas and Margaret sat in front of the picture window and looked out to the empty lot across the street. Two more duplexes were planned for next year, but now it was still the best playground in the neighborhood. Two ten year-old boys were teamed against two girls about the same age, playing "Kick the Wicket," a form of baseball that had the batter kicking a stick held off the ground by two bricks, then racing to first base before the two opposing players could put the stick back on the bricks. The girls were winning. They kicked the wicket where the boys weren't. The boys kicked it as hard as they could, right into the hands of the girls.

Margaret smiled, wished she was in a game that had such simple rules, where her own personal strength and commitment made a difference. What she had before her was a scary blend of what she knew about this man, a man she loved, with a job, that loved his family, was committed to caring for them till they died, that said he loved her. And, what she couldn't see under his orderly habits and vibrant personality, maybe never would.

"Fr. Conlin tells me that if we get married, I can't become a Catholic and you can't receive your sacraments. And, I find it a bit strange that he talked to me about this before you even *asked* me."

Margaret looked at Thomas with mock confusion on her face.

"Then we raise the kids Catholic? That means we sort of go Through the motions of being Catholic for their sake, and they're not even here yet. I am a Christian. I was baptized in the Episcopalian Church, I believe in the same God and in Jesus Christ." She shook her head.

"Maybe I'll try one of your cigarettes."

Thomas sat listening, his back to the front steps, but aware of sudden bursts of air, as if somebody was racing up and down the front stairs, not even trying to be quiet. There were two distinguishable rhythms. One deliberate, monotone, up to the second floor, back to the first, the sound of a priest walking quickly down the center aisle of a church, throwing holy water at the congregation. The other bouncing down the steps, then crawling back, as if it was trying to break through a skirmish line. For some time he had expected these two rivals to appear again. It seems they didn't want any part of him since the divorce. Maybe they only appear when they can affect his decisions. That dark night a year ago, he had acted too quickly for them to materialize.

"The important thing is that we love each other, trust each other, right?"

Thomas took her hands in his, their knees touched.

"Margaret, I love you, that's the only thing that I know for sure. I trust you, I want to spend the rest of my life with you." The noises on the stairs stopped as he spoke, as if waiting to see what would happen next.

"I also love the church. I believe in their rules, the importance of following them. I made a mistake before, I married the wrong woman. She's gone now, I'll never see her again."

Tell her now, the sound came from the step, a leaf on its way to the ground.

Live your life with Margaret, not behind bars, pushed the first thought away, forceful as only a lie in battle could be.

He still had a choice, the rest of the lives in the house and the lives of the unborn depended on his own passion.

"I am willing to live with the church's sanctions so that I can live with you. Will you marry me?"

Margaret looked into Thomas's eyes and said,

"You are willing to put up with the penance the church gives you for the rest of your life, so that you can marry *me*?"

"Yes."

Margaret put her arms around Thomas, kissed him tenderly on the lips,

"What are we waiting for?"

"Is that a yes?"

"Yes." Margaret looked over to the steps, thought she heard the rustle of Ann's dress retreating into Julia's bedroom. How long would she have to care for these two women? Both in their seventies. Her life was just beginning. A small sacrifice compared to Tom's.

Harvey T. Minas, Justice of the Peace, witnessed the marriage of Thomas Stone and Margaret Nelson in Crown Point, Indiana, on November 14, 1936. The small chamber felt more crowded to him than usual, with the bride and groom, Harvey's wife and brother acting as witnesses. As Thomas kissed Margaret, he looked over her shoulder and saw the Youngest Martyr shaking Henry Fleming's hand. Thomas never saw them again.

Thomas placed eleven ledgers into the empty wooden box, put it in the back of his closet. He had written a simple entry on page 156. The remaining 134 pages were left blank.

November 21, 1936

Writing doesn't change anything, it just records a memory. My life changed because of these people, and my own decisions. But I know them without looking at the page. It is time to put them to rest. I have made my best decision. She is my courage, my humility, my life.

THE SINGING BONE

PART FIVE

1982

CHAPTER ELEVEN
FINISH

Liam Stone pulled the last sheet out of the typewriter, shuffled it to the bottom of the neat pile of paper in the box next to his desk. He was finished, he knew that. There was no more to write. He expected a sense of accomplishment, some emotion that would justify giving into the seduction of his story. Instead, there was a complex silence that disturbed him. His ears were quiet. There were no footsteps, no door closing, no radio or T.V. voices floating up the stairs.

An empty feeling closed in around his eyes, a sting at the edge of his cheekbones that he could not wipe away. Nothing appeared. His shoulders were slightly slumped forward. His hands were quiet resting in his lap. How long had he been in this room? One month, two months? All the attachments to his writing were neatly organized in an inner circle, the prized Selectric with auto correct, a fast pen, a pad of pre punched three- hole paper, a leather writing folder, dark blue coffee cup, slippers. He turned to the empty chair in the corner, saw for the first time that it was surrounded by piles of t shirts, sweaters, jeans and socks.

The novel was his America, his grocery store, his championship basketball game, all seductions, all temporary. Now what? He knew he couldn't just turn and leave, but it would be easier. Walk away from the room, the shelves of books, the ledgers filled with history, the piles of clothes. His foot hit the manuscript box. One more trip downstairs, into the car, drive to White Cloud, leave the box with Amy

Brown. Find Kathryn and Colin, commit to them what he had put into the book. They'll see, it's not too late.

He untwisted a sweater from two pair of faded jeans, pulled it on over his t shirt, grabbed the box and went out into the hall. The door closed as if pulled from the inside.

Liam delivered the manuscript to White Cloud's office. The new receptionist, Ms. Black, turned the book over in her hand, as if she was weighing it, frowned as she dropped it with a thud into a pile of boxes next to her desk,

"I'll be glad to give it to Ms. Brown when she comes in. She might not read the whole book, but for sure the first chapter, she always reads the first chapter."

"Just tell her that Liam Stone finished his project and please hand her the book."

"Oh, you know Ms. Brown?"

"Yes, I know Ms. Brown, in fact, I am under contract with her for this book."

"Sorry, you know how many unsolicited books I get every week? And I haven't been here long enough to know all of our authors. I'll be sure to give her this book." She walked over to the box, pulled it out and placed it carefully on her desk.

A week later, Amy Brown called,

"Well Liam, it's been worth the wait. I think we can do something with this. Can you come in tomorrow?"

The next day, Liam sat in front of his publisher. He could see her shoulder blades outlined under her turtleneck sweater, narrow wrists that somehow connected to long finely shaped hands. Her voice was soft, but brisk, no hint of a smile. This was not a negotiation.

"You know we only publish eight to ten titles a year, this manuscript has a bit of promise. I'll work on it myself. Maybe we can get it out by Christmas. We'll start with eight thousand five. Give you a little promo package." She looked at a large calendar on her desk, a line had been driven through two weeks at the beginning of December.

"It's short notice, but we'll start you in Peoria, at the Blue Bird Book House, give them a chance to see a home town boy, then St. Louis, Kansas City, Des Moines, Rock Island, end up in Minneapolis. You'll drive of course. That OK with you?"

"Fine, driving is fine. It's pretty tough to get flights this time of year." Liam wanted to sound disappointed, but the idea of driving through the rural mid west, tracing some of the roads that his father had driven, excited him, and yet he just wanted to get the tour over. Publishing the book was enough. The most important thing now was to get home and patch things up with Kathryn. He was very scared about losing her. She seemed to be happy with this separation.

"Finally, I'm doing something for myself. We'll talk about what's next, after I finish my course work," she told him after his proud announcement that he was about to be a published novelist.

Once the tour was over, he would make up for the last year. Colin didn't seem to be a problem. He actually saw him more now. Putting his guilt to good use he had been helping his in-laws with driving to guitar lessons and movies. But one recurrent question bothered him,

"What'd you bring me, Dad?" His only value was being the guy that came around once in a while with a present. What kind of a father was he? Once they got back together, he would break him of that expectation, become a real father.

CHAPTER TWELVE
READING
1982

Before the reading at the Blue Bird Book House, Liam was to meet with a local public radio interviewer. White Cloud even had the hotels booked and paid for; not bad preparation, a radio station, bookstore *and* a hotel. He wasn't used to this treatment.

Liam walked into radio station KDQW the afternoon of the reading, sat at a table facing an empty chair. Two lavaliere microphones were placed next to a pitcher and two glasses. He hooked one of the microphones to his black sport coat and waited. He could hear voices from behind a production room window. A door opened and a man about ten years Liam's senior, stepped into the room. He looked oddly familiar to Liam. Even his voice sounded familiar, a little slower perhaps and with more inflection than the voice he was trying to connect it with.

Liam tried to remember where they could have met. Too old to have gone to the same schools, maybe New York, or LA, at some trade convention from the apparel industry. He stood for a second with the book in his hand, adjusted his rimless glasses, still talking to the man in the production booth. His black hair was combed straight back, clean over the ears, with a slight curl at the nape of the neck. He had on a dark navy double breasted pinstripe suit, dark gray shirt and solid burgundy silk tie. Liam heard him say,

"Thirty minutes, we'll run it during drive time this afternoon." He sat down, put on his microphone, stared intently at Liam, shook his hand and said,

"I'm Nathaniel Atchison. I have a little program on the local Public Radio stations in the area. This is a very good book community, publishers, universities, book stores. Normally, we don't bring first novels onto the show, but I asked for you after reading your book."

The next thirty minutes went by quickly, Nathaniel Atchison

had not only read the book, but had evidently done a lot of research, asking questions about a number of things Liam had not put into the final draft. He and Amy Brown had cut a good fifty pages before it went to press. Maybe Nathaniel had called the publisher and done a little homework. Liam expected a very positive program after they had finished. Hopefully, it *would* run during drive time and *before* tonight's bookstore reading.

Nathaniel took off his microphone, gestured to the booth with a thumbs up. Liam smiled, started to stand, when he felt Nathaniel's hand on his arm.

"I'd like to ask you a few questions off the record about the book."

"Sure. You must of done a little research. Did you call "White Cloud?"

"No. I just kn......., Listen, please don't take this wrong, but you did make a mistake in the book."

Liam wasn't ready for a critique, even if it was off the record. Wait until he got on the phone with Amy Brown. No more ambushes. He got enough of that with his own editors.

"Oohh, what did I do wrong?" He sat back, forced a smile, waited for the comment on sequencing, character development, point of view, even grammar. He would make the best of it.

"It's about Irene."

"What do you mean, a mistake about Irene? It's just a novel. I make this stuff up."

He could be sitting across from some well dressed maniac, some strange reader that obsessed with characters and took it out on the author when he didn't agree with how he handled them. Liam looked to the production booth, mouthed the word 'help,' but the booth was empty. As far as he knew, they were the only two in the building. He looked around for a door.

Nathaniel's even radio tone had disappeared, replaced by a rising and falling barrage of words. His shoulders, that had been squared to the back of his chair, now curved forward, his hands held Liam's book as if the words might escape if he let go.

"Listen, Liam, I know it sounds strange, but everything you wrote about Irene, up until you put her in the river, I knew about. And all the stuff about Thomas, I knew about, up until Irene left. Now tell me, did you write a novel, or did you write a biography of your father in the form of a novel?"

Liam sat back in his chair, tried to look in control, as if this was just part of the interview. But the sudden revelation that his father might be more than his blood memories revealed, scattered his resolve. He rubbed his wet palms on the sides of his wool trousers, his heart raced. He broke the silence,

"This is a lot more than I expected from this interview. How do I know what you're saying is true. You know a lot about my book, and evidently, my Father. But what about you? Who are you? What do you want from me?"

"Then you are writing about your father?"

"Of course, I'm writing about my father, but it still comes out of my imagination. He never talked to me about his past, hardly spoke to me about anything other than sports and school and getting the oil changed in the car. He did talk a lot about not lying to people. And I'm not sure this isn't some scam you're cooking up for God knows what reason. I sure don't make enough money to pay you anything, this book will probably sell to my friends and relatives. What do you want?"

"The same thing you do. I want to know about *my* father. I thought I had a father until I realized that the guy that came home every night, that I called Dad, was a man that I loved, but not my *real* father," Nathaniel hesitated for the first time, appeared unsure. The silence twirled on the table between them.

"Nathaniel, you've started this, I'd like to know how it ends, maybe I can use it in my next book," Liam said with a hint of sarcasm, trying to calm himself, thinking that he might get something out of the exchange.

Nathaniel's voice returned to his Public Radio drawl, as if he was telling his story for a Saturday morning program entitled, "Sons Looking for Their Fathers." He cleared his throat, took a lozenge out of his pocket, offered one to Liam.

"Sorry, just a little bit of the radio curse, dry throat. There's something I want you to see. I'll get you back to the hotel in plenty of time to get to the book store for the reading." Liam hesitated, but he was starting to trust, if not believe, this passionate man that reminded him of someone coming out from behind a cloud.

"I'll go, but I want to call the bookstore and tell them that you will be dropping me off. That I'll need a ride to the hotel after the reading."

As they drove away from the radio station, the first snow of the season fell and melted on the concrete streets leading to the Illinois River. Nathaniel turned onto a parkway with a row of scrawny poplars planted in the spring along the median. He followed it north for a mile then turned into a parking lot and stopped the car facing the widest part of the river. The low rumble of the current was clearly audible as they got out of the car. There was no horizon, just a flat sheet of white sugar that Liam thought would have satisfied his hunger as a child if he could have held his mouth open to the sky long enough. They sat on a picnic table, their feet on the plank seat. Liam saw Nathaniel rub his hands together, oblivious to the flakes that had suddenly turned moist and heavy, accumulating on his knees.

Nathaniel's voice started in his Public Radio monotone, trustworthy, rhythm.

"When I was ten, I heard Mom yelling at him. 'He's not yours, don't *you* wish he was?' I sat outside the door crying, thought she meant I was adopted, that was the big deal fear when I was a kid, thinking you might be adopted. She came out and almost tripped over me. I asked her about being adopted, she said she was my real mother, she delivered me in a hospital like all my friend's mothers. I asked her why she was mad at Dad. But she wouldn't answer me. Said I wouldn't understand, that Dad loved me and that's all that counted. I started having these dreams, not ones that I forgot, but ones that stayed with me through the morning, and came back again and again. I have a three ring binder full of them. I finally figured out that she had been pregnant by another man and married the guy that I called Dad, out of desperation. Mom died years ago, Dad died last year. I gave up the hope of ever finding out about my real father. Then, I read 'Stone and Son.' The dreams made sense for the first time."

"Where did you grow up? In Illinois?" Thomas asked.

"Yes. In Ottawa, on the grounds of the T.B. sanitarium. My father, my adopted father, was the chief of the medical facility."

Liam walked back and forth as he listened, his coat tight around his neck. His feet left a muddy brown trail in front of the picnic bench.

"What about the dreams?" Liam asked.

Nathaniel's voice deepened and rolled as if he was hanging onto the gunnels of a rocking row boat.

"In the first one, a baby falls into a river with no banks. I don't know if it is a boy or a girl, how it got to the river. The baby is pulled under the water by a griffin that is chained to a pillar under the river.

The griffin pushes the baby towards a white light just above the surface. It's like a picture, no movement. Similar to your great grandfather's story about losing his child, don't you think?"

"There's more hope in your dream, your baby might live."

Nathaniel nodded.

"The second is one that is not in your book, if I'm right, there is no way you could know about it."

Nathaniel reached under his jacket and pulled out a copy of Liam's book. He easily found a worn page;

.......Then on his right was a gravel road that he recognized as leading to a seldom used beach of dirt and sand. It was posted,

'No Swimming, Treacherous Currents."

He backed the Ford as close to the water as he dared. Untied the twine and pulled Irene's body out of the tarpaulin. He walked into the black water until he was chest deep, felt the current pulling at his legs, and pushed her out as far as his arms would extend. She bobbed momentarily like a cork on a fish line and then disappeared under the oily surface.'

Nathaniel stopped and appeared to be catching his breath.

Liam recognized the staccato rhythm of a eulogy, or, evidence being presented by the prosecutor in a murder trial. Where was this going? Isn't there a statute of limitations? What had he gotten himself into?

"Then you leave her, we don't know what happened, except we assume she is dead and the river is her grave."

"That's the idea, her character has played its role."

"This is where my dream starts. A woman with a suit of shells And fish heads crawls out of the river into a wall of flames. She emerges on the other side carrying a screaming baby. A man in a long white coat puts them into a shining tent. I don't think Irene really died."

"It's a novel, I made it up." Liam said without conviction. He wondered for the first time if Irene could have been alive when Thomas pushed her into the river? Could she have been rescued, returned to Ottawa, married, and given birth to Thomas Stone's first child? Could this Nathaniel be my half brother? Was my father *not* guilty of a sin that he carried with him his whole life?

"What shall we do with all this?" Liam asked.

"I don't know. Do you know where we are?" Nathaniel asked.

"This could be the spot that I wrote about, where he walks out and lets her go. But it wasn't a cove like this, it was wide open."

"Come with me, just the other side of those trees."

Liam followed Nathaniel back towards the car, turned onto a narrow path and walked through scrub pine and bare oaks.

"Look at this clearing, it's the mirror of the place we just left, two coves, fifty yards apart. It was known as "Hobo Park" during the depression. If you dig down, I guess we'd find the remains of a thousand fires and a few lost men. Can't hear or see the other side of that finger going out into the river. Isn't it possible that the woman your father pushed out into the river was pulled by the current and washed up into the camp? Somehow, she survived?" The two men stared into an empty gray sky that silently fused with the river.

"Do you think it is possible that you wrote about my real father? That's all I want to find out. Do my dreams, your Singing Bone, have anything to do with each other?" Nathaniel slumped to the ground, his face flat and gray as the sky. A cold wind swept across the water's edge,

"Nothing will change. I'll go on with my interviews, you'll finish your book tour, go back home to your family. They're all dead, nothing we do will change anything."

Liam looked at Nathaniel, tightened his coat at the neck.

"I don't know. I don't know if 'Singing Bones,' exist, if 'Blood Memories' are real. Maybe I just wanted more of him, wanted to see him as vulnerable as the rest of us. His blood is in me, maybe in you. Are you my brother? I don't know. Is he your father? Sure, why not. Your Dad loved you, probably spent more time with you than my father did with me. Maybe you have the best of it. The blood of one and the love of another."

Liam could learn nothing of Thomas from Nathaniel. He could not help Nathaniel in his quest for a father. Their searches were messy, isolated affairs, with no clear answers.

Liam knew his ending. Do the reading, go home, piece his family back together. He finally had what he wanted, what he knew from the beginning. Thomas Stone had done the best that he could, now it was his turn.

He looked out over the dark rippled water, the sun shone over his shoulder into the faces of three men moving towards him. They seemed identical in the way they carried their shoulders, straight and square. But there were differences he had never noticed as he created them. Michael Stone's right cheek was concave, the skin sunken against the upper jaw. William Stone was missing an arm and leaned slightly to the left. Thomas Stone was shorter than Michael and William. Each different, but the same in their eyes; clear, unafraid, sure of their courage. They said nothing, then faded into a mist that had risen from the river depths. Liam bent down and picked up a handful of dirt and sand, damp from the slow lap of the river's tongue, dropped it into his pocket, sure for the first time that he was one of the men he had listened to.

www.ingramcontent.com/pod-product-compliance
Lightning Source LLC
Chambersburg PA
CBHW051538260626
47170CB00003B/996

9780615890319